I0760525

CRIME QUEEN OF L.A.

TIMOTHY WURTZ

ONWARDPRESS.ORG
LOS ANGELES, CALIFORNIA

This book is a work of fiction. Names, characters, places and incidents are the product of the author's imagination or are used fictitiously. Any resemblance to actual events, persons, living or dead, is coincidental.

Library of Congress Control Number: 2021948238

Published in the United States by Onward Press, an imprint of United States Veterans Artists Alliance, a 501-c-3 non-profit organization.
5284 ½ Village Green
Los Angeles, CA 90016

www.onwardpress.org
www.usvaa.org

Edited by Christina Hoag
Cover design by Teddi Black
Formatted and designed by Megan McCullough

ISBN Hard Cover: 978-1-954988-12-5
ISBN Paperback: 978-1-954988-11-8
ISBN E book: 978-1-954988-13-2

"Not until we are lost do we begin to understand ourselves."

Henry David Thoreau

CHAPTER 1

"How's about a little holiday squeeze and squirt, sweet thing?" The emaciated, thirtyish male hooker said. He worked a stroll at Hollywood and Highland. And worked hard. Long past his prime, he twirled a glittery ornament tied to an eight-inch piece of ribbon. The guy puffed his tight green tee and swayed his boney ass in red skinny jeans. All he managed to do was show off ribs and a pointy pelvis.

"In your dreams, sweetheart," Johnny Lincoln said. Floppy, gray fedora pulled low, he buttoned and belted his khaki trench coat and scooted by.

The slim hooker, a head-and-a-half shorter than Johnny, hitched his hip, tossed baby-thin, multi-hued, candy-dipped hair and scoffed, "You tourists are all alike. Fa la la."

"Yeah, yeah, yeah," Johnny said.

The streetwalker sneered, stuck out his tongue, and continued to prance and parade on that chilly December night.

Johnny trudged on, hands shoved in pockets, chin tucked against the wind and drizzle. He was oblivious to a million twinkling lights and the tawdry nocturnal sites on Hollywood Boulevard—gawkers and hawkers, shakers and fakers, wandering visitors and scam artists. He bumped a massive, three-hundred-fifty-pound bald dude draped in an ankle-length fur. "'Scuse..."

"Don't make me no never mind." Baldie shimmied and hiked his pleated chinos over his balloon belly. He wrangled a dozen foreign sailors ogling faded posters of bare-breasted strippers. Displayed a gap-toothed smile and laid it on thick. "Gentlemen, gentlemen. Your rendezvous of a lifetime is upstairs. Glamour, elegance, sophistication. A single Jackson and it's abracadabra."

Johnny hurried on. He slalomed and dodged strange beings. A Busker strummed a guitar, huffed a harmonica and pedaled a drum into a song.

A twelve-year-old girl in need of a scrub offered a smoke to a ten-year-old.

Superheroes, most of them Batman or Spiderman, wore masks and grimy costumes. A blonde-wigged "Marilyn" in a knock-off of the iconic, white, subway-grate dress, shivered. A buxom "Wonder Woman" wannabe rubbed goosebumps on her bare arms. They both forced smiles, posed for photos and plied the meager, winter crowd of sightseers for tips.

"Marilyn" embraced Johnny's waist, leaned in and hugged. "Welcome to the center of the universe, handsome. Where you from?"

"Here and there." Johnny did not slow his pace as he dragged a twenty out of a pocket and stuffed it in Ms. M's bra.

"You're the best." She smooched him on the cheek and peeled away in search of other marks.

Five yards later, Johnny stopped, examined buildings and signs to catch his bearings, thumbed pages in a small notebook and wrote in it. He glanced back at the future, a modern movie palace built for one purpose, to be the home of Oscar. A pack of vacationers rubbernecked and snapped pictures.

Ahead was a Golden Era shrine, the Roaring Twenties Chinese Theater, and more out-of-towners. They oohed and awed. Compared their hands and feet to world-famous spread-finger hand and shoe imprints cast in cement and immortalized forever, or until The Big One hit. Johnny had done the tourist thing and visited the poured concrete when he arrived in LA. He was surprised by how diminutive the stars were in real life, unlike their on-screen visages.

He jotted in his pad and hustled to the intersection at Orange Avenue. Johnny defied a *Don't Walk* signal. Dashed kitty-corner across the Boulevard under the glow of a plastic Santa, sleigh and reindeer that spanned the busy street. He evaded pissed-off drivers who buzzed down windows, shouted, "Asshole," shook fists or flipped the bird.

"Right back at ya." Johnny blew kisses, glad California wasn't an open-carry state. He made it to the sidewalk and continued towards a vivid, lime-green sign that flashed *Gee Spot.* It was a retail establishment. He marched inside, raised his fedora an inch and endeavored to adapt weary, man-of-the-world posture.

A splash of chartreuse neon revealed Johnny was tall, six-four, easy on the eyes, and twenty-four since the twenty-fifth – three weeks. His baby blues widened as he eyeballed the place. Well lit. Loads of shiny chrome.

"Hey, hey. You hit the *Spot*. Aren't you something to behold? Dive in, baby. I'm Kalessi, your hostess." A cute blonde in a clingy top and Daisy Dukes the same color as the sign curtsied. "Got hot coffee or cocoa for ya. It's burr cold."

"I'm good. Thanks anyway."

"And free yummies while you browse." She motioned to a tray of donuts, bear claws and strudel on a table.

Johnny patted his tummy. "Already ate, but I appreciate it." He ambled further into the store. It was dotted with holiday shoppers, an even mix of young and stylish men and women. One woman's mouth formed an "O" as she clutched a giant-sized, dayglow demo dildo. She stroked it once, shuddered, and peeked to see if anyone noticed. Johnny knew she gave a purchase serious consideration – she held onto it.

He surveyed sex toys designed for every imaginable kink and a few that had never crossed his mind. Several lay beneath a Christmas tree, others beside a Menorah.

Kalessi joined him. "And for the extra adventurous?" She grabbed a handful of his wavy, dark-blonde hair and yanked. Forced his gaze to the ceiling.

Ribbons adorned implements of bondage and torture suspended from rafters and heating ducts. Bows were strategically pasted on life-size dolls outfitted in erotic lingerie.

"Not a fan of beat me, hurt me, love me," Johnny said.

"You might enjoy this." Kalessi lobbed a shrink-wrapped, silicone vagina to him.

He caught it and fumbled the package. "Wow. Okay…"

"It's the official, authentic, perfect replica of Vicki Venom."

"Who's that?"

"She's huge."

Intrigued, he appraised Ms. Venom's lady part and returned it. "Like I told you. Cruising."

"I'm here when you need me." She bopped to her post at the entrance.

Johnny scanned the merchandise. Where to begin? The *Gee Spot* was not your father's sleazy porn shop. He moved to a magazine and DVD rack. Perused rows and rows of porn vids and glossy publications that featured perfect bods and crazy freaks. Lifted a copy of "Tinsel Town Thangs," but reconnoitered.

Stationed at the rear of the store behind a counter, next to a cash register, was a smokin'-hot college-age babe in blue denim short shorts. A name tag pinned to her red crop top stated MANAGER. Perched on a bar stool, she boasted legs as long as highways.

A secured cabinet bolted to the wall exhibited select playthings. A printed label purported they were genuine, 10k gold plate. The Manager swiped a credit card. "For you or him?" She said, and passed a spiked collar to a furtive, middle-aged dowager. The customer blushed.

Johnny kept an eye on the transaction and observed a stylish, well-groomed businessman slip a DVD box to the Manager. She swept her straight, black hair into a ponytail, twisted a scrunchie then peeped inside the box. Voila – a couple Jacksons. She plucked the bills. "You're the greatest." Slipped fingers under her bra, tucked the money in a private place and hopped off her seat. She rose to her toes and stretched her arms above her head. Flaunted a figure that would drop an army to its knees. She winked. The biz guy patted her butt. She parted midnight-blue curtains and he disappeared through the partition.

Three hopeful geeks stared at her and dreamed.

Johnny admired her too as he leaned against a waist-high case jammed full of bedtime party favors. He was inclined to tail the dude in the suit but stayed put.

"Purtty sure I knew her. Bouncing Betty," a rummy wino said. Stringy, greasy bangs fell on his forehead. He wiped his nose with a filthy sleeve as he leered over Johnny's shoulder at the nudies in the magazine. "Yep. When she first got to town. Baptized her, I did. Bouncing Betty." Wino hit the Bs hard and exposed corn-colored teeth. He was blessed with what radio announcers called a four-ball voice – deep, resonant. Too bad it'd been squandered.

"Geez, Mac. Gonna singe skin. Brush and floss." Johnny recoiled and knocked the display. It teetered. He lunged at it, lost his balance and tripped. The case collapsed and shattered. Adult toys littered the floor. Some buzzed. Johnny sprawled and grinned.

The Manager heard the crash and saw the mess. "Goddamn piss ant."

Patrons scattered. The wino kissed a twenty. Johnny nodded at him and scrambled. He attempted to scoop an armful of dildos, vibrators and nipple clamps. Instead, nicked a pinkie on a shard of broken glass. "Ow."

The Manager scowled. "Transport your ass and clean this up, dick wad," but she'd lost him. "Fuckawala… Anybody see where that big shit went? Kalessi?"

In the confusion, Johnny vanished. He lingered in a corridor beyond the register and drapes. Looked in both directions. Nobody followed. He stepped along a row of closed doors. Rattled half-a-dozen knobs. All locked. At the end of the hall was a seventh. He gripped it. It turned. Relieved, Johnny eased the door open. Not a sound. He wasn't sure what he was supposed to hear but hadn't expected silence.

He entered a dimly lit, closet-sized room. Took two steps on sticky linoleum. Rested a hand on the arm of an easy-to-scour black or dark blue Naugahyde recliner. He sat and faced brown, floor-to-ceiling swags. A three-inch-wide horizontal slot was cut in the wall to his right. Above it, a doorbell button. He pushed it. A harsh ring jolted him, but not a thing happened. He waited a moment and pressed again. Identical non-result.

Impatient, Johnny drummed the chair arms. What a crapshoot. A monumental waste of time, effort and energy, but he was there. He dug in a pants pocket and extracted a substantial flash roll. Remembered how much the biz man spent, snapped off two bills and fed them in the slot. Paused. Inserted another. Silence. Added a fourth. Not the magic number. Okay, one more. That brought the total to a hundred.

Trumpets blared a fanfare. It startled him but sounded familiar. Maybe a movie theme? The curtains separated. Johnny scooted his butt and sat at attention.

A key light revealed a gum-chewing bottle-blonde on a swivel stool. She may have graduated school, or not, and in her past, he guessed Sophomore year, was a hottie, but even at her tender age, the girl had blown past her expiration date. Makeup didn't hide eye bags and frown lines.

Legs crossed, she wore scarlet, six-inch fuck-me pumps and swung a foot in rhythm with the tune and the chomping of her jaw. The "model" was laced into a black corset, all the curvy parts ready to burst. She tweaked her garter belt, flicked the tip of her tongue between chapped, ruby-red lips, then offered Johnny her version of a wistful gaze that resembled an "Elvis" sneer. The music petered out. She hunched and crushed her boobs together, suggesting bottomless cleavage. "No artificial ingredients," she said. Bounced her tits. "You approve? I'm Luuu-cie."

"I'm, uh..."

"It's cool. Don't tell me if you don't want, 'kay? But I'll tell you everything, 'kay?"

"Hope so."

Lucie smacked her gum. Giggled. "Don't be shy. I'm barely legal, a Pisces, and I'm shaved, Daddy." Spread her thighs.

"Getz. Clue me in about Getz."

Lucie folded her arms and fine-tuned her cleavage. "I'm all grown up, 'kay Daddy? What do you crave? I'll make it special for you."

"Cut me a little slack here. You know who I mean."

"Nuh unh." She forced a smile. Braces.

"Sure you do. C'mon, doll. You got my dinero. Spill."

Lucie jumped down. In the spike heels, she stumbled and staggered behind a scrim.

"Hey." Johnny sprang to his feet and pursued. "Getz." Discovered a padlocked door, retreated the way he'd come in and rushed into the passage. No Lucy. He didn't bother with knobs until he reached the end of the hallway. The last one opened. He lurched into a dank, trash-filled alley. The latch clicked. He spun and shook the handle. It didn't budge. Aggravated, Johnny kicked it. A lot of good that did. He glanced towards the Boulevard and there was Lucie, bundled in a fake leopard-skin jacket, sneaking out an exit.

Johnny hurdled ruts and puddles and raced to the bright lights. At the street, he was jostled by a cluster of eager Japanese tourists. They bowed, he bowed. Johnny craned his neck. Strained to spot Lucie and her faux fur. He avoided cars, stood on the double-yellow line, and did a nimble three-sixty. Furious motorists shouted. Astonished onlookers watched from the curb. A plumper captured smartphone video and elbowed her friend. "Any idea what TV show they're shooting so we can see it?"

Frustrated, Johnny angled his fedora high on his head. Where'd Lucie get herself to? He ignored honking and began a slower turn in the opposite direction. Bingo. He tugged his hat and ran, trench coat flapping.

A block east, Lucie carried her shoes as she hauled ass beneath a rainbow-colored awning and into a building.

Johnny darted to the sidewalk and veered left. Sprinted. He stopped under the canopy. Breathed hard as he scoped the entry. No sign, no brass plaque, no indication as to the type of enterprise. Nothing ventured, nothing gained, he dipped in.

A spacious lobby. He felt the thump, thump, thump of a bass guitar as he faced a large, decorated tree in the center. Its crowning angel touched the twelve-foot ceiling. Beside it was a poster on an easel.

Guess Who? Club
$1,000 – 24/365
$100 – just for tonight
plus
$100 cover

Guess Who what? Odd, but hey, it was Hollywood. However, no Lucie.

Johnny moseyed across a lush carpet, around the tree to a saloon bar backed by multi-hued, velvet curtains. On the walls were five rows of publicity stills. He counted eighteen headshots per. Examined them. All were familiar females. Some famous. He feigned amazement here, a bit of revelation there, and treaded backward. Bumped something soft and mushy. Pivoted. "Woah!"

He was belly-to-belt with a super-sized, bare-chested, blubbery guy who sported purple mascara and lipstick, a matching purple cape and leotard. Johnny recovered his composure, located his cash, peeled four bills and tendered them.

"Private club, junior." The purple Bouncer sneered. "Leave, or I learn ya how to fly." He flexed. His waxed tummy jiggled.

"Better idea." Johnny indicated the prices. "I score a membership." He skinned six additional twenties from his roll for a total of ten. Fanned them to prove he had the two hundred.

An average-sized dude joined the Bouncer. At least Johnny thought he was. A dude. He was made up in whiteface, garbed in formal wear. Impossible to distinguish if he was thirty or fifty. "Look at you. Um, um, um. Welcome to the pot of gold, gorgeous. This must be your inaugural visit. And you are?"

"Johnny Lincoln. What're you supposed to be?"

"The maître d'hôtel." Hands clasped, he strutted to Johnny, affording an opportunity for a critical inspection. The Maître d' spoke with a clipped, east-coast, boarding-school cadence. "If you've ever voted Republican, we probably aren't your cup of tea, unless of course, you're digging in your closet. But my colleague and I will be delighted to provide you an application. Approval won't take but a moment." He winked. The Bouncer used his gut to bird dog Johnny into a private tete-a-tete.

Johnny grinned and played along for a heartbeat. "Fantastic." He feigned a move one way, deked the other and slipped through the curtains.

The Bouncer chased him. His fat flopped and his tights slid down his ass. Not pretty.

On the far side of the velvet, Johnny loitered at the rim of a dim, smoky area. He heard chats and chuckles. As his vision adapted, he saw two dozen circle-top tables all three feet wide surrounded by chairs and people. Crammed theater-style, they faced a small stage. Red Venetian candles lit dapper men of a certain age, between forty and forever. They sat shoulder-to-shoulder, puffed cigars, laughed, scratched and slurred toasts. Arms and elbows competed for space with bar clutter – tumblers, snifters, Champaign flutes, nut bowls, ashtrays. It was a private club, smoking permitted.

Johnny glimpsed the Bouncer and edged deeper into the dark.

"It's time for Christmas treats and New Year's wishes." A brunette Mistress of Ceremonies glided on stage in a floor-length, off-the-shoulder, emerald-colored dress. The MC stroked a microphone and in a husky tone said, "So – are you ready? Are you?" The Audience settled. "Okay, gang, let's give it up for the maahvelous, the one and only – Diana!"

Johnny stared as "Diana," at her Motown best, shimmied to enthusiastic applause. Wrapped in a sapphire gown, she raised a sprig of mistletoe above her head, flashed that legendary, toothy smile and laid a scrumptious holiday lip lock on the MC. The spectators roared approval as Johnny noticed leopard spots approaching the stage. He did a double-take. Lucie. Hustled after her.

"Stop!" "Diana" sang on the downbeat, and Johnny slammed on the brakes. The music continued and he recognized it was a song, not a command. He skirted tables and zipped backstage.

The wings were congested. Costumed performers stretched or quietly sang scales. Crew members issued hushed instructions and urgent prods as they herded a swarm of entertainers.

Johnny jolted a near-perfect "Dolly Parton." Snagged "Cher." Uttered, "'Scuse me. Sorry," then saw a frantic Lucie gesturing to the Mistress of Ceremonies who urged her with hand signals to chill. She didn't.

Lucie struggled to light a smoke. Annoyed, the MC held the match to the tip. Lucie sucked instant relief until the MC yanked her out of sight.

They were in a six-by-eight dressing room dominated by a vanity. Johnny charged in. Freaked, Lucie flipped the cigarette on his shirt and blew by him.

Johnny swatted embers and ashes.

The Brunette, a bombshell in stiletto heels, relaxed on a padded bench, studied herself in an oval mirror and slowly crossed her legs. Image framed by fluorescent lights, the Brunette examined artful makeup that popped cold, green eyes below plucked, shaped brows, highlighted cheekbones and accentuated thin, unsmiling, crimson lips. All in all, an attractive package. She nodded approval and removed her wig. Uncovered a military buzz cut. Explored Johnny's reflection for a reaction.

He gulped. "Uhhh – I'm searching for somebody."

"Aren't we all." The Brunette's voice was low and male.

It caught Johnny off guard, which was unexpected, considering what he'd seen in a few quick minutes. "Getz," he said. "Looking for Getz."

The Brunette fitted a new wig, rose and smoothed the dress over the curve of his hips. Very Audrey Hepburn. Stunning.

"Wow." Johnny whipped out his money.

The impersonator fired a mean-ass snarl, put on a mink stole and blended into the backstage commotion.

Johnny hesitated, then hurried. "Miss? Mister?"

The Brunette shoved open an emergency exit and departed.

The Bouncer materialized, poised to pounce. Yelled, "Intruder. Intruder."

Johnny bolted. Dodged cast members and singers. "Sorry. Oops. Careful…"

The caped, purple enforcer was in hot pursuit, 300 pounds of angry shake and jiggle. "Intruder. Intruder…"

Johnny tried the door used by the Brunette. Locked. He reversed field and ran past "Judy and Liza" to the showroom. Banged into paying clientele as "Diana" sang about a lover treating her bad, breaking her heart and leaving her sad.

Johnny tore through the lobby and outside. Spotted the Brunette as he swung his legs, lady-like, inside a black Mercedes limousine.

The Bouncer hurtled to the *Walk of Fame*. Gasped for air. Watched Johnny run in front of a taxi, point at the cabbie and shout, "You!"

The cab, a yellow Prius, halted. Johnny dived in the back. "Follow that car." The Ethiopian driver froze. "The limo." Johnny tossed a couple twenties at him. "Go."

The Bouncer crumpled to the sidewalk and puked.

CHAPTER 2

"Perhaps we can facilitate each other," she said. Wet and raspy with a slight accent. American, but the Brunette MC couldn't place it.

"It would be a privilege and a pleasure." The Brunette sat in the limousine's back seat, prim and proper, hands in his lap. There was adequate, ambient glow from outside for him to see the profile of a thin woman.

The silence was uncomfortable as they drove under the 101 Freeway at Argyle. The small flame of a solid-gold Dunhill lighter provided the Brunette a glimpse of someone in her deep fifties. Or sixties. Tough to determine, but in the glimmer, he saw a single strand of pearls around her neck and a shawl draped across her shoulders. He assumed Cashmere because of the Benz. She lit the cigarette. The tip flared, revealed aging beauty, faded. She eyed the Brunette. He appeared calm, but his fists were balled and blood pressure ballistic as they approached the Hills. He managed a grin, then stared outside at anything but his seatmate.

Bumper-to-bumper traffic yielded to sparse residential. The limo climbed Beachwood Canyon, passed six and eight-unit apartment buildings, then duplexes and finally, single-family dwellings. Some were decorated for the season.

The trip felt like an eternity. The Woman allowed tension to flood the passenger compartment. She lifted a digital tablet off a console. Touched it with a bony index finger. "About you, I hear promising stuff." She inhaled and floated smoke rings.

The Brunette shifted his knees towards her. "Much obliged, Ms. Getz."

Getz angled the pad and presented an image of a magnificent teenager in a meaningless bikini.

"Nice."

"Yes. Of course. The finest." Getz coughed. Bubbly. A life of too many cigs and too much booze. She covered her mouth with a tissue, hacked phlegm and tapped the screen. They admired a ripped boy in a Speedo. Another tap. A naked girl. More taps, more models, the majority female, all in their prime.

"These are available? Or did you already move them?"

"It's LA."

"Seems to be a never-ending supply."

"It's LA."

The partition separating driver and passengers lowered. The Chauffeur glanced in the mirrors. "And, we have a tail." Female. Sounded young.

Getz sighed, dropped the device on her lap and gazed straight ahead. Contemplated how she hated betrayal and whether this counted.

The Brunette tensed. His mind raced. Who was tailing them? Why? No ideas. He kept his yap shut and showed no fear. Easier said than done.

The tail was the Prius taxi. Johnny, forehead against the back window, peered outside. He wasn't sightseeing or admiring the scenery. He kept tabs on his whereabouts and conjured contingencies. The cabbie pumped the brakes and navigated a sharp bend.

"There," Johnny said. "Pull over." The Prius slowed and stopped.

The Benz was parked.

"Cool your jets. Won't be but a minute." Johnny got out.

The cabby adjusted his ass and turned for a better look.

They were near the top of Beachwood, but Johnny wanted precise coordinates. Or an intersection. He selected the map on his smartphone. As it calculated, he checked his environs.

Four paces in front of him, the big car idled at the curb. The engine hummed, but Johnny saw zilch through tinted glass. Beyond, the city sparkled.

Behind him, upslope McMansions obstructed all vistas of the *Hollywood* sign. Perimeter gates, fences and walls were lit. Various residences were trimmed with holiday bulbs. In many, a Christmas tree was centered in a large picture window.

Johnny pressed the app. The GPS put him on Hollyridge at 11:02 p.m. He knew the location - a steep, winding street, as were most in the hills, but it had a landmark – the five-story turret house that flew a pennant on the pinnacle of a coned roof. In the still and quiet, he stepped downhill to the limo.

An arm shot out of the dark. Clamped Johnny in a chokehold. The cold muzzle of a gun kissed his brow.

That was enough for the cabbie and he rolled away on silent battery power. Being a witness was not on his to-do list.

Dragged backward, Johnny flailed. He needed to grab something - pants, sleeve, anything - and fight. Bicycled his legs. His running shoes bounced on the asphalt. "C'mon, we can work this out."

"Not my gig." Female. For Johnny, a nano-second of hope until she flipped him and tightened her grip on his throat. She rested her pistol on his chin long enough for him to wonder if this was it, then felled him with a sweep kick. He collapsed on his kneecaps. Ow. Swallowed the hurt. Didn't make a sound but grimaced, gritted his teeth and caught a peek of her.

Petite. Five feet and a smidge on a good day. She wore a white, skin-tight wife beater, black breeches and riding boots. Her hair was a dark, wild mess capped by a cavalry-blue Stetson. Exotic. Polynesian? Hispanic? Either was possible. Gym-rat body. Short torso, muscular quads.

She smiled and leveled a Glock 19 at him – a small semi-automatic but 9-millimeter deadly. She spun him and smashed his gut on the guard rail. Knocked the breath out of him.

"Ahhh..." He sucked air. "Got cash."

"Me, too." She forced Johnny forward to the rim of an abyss. Seventy yards to the closest roof. Jerked his collar. "Talk."

"Reporter," Johnny gagged. "I'm a reporter,"

"Prove it."

"Pocket." She kneed a kidney. Intense pain radiated. Bile burned his throat. "Right. Right coat pocket."

She rummaged in it and found a business card. "Fucking joking?"

"Scout's honor. Can I go?"

"Sure." She heaved him over the steel barrier.

"Holy damn!" He snagged the rail. Couldn't find a toehold.

She brought the full might of thick shoe leather and stomped his knuckles.

"Ah geezus." Pain blasted. Johnny's hand slid.

The shriek of a security alarm ripped the night.

Getz, in the Mercedes, yelled, "Let's go."

A siren wound its way uphill.

"Now."

Johnny's tormentor faked a last punt. He cringed. She giggled and hustled to the limousine. Inside, the driver stomped the gas and swung the wheel. Navigated a curve with one hand.

"Stop," Getz said. She turned to the Brunette. "Out."

Before the limo stopped, the Brunette opened the door. The car halted. He disappeared into the night. The door slammed and the engine roared.

The siren grew louder. Police? Fire? Paramedics? Help? It was on top of Johnny. The road above. It faded, and an uneasy quiet permeated Hollyridge. Crickets chirped.

A terrified human wail shredded the calm. It was Johnny. He held onto the guard rail with his left hand. The edge of the girder bit his flesh. Eyes slammed closed, he said, "I can do this. I can do this," over and over. It required immense effort, but he raised his right arm. The thumb skimmed the bottom of the rail. So close.

"Oh God." Johnny hung on by his nails. Strength circled the drain. He glanced into a canyon. The nearest speck of light was seventy-five yards away. Was that all she wrote? End up a pile of bones in a gully, skull discovered by a hiker's dog in ten years? Desperation set in. A finger slipped. Panic. Then another. Terror. He summoned every ounce of energy and confidence. Lunged. Missed.

CHAPTER 3

"Ohhhhhhhh.... N'..." Johnny plunged a yard. No time to even scream. He landed on a safety ledge constructed of railroad ties. "Thank you, God. Thank you, thank you, thank you. I'll start Sunday." Before he had a chance to ponder his luck, a hand swooped, grabbed his wrist and hoisted him up and over to the pavement. Johnny clung to his savior as he scrambled for balance. "I so owe you." Then surprised. "You?"

The Brunette MC slapped cuffs on Johnny. "Busted. Correction. You are under arrest." He bent his knees, spread his thighs, reached beneath the gown and removed a small flip phone.

"Impressive," Johnny said. "Hiding anything else?" It was an honest question, no quip or insult intended, but the Brunette took exception. Pushed him.

"My weapon. Tuck it up in there between the angle and the dangle. Wanna see?" Instead, he punched in a number, ID'd himself, recited an address to whom-so-ever at the dispatch center. Pushed Johnny again. "Why'd you tail her?"

"Her? Who her? I was tailing you."

That cranked the Brunette's anger. He clenched a fist. Wanted to pound Johnny but had an audience and no desire to be tomorrow's viral video. Residents recorded every word and gesture, aiming devices out windows and from balconies.

"Who's her, officer?"

"Detective."

"Sorry."

"Baby Doll Getz."

"For real? Hot diggity damn, Sam. Knew I was on it."

"Shut it." The Brunette pushed Johnny to a curb, paced and made calls. He had three conversations in the fifteen minutes it took a patrol SUV to arrive. Mindful of spectators, he escorted Johnny to the black and white, laid a hand on his head, shielded him from the roof, and lowered him to the backseat.

"Whoa, whoa, whoa." Johnny was rattled. "You're taking me in?"

"Complimentary sleepover at the Gray Bar."

"How was I supposed to know you're a cop?"

At Hollywood Station, the Brunette carried his red-soled, counterfeit Louboutins. He smacked Johnny's shoulder blades with them and herded him through the non-public entrance of one of the Los Angeles Police Department's more flamboyant garrisons.

"Easy does it," Johnny said. "I'll do the amends. Promise. But seriously, all prettied up? What'd you expect? You rock that look."

"Yeah, definite badge bunny material," a handsome guy said. He was the shade of latte, heavy milk, sported a three-day beard, was taller than the Brunette, but shorter than Johnny.

"Eat me, T," snarled the Brunette. His voice didn't fit his outfit.

T flashed the peace sign and wagged his tongue between his digits as he sauntered in the opposite direction.

"Who dat?" Johnny meant T.

"Nobody."

"Sure he is. Bet he's your sidekick. Partner? Gotta be. He's not stylin' like the police, either."

T resembled a tourist. Faded jeans, worn Army field jacket, desert combat boots. A camera on a nylon strap hung around his neck against his chest. A photo-ID was fastened to a brash, Hawaiian-style shirt. As he swaggered by, Johnny read the name – Taylor N. Quigley.

The Brunette, barefoot, clutched his wig and heels as he steered Johnny. They passed Tinsel Town night crawlers shackled to hard-shell plastic chairs. Two well-fed hookers hauled in off the stroll, a teen and one who could've been her mom, were happy to be warm. Sleeveless, micro-minis on a shivery evening did little more than meet the legal definition of clothing.

A terrified Asian tween, no older than twelve, in torn denim jeans and stained hockey jersey, was probably a runaway. She wiped a tear and snuffed.

A blonde boy, maybe eleven, no shoes, socks filthy and stiff, bobbed to something only he heard.

A swarthy lady sat with a grimy, cable-knit sweater tented over her knees. She babbled the preamble to the Constitution. "In order to form a more perfect union..."

All in all, low attendance. Even the crazies stayed in when it was wet. Most of them, anyway.

The Brunette yanked the belt on Johnny's trench coat, guided him past the empty shoe-shine stand and reined him to a stop at the check-in desk.

"Easy on the tug, sweetheart," Johnny said.

The Brunette rolled his eyes at a cute, Black officer. "Taking him to the trophy room."

She primped. Said, "Merry, merry," to Johnny, and attached a shiny, scarlet ornament to a Banzai tree.

"You, too, doll."

"Shut it." The Brunette whacked Johnny's ass and prodded him to a fluorescent-bright hall. Black, red and blue stripes were painted on the dull, gray floor. "Red one."

Johnny followed the line but had to ask, "Getz. You get her on something? How'd she look?"

"Bummer, dude. Forgot the autographed mugshot. My bad." The Brunette poked Johnny. He grimaced but stood as tall as the beating and bruises allowed. Cuffed, he marched along the corridor. Official portraits of the Police chain-of-command hung on a wall. The mayor, grizzled Chief and his subordinates seemed to watch every step. The Brunette turned at *Booking* and drove Johnny in.

A stout woman placed her elbows on a hip-high counter. Rested her chin on her fists. "Bagged yourself a full-sized one." She raised her head and sniffed. "Um, um, um. Smells good, too. You sure he's the guy?"

"Ring him up for felony tampering."

"What?" Johnny was shocked. "You a tad bonkers 'cuz of the nippiness? Cold curdle your brain? I'm not messing with your case. Not on purpose. There's absolutely no intent to screw with it or you. None." Anger sparked but didn't ignite.

"Fooled me," the Brunette said. "So far, I'm in eleven weeks of shaving and waxing and talking funny. Practically douche once a month and I'm this close." He held a thumb and finger a quarter-inch apart. "This close to nailing the bitch and you show up."

"I'll make it copacetic. Promise."

"Fuckin'-A right you will."

"Ohhh-kay, sugar," the clerk said. She smoothed a gaudy, brown and green holiday cardigan featuring Santa, elves and the red-nosed reindeer, cracked her knuckles and positioned a keyboard. "Name. Last first, first last."

"Lincoln. Johnny."

"Spell it."

"Same as old Abe. L-i-n-c-o-l-n. Johnny. J-o-h-n-n-y."

She did a hunt-and-peck. "Middle?"

"N-M-I."

"Huh?"

"No middle initial."

"Clean him out and gimme his junk." The Brunette didn't move. The clerk offered, "Please?"

"Dig in there? Unh unh. No way."

Miffed, she plucked Johnny's fedora off his head. Hummed a carol. Waited.

The Brunette caved and uncuffed him.

"Wallet?" The clerk said to Johnny as she set his hat on the counter. "License up to speed? Particulars?"

"Yes, ma'am." He put a thin, ox-blood billfold beside the hat and rubbed his wrists.

She opened it, compared him to his ID. "Yep. That's you. Date of birth?"

"November two-five."

She confirmed. "Empty 'em, young man."

Johnny extracted his cash roll.

"Where you get all those bucks?" The Brunette said.

"Savings."

"Gonna make me count it?" The clerk said.

"Roughly a grand."

"Can't write that on here, honey." She slapped a multi-copy LAPD personal-possession inventory in front of him.

Johnny thumbed his money. "Forty, a hundred…"

"Best guess."

"Eight-sixty."

She jotted the amount, flattened the bills and fanned them. "The rest of your things?"

Johnny dragged notebook, pen and another thin, rectangular device from his coat. A bit larger than his smartphone, five red LED dots at the top blinked in sequence from left to right.

"Not a bomb, is it?" She half-joked.

"No, ma'am. Portable police monitor." He showed her an earbud as she wrote.

"That it?" She eyed his property, then him. "Come on, now."

Caught holding out, he shrugged, dug deep and laid his phone on the pile.

"Nothing else living in there?"

"No, ma'am."

"Remove your coat and tie." Johnny tossed his coat next to the hat. Unknotted a maroon knit necktie and tugged it from under the collar of his burgundy-check tattersall shirt. "Unroll them sleeves. And unload your pockets. Leave 'em inside-out."

Johnny drew a dozen keys, breath strips and a few coins. He let the linings hang.

She finished writing. "That all of it?"

Johnny nodded. "When do I get my things?"

"At check-out."

"When's that?"

She didn't answer. Swept his possessions into a nine-by-twelve Manila envelope. Slid the inventory to him and tapped her pen on the paper. "John Hancock." He scribbled a signature. She tore off the white original, gave it to him, stuck the pink sheet in the packet and sealed it. Dropped the bottom golden-rod copy in a drawer. "Time to spread those fingers."

Johnny didn't respond with hustle, so the Brunette slammed him against the counter.

"Ow..." Knocked the breath out of him. He gulped air.

The clerk placed Johnny's palm on a flatbed scanner. "No ink pads in the twenty-first century." His hand was scratched, bruised and swollen. She raised her brows, surprised by the injuries. Shot the Brunette a scowl.

"Don't blame me," he said. "I didn't do it. Dude got himself beat up by a girl."

The clerk, skeptical, tapped a computer key. A life-sized print materialized on a monitor. "Other one now." Johnny switched and they viewed his digits on screen. "Congratulations, honey. You are now in the system. Ready for your close-up?"

The Brunette shoved him. "Toes on the stripe."

Johnny stumbled to a foot-long strip of dirty, yellow duct tape. He slouched between a height chart and a boxy camera. Behind him, numbers and horizontal lines marked 4'6" to 7'6". Midget to monster, he thought. Johnny rounded his shoulders and registered six feet.

"Stand straight." Mom voice.

He snapped to attention – and measured seventy-six inches.

"Let me see them chiclets, sonny, 'less you wanna get hung."

"Say what?"

She pointed at a wall. Mugs of whackos produced a tapestry of Hollyweird crazies. All ages, races and genders.

"So that's why it's the Trophy Room."

"Nope. Smile."

Johnny offered a lukewarm grin. The strobe flashed and she appraised her effort. "Good enough for your greeting card. Let's shoot your profiles." She made a circular motion.

He turned ninety degrees. Saw rows of photos of the famous, once-famous and nearly-famous. Not to mention studio moguls, a network honcho and a former United States Senator. "Oh wow."

"Those're the trophies." Flash. "Okie-dokie then… He be all yours."

"Where to now, bub?"

"Told ya," the Brunette said. "All expenses paid at the Gray Bar Motel."

"Twin Towers?"

"They'll love you downtown."

"Oh, boy." Johnny searched for options. "And you, all glammed and struttin' your, uh, stuff at that club. You're used to coloring outside the box. No reason to change on my account. How can I help? You want it, you got it. It's all on the table."

"A tit for tat? What do I gotta give you?"

"Me? From you? Tips. Clues. Leads. Nothing too heavy. You know, quid pro quo." The Brunette jerked Johnny's arms and cuffed him again, too tight. "Easy, princess. You bulls puttin' the works on me makes me wanna play hardball." Bluster was all he had.

Cop and clerk laughed. "Batter up." The Brunette grabbed the scruff of Johnny's neck, gripped his waistband, and frog-walked him to the door.

A hint of desperation snuck into Johnny's pitch. "I can get you front page. That's a big deal."

"And blow my cover?"

"Recalculating. Tons of choices here. Really." He twisted and faced the detective. Concern, maybe a little fear, sprouted. "I have people."

"It's okay, darlin'. Just punking you. You'll be here with us."

"No Towers?"

"Not tonight. Next visit."

Johnny was relieved. "Then give me my call and some respect."

The Brunette chuckled. "A comic in La La Land. Who knew?"

CHAPTER 4

"You a nutter? Wanna end up coyote crumpets in Griffith Park?" Jolly Duncan said. Short, bearded, bald, nudging fifty but in decent shape, he paraded past the cop shop. A Londoner by birth, he'd lived in the US twenty-six years but maintained his accent. "I do not remember giving you this assignment, mate." Veins throbbed at both temples and sweat beaded on his scalp as he squinted into the morning sun.

Johnny, in desperate need of a shower and shave, protested. "But it's the Big Story, Chief. You Okay'd it."

"But not on my clock. Or my ledger." Duncan gestured at the bail-bond joint across the street.

"I'll hit you back, whatever it cost."

"Five hundred big ones, and you're late for the rundown. Made me late."

"Not to worry. It's worth every penny. C'mon, Getz controls the town. She's got it wrapped up like a Hanukkah present."

"I don't even wanna hear her name." Duncan paced, fingers in his rear jeans pockets, black leather jacket zipped against the chill.

"But..."

"Not a bloody peep." Duncan clutched Johnny's lapels. Stood on his toes. "Listen, Harvard, your gig here ain't to win a Pulitzer. It's to publish items of interest for our readers. Right?" He released him and stomped away. "Another cock-up. That's twice in the four months you been here. I okay'd you a start, but three strikes, you're out, mate. Even I know that."

"So I fouled one off. Keep making contact, you get to keep swinging."

"In LA, they, them," Duncan aimed a fist at the Station. "Coppers nick criminals." Anger and volume surged with each word. "We. Only. Write about them."

"Sure, Chief. Where's your car?"

Duncan traipsed towards Sunset. "You buy fuel lately?"

"No. Let's get a hack."

A block later, on foot, Johnny and Duncan arrived at a "Rapid Express" stop on the Boulevard at Wilcox. They had it all to themselves but no time to relax. A red, articulated bus fifty-nine feet long, halted. White letters between windows and roof proclaimed, *"Nation's Largest Clean Air Fleet."* A placard advertised a Zombie film – a craze Johnny did not appreciate. He and Duncan boarded. The operator, behind the wheel for too many years, checked her mirrors and maneuvered the giant vehicle.

"Can you take care of it for me?" Duncan said. "There's a good lad."

Annoyed, Johnny reached for his wallet. Plucked two singles, fed the farebox, then tapped a plastic card on a scanner to pay for his ride.

"Why didn't you use it twice?"

Johnny ignored him and dropped onto a three-butt bench. He flipped pages in his Reporter's Notebook – a brand name for a half-inch-thick pad of ruled paper, seven inches by three-and-half, with stiff covers, spiral-bound at the top. He wrote impressions about Lucie, the Brunette, jail.

A dozen commuters were scattered in forty-eight seats, a mix of school kids and adult Latinas. The ladies chatted, the students sent texts.

Duncan plopped next to Johnny and watched the sights. Ten a.m. raised the curtains and shed a different light on Hollywood. Seedy, long-in-the-tooth, it struggled to evolve but never found the right cast of characters. Holiday decorations flapped at the mercy of the wind. Denizens of the "Entertainment Capital of the World" slid by. Residents represented a mini UN. The western border was a north-south avenue locals dubbed "Kosher Canyon." East was Little Armenia and in the middle were the Thais, Salvadorans, Filipinos and Russians.

It was lost on Johnny. He dozed, lulled by the rhythmic sway. As they rode in the direction of the downtown LA skyscrapers, the Rapid stopped at major intersections a mile apart. Duncan tracked their progress on a GPS display mounted on stainless-steel poles near the front. A bus icon traversed an electronic map.

They took on an elderly man and woman at the Hospital District and cruised by the bright blue Scientology headquarters. Further on, they picked up an assortment of passengers at the confluence with Hollywood Boulevard, across from the historic Vista Theater. It was one of the few silent-era movie palaces that had escaped the wrecker's ball and survived progress. At the Vista,

Sunset made a half-right and traversed the city at a forty-five-degree angle. But Johnny slept through it all. A mile-and-a-quarter and nine minutes later, Duncan tugged the cord draped above the windows. An automated voice that sounded female announced, "Silver Lake Boulevard."

Duncan kicked Johnny's ankle. He stirred, woke and patted his coat. Panicked for an instant. "Where's my shit?"

"Where you left it."

The notepad was cradled between Johnny's shoes. He recovered it as air brakes hissed. The bus vibrated, slowed and halted. Johnny rose, hung onto grab handles, and shuffled to the exit. He hopped to the curb. Jolly followed.

They stood on a corner at the Café Tropical, which was, in fact, a bakery. It was opposite Murder Burger. Locals awarded it that moniker due to several fatal, drive-by shootings at its take-out window.

The traffic signal changed. The Rapid rumbled away. There was sun, clear sky and a cold, gusty breeze. Trash swirled as Johnny yawned and trudged a yard behind Duncan.

It was a rough, iffy section of town. No trees or decorations to celebrate glad tidings. Years of attempted gentrification and urban renewal helped, but it was where Silver Lake and Echo Park bumped asses. Multi-million-dollar houses rubbed butts with the most dangerous neighborhoods in LA. Heavily-armed gangs fought to retain power and influence even as waves of urban hipsters swamped the area with exotic food, gourmet beans and leaves, and pricey boutiques.

Duncan led as they traversed Silver Lake Boulevard and walked east on Sunset. He ignored a vacant locksmith shop and lingered at a tiny liquor store. "Hair of the dog, mate?"

"Not hungover." Johnny concentrated on his notes for a couple blocks, composing potential first sentences for the piece he'd write.

At Occidental Boulevard, he stepped into the crosswalk and stopped the stream of cars. All of them. Johnny was always amazed by that. "I love LA," he said. A single toe on the asphalt and everything came to a standstill. Reminded him of Moses and the Red Sea.

They hurried to the far side of Sunset and a sizeable, two-story brick building, ancient by local standards. Los Angeles banned brick construction after the 1933 earthquake, but that one was a survivor. The faded logo of long-gone and forgotten "Angel's Halo Chocolates" was visible. No contemporary notices indicated the structure's current function.

Boss and employee arrived at a black garage door wide enough for a delivery truck. A human-size entrance and been cut and hung within it. Duncan jammed a key in the lock of the normal-sized entry.

"Catch you in an hour," Johnny said. "Gotta splash a shower and throw on clean undies."

"You are on the clock."

Johnny sniffed his pits. Shrugged. "Your choice." He scooted ahead and entered an expansive, cluttered space, last painted the summer Nixon quit. It was filled with a Christmas tree, eight people and thirty stacks of tabloid-size newspapers, each pile about two feet high.

Duncan used his outside voice. "Let's get to it."

Three men and three women of diverse ages, sizes and ethnicities, glanced at him but didn't pause. They sat at old wood desks, ancient landlines balanced on shoulders as they talked and pounded on computer keyboards. It was noisy.

An obese male answered an obsolete, yellow touch-tone. "*True Crime LA*. You stab it, we blab it, Mass speaking." He disregarded a *No Smoking* sign as he puffed a cigarette, fouled the air and broke a bunch of laws.

A muscle-bound staffer, too tan for December, parsed the final, interminable minute of a pro basketball game. "And the buzzer-beater. Wow."

A nattily-dressed, well-coiffed African-American schmoozed on his phone. "Yes indeedy-do. Those four sisters. The reality-TV princesses. Wild. Had to be the youngest. Yeah, her. Eighteenth birthday bash. Makes her legal, so she pulled a train at her party, not that being underage ever slowed her before. We just couldn't report it. Legal issues and all." He listened. "Both. Boys and girls. One for every year. Fantastic fodder for us."

A skinny, mousy, forty-ish Hispanic woman explained to someone on the line, "No, no, nothing like that. Not even close. It was an ordinary, garden-variety heist, not a hall-of-fame cast of thieves. Sadly. That dung-waste of a video is basic-cable farting on a perfectly respectable urban legend."

A nosh vendor did her best to channel a ragtag, Summer-of-Love hippie. She sold an organic beverage to the weightlifter, then hauled an orange wheelie cooler to Mass. "You choose," he said.

She bent at the waist, flashed braless boobs under a loose, violet, tie-dyed top, and swept pink tresses off her forehead. The colors clashed, but her customer enjoyed the performance. The food lady selected a soda and bagel sandwich from her inventory and plopped them in front of the fat guy. "Mucho thanks," he said and graced her palm with a twenty. She slipped it in a pocket of her faded jeans and didn't offer change.

"Get 'em while they're fresh," Miss Edna said. A skinny gofer at least sixty-five, she sported heavy makeup, some of it permanent, and fuzzy reindeer antlers. She wore a Persian-red tee too snug for her age and a tartan skirt that exposed knobby knees. Edna distributed copies of the *True Crime LA* tabloid to the assembled and hollered, "Hot off the press. Hot off the press."

Johnny snatched the latest issue.

Jolly Duncan grabbed a copy, too, and admired a posed pic of a "cop" in a tunnel, straddling an attractive "corpse" in a toga. The banner headline blared:

SUBWAY SURPRISE – STAR'S DEMISE

"Boffo. Who's she remind you of?" No one answered. "America's Sweetheart, yeah?"

Johnny ripped through pages of sleazy, racy photos and lurid captions. He reached the end and slammed the publication in a trash can. Nobody reacted.

"Maybe you'll make the rundown next week, Harvard," Duncan said. "We'll have to see."

Johnny stormed past a glass-walled office. Printed on the frosted upper pane of a door was *Editor in Chief.* He banged a drafting table and knocked a laptop. Caught it. Shoved it out of the way.

"Dammit. The holiday special's in there."

Johnny glared as he zigzagged around the Christmas tree.

Duncan cruised his domain. "Mass."

Mass yapped on his telephone and brushed ashes off frayed, dung-colored, polyester slacks. Friends, associates, everybody he knew, thought he was in his forties. It was impossible to deduce an exact age because of his bulk. He crushed a cigarette in a full ashtray, clamped another between his teeth and lit it. Used a classic Zippo with its familiar clink-and-clunk open and close and inhaled.

"Mass," Duncan repeated.

"Stand by." Exasperated, he said, "What?"

"How many bodies on that cult slaying?"

"How many to make the cover?"

"How many you dig up?"

"So far, four."

"Keep on it."

Mass drew a deep drag. Resumed his conversation.

Duncan moved on. "Heat? Hit on a hook yet? Orgies? Wife swapping?"

She glanced up from her computer screen, dug fingers into frizzy, semi-long, fire-engine-red hair and scratched her scalp. Turquoise dayglow hoops dangled from pierced lobes.

"Last week's piece was boffo," Duncan said. "'*Who Gummed Granny At The Rodeo?*' Monster."

"PG thirteen," Heat said. "This one'll curl your digits, Chief." She winked. Asian-influenced multi-racial, her aquiline nose complimented chiseled cheeks, dark eyes, full lips and a slightly cleft chin that blended into a beauty. She crossed legs sheathed in turquoise yoga tights, tugged her brown, leather mini and twisted the tail of a shapeless, beige bowling shirt. Heat hadn't hit thirty. That dreaded event would punch her the day after taxes. Co-workers pep-talked her not to worry - the big three-oh wasn't a matter of life and death. Plenty of opportunity remained to prospect for a partner. She was a stunner, but they neglected to mention she needed an overhaul. The hair disaster should be the initial fix. Second was, she seldom, if ever, used cosmetics, which was okay, she had great skin but ought to try lipstick. Couldn't hurt. Might even help her brand. And third - a mani-pedi. Her nails were chewed and the polish chipped. She didn't give a hoot.

"Head?" Duncan asked anyone within the sound of his question.

"Grinning Ghouls Of Gardena," Mass said.

"No zing."

"California's Kinkiest Cult?" Heat said.

"Better."

Mass shot her a nasty look, so she "nah, nah, nahed" him.

Duncan poured a mug of coffee, gulped and spat.

"Killer Coffee Creams Crank," Miss Edna cackled.

Duncan growled at her and skulked into his tidy, one-hundred-forty-four square feet of office. He slid out of his jacket, laid it on a neat, organized credenza and reclined in his pride and joy - an ergonomic executive chair. It had been a significant out-of-pocket purchase, but Duncan padded his monthly expense account to bury the fifteen-hundred and nineteen bucks.

The reporters – an older blonde woman, the thin Hispanic, Heat and the men, faked frenetic activity until the Chief snapped open *Frisco Felons*, his Bay Area counterpart.

The team surrounded a dejected, exhausted Johnny who swiveled his seat.

"Getz again?" Asked the blonde.

"Yeah," Johnny said.

"Tell us all of it." She was 50-ish with a coif that dinged her at least $400 a month. She preferred to think of it as an investment. Perfect highlights cut to the shoulders swayed when she moved and framed a sharp, natural jawline gallantly resisting the ravages of time. Wrinkles were minor and difficult to detect beneath expert makeup. Her practical, pastel-green, pin-point-cotton blouse strained a couple strategic buttons and was tucked into a tweed skirt. Winter boots put her in the "tall" category and the lift from four-inch heels accentuated diligent workouts. "Let's see if you're any closer to a cherry-popper by-line, Johnny."

"No thanks to chrome dome." He scowled at their editor.

"Or the police," Heat, the Asian-ish redhead, said.

"I'm fine, doll. It's a stretch since I burst out cryin' 'cuz the bulls don't love me."

Staffers chuckled. Mass, vertically challenged at five-two - even Edna was taller - retrieved a battered hard pack of Marlboros. He shook one free and offered it to Johnny.

He took it, placed it between his teeth and bit the filter.

"What're you doing?" Heat said.

Mass flicked his Zippo and touched the flame to the cigarette. Johnny sucked, coughed and hacked. Heat tenderly removed the smoke and stubbed it.

"Have a snort." Miss Edna wagged a sterling silver flask under Johnny's nose. He gagged and waved her away. Too early and too tired.

"Gotta avoid Getz's line of sight, Johnny," Mass admonished.

"True dat," Miss Edna said. "If'n ya don't, sure as shit she'll whack ya, then squat and piss on ya for good measure." She guzzled a swig and smacked her lips. "Ahh…"

"And this is like the worst week for you," Heat said. "Your moon's in Cancer and Mercury's in definite retrograde."

"Again?" Captain Showbiz said. He was chic and pressed. Resembled a department-store mannequin. Clean-shaven, a helmet of precision-cut, straightened, dyed-black hair, he pushed the seams of the middle-age envelope. The Captain clucked his tongue. "T'were I, I'd settle into bed with a bottle of Bordeaux for the weekend, young friend."

"Not a snowball's chance. Getz is my rocket outta here." Johnny's colleagues frowned. "You mooks know what I mean."

"You get hit with a case of the 'I'm betters?'" The blonde said.

"Even I get those, Madam Speaker," Heat said.

Jolly Duncan folded *Frisco Felons* and glowered at his employees. "Deadline?"

They scattered. Duncan's phone rang. He was irritated by the interruption. Answered. "Speak."

"Johnny. How you spell gruesome?" Mass said.

"Use the spell check."

Mass sneered and mouthed, "Use the spell check."

Johnny recognized his mistake. "With an 'e.' G-r-u-e."

Electronic feedback screeched as Duncan's voice boomed from a public-address system. "Attention, attention." Another screech. "This is your editor." He clutched an outdated broadcast microphone and paced behind a gleaming, shipshape desktop. "We have a stiff. Whitley Heights. Semi-ritzy Hollywood."

All pretense of work ground to a halt. Johnny, Heat, Mass, Captain Showbiz and Panther, edged forward. They coveted the story. The more by-lines, the heftier the New Year bonus.

Duncan's gaze taunted as it fell on each reporter for a moment, then shifted to the next. He enjoyed the suspense.

Panther squirmed. The Captain wrung his hands. Mass chain-lit another cig. Heat fiddled with her pen. Madam Speaker never participated in such nonsense, and Blitz, the muscled sports-crime writer, didn't care.

The tension ratcheted up as silent seconds ticked. "And…" Duncan decreed a winner. "Harvard. Come on down."

"C'est la vie," the Captain said.

Mass and Panther muttered curses at Duncan, but Heat was pleased for Johnny.

Excited, he smelled his pits again. Passable. His fatigue evaporated as he hustled to Duncan's office and stood on a red, six-inch circle a yard in front of the desk.

The Chief awarded him a sheet of paper. "Jump on it."

"Copy that." He put on his fedora and strutted to the exit.

"Hey, Johnny," Heat said. "Catch up with you later?"

"Yeah. 'Course." But didn't give her a thought as he reached daylight, jogged all the way to Murder Burger and cooled his heels as he waited for a west-bound bus.

CHAPTER 5

"Can I sneak a peek?" Taylor Quigley said as he approached a blonde. Weren't they all in that part of town? The female victim was on her right side, a cello curve with no tats, piercings or blemishes. She was curled on a rug in an alcove of an elegant living room. He faced her perfect, naked butt and noticed a small puddle of blood congealed near her left wrist, which rested in front of her tummy.

"Whoa. Intense colors on the shirt, T," a cop said.

"Hawaiian neon."

"Bold and ballsy. You should pass out free sunglasses."

Taylor rummaged in a canvass tote hanging on his shoulder and gave her a pair.

"Cool, dude. Thanks."

He greeted the assembled. "Hola, group, top of the mornin' to ya. Hear the one about the honeys headed to the beach?"

"Yes," all of them said in a chorus. Plainclothes, uniformed officers, Scientific Division techs, coroner's investigator.

"Sure? The one about sucking lifesavers?" Taylor winked. He was partial to those folks, though they teased him about his desert-camouflage field jacket and poked fun at his vibrant wardrobe. He extracted a light from his tote, attached it to his expensive DSLR and focused on the body. The strobe flashed three times. He stepped two paces and grabbed photos that concentrated on location, perspective and context. "Well, well, well," he said to himself. "What've we got here?"

The forensics team, aka SID, aka Scientific Investigation Division, processed a spacious, exquisite, Spanish-style home. Textured, white-washed plaster walls and ebony-stained beams adorned with faded, stenciled flowers put the era of the manse in the late 1920s, early 30s.

Taylor photographed tasteful leather sofas and Stickley furniture. Turkish carpets dotted the hardwood. None of it was arranged or situated. Packing boxes were stacked and scattered. "She just moving in?"

"Or out," someone said.

Taylor squeezed off additional images of lamps, sculptures and paintings that memorialized their physical relationship to the decedent. Distance, proximity. "Check this." A stylized, colorful depiction of field workers appeared to be a Diego Rivera. "Think it's real?"

"We'll get the art squad on it," a detective said.

Taylor shot the home's main entrance, an oak Dutch door, divided horizontally, top half open. He stepped to it and aimed outside. Patrol cars, a plain-wrap sedan and Medical Examiner's van jammed a narrow lane in Whitley Heights.

He framed a gaggle of media types who stretched the crime-scene tape. Frumpy print and radio people, camera-ready TV news babes and their videographers crept closer as they jostled for position and attempted to snatch a glimpse of the corpse. They didn't shout questions because no spokesperson was present.

Taylor re-focused on a couple dozen lookie-loos, several in pajamas.

"How much more you gonna clog the street?" A middle-aged female in a dressing gown said.

"Some of us work for a living." A male in an expensive suit chimed in.

A majority of the neighbors recorded cell phone footage, and all of them swarmed the reporters demanding information no one had.

A florid, forty-ish woman weaved through the throng. She wore a navy-blue windbreaker and lugged an aluminum Halliburton briefcase. She signed the log held by a policeman who lifted the yellow plastic boundary. She stooped and stumbled. "Damn all…"

"Upsy-daisy." A fellow in a trench coat and hat said. He gripped her elbow and prevented a belly flop.

The woman, CC Rademaker, resembled somebody who'd kissed a bottle instead of a human the night before. A ball cap covered her head. The bill shaded her eyes, and six inches of auburn curls were pulled into a loose ponytail that brushed her collar. She managed what she assumed was a "yeah, okay, thanks" smile, but to the world smacked of a too-early-for-this-shit snarl. She squinted. Dark crescents pouched, and smoker's crow's feet radiated from her hazel eyes.

The guy in the khaki London Fog gave her a boost and up she went. She swayed, found her balance, and together they entered the house.

"Hey there, doctor sunshine," Taylor said.

Rademaker sneered at him as she droned greetings and apologies to the crew. "Hope you started the party without me."

Taylor ambled to a picture window. Huge. Twelve wide by eight tall. Magnificent vistas, especially in that weather. The city was scrubbed crisp and clear by December rain. He snapped jetliner views of the Los Angeles basin, then found a telephoto lens in his canvas case and swapped.

He trained the Nikon on two buffed black men lurking on the periphery of the crowd. They stuck out in bold, green track outfits. Drawn to the bustle, one captured smartphone jpegs of officers and gawkers. The second kept watch.

"Enough," Taylor said to himself. "Time to deal with the dead."

An overweight male orbited the human remains. He carried a notebook and a pen. Jotted an occasional word and unzipped his nylon windbreaker with Department of Coroner Investigator stenciled in white on the back.

Three criminalists in disposable lab smocks dusted, bagged and tagged all items.

A mismatched twosome of detectives contemplated the deceased. Known to their colleagues as "The Long and the Short of It," each carried a Posse Box storage clipboard.

A vertically challenged Bruno Morales rose on his mock-suede chukka boots. "She is a goner? Right, Doc? We don't need a 9-1-1 RA?" No one bothered to respond. Or laugh.

At thirty-seven years old, he topped out at five-six. A thick neck and bunched biceps were evidence that Morales humped weights to compensate. He possessed the hairline of a twelve-year-old and was respectable in a pin-striped, off-the-rack, charcoal-colored suit complimented by a red power tie.

"We absolutely got to score you some new material, partner," Alita Walsh said. Wrinkle-free as her middle years loomed, she had four inches on Morales which put her at five-ten in stockings, an even six in her regulation, PD-approved heels. Walsh stood ramrod-straight and hid what cop shop tongue-waggers claimed was a killer bod beneath a navy blazer, gray, gabardine slacks and a starched, pink cotton shirt. A hint of magenta emphasized her lips and her "do" was cut wash-'n-wear. "So, what's up, doc?"

"Bad jokes from everybody today," CC Rademaker said. She knelt. *Deputy Medical Examiner* was in block letters on the back of her jacket. She stifled a yawn as she probed the corpse and recorded her observations on a form. "Definitely history. Definitely female."

Taylor navigated the space, stopped beside Walsh and switched lenses again. He nudged her, wiggled his brows and whispered, "Happy birthday."

She held a finger to her mouth. Nodded towards Morales.

"So how many?"

"If I told you, I'd have to…" She ran a pen ear-to-ear over her throat.

"Let me guess."

"Only in private."

"Pick the place, I'll be there." He winked. "Crack it yet, doc?"

"Suicide. And a dreamboat," Rademaker said. "But that's not the official pronouncement. 'Til I get her to the shop and look under the hood, a little birdy clued you. Dearly departed is young. Late teens, maybe twenty, but I doubt she's that old."

"You done for now?"

"Pretty much."

"Can I shoot the glossies?"

"Sure."

"Let's flip her sunny-side up."

The M. E. rolled the stiff. The arms flopped. "No rigor."

"So expired less than two hours," Morales said. He smiled. He knew the answer.

"Gold star, Bruno."

"You taught me good, master."

"That would be mistress."

"Details, details."

The victim was a knockout. A pouty, silky blonde with azure eyes. She appeared asleep, not lifeless, as did numerous non-violent deaths.

Taylor gasped and dropped his camera rig. The strap prevented it from crashing on the floor. His knees buckled. He staggered, caught his balance. "She's – she's – my ex."

All activity halted.

"Wife?" The ME said.

"Almost."

"Cradle-robber," Morales said. "She legal?"

"When did you..." the detectives said in unison and snickered.

An impatient CC Rademaker spit the question. "When'd you end it with her?"

Taylor was fixated on the victim's face.

"Taylor!"

"Uh, near when I joined up with the PD, I suppose. A year?"

"You asking or telling?" Morales said. His tone had an edge.

"Yeah. Year ago." Taylor's brain screamed. Did not comprehend what he saw – her beautiful, familiar features and Hi, Baby expression. "She… she's so normal. Like there was no surprise." Or shock. "Seen her that way a gazillion times. Let me read the note."

"Ain't one," Morales said.

Taylor scrutinized the body. Saw no evidence of lividity – bluish, purple, discolored skin caused by internal settling and pooling of blood. An ugly gash was slashed across her right wrist. He reached for it.

The ME slapped his hand. "No touching."

He fought tears. "No way she offed herself."

"Shoot the pix, T. It's the easiest way to deal," Walsh said.

"He can't," Morales said. "He's a person of interest."

"What?" Taylor said.

"Ex-honey. We clear you or arrest you. Might arrest you anyway if she turns out to be underage."

"Ease up, Bruno," Rademaker said. "You wanna hang all day for his replacement? He's family."

"Debatable," but Morales relented.

"Shut her eyes, could ya? Please?" Taylor said.

"When I'm done with her," CC Rademaker said.

"Be helpful, T," Walsh said. "She own a name?" Not much compassion, but no cop-suspicion.

"Emma." Taylor fumbled his gear. "Emma McConnell."

"Age?"

Taylor stared at the blonde.

"How old, T?"

"Looks fifteen, sixteen," Morales said.

Taylor twisted his camera lens. "Twenty-three."

"You shittin' us?"

Taylor shook his head. "Who phoned it in?"

"She did."

"I meant the nine-one-one."

"She did," Walsh said.

"No way. How's that even possible?"

"Anonymous nine-one-one. Female. Said she was checking out. We figure it might've been her."

"Called from here?"

"Probably. Cell pinged a tower just down the hill."

Johnny observed the early investigation as he loitered next to a coffee table. He tugged his hat brim and attempted to blend in, but that was easier in thought than deed. Six-four? Crowned by a chapeau? He slouched. Spied a tabloid-sized newspaper. A wild-haired, grandma-type flew off a bull. It was a photo-shopped Miss Edna. The headline was…

Who Gummed Granny At The Rodeo?

It was the previous week's *True Crime LA*. He picked it up, hoped to find a clue, but instead, ruffled pages and made noise.

Walsh heard and noticed him. "Yo. You. Who the hell are you? Get outta my scene."

Johnny folded the *TCLA*, stuffed it in a coat pocket, saluted and rushed away.

She realized her mistake. "Bruno. Go get him."

Taylor raised his camera and brought Emma McConnell, his ex-lover, into focus.

CHAPTER 6

"Ex-G.F. is in fourth position after wife, mother, sister. Fifth, if you count ex-wife. Resources, T. Consider our pov." Words of wisdom from Lieutenant Cederick "Cedar Tree" Hoffman, head honcho of Hollywood Detectives. He commanded from a government-issue metal desk. Behind him, a brag wall featured a dozen 8 x 10s of the LT, prominent politicians and celebrities doing grip-and-grins.

"But I'm trying to enlighten you," Taylor said. "Nothing was going to knock her off track." He was pissed, paced the boss's cramped office, gestured to prove the point and banged a half-glass partition with an elbow.

"Long and Short declared it a suicide." Hoffman coughed and wheezed. "So'd Doctor Death."

"No, no, no. She was zoomin' to the top. You see that house? She was a comer."

"Screw it on tighter, Quigley. You buy that it was her place?" The Lieutenant scooted his chair and rose. Broad, stocky and dark, a bit of gray flecked his trimmed mustache. At fifty-two, Cedar Tree was the clichéd "grizzled veteran." His desire was to die with his boots on, but trapped inside most days, he'd lowered his hopes and expected to be carried out of the Station on a flag-draped gurney.

Cedar Tree slipped on the charcoal-gray jacket of a $3,000 bespoke suit. Fashionable, with the faintest of pinstripes, it hid his old-school shoulder holster. It also concealed a multitude of other sins and extra pounds. He knew he should lose at least twenty, but never set foot on a scale unless required. Lieutenant Hoffman smoothed a silk rep tie over a crisp, pale-blue, monogrammed, French-cuff dress shirt.

"Not pulling rank, T, I'm pulling age. More than Thirty years I've been doing this. Sixteen, pushing troops here in Hollywood." In sympathy, he clasped Taylor's left forearm. "It's never-ending. You know that. Girls go from the bus terminal to the hills, then the morgue. Specs change - names, tats, weight, hair. And in between? Hot ones go to Chatsworth. The others? They hit the stroll 'cause that's all they got. But the ending is always the same."

"No, no, no… Not a chance. She was my ex."

"Girlfriend. Ex-girlfriend. She meant a lot to you. I get it. But we'll do the sleuthing. Capeesh? And we determined suicide. Sorry for your loss."

Furious, Taylor shook him off. "Gonna wrap it quick so you won't be late to happy hour? Spin a new boo-hoo sob story for the badge bunnies? Even I ought to be a suspect."

"You are. In fact, you're number one with a bullet. And we'll write it up the way it is, thank you very much."

Taylor stormed out and slammed the door. Picture frames rattled.

Walsh, Morales and twelve others, seven men, five women, paid no attention as the photographer stalked across the squad room. Desks were in cubicles, detectives obliged to stand or lean past partitions to see each other. Some work areas were messy, a few neat and tidy, all had a flat-screen monitor, keyboard, mouse and a landline.

Taylor ignored a blue and white Hanukkah bush. Swatted a sparkly ornament on a green and red Christmas tree. Didn't break it. Passed floor-to-ceiling particle-board bookcases that lined the walls. They were jammed with three-inch binders and creased, dog-eared, pre-GPS Thomas Guide maps of LA County. The bottom shelves were anchored by city directories, reverse directories and thick, residential phone directories. It was info available online but would remain until the last of the pre-digital police retired.

"Let's open the murder book, Bruno." Walsh slid an empty binder off a shelf and tossed it to her partner as she continued to eye Taylor.

"Wanna crack the seal on a computerized one?" Morales said.

"Only when we're forced to."

Disappointed, he printed a label. Stuck it on the spine.

LAPD death investigations were cataloged in chronological order. First were the crime-scene photographs of the victim or victims, followed by diagrams, preliminary findings of the Coroner's Investigator and Medical Examiner, interview transcripts and voluminous notes. If necessary, Confidential Informant tips, street rumors, even scribbled messages. The digital age added computers, smartphones, e-mail, voice mail and relevant video.

Morales hailed Taylor. "Shoot me all your Whitley Heights glossies."

"Already up-loaded." Taylor smacked his forehead on an ornament dangling from a ribbon taped to a light fixture as he rounded a partition and flopped in his seat. He was on the perimeter. Alone. Not a sworn officer, not quite a civilian, but necessary and nearby. He yanked a drawer and removed several photos. Lamented a selfie of Emma and him at Will Rogers beach. Wet and sandy. He remembered the fun. The next pic caught Emma in a kitchen as she laughed, ready to fling limp spaghetti. A third presented her in the fountain on Avenue of the Stars. She fanned a dress, bared tan thighs and flashed a come-hither smile as she pranced, splashed and kicked water.

"The blonde was a homicide."

Taylor turned. Eyeballed Johnny hat to shoes.

Decked out in trench coat and fedora, he looked eighteen and needed a wash and dry after his night in the lockup. "Emma McConnell," Johnny said. "Not a snowball's chance she killed herself."

"What the fuck brand of crazy are you?"

Johnny flicked his business card onto Taylor's lap.

The photographer glanced down. Saw *True Crime LA*. "This a joke?" He flipped the card into a wastebasket.

"Seriously? I'll spring for a cuppa and explain it."

"Climb in your rocket ship and blast off." Taylor stowed his memories of Emma in the desk and walked to the elevator. Pushed the button. Doors opened and he stepped inside.

"Cut me some slack." Johnny dogged him, but wasn't quick enough. The elevator closed.

Walsh looked up from her paperwork and recognized Johnny from Whitley Heights. She jumped out of her chair and hustled to catch up. "Hey. You. With the hat."

Johnny hurried to the stairwell. He took the steps three at a time, zipped through the main lobby and out.

The Brunette, in a skirt and sweater but no wig, jawed with a cute desk cop. Did a double-take as Johnny ran outside.

Walsh charged in. Bumped the Brunette. "Sorry," she said, and pursued as far as the sidewalk. In the almost-dusk of 4:30 p.m., she watched Johnny board an east-bound Sunset Boulevard Rapid and wondered who he was.

CHAPTER 7

"Your toaster's possessed?" Mass said. "And it's demanding you to do what?" He cradled the yellow telephone receiver between his left ear and shoulder, clutched a red pen, and doodled. He pulled a drag on a cigarette and exhaled smoke. "Whack-a-doodle. Bat-crap-crazy whack-a-doodle." Throttled the phone. Wanted to slam it, but hung up. "Ain't exactly how I planned to start my shift, Chief."

"Do not insult our subscribers," Jolly Duncan said as he meandered from one reporter to the next in the noisy newsroom.

"They pay your salary," recited the entire staff, without enthusiasm.

"Whack-a-doodles." Mass sulked and hugged his round jelly belly.

Duncan wore a puce polo with logo, ironed designer jeans and Gucci loafers, no socks.

Miss Edna scoffed at his wardrobe. "This Throwback Thursday? The eighties rang. Needs its costume. Sooner the better."

He ignored her, paused, and inspected his minions as they talked and typed.

The interior of the aged *True Crime LA* building was large. High ceilings, a lot of square footage, but the space was crowded and cluttered. The piles of back issues created mazes and obstacle courses. On top of each was a tent card with a year written on it. 1988 was in the far corner close to a desk with a hand-scrawled sign, "Rookie Haven" taped to it. The decades progressed and snaked a trail to "NOW," the stack closest to Duncan's office.

The Chief stopped at Captain Showbiz. Lifted a plastic nameplate, "Celebrity Crimes," and listened.

"Okie-dokie," Showbiz said into his phone. Oh-so polite, he filled in the blanks on a form and confirmed, "You wish to sell a chain saw?" The Captain's white long-sleeves were starch stiff. He shot his cuffs, revealed antique, gold links and adjusted the full-Windsor knot of a lavender, paisley necktie. Every strand of straightened, dyed hair was slicked back, glued to his head with spray, and his teeth were whiter than white. "A Gatling gun, as well? Vintage, you say?" He raised his eyebrows at Duncan, who nodded. Showbiz said, *"sehr absolut."* He loved to use his high school German. "Ab-so-lut… ab-so… it's perfectly fine. That'll be an even thirty-five. Dollars. Credit or debit?" Waited for the answer. "Credit it is. I'm ready." He pecked sixteen numbers. "And the security code? The three numbers by your signature?" Poked more keys. *"Sehr gut. Ja wohl.* Your ad'll be in next week." He dropped the phone in its cradle. "Why oh why do they persist?"

"Loyalty," Duncan said. He returned the nameplate to Captain Showbiz's neat, organized space, admired the sandwich vendor's ass and strode to Blitz.

It was apparent the sportswriter spent many of his non-*TCLA* hours in a gym. His too-small black tee flaunted sculpted, waxed biceps and pecs, and skinny jeans hid nothing. "Uh-huh, uh-huh, you found a toe? Where? Uh-huh. A big one. Uh-huh. Left or right? You can't tell. Interesting, but not my beat. I don't do body parts. Not that kind. I do sports crimes." He brightened. "Correct. Blitz. Isn't that nice. Glad you enjoyed it, ma'am." He covered the mouthpiece. "Madam Speaker? Severed toe?" She gave him a thumbs-down.

Duncan slide-stepped to Heat. Feet propped on a drawer handle, ankles crossed, she chatted, using a headset plugged into a red, multi-line touch tone. "Seriously? You expect me to know that?" She became aware of Duncan lingering. Wagged fingers at him. "It's great you're a fan and all, mucho appreciated, but I'm not a counseling service. If your little heart's pining to get into internet dating? Go for it. 'Til then, you get a classified ad."

She rifled files on her lap and checked her computer. "Hang on. Coming up with a word count." Heat used her fingers as she recited an ad. " 'Well-equipped ex-dick, into life hunting foxy blonde to get into.' Thirteen, 'less you thought 'ex-dick' was a single, which it most definitely isn't. Hyphens equal two. It's gonna cost you plenty. Stand by." She pushed the red hold button and snapped at Duncan, "How come I feel like I'm riding a dinosaur?"

" 'Cuz you are," Captain Showbiz said. "Giddee up."

"This is not in my pay grade."

The Chief didn't want anything to do with her attitude. He scooted to Johnny who loitered at an unused workstation and drummed a boxy CRT monitor. The kid had bathed and shaved and was clad in fresh, no-wrinkle plaid with the knit tie. His khaki chinos were rumpled but clean.

"Ad time, Harvard," Duncan said. "Gotta keep the power on and the roof patched."

"Tracking the new AMW story you assigned me yesterday, Chief." Johnny ground his molars as a nasty, ancient, dot-matrix printer buzzed and spat paragraphs.

"Dead Actress, Model, Whatever. She ain't headed over the rainbow. Pull your oar same as everybody else." Duncan hovered above Panther. She fidgeted.

"I'll get crackin' on it ASAP." Instead, Johnny said to Heat, "Emma McConnell?"

"'Weekly' clip from a year or so ago. 'Soon To Be A Big Thing' kind of thing."

"That's it?"

"And, Emma was a Virgo."

No response or reaction.

Exasperated, Heat explained, "Astrology? Means she was neat. Anal-retentive-compulsive, if you're up on Virgos."

"I got a grip on Virgos."

"Then consider it. Might be important."

He pondered. "How?"

"Personality typing? Traits?"

Johnny squinted. Contemplated. "Don't see it."

"Try this on for size. You're a November Sagittarius."

"So?"

"Gives me a solid place to start."

"Yeah?"

"Sure. You're spontaneous. Playful. Even sexy."

The entire staff reacted with, "Ohhh..."

Heat rolled her eyes at them. "So maybe later, when we get outta here..." She twirled an earring. "I'll, uh, explain it all to you."

"Explain what?

"You."

"Explain me to me?"

"Sure. Do a chart and a reading. You'll love it."

Johnny's printer finished. He scooped two yards of sprocket-holed paper and folded them into pages.

"So, Johnny?" Heat said. "Drink?" Forget coy.

"Have to boogie on out. But you're a good man, sister. Later."

Heat frowned as she hauled her hands through her mess of hair and pulled. Punched the blinking button on her phone with a knuckle. Reconnected the dating-ad call. "Okay, honey bunch, you there? Terrific. Ex-dick hunting..."

Johnny rushed to the exit. Miss Edna cut him off, boobs thrust, arms wide. He skidded. Missed her.

She pouted. "Hey. How's about some contact? Kidding. Wink. Wink. Don't be hollering at HR." Edna waved a classified-ad insertion order and sang, "Harvard's got a girlfriend. Harvard's got a girlfriend."

Curious, Johnny grabbed the sheet.

"Spill," Heat said.

"To JL, cub reporter. Close but no cigar. Soon. Best, BDG."

A collective gasp from the staff. They knew what BDG meant and were impressed. Even Duncan.

Johnny saluted and departed.

CHAPTER 8

"You're hanging a huge pair, coming in here," the Maitre d' said. He was out of uniform. No white-face, no bow tie and tails. He spread the curtains behind the bar and glared as he strutted into the lobby of the *Guess Who? Club.*

Johnny assessed the publicity stills of the female impersonators. " 'Diana.' She's incredible." He extended an arm and sang, " 'Ain't no mountain…' " Hummed and thumped a different photo. " 'Dolly.' " She was a row below and a headshot to the right of Diana. He sang, "Nine-to-five..." Said, "Ran into her backstage. Literally."

The Maitre d' rested against the mahogany bar. A pretty boy gone to seed. An abundance of those in La La Land. Black Tee, pressed jeans, buffed, cordovan penny loafers. Johnny hadn't seen shoes like that in years. The Maitre d's mane was highlighted in ways only his colorist could describe, and his hips were liposuctioned to the bone. He sucked in his cheeks to appear thinner. Johnny wondered if the Maitre d' clenched his other cheeks to tighten his butt. Gross. That was a notion he needed to chase before it kept him awake at night.

He pointed at the gallery of black and white headshots. "Kind of similar to a giant game of 'what's wrong with this picture.' 'Specially this one. Smokin'." He rapped a knuckle on the Brunette's image. Whoever the undercover cop was, the camera loved him. "Clue me in about the MC." Not a peep from the Maitre d'. "Come on. A couple answers to a few questions and I'm out of your life."

Three-hundred pounds of scary stomped in. The Bouncer wore his full purple regalia. Face paint, cape and leotards. "You."

"Geez, fellas, don't go gettin' your panties in a twist. Your MC. What's his *nom de plume*?"

"Her's," the Bouncer said. He balled his fists.

"Eddie," the Maitre d' said. The Bouncer shot him a look of disapproval.

Johnny remained calm and cool. "Got a last name to go with that?"

"Sullivan."

"Eddie Sullivan? Seriously? I've watched those pledge-week specials on TV." He flashed cash.

The Maitre d' snubbed the money.

"I suspect he gets a paycheck. Unless you do direct-deposit."

"She," the Bouncer said. It was almost a growl.

"Six, one-half dozen… the person has a legal name and a social."

"Which are beyond our professional purview," the Maitre d' said. "You'll have to ask corporate."

Johnny fired his meanest scowl and stretched to his full height. "So who owns this dive?"

The Maitre d' sneered. "Club, tough guy."

"Joint."

"Establishment."

"Paint."

"Okay. All right." The Maitre d' flinched as if he expected a bullet. "Who owns everything around here?"

"I have to hear it. Can't assume it." Johnny presented a business card. "Tell me. For the record."

The Maitre d' trembled as he peered past Johnny at the glass doors that led to Hollywood Boulevard. The Bouncer glanced at an emergency exit, embraced the Maitre d's waist. Terrified, they stumbled backward into the showroom, and that was that. Johnny knew he couldn't pry one more syllable from them.

Outside, he hurried west on the *Walk of Fame*. The mid-day, mid-week, mid-December crowd was sparse. Clusters of tourists took photos of the terrazzo and brass stars that celebrated past and present stars of film, TV, radio and music.

A husband and wife in matching olive-drab cargo shorts and wax museum souvenir T-shirts shivered. She snapped a pic of Donald Duck's star. "Thought LA'd be something close in weather to when we went down to Florida," the frumpy, pale woman with flappy upper-arms said to her chubby hubby.

Hubs made a bee-line for the *Gee Spot*. "In here. It'll be warm." The vacationers scurried past Kalessi into the porno palace. The husband had a change of heart. "No, no, honey." Too late. Wifey smiled and went deep.

Johnny followed.

"Hello, babe. Nice to spy you again," Kalessi said to Johnny.

He waved at the perky hostess and marched towards the counter and the Manager, balanced on the stool. Frayed cut-offs showed her toned legs. To celebrate the season, she wore dainty, green, curve-toed elf slippers and an anklet of bells that jingled as she shifted her ass and crossed her legs. She recognized Johnny and shouted, "Leave." Jumped down, reached under the register and came up swinging a fungo bat. Twenty patrons cleared a path as she targeted Johnny. "Get your ass outta my store."

"Yours? Getz give it to you?"

She set course for him. Her ankle bells tinkled.

"Baby Doll owns it, doesn't she?" He moved backward. "Am I on track? Simple nod to confirm. An out loud 'yes' is best. Take your pick and I'm gone."

Instead, she raised the bat.

Johnny decided he'd live to fight another day and executed a strategic retreat – he bolted to the sidewalk and sprinted east. He knew it wasn't smart to run in an area patrolled by masses of cops, but he was Caucasian and wanted to put distance between himself and the bat. At the next intersection, he slowed, saw no police, continued to Wilcox Avenue and jogged south.

Three blocks later, Johnny ambled past the Hollywood Station pedestrian entrance to the steel parking lot gate. The lot was inaccessible to the general public. He leaned against a concrete wall crowned with spiraled, razor-sharp concertina wire and checked his cell phone for mail – voice, e and texts. Didn't have any.

The motorized gate vibrated, screeched and opened. A van rolled through. Painted the same scheme as the black and whites, the city's seal and LAPD motto, "To Protect And Serve," were on the doors. A light bar spanned the roof. On a side panel was:

Los Angeles Police Department
Crime Scene Photographic Unit

Johnny stepped in front of it.

Taylor braked and lowered the driver's window. "You my new bad dream?"

"Let me buy you that cuppa."

"And do what?"

"Talk about the blonde."

"Emma."

"McConnell. Yeah."

"You can't help me."

"I know she was murdered."

"Aren't you the smart one."

Johnny gestured at the Station. "They seem to disagree."

"And you're the dude to set 'em straight?"

"You bet."

Taylor drew his head into the van and gunned the gas.

Johnny stepped out of the way. For all the world, he didn't understand why the photog blew him off.

CHAPTER 9

"Quittin' time. Who's Hordin'?" Mass said. He lumbered to his feet. It was December dark, and he needed to refuel. "Let's go love me some Horde."

The *TCLA* editorial staff groaned in protest.

"Ah, come on."

"Sorry." Blitz clutched his gym bag and hustled out.

"I'm in," Miss Edna said.

Madam Speaker picked up her digital devices. Dropped a laptop and a pad in an expensive leather shoulder bag and palmed her phone. Captain Showbiz swung a blemished briefcase, and Panther gathered a backpack. They looked to Heat for inspiration or at least a better plan. Nope. She concentrated on her typing.

"You banging out an opus?" Panther said. Heat ignored her.

Showbiz tried a different tack. "Silver Lake Lounge has a nifty *hors duvers*."

"Just those crappy baby weenie thingies," Mass said. "Yuck."

"Do I exude an inkling that I care?" Captain Showbiz was as svelte as he was well-dressed. "Twofers on the hard stuff 'til seven."

"We can scoot in under the wire for the early-bird at the Horde, so let's git while the gittin's good." Mass nodded at Duncan.

The Chief's nose was buried in "*Boston BOLO*."

"I'll hang for Johnny," Heat said.

"Text him. He'll meet us."

"How about we call it a day and all go home?"

"Where's the fun in that?" Showbiz said.

Heat gave in, sighed, powered down her computer and joined the crew. She waved to Duncan. No one else bothered.

A block and three minutes west, Heat, Madam Speaker, Showbiz, Mass, Panther and Miss Edna arrived at their destination - The Mongol Horde BBQ. It was p.m. rush hour. Traffic jammed Sunset in both directions. The stroll smelled of wet asphalt and exhaust. Most engines idled, a few revved, but no horns honked. In LA, no one honked. That was the perception.

The restaurant was shoe-horned into a mini-mall flanked by "Little Bundle of Joy Birthing" and "Immigration Counselors – First Hour Free." Captain Showbiz held the door, bowed, and gallantly ushered in his colleagues. Mass sniffed. "Mmmmm… Garlic."

Heat patted him on his butt. Panther, thin and nervous, wedged herself inside a semi-bright dining room. Six four-tops were covered with oyster-gray linen. Early diners sat at three. Two unoccupied, red-vinyl booths lined a wall and in a rear corner was a banquette, comfortable for ten.

"Ambrosia." Mass inhaled. His tummy grumbled.

"My friends," a wiry man said. It was difficult to pinpoint his age. His skin was smooth, and he took pride in a full complement of shiny, black hair. A sheep-skin vest exposed most of his chest as he spread bare arms in an exaggerated welcome. Baggy, beige pants crammed into tan cowboy boots were secured by a knotted rope.

"Howdy ho, Genghis. Hitch your horse out back?" Mass said.

Genghis laughed and slapped his hips as if he'd never heard that. "Your boot is waiting." Heavy accent. Customers presumed Mongolian. He meant booth. "No Meester Johnny?"

"He's on a story," Heat said.

"He's playing with matches," Madam Speaker said as the group settled. Panther, Miss Edna and the Captain slid in on one side of the booth, Mass, Speaker and Heat on the opposite.

"Madam Speaker nailed it." Panther flapped a menu open and closed as she talked. "You know Johnny's gonna start a fire, and then he and that Big Story of his'll be trapped."

"And we're supposed to gallop in and white-knight him," Showbiz said.

"Mixing metaphors."

"Sorry. Hose him off before his ass fuzz gets singed."

"We'd do it for you," Heat said.

"I have a clue about what I'm doing. Johnny, sweet as he is, has to experience the sting and the tingle for himself. Builds character. I bet a stint in the lockup was on his bucket list."

"You ever spend a night in jail?"

"An Black Boomer sired and nurtured in the urban environment?"

Heat laid a stink eye on him.

"Okay, no. Not really." She frowned at him. "Not ever."

"Me, neither. So when we do, we'll decide if it builds character."

"But we can't do it for him," Speaker said.

"Don't want to, but we can have his six. You and me, hell, all of us, we've reported and written about Getz. We can help him crack her."

"The *Times* hasn't."

"Even the gods at RHD haven't," Mass said as he munched on a piece of flatbread. "Not to mention the Fibbies." Slang for the FBI.

Heat pushed. "Maybe Johnny's it."

"Beginner's luck?" Showbiz said.

"We'll see."

Genghis licked his pencil lead and pressed it to an order pad. "What's to be tonight?"

"A round of lubrication, then shoot the works. Horde's Feast on me," Miss Edna said.

The gang thanked her profusely. Under the table, Miss Edna put one hand on Captain Showbiz's right thigh, the other on Panther's left, and squeezed. Both snapped to attention.

CHAPTER 10

"Original dispatch was a two-eleven. Morphed into a one-eighty-seven," a cop said. Bored, he rested against Taylor's van and chatted.

"'Nother one bites the dust," Taylor said.

"Copy that."

They were in a dirt lot. Headlights from a row of three patrol SUVs, an unmarked, late-model Crown Vic and the Medical Examiner's van lit the fifty-foot, one-level, peaked-roof, corrugated-steel structure. Its best days had been in WW deuce.

Taylor stepped out of his van and scanned the vicinity. Grabbed a couple pictures. The strobe lit an urban scar. "Where're we at, exactly?"

"Atwater. Frog Town."

"Why they name it that?"

"Frogs in the river, I guess."

"What river?"

"LA. Behind there." He pointed to an assortment of warehouses constructed too long ago to be deemed an industrial park. The buildings shared ground with ramshackle, stucco cubes gussied up as the American Dream by a 1950s-era developer. Taylor suspected people lived in them because iron burglar bars screened all the windows.

Tuck-and-roll upholstery shops and chrome-plating fabricators also blemished the area, divided east from west by the cement-lined slit trench known as the Los Angeles River. And on summer evenings, the frogs still croaked.

As they approached the assembly of official vehicles, Taylor noticed the DTLA towers to the south. "How far to downtown?"

"Five miles, about."

Taylor signed the always-present log and forced himself to acknowledge the officer on clipboard duty with a half-hearted grin, not his customary big smile. That was clear evidence he was off his feed. A year after the breakup, Emma continued to occupy a large plot in his brain.

"Plus-one for you," Clipboard said as she eyed Taylor. "We have a Mr. Gaspard."

"Doctor."

"Duly noted. Doctor Gaspard, you'll be escorted by Officer Tripp, here, and accompanied by the shooter."

"Shooter?" Gaspard was a nervous, fifty-ish man with a dreadful comb-over. He tightened a belted, terra-cotta-orange cardigan and pushed up goggle-sized, tortoise-shell glasses that had slipped to the tip of his pug nose.

Taylor held up his camera.

"Oh. I..."

"Sir, it's recommended you hang on to all your thoughts and information for the interview," Clipboard said.

"But..."

"Appreciate your cooperation." She eased him towards the entrance. Gaspard again raised his specs with a thumb.

Tripp, dubbed "Road" since high school, was a slick-sleeve. Average height, nervous-thin, a decade beyond prime. He led the way.

"What's shakin', Road?" Asked Taylor as they entered a small reception area.

"Nada, boychick."

The usual personnel - patrol, criminalists, detectives and CC Rademaker, the Deputy Medical Examiner, made for cramped quarters.

Gaspard was a step behind. "Oh my. What's all this?"

"Investigators'll get to you in a sec, sir." Tripp said. He led them into a twelve-by-twelve office.

The ME wore her windbreaker and baseball cap. Portable, battery-powered LED illumination added to the congestion and lit the place like a movie set.

"Oh no." Gaspard chewed his lower lip.

A bald male white was spread-eagle, ass up, belly down, face flat on the floor. The seat of his olive-drab trousers was scraped and ripped as if he'd been dragged across a rugged surface. An inch-wide red stripe hid the outer seams of his pant legs. A heavy police utility belt encircled his ample waist. Blood pooled on cold, polished concrete beneath a khaki uniform shirt. It had sergeant's chevrons on the sleeves below shield-shaped patches that touted an armed security service.

Gaspard babbled, "Never actually witnessed a dead body. Oh, this is terrible. Terrible. My insurance rates."

"Who you got there?" Alita Walsh said. She squatted opposite the ME.

"Doctor," Tripp emphasized doctor, "Gaspard. Property owner."

"A doc that's never seen a stiff?" Bruno Morales said.

"A little less colorful, Bruno," Walsh said.

"I'm a chiropractor," Gaspard said.

"Look who's here," Taylor said. "You pulling a double?" He attached a lens to his camera.

"Yeah," Walsh said. "Overtime dinero for Bruno. New belly to fill."

"Oh? Blue or pink?"

"Most definitely pink." Morales puffed his chest. "Brunette over hazel, five-eight, one-thirty-five, younger'n me."

"Taller, too," Walsh said.

"I make up for it," Morales protested.

She laughed. "What's your excuse for being here, T?"

"Same."

"You ain't waitin' on me?"

"Yo. Kids. I had plans," the ME said. Odds were, something solo. Her curls were packed under a yellow ball cap, lipstick faded and cracked, crow's feet dug in at the corners of her eyes.

"Any idea who he might be?" Dr. Gaspard indicated the body.

"Kind of seems to be your night watchman," Walsh said. "According to the uni, expired dude was a rent-a-cop."

"I don't employ any."

That tweaked her senses. "Oh?"

The ME rolled the corpse. "Fresh. Warm." She probed entry wounds. "Double-tap to the valentine." Searched pockets. "No wallet, but I bet he was ready to collect. It'll save the taxpayers."

"Collect what?" Walsh said.

"Social Security." Rademaker sliced the victim's blood-stained shirt and bared a round, hard stomach the size of a basketball. "Behold. A Milwaukee tumor." Beer belly. She punctured skin at the bottom of the rib cage with the spiked end of a liver thermometer and slid it in. "Whenever I poke one of these, I kind of expect it to pop."

Taylor shot pix of industrial-grade furniture – all gray steel and vinyl, plain, no decorations. Against the far wall was a vintage, stand-alone safe. Gold, scroll letters spelled the name of a defunct manufacturer. An evidence tech knelt on the polished concrete and dusted for prints.

"Maybe he barged in on a robbery," Taylor said.

"I don't keep anything of value here," Gaspard said.

"There a reason you own a vacant building?" Walsh said.

"Inherited it."

"Why keep it?"

"Tax write-offs." As if everyone knew.

Walsh didn't but accepted his answer.

"Tough break for the old fart," Taylor said as he redirected his camera.

"Hey, photog."

Taylor saw Johnny's hat brim, nose, and chin peek around the door jam. "You?"

"Shhhh," Johnny put a finger to his mouth. Whispered, "His gun?"

"You say something, T?" Walsh said.

"Uh, no." Taylor focused on the deceased's girth and an empty holster, but curiosity snagged him. He backed into the hall and spied Johnny deep in the warehouse. The reporter, holding his scanner, waved at Taylor. He glanced at the crime scene activity, then at Johnny, who signaled a second time. Urgent.

Taylor cogitated, weighed pros and cons, but couldn't help himself. He walked towards Johnny. Mumbled, "What am I doing?"

"Get snapping here T," Walsh said. She didn't spot him. "Doc, you see Taylor?"

"Nope."

"So where'd he get to?

Johnny led Taylor through the unused space to an exit and onto a service road. It was a glorified alley - dumpsters, litter, potholes, puddles and a wet stink. Wasn't much of a moon. Only a few shadows and the roar of the river, full, due to the recent rains. Johnny removed an earbud and prodded Taylor.

Thirty yards ahead, mounds of shipping containers filled a loading dock. Flush to the platform was the rear of a truck, doors open, interior lit.

"Pick up or delivery?" Johnny said.

Taylor shrugged.

"So let's rock." Johnny led. He bent his knees to shrink his profile. Advanced a step. Bright lights nailed him. He froze. "Motion-activated sensors."

"You think?" Taylor shook his head. "Blows the surprise."

"Nah. Whoever's there can't make us." Twenty feet of flat ground were between them and the next structure.

"That's a theory."

"So c'mon."

"I have a job to shoot."

"Ain't as if your subject's in a rush." For the benefit of any hidden eyes, Johnny played BFF, smacked Taylor's shoulder and urged him on. They strolled halfway. Johnny stooped and dipped a finger in a smear of dark red on the pavement. Rubbed it with a thumb. Sticky but liquid. "Fresh. More or less." Sniffed it. "Kinda metallic."

"Blood?"

"Leaning that direction."

"Dead guard's?"

"Possible. I'd make the bet." Johnny lifted a 40-caliber, long-barrel revolver off the asphalt. "Upgrade it to probable." He surveyed the distance from the truck to Gaspard's. They were midway. "Bet the codger was capped here."

Codger? Capped? Taylor forced down a smile, but for the sake of argument said, "Diversion?"

"Might be." Johnny clutched the gun butt. Whiffed the muzzle.

"Christ, man, be careful."

Johnny rotated the chamber. Counted. "Four hot, two spent."

"Best leave it for the Ds. Evidence."

Johnny shoved the large six-shooter in his waistband. Taylor started to protest but didn't. Not worth the aggravation.

Johnny scooted past the middle building to the third. A mountain of cartons, all twenty-four by eighteen inches, were heaped high. He counted. That was a wasted effort and guessed at least a hundred. "Need a plan." He thought he was talking to Taylor, but the photographer hadn't moved. Johnny gestured at him to hustle, then boosted himself to the dock.

There was adequate illumination to read shipping labels. He gripped his notebook, a pen and printed, "Borrachero." Inspected another. Sounded out, "Osteopilus Dominicensis," as he wrote it. Latin? Double-checked the spelling. He'd Google it later.

Taylor hadn't budged from the alley. He'd fought his better judgment to a tie and stayed put. Then saw Johnny gesturing. Damn. Couldn't leave him in the lurch. He jogged to the loading dock. Zig-zagged, just in case.

Johnny heard Taylor hoist himself and slipped pen and pad in a trench coat pocket. They eased along a path created by columns of boxes and ducked around a pile. A delivery truck loomed several yards away. Two hefty, male African-Americans, assault rifles slung across their chests, humped stuff into it.

"Gonna get the cavalry," Johnny said. He turned. Bumped a ten-foot stack. Lunged and attempted to steady it, but made it worse. Their cover teetered, fell and propelled a chain reaction of crash and collapse.

"Brilliant," Taylor said.

Military-grade M-4s spit lead at them. They were in a firefight. Half a firefight. And exposed. Johnny was fascinated, full of awe, but wondered why he didn't smell gunpowder.

Taylor dropped and flattened. Grabbed Johnny's sleeve and dragged him down. "Stay with me." Crawled.

Instead, Johnny leaped to his feet.

The thieves retreated.

Taylor hugged the ground and took photos. Rounds zipped above his head, shredded cardboard and pierced corrugated aluminum. He sensed he recognized the shooters but had no time to ponder it. He was in non-stop motion – right, forward, left – never a fixed target.

The thieves scrambled to the truck cab.

BANG. A blast rattled Taylor's brain. He ducked. BANG! Louder.

Johnny knelt, sighted and aimed the 40-cal. Or tried to. It wobbled as he squeezed a third shot. Wild. Pulled the trigger again. The slug ricocheted. Kind of a "zing" or "zzzzt." He'd decide later when he wrote his story.

A tire blew. The truck veered, tilted and caromed off a temporary K-wall. Crumpled the grill.

"Great, huh?" Johnny was so proud.

Taylor, on his stomach, labored to pop his ears and restore hearing.

The bad guys crawled out of the cab, sprayed a burst towards the dock and ran a forty-yard dash to a Mercedes limousine idling at the entrance to the alley. Dived in.

A tall, thin, 50-ish woman in a belted duster stood at an open passenger door and trained a pistol on Johnny. A moment later she lowered the weapon and raised a salute to concede a job well done. At least that's how he interpreted it as Getz stepped inside the Benz.

"This wasn't a diversion." Johnny watched the limo back up, make a U-ie and disappear. "It's a Christmas present. For me."

"Some present. From who?"

"Queen of the jungle." Ecstatic, Johnny slapped the firearm into Taylor's hand and dashed.

"Jesus H," Walsh said. "T?" She clambered to the dock trailed by Morales and four patrol officers. All had their weapons drawn. Walsh eyeballed the destruction, bullet holes and wrecked truck. "Explain."

Taylor waved the revolver. "Me and the kid, here, busted a heist."

Walsh stuck out her hand. "Better give that thing to me. What kid?"

"Uh, the kid from *True Crime LA.*" Taylor scoped the area. Johnny was gone. Vanished. "He was there." Pointed to the dock with the gun barrel.

Walsh ducked out of the line of fire. "Hand me that thing." He did. Barrel first. "Whoa. Other end. Thought you were in the Army."

"Sorry."

"Yeah." Walsh shut her eyes. "Gonna be a long-ass shift."

CHAPTER 11

"Let's discuss payback motherfucker," the Brunette said. He emerged from the brilliance of the AM sun. Threw Johnny against the *TCLA* building. Smashed a forearm into his gut. The force of the blow bounced Johnny's skull on the bricks. "You're crapping on my show. That's twice. The hell were you doing there last night?" The cop strained to maintain and contain.

Johnny knew not to retaliate. He'd end up in jail. Or dead. So he laughed. "Love the look."

Pigtails hung halfway to the Brunette's butt. They were braided with red and white ribbons that matched a short, pleated pep skirt and saddle shoes. Falsies tented a red "O" on a white sweater.

"I'm deducing your get-up is supposed to be college. You're way too crusty for high school. Yay team."

The Brunette clenched a fist. "Who you think you are? The fuck you playin' at? You screwed my deal. Had a team on scene set to track that shit all the way home to papa. And the boxes? That got shot up? Evidence. Was evidence." It took every ounce of self-control not to hammer Johnny's gut.

"Borrachero?"

"Same to you."

"Borr-a-cher-o. What is it?"

The Brunette lodged a knee in Johnny's crotch and applied tactical persuasion. "Stay. Out. Of. My. Way." Angry. Emphatic. His wig slipped.

"Rah, f-ing rah, baby." Johnny stated his position. "It's my story, too. You don't get dibs."

The Brunette tore off the wig. Leaned in. "You a rookie? Must be, otherwise, you'd know there's no story for you 'til I close my case. You skip that class at reporter training? Who told you about my heist?"

"Come on now, you know better than to ask."

"Oh?" The Brunette jabbed Johnny's privates with enough vigor to send a message but not hurt him.

Johnny kept a straight face. "Definitely not one of yours."

The detective applied more pressure.

"Okay, okay. Lucky guess. I was chasing the one-eighty-seven. Picked it up on my scanner."

"Course you did. From right this very minute, you get anything, I mean any-fucking-thing on Getz, even the color of her thong, I hear first."

"Next. You would hear next."

The Undercover flexed his leg.

Johnny didn't twitch a muscle. "Oh absolutely, Eddie. Yes, ma'am. You hear first."

The Brunette was surprised. "What'd you call me?"

"Sullivan."

He eyed Johnny. "You trying to get me killed?" And laid a juicy kiss on him. Held it - one one-thousand, two one-thousand, three one-thousand. Johnny squirmed. The Brunette nudged the family jewels again. "Don't forget me." He used a thumb and smeared the lipstick he'd planted on Johnny, clutched his wig by a braid and sashayed down the sidewalk.

Johnny grinned, wiped his mouth. Excellent. He'd struck a nerve. None the worse for wear, he stepped inside the *TCLA* entrance but paused in the shadows.

Jolly Duncan stormed out of his office. "How on God's little green earth did we miss this?" He flapped the morning paper. "Why do I bother paying you?" Silence. "A stiff? Machine guns? A truck crash? I'd die for this kind of piece."

"That can be arranged." Whoever said it was veiled by a page of newsprint. Mass? Showbiz? Definitely male.

"Why in bloody 'ell am I not reading it in our rag?"

"'Cuz we're a weekly?" Heat said. "Unless, of course, somebody in management coughed up the dinero to pay for a website or even a blog. Then we could do daily stories."

"No excuse. Is Harvard hiding?"

Heat waved Johnny off. He departed, crossed Sunset, hustled to the bakery and the bus stop.

CHAPTER 12

"Been in here since the ass crack of dawn and you keep lying to us?" Bruno Morales said. He sighed.

"Never lied. Not once." Taylor sat on the opposite side of the cold, steel interrogation room table. Hands clasped behind his head, he scowled at his reflection in a four-by-six mirror. Eyes bloodshot, clothes wilted and sweat-stained, he ran the tip of his tongue on the front of his teeth. Felt fuzzy. After grueling hours of questions thrown at him a dozen different ways by The Long and the Short of It, he needed a triple S – shit, shower and shave. Those two were relentless. They deployed all the protocols - brow-beat, good cop-bad cop, I'll-be-your-best-buddy cop, and a bunch not in the manual.

Bruno wasn't finished. "We pull an all-nighter and you're still slingin' a gigantic, fat fucking lie."

"No, not me. Must be talkin' about your sister. The big, fat, fucking lay."

"Asshole," screamed Morales as he climbed onto the table-top, arm cocked, ready to pound Taylor into submission.

"Easy, boys." Walsh grabbed Morales's shirt. Hung on as he tried to reach Taylor. "T? Something to add, maybe? The dude from *True Crime*?" She struggled with her partner. "How 'bout the shooters?" Silence from Taylor. Morales ceased his effort, but Walsh clung on. "No? I'd say he's on the up-and-up, Bruno. You on the up-and-up, T?"

"You are super lucky, bro," Morales said.

Taylor glared at them.

Walsh released him. "We're done here."

"Saved your ass from the fire, Kemo. Kept it in-house," Morales said. "No swinging dicks from RHD." He meant LAPD's world-famous Robbery-Homicide Division. "No hard feelings?" Bruno wiped his palms on his suit pants and offered to shake.

Taylor snubbed him. "Schmuck..."

"Back at ya."

"Crap all mighty, it's just business," Walsh said. "Shake, goddammit."

So they shook. Once.

"There ya go." She led them out.

In the squad room, they were met with applause. Seven Area Ds clapped. It was a modest assembly. A lot of empty cubicles. Burglary, Auto-theft, Juvie and Sex Crimes were on the street. Or lunch break. It was noonish.

Cedar Tree Hoffman joined in. "Man of the moment. Congrats, Quigley." The boss taped the newspaper's *City* section to his office wall. The official PD portrait of Taylor in blazer and tie posed with Old Glory was below the headline...

Police Photographer Halts Heist

Taylor bowed. "Thank you, thank you, thank you very much." He beamed a smile. Rare since Emma's demise.

Walsh and Morales, as rumpled and drag-ass as Taylor, clapped, too.

Hoffman and his troops continued to applaud. Except the Brunette, at his desk, no wig, but in his cheerleader gear.

CHAPTER 13

"You planted her already?" Johnny said. He stood in a white tile autopsy suite. Watched as CC Rademaker bopped and slid across the slick, blood-splattered floor in time to a loud rendition of the Grateful Dead. The Deputy Medical Examiner sported mauve scrubs and wore a spatter shield - a full-face protective visor. Johnny raised his voice over the music. "Tell me why you boxed and shipped her so soon." He held a pen and his Reporter's Notebook.

"Who?" Rademaker dug in a body. Tugged. Made nasty, slurpy sounds. The corpse on the ME's stainless-steel dissection table was the rent-a-cop killed at the Frog Town warehouse. Rib cage sawed and spread, shiny-wet, mottled, dark-gray lungs, red heart, brown liver and kidney were exposed.

Johnny's attention was riveted to the guy's thick belly fat. "Wow... it's so yellow."

"Well-marbled." Rademaker reached into the torso and generated more gooey noises as she excised a lung and laid it on a scale. She logged the weight, transferred it to a cutting board, sliced the tissue with a scalpel and revealed the interior. Black, coated in tar. "Decades of cigarettes."

Johnny grimaced. His stomach flipped, but he stared. "Emma McConnell," he said.

The ME faked contemplation. "The model babe? Meh. Tough to say. I get a ton of 'em. Who're you?"

Johnny presented a card.

She glanced at it. "Huh. *True Crime LA*?" Smeared goo on it with a gloved thumb. "I see it all the time at the market."

That pleased him. "Just so you know, I keep my sources confidential." He would, once he cracked the lineup.

"You really work there?"

"Absolutely."

Rademaker flicked Johnny's card. It fluttered into the muck. She stepped on it.

"There's no need..."

A mental bell rang for the ME. "We met?"

"Possibly." Johnny shifted his weight from foot to foot. Shivered. Shoved hands in pockets, but that didn't help. The LA County Morgue was a giant, walk-in refrigerator.

She tried to place him. Couldn't, and he didn't remind her. Instead, she unpacked yards of intestines and coiled them in a metal bowl.

He crinkled his nose. "It always reek so bad?"

"If we nick the bowel. You a morgue virgin?"

Johnny hated to admit it but nodded.

"You've now eyeballed and whiffed the part of homicide never ever mentioned on all those TV shows. The stench." Death rot and heavy-duty chemical disinfectants. "No stink on the tube, so they figure let's keep it secret. Right? In their genius minds, the issue becomes - do people tune in if they know what murder smells like? It's the reason for my aromatic assistance." Rademaker pointed a latex-covered finger that dripped body fluids. Incense burned in the corners of the room. She snagged a jar of Vicks from the instrument tray. Tossed it to him. "Here. Stick some up your schnoz."

Johnny twisted off the lid, dipped a glob and smeared it in and under his nostrils. Potent, mentholated and cool.

"Inhale through your mouth." He did. Better. She displayed the watchman's liver. Poked it. Spongy. "Swelling. Means a megaton of booze. Mine probably resembles this." Her flushed cheeks and wrecked capillaries agreed. She set the bloated organ on a ruler.

"C'mon," Johnny said. "Emma McConnell."

"The natural blonde."

"Yeah. Whitley Heights. Got a clue where she is?"

"Not my job." Rademaker scooped the heart out of the chest cavity and weighed it. Documented the numbers on a chart.

"So why wrap her so fast?"

"We're dealing in volume here. We forward 'em on quick, otherwise, it's gridlock." She swayed to the tune.

"Breaking news. We're in LA. You look at your hallway lately? There's stiffs stacked up since the turn of the century."

Rademaker shrugged. "They haven't been there that long."

Johnny persisted. "Lay the AMW's headlines on me. Her tox screens, your analysis, all the pertinents."

"Profiled exactly how you'd expect for a girl on that career path. Blow and snow. Booze. Benzocaine, casein and that dry-dusting powder on condoms. She had a pricey dinner the night before, then cashed her own check. Don't need a rocket scientist to unravel this one. Absolutely nothing to see here."

"Can I scope your report? Have to corroborate everything. Make sure I get all the facts."

"Nope. 'Less, of course, you're next-of-kin, which we don't believe she has any. You can petition the court. It's a public record and I suppose the press is public."

"We are. It's in the constitution."

"But it takes a while."

The ME carved the heart. Used the tip of her scalpel to dig fat deposits. "Let this be a lesson to you. A lifetime of burgers and fries."

"I'll keep it in mind." Johnny whipped out his money. "Prime-rib at Musso's for a gander at the AMW's autopsy and your conclusions."

Rademaker scoffed, touched her phone's controls with a clean pinkie finger and cranked the Dead from loud to earsplitting.

CHAPTER 14

"See the man. Six-thousand Santa Monica Boulevard." The disembodied voice of a female dispatcher caught Taylor's attention. He wondered for the zillionth time if she was hot or not as he drove the Photographic Unit out of the Station lot. There were five hundred of them and they all sounded sensual, even suggestive. Someday, he'd scratch that itch and trek to the emergency operations center. Taylor keyed his radio mic and said, "Repeat, please."

"Six-thousand Santa Monica Boulevard." Resonant radio pipes. An alto.

"Hollywood Forever?"

"Affirmative."

"A body?"

"No indication."

Taylor was dubious. "Has to be a joke."

"I'm just the messenger."

"Copy that. Sorry." If it wasn't a homicide, they wouldn't need him.

Police radio chatter filled the van. Holiday-heavy traffic jammed the streets as he navigated Wilcox, then Santa Monica. The TV weather mavens had predicted sprinkles turning to rain, but it was dry as pedestrians dashed from store to store and blustery gusts blew Christmas and Hanukkah decorations.

A mile south and east of the cop shop, but seventeen minutes on the clock, Taylor stopped the van at an unoccupied guard shack. Behind it was a wrought-iron gate two lanes wide. The right side was open. On the left were a pine-bough wreath and a placard topped by the infinity symbol. It announced *HOLLYWOOD FOREVER*, the wannabe's dream when they arrived in LA, except that particular dream was a well-known cemetery and forever was six feet under.

Taylor scanned the area for "the man" but didn't spot a soul. He steered through the entrance and followed the main road to the final resting places of Valentino, Douglas Fairbanks, Tyrone Powers and other golden-era luminaries. The narrow track curved, bypassing a statue of rock god Johnny Ramone and a pond. On an island, an imposing, smog-stained Greco-Romanesque mausoleum with eighteen columns was home to the earthly remains of the long-forgotten Clark family.

Taylor searched for the vehicles and personnel that swarm an investigation. No such luck. He heaved a sigh, draped his camera strap around his neck, dug in his equipment bag and located a heavy-duty MagLite. He eased out of the van, zipped his Army field jacket and scouted the deserted boneyard. Grouchy, sleep-deprived, Taylor preferred anything to wandering among the graves. He slid the switch and swept the beam of light in an arc. Headstones and monuments. All Taylor craved was shut-eye but thought he noticed someone. Yep. There, on a rise, fifty yards away. An arm waved. He sagged, notions of a toddy and bed, gone. None-too-happy, he hiked the slight incline and recognized who signaled him. His bad attitude amped. "What kind of BS you tell nine-one-one, Scoop?" He nailed Johnny with his flashlight.

Johnny winced. "Don't call me that."

"What load of crap you give them?"

"Not important."

"You can catch a serious sentence in the lockup for screwing with comms."

"Cost of doing business."

"Wow. You kidding?"

Johnny stood on a mound of dirt covered by a green canvas tarp. He was lit by a camp lantern propped up in a wheelbarrow. "Any problems finding it?"

"Hollywood Forever? Been here. For the movies. Me 'n Emma, actually." Cemetery management staged outdoor screenings of classic films. The Halloween event was world-renowned.

"Don't I get a thank you?"

"You serious? For what?"

"The terrific front-page pub."

"Okay. You did good."

"All in the course of a normal week at *True Crime LA*."

"It's not movie night, so why're we here?"

Johnny yanked the edge of a second tarp and uncovered a grave.

"Been puttin' in some overtime."

"Nah, I distributed X-mas cheer to the diggers."

Taylor aimed his MagLite at the hole. Saw a cheap pine coffin. Stenciled in white on the lid was a representation resembling a crude coat of arms. Two elongated snakes, both shaped in a lazy "S," not coiled, faced each other. The serpents were separated by a rectangle, three feet long and one wide. Inside the lines, vertical and horizontal cross-hatches intersected every four inches at ninety-degree angles and formed a grid. "Okay. You get another minute."

Johnny pointed at the grave.

Taylor shined his light at a temporary marker - a hand-written name on a small piece of cardboard stapled to a stake.

EMMA MCCONNELL

He fell to his knees.

"That buy me a few more?" Johnny paced. "Here's the press release. It's *dos, deux, zwei* days since they found her, and she's already in the ground. Gotta be a new speed record for the LA County Coroner."

"Not my issue. How'd you trace her?"

"Emma have a family?"

"Yeah. Back east." Taylor directed his MagLite on Johnny.

"Want you to dig them up."

"Excuse me?"

"Mom and dad. Granny and Gramps. The who and the where. Can you?"

"Suppose so. Yeah."

"*Excellent.*" Said it with a French accent. "All right. Moving on. Emma would never slit herself in the living room. She'd slice her arm in the bath, over the sink, or in the tub."

"That's true, but there's no way you picked that up at the crime scene."

"Actually, I did."

"Not buying it."

"It's my racket. You study certain subjects. For example, the cut? On her wrist? Perpendicular to the artery? Can't off yourself like that 'cept on television."

"Meaning?"

"Same as you're thinking." Johnny gave Taylor time to agree. Received nothing but silence. "Ohh-kay... Pin this on. The homicide dicks undoubtedly understand the slash didn't kill her. And the Medical Examiner, too. The doc's being cagey about the autopsy. And the detectives signed on to the whole suicide motif." Case presented, he folded his arms.

Taylor considered all of it. "Somebody's gone to heaps of trouble." He touched the grave marker. "What's the deal here?"

"Ain't suicide, and the lid, the drawing, means something."

"Goddamn vulture." Taylor grabbed Johnny. "What're you after?"

Johnny cocked a fist, ready to punch. "Answers. No different than you."

"Bull." Taylor knocked him on his ass.

"I'm chasing a story. A huge one. Ginormous." Johnny hopped up and brushed himself. "But I ain't going to catch it unless…" He dropped into the grave. "Shoot me some bright."

Johnny pried the coffin lid with a pocket-knife blade and raised it a couple inches.

"The hell?" Taylor was shocked but raised his camera. In rapid succession, his strobe lit five shots of the serpent symbol.

Johnny lifted the lid. "Knew it." Did an arm pump.

"Geezus H. Christ!" Taylor snapped pictures.

A hundred-twenty pounds of sandbags packed Emma's casket.

CHAPTER 15

"Who're you, sweet cheeks?" Miss Edna, the ancient-age gofer said. She leered at Taylor. Goosed him in the ass.

He jumped. "Who're you?" Taylor looked better than he had at the cemetery. Restored. Fresh Hawaiian shirt. Clean jeans. Scuffed combat boots, a spring in his step. Eight hours of sleep, a triple S and coffee, elevated his mood.

"Meet Miss Edna," Johnny said. "She's a fixture."

"I own the joint." Edna fanned her pleated, tartan kilt and curtsied.

"That's her story."

"And I'm stickin' to it."

Taylor winked at the old dear.

She swooned. "Can I follow you home?"

Johnny continued the tour. "And this is Mass. Mass Machado, Taylor, Taylor…"

"Quigley. Taylor Quigley."

Mass yapped on the phone. "Uh-huh, uh-huh." A cigarette bobbed between his thin lips.

Taylor read an In Basket.

MASS MURDERS / SERIAL KILLERS

"This real?"

"Abso-freaking-lutely." Mass aimed a locked and loaded finger.

Taylor threw his hands over his chest. "Got me." Whispered to Johnny, "Thought it was 'cuz he's so, uh, so..."

"Ample," Johnny said. He continued the intros. "The chiseled boulder there is Blitz Bergen." Bulging biceps and pecs encased in a bodybuilder's long-sleeve muscle jersey, Blitz elevated the left side of his mouth a quarter-inch as he typed. "And the tall drink of water behind him is Panther, as in Pink, Perez. She's the scams, cons and capers desk."

Panther clutched a gray cardigan and chewed the ends of her limp, mouse-brown hair.

"To her left, that's Captain Showbiz."

"Let me guess," Taylor said.

"Not necessary. My by-line captures it all." Showbiz leaned forward, cupped his chin in a palm and appraised Taylor tip to toe. Approved.

"In Center Court is Madame Speaker. Senior reporter, political larceny, graft…"

"And so much more," she said.

"Mentor to us all."

"Must keep you busy," Taylor said.

"Never a dull moment." Speaker crossed her legs. Her tweed skirt snuck above her knees.

"What's your specialty?" Taylor asked Johnny.

"We call them beats."

"So what's yours?"

Johnny hesitated. "Uh, General Assignment."

"Means he's waiting for one of us to die," Showbiz said.

Johnny ignored the snark and led his guest to Heat's empty chair.

Taylor picked up her nameplate.

Crimes of Passion

"Seriously?"

"Seriously," Johnny said.

"All crime, all the time?"

"Pretty much, yeah."

Taylor, at best skeptical, often cynical, said, "Insane." He ran his fingertips over the letters on the plastic plaque. "I appreciate all you did, working the Emma angle, getting me in the paper 'n all, but I don't see it happening here."

"And you do with the police?" Johnny challenged.

"Been a tough day…" Taylor set the plaque next to a framed certificate and turned for the exit. Made it a yard.

Heat, stooped at the waist, searched the bottom drawer of a file cabinet. She reached deeper. Knelt. Her green leather mini stretched across her butt.

Taylor scrutinized every square centimeter.

"Lots of ways to go, Johnny," Heat said. "Mucho possibles."

"She's digging on McConnell."

"I see. Yes, I do."

"Who the what…?" Heat, caught derriere up by a stranger, was flustered. She rose, blushed and pulled her hem. "An FYI would've been nice."

"Taylor, meet Heat," Johnny said. "Crimes of Passion."

"Arrest me," Taylor said.

Captain Showbiz flapped a dollar bill. Heat snatched it.

"Win a bet?"

"You could say that," she said.

"Own a name to go with the title?"

"Weren't you listening?"

"Last name. Case I wanna get in touch."

"And you'd need to do that, why?"

"Use your imagination."

"Easy, big fella."

Johnny was impatient, bored by the banter. "O'Leary. She's O'Leary."

"Not your question, Johnny."

"O'Leary?" Taylor said. "You married?"

"Excuse me?" Polite words, angry eyes.

"You hitched?"

"What's that have to do with the price of anything?"

"You don't resemble an O'Leary."

"And an O'Leary is supposed to resemble…?"

"The Irish?"

"Fight on for old Notre Dame?" Heat assessed Taylor's latte-colored skin and hazel eyes. Dude was hot.

"Ireland Irish," he said.

"And you recognize this how?"

"My dad."

"Ahh. He the one that gave you a preppy-girl handle?"

"Taylor's a family thing. At least one in every generation back to the beginning. My dad's a wannabe WASP."

"Wannabe?"

"He's missing the P."

"Mine's Army."

"Say again."

"My dad. He's Army."

"So?"

"Never met a military brat?"

That was unexpected.

"Harvard!" Jolly Duncan scurried into the newsroom.

"And this..." Johnny performed a stage bow. "Is the center-mass of *TCLA*, our leader, our spirit-guide, our Editor-In-Chief, Jolly Duncan. Chief, Taylor."

Taylor offered a shake. "Nice to meet you."

Duncan, suspicious, paused and shook. Acted as if Taylor might steal his watch and wallet. He broke the grip and nudged Johnny to the coffee pot. "Who's the bloke and why's he here?"

"He's a friend."

"You got no friends, mate."

"He's part of the AMW story, Chief. Trust me."

Duncan invaded Johnny's personal space, ready to lecture and admonish. "Harvard, I get it. Trying to lose your virginity. Nail your first piece."

Johnny shut him up. "He's the dead model's ex and an LAPD crime-scene shooter. Actually grabbed the glossies on this one. It's all hunky-dory." He had an urge to pat Duncan on his slick noggin but instead fist-bumped his shoulder.

"Breeding sources. I uhh... great, Harvard." Duncan ducked into his office. No one paid attention, least of all Johnny.

Taylor observed Heat with a critical eye. She lowered herself to a kneel, tugged her skirt to mid-thigh, aimed her ass away from him, for all the good it did, and resumed her search.

"So - been here long?" Taylor said.

"Wasting your smile."

"Only being sociable."

"Didn't your squeeze just buy the farm?"

"Ex, and now it's anybody's guess. Scoop, here..."

"I'm aware of what he did." Heat indicated a worn folder. Old notes and titles were scratched out and Model Murder added. She tapped a key on her laptop and said to Johnny, "So... Soldier boy and the wannabe found each other when they landed in town. Couple years ago. Love-in-the-loft. She'd graduated, or so she claimed. My money's on dropout. Jailbait. A runaway. Or all of the above.

"He claims she's twenty-three."

She laughed. "Next lifetime, maybe. We'll pin it down. So he generously provides the rockin' little babe a boost. Even more, by the looks of it. I suspect co-habitation and he shot her book." Industry-speak for a model's portfolio.

The recitation had a familiar ring to Taylor.

"Heat's aces," Johnny said. "Absolute cream of the crop."

To hammer it all home, Heat locked onto Taylor. "But after a while, you two hit the skids. You joined The Man and Emma circled to the dark side. Took just about anything and everything for a buck."

"Such as..." Johnny prompted.

"She bought a ticket to Chatsworth instead of TV City."

"You don't know squat," Taylor said.

"Squat?" Heat swallowed a laugh.

"And who'd Emma hook up with out there in Chatsworth?" Johnny said.

"Michael Le Roux. Coke. Meth. Porn. Your basic scum merchant. We can probably find him at The Baths in Silver Lake. It's a haunt of his." She presented a picture of him. "Pulled this off the 'net. Not sure how current it is." Le Roux was soft, pudgy and into age denial. Expensive haircut and dye-job, Botox forehead, capped or professionally bleached teeth. A bevy of beauties-for-hire fussed and fluttered.

"You're tripping," Taylor said. "Emma? Porn? Not for a New York minute."

"Let's check it out. Easy to confirm."

"Not tonight." Johnny swiped the photo from her.

"Hey." Heat launched out of her chair. "It's my lead."

"The Baths ain't exactly lady-friendly."

"So why do they let women in free?"

"Use a mirror."

Before Heat killed him, Miss Edna waved a sheet of paper at Johnny. " 'Nother hoochie koo letter, Harvard. For the classifieds. You're on a roll."

Johnny snatched the ad order.

"Spill, dammit," Heat said.

" 'Dear J.L. Hope you aren't too involved. I'd hate it if you were hurt. XOXO'? What's that mean? XO."

"Means love and kisses," Miss Edna said.

He didn't know that. "Okay. 'Love and kisses, BDG'."

A collective "Ohhh," from the reporters.

"Shakin' a cage, kid, shakin' a cage," Madam Speaker said.

"Keep slinging," Heat said.

Even Taylor was impressed. "BDG as in..."

"Don't say it." Miss Edna plugged her ears.

"Not in here," Speaker said.

"Never in the newsroom," Panther said. "Not 'til the issue's put to bed."

"Whew. Too close for comfort," Mass said.

Taylor raised his palms in front of his chest. "Sorry. Won't happen again." But he was clueless about what he'd done to ignite them.

Johnny scribbled a sentence on the ad form. "Can I still make the holiday special?"

Miss Edna said, "Oh sure. I'll stop the presses for you."

He remembered his manners. "Pretty please?" She didn't move or react. "With sugar on top?" She nodded. He gave her a big smooch on the cheek.

Taylor winked at Heat. "Never answered my question."

"No?"

"No."

Staffers inched forward in their chairs. Except Heat. She propped red, Jack Purcell tennies on her desktop. Flashed leg at Taylor. "And what question might that be?" The corners of her mouth edged up a millimeter.

"You married?"

Before she responded, not that she was inclined to do so, Johnny escorted Taylor to the exit. "C'mon. Story won't buzz the bell on its own."

"Sizzle, sizzle," Captain Showbiz said.

CHAPTER 16

"She involved?" Taylor said as Johnny latched the door-within-a-door.

"With what?"

"Not what. Whom. She have a whom?"

"You asking me?"

"You're the one sits beside her. How do you concentrate with her filling your frame all day?"

"You didn't split to go back to the cops 'cuz Heat's got a great bod?"

"You said it. She certainly does."

"But all the relevant material we dug up? Plus your pic on the front page? Don't you wanna be a hero?"

"Sure. Already told you."

"I ain't feeling the love."

"Rather work on what became of Emma. Wouldn't you?"

Johnny walked towards the street corner.

"Hey," Taylor said.

"What?"

"Where you headed?"

"The Baths, remember? Need to catch the bus."

"Keep your change." Taylor unlocked a compact, burgundy Kia. It wasn't too ancient. "Hop in."

Johnny bent his 6'4" into the passenger seat. Knees pressed against the dash, he reached for the adjuster lever, lifted and pushed. It didn't budge.

Taylor swung the wheel and melded with the rush-hour crush. "Left, right, straight?"

"Right at Murder Burger."

"Huh?"

"The hamburger joint at the light."

Taylor turned and drove into the core of the hipster universe. Silver Lake. Spawning-ground of all things black and tight - jeans, sexy tops and accessories – biker boots, watch caps and heavy, oversized spectacles.

The area, north and west of downtown, was the heart and soul of capital "I" "Indie" LA. Recording studios, record labels, production companies, publishing concerns and video editing facilities sprouted on every block, all with an over-used descriptor – boutique. Whether they were profitable or not, no one knew or cared.

Tuesdays or Saturdays at the local farmers markets, it was possible to wrangle anyone required to crew a low-budget feature film. "Producers" dangled the promise of deferred compensation, free food and a screen credit, which dripped paradox because it was LA. The living was easy, but not cheap. However, Silver Lake residents possessed an irony level ten times cooler than the rest of LA, and their sense of boredom was off the charts. Unofficial motto - Unless you lived life on the edge, you occupied too much space.

Taylor glanced at Johnny. Pretended the glow of taillights crawling at a snail's pace added to the holiday vibe. "Kinda Christmas-ish."

Johnny stared into the night at expensive houses. He didn't react as they crept past the larger of two reservoirs – the lake in Silver Lake.

Taylor had no desire to endure an uncomfortable silence. "Tell me about the hissy-fit when I started to say Baby Doll Getz?"

"It's negative Ju-Ju to mention a subject's name in the newsroom before you go to press."

"Never heard of that. Is there more I ought to know?"

"Let me dig out my list."

A mile and fifteen minutes of silence later, the four lanes rounded the base of a hill as Johnny gazed at a mix of multi-million-dollar, ultra-modern houses and old brick buildings.

"Ohhh-kay. I'm not going to the cops 'cuz you asked important questions. Even answered a few." Taylor slid the car in a spot. "Parking gods are with us." He fed the meter.

Johnny emerged. Stretched the kinks. "It's directly across."

Lit windows dotted the first and second floors of a three-story brick structure half a block long. It was streaked by a century of smog, punctured by earthquake retrofit rods. The third floor was dark.

The Baths, in faded letters, arched above a dull-red entrance. A trio of whippet-thin Boho boys lurched to the sidewalk. Their skinny jeans and tie-dyed T-shirts afforded no protection as winter raindrops resumed. They managed to buttress each other and staggered away.

Taylor and Johnny caught a break in traffic, jogged to The Baths and entered a worn lobby. They sauntered ten yards on frayed, 1970s avocado-green shag. Paint peeled off unadorned walls, and there were no chairs or couches. Johnny sniffed. "Mold."

A reception desk of sorts – waist-high, ten feet of raw plywood - was built next to double doors. Behind it was a pair of black-clad women. The only hints of color were their spiked tresses - one emerald, the other crimson. They enjoyed a tentative peck, then bam – lip lock.

Laughter erupted. Two couples stumbled into the lobby. They fondled, tickled, played tongue hockey, unaware of Johnny and Taylor. The men, a natural gray and a brown dye job, both in blazers and khakis, waved what Johnny figured were membership cards. Gray bowed, and with a flourish, opened the doors to the roar of a crowd. Sounded like a ball game. The young sweeties wobbled on stiletto heels. Their animal-print bandage dresses required minimum imagination as they giggled and led the charge.

Emerald and Crimson pawed and groped as the doors closed and noise subsided. Johnny showed his cash. Crimson released her friend's boobs and pointed to a poster.

Admission - $20.
Annual Relationships Available - Inquire

"Apiece," she grumbled.

"And for a relationship?" Johnny said. No reply, so he skinned two bills from his flash roll. Emerald stuffed them in a drawer.

"Seen him?" Johnny displayed the photo of Michael Le Roux and the party babes.

Emerald and Crimson didn't bother to break their smooch and dismissed the guys with condescending gestures.

Johnny and Taylor passed through the doorway and walked along a congested corridor towards a jumbled, unintelligible din of voices and noises smashed together. Ahead, folks cheered as if they were fans at a game or an event.

Johnny held the picture of Le Roux at arm's length as he checked it against the throng. Some faces were fresh and eager, others worn and faded. Several swapped money for tiny plastic baggies. Most cooed for favors.

Negotiated transactional hook-ups. Kids for sale or rent. A body for a fee or a fix. A pale girl of indeterminate age said, "Come on, daddy…" clenched a gentleman's silk cravat and led him to a shadowy nook.

An older white dude chucked his suit jacket in a heap. He signaled to a naked, bald chick and said, "Finders, keepers."

She swooped in and scrounged the pockets. Empty. Shrieked, "Cocksucker." Tried to punch him. Swung wild. He tossed her.

Boys of all major races and a smattering of mixed pedigree also worked the scene. Those who were clothed wore classic thrift store. They performed various roles - stud-muffin, nasty-nephew, son's BFF, for middle-aged mothers parading and prancing in thongs, nylons and garter-belts.

"Won't locate Le Roux in here," Taylor said. He and Johnny moved on and encountered a rectangular hole, one-hundred feet by seventy. People were jammed cheek-to-jowl on the coping. "Got a guess as to how many souls?"

"Tough to peg. Two hun?"

"Double, at least. What is this place?"

"Depends…" a blonde MILF said. She draped her arms over Taylor's shoulders and curled a stocking-covered leg around his calves. Outfitted and coifed to conjure a 50s-era sit-com mom, her hair was drawn into a ponytail. Petty-coats puffed a hot-pink, knee-length poodle skirt. A red, scoop-neck sweater offered serious cleavage shaped by a faintly visible bullet bra. "You want to eat it, drink it, smoke it, or fuck it, we got it." Slow and sultry.

Balanced on a single foot, she smushed a full-court-press on Taylor - lips to hips, tits to toes - and nodded at a nude cutie in a canvas beach chair. "Choices, baby." She licked his ear.

Johnny shoved the image of Le Roux at her.

"Damn. You know how to screw a moment." But the MILF studied the shot. "Try the Hole." Each resonant syllable dripped double meanings and unknown secrets as she hugged Taylor and swiveled her core.

"The hole?"

"The pool."

"Appreciate it."

Taylor shrugged an apology. The MILF pouted, slipped a business card in his shirt pocket and tucked another into Johnny's. She caressed a passing honey's butt and stroked a hunk's package. Both kissed her.

Johnny and Taylor navigated the crush of partiers. They nudged, dipped, swayed and shoved their way to the Hole. Once a swimming pool, it was almost Olympic-size and sloped from a depth of three feet to twelve. Steps in the shallow end were the way in unless, of course, one dived onto a slab of rock-hard, faded-blue gunite. The Hole was partitioned. A maze of vinyl panels divided it into sections filled with king-size mattresses. Half was for groups and gangs, a quarter for couples, and the deep end was orgy-sized. Wherever the guys looked, limbs thrashed, hips undulated, and glutes humped.

"Kind of Fellini-esque,"Taylor said, "'cept hotter." Rhythmic moans and gasps reverberated. "Whoa..."

He saw a woman spur an enthusiastic cowgirl as she yelled, "Yee-haw, pardner," in response to spirited applause and cheers.

Johnny assessed the males in the Hole. Compared them to the print of Le Roux. He altered perspective and took advantage of his height. "*Pas bon.*" No good. He eased away and ventured into the swarm of revelers in various stages of undress. They inched in the direction of the Hole or climbed out of it. Must have been hundreds, but an accurate count was impossible.

Six masked, bare teens wielded feather dusters and tickled a plump, naked gent. They tormented him until gold beads of pee dribbled down his flabby thighs. He was oblivious. The kids giggled.

Johnny presented Le Roux to a matched pair of stripped, collared and leashed subs. Their Dom jerked leather reins and they lowered their eyes. The Master scowled at Johnny but scrutinized the photo. He wagged a bullwhip over a hundred heads at a far wall.

Johnny suppressed a laugh. "Thanks." He waded around pulsating bodies to a row of a dozen wood doors. Yanked the one on the far left. Scoped out a ten-by-ten sauna. Vacant. Taylor opened the second.

A shriveled human slouched on a bench, surrounded by rough, pine siding. His tongue lolled. Small, grimy feet rested on a pyramid of smooth, oblong stones. There was no suffocating heat nor sticky humidity. Cigarette smoke hovered at the ceiling and refracted the light of an incandescent bulb into bands of red, yellow and green. Slack-jawed, the man clutched a cold crack pipe and stared at his toes. Wiggled them.

"Michael Le Roux?" Johnny said.

Red-rimmed eyes darted sideways as the guy sucked on a cigarette.

Taylor compared him to the photograph. "Drug diet. Lost a bunch of weight, but yeah, it's him, sorry sack a shit."

Le Roux's hair was greasy and matted, his face blotchy beneath a week's worth of salt and pepper beard. "I'm tapped," he whimpered.

"Not looking to score."

"Me neither, comrade, me neither." He ground his teeth. Mopped drool with the sleeve of a dingy, sweat-stained terry cloth robe. Gnawed it as he struggled to focus bloodshot browns.

Taylor was disgusted. "So who chewed you up?"

"And spit you out," Johnny said.

Le Roux, confused, shrugged.

"What happened to you?"

"Craved a steady cash flow."

"How's that working for you?" Taylor said. He and Johnny sat and bracketed Le Roux. "Fragrant."

"A pit spritz wouldn't hurt." Johnny breathed through his mouth to avoid the BO. "So – Mr. Le Roux. Maybe you can assist us."

"And maybe I can't." He slumped. His chin hit his chest.

"We're pals of Emma. Emma McConnell."

Le Roux jolted. Dropped his pipe. His heels slid off the rocks. "Didn't do it. Got nothing to do with it." Sulked as if he'd lost his lover.

"With what?" Taylor said.

"Whatever it is you're here for." Le Roux lunged for his pipe. Johnny kicked it.

Le Roux watched it skid across wood planks. He teared. "What're you here for?"

"You tell us."

He slurred, "You the ones who's here. Why're you here? The hell you doin' here?" Made fists. "Don't fuck with me." Flailed.

"Easy," Johnny said as he and Taylor scooted out of elbow range. "We're friends of Emma's."

Le Roux calmed. "Me, too, comrades, me too." His hands fell to his lap.

"How'd you know her?"

"Who?"

"You stuck on stupid?" Taylor said.

Le Roux was lost. Johnny prompted him. "Emma McConnell."

"Oh wow. Incredible."

"How'd you meet her?"

"Discovered her."

"Where?"

"Chatsworth. Freed her. Took her big time. To her A-game. But you knew that already, didn't ya? Who are you?"

"What'd you do to get her there?"

"Where?"

"Geez. The big time, numb nuts. Pay attention," Taylor said.

"Oh. Easy. Staked her, comrades. Flew her up the stairway, man, to heaven. You know? Like the song? Orbiting. Felt it. Sparks. Still feel it." Le Roux exposed his forearms. "Goosebumps."

"What did you do to her?"

"Loved her."

"Bull. She was your meal ticket. No way you'd let her go. You killed her."

Le Roux shook his head. Slow, then faster, and finally in a frenzied back and forth as he screamed, "She killed me, comrade, she killed me."

Taylor stormed out.

Le Roux collapsed, brain dormant. Insignificant and alone, he tightened his filthy robe.

Johnny retrieved the crack pipe. Le Roux snatched it, swabbed it on the cloth. Lost in a memory, he frowned. "She killed me, comrade. Emma killed me."

CHAPTER 17

"We going to Porn Valley next?" Asked Taylor. He zipped his jacket.

"Chatsworth? No." Johnny's coat flapped as they dodged puddles and potholes and hustled to the car.

"So where?"

"Scene of the crime."

"Whitley Heights?"

In the Kia, Johnny flipped pages in his notebook. Found what he wanted. "Nope. Onward."

"Vague..." Taylor twisted the ignition key. The motor rumbled. Worn blades smeared the windshield. He switched them off. Waited for rain to collect. Turned the wipers on again and cleared a five-inch swath, ample to evade death. "Address, directions, something, Scoop."

"Don't call me that... Back a few blocks on Silver Lake."

Taylor swung a scary, four-lane U-turn.

Johnny gripped his seatbelt, but gravity thumped him. "Could've walked."

"It's wet."

"Trust me, you ain't gonna melt."

"Still waiting for where we're going."

"Up on the right?" He pointed. "Six stories?"

Taylor whipped his ride into a space. Fought a smile. "Let's walk."

Johnny put on his fedora. "No coinage for the meter. Sorry."

"It's after eight. Don't need any." Taylor jogged less than a block to a mid-century, glass-and-steel cube.

Johnny tugged his hat to fight the drizzle and scanned the building from roof to street. Neglected. Two-thirds of the windows were dark. All needed Windex.

They entered, crossed fissured, gray terrazzo, passed a barren planter and a rack of throw-away tabloids. "Not a great start for the bigs," Taylor said. The remainder of the lobby was unadorned, except for a droopy, potted palm by the exit.

Johnny ran a finger over a directory. Read white letters on black. Dozens of listings ending in "productions," "media," or "group." He knocked the clear plastic with a knuckle. "Gotchya."

Taylor pushed a button. The elevator arrived. Vintage, puke-green interior. Johnny touched "4" on a panel of faded numbers above an emergency telephone.

Up they went, lost in their own worlds. Taylor expected to solve Emma's murder and the mystery of the empty coffin in a matter of minutes. Johnny crafted the lede of what he sensed in his bones would be his maiden cover story, "El Nino scoured Los Angeles," but remembered Dutch's first rule - never begin with the weather.

Orange digits below the elevator ceiling blinked on, then off - 1, 2, 3, 4. The Otis bounced as it stopped, opened and revealed a well-lit corridor.

Johnny stepped into the hall. Surveyed his surroundings. Eight offices. Saw 412 on a cheap plaque. "There. Third one." He stepped along the hall. Decorative cursive declared …

LE ROUX PRODUCTIONS

Taylor whispered, "We get the goods to nail the SOB and give him to the police. Okay?"

"Shoot me a beam."

"Okay?"

"Sure." At 412, Johnny knelt and removed a calfskin trifold wallet from a pocket. He studied the deadbolt. Selected a burglar's pick. He had seven. "Light?"

Taylor used his phone. "You didn't mention anything about B and E-ing."

"Happen to have a key?" On his knees, Johnny inserted the short side of a thin, L-shaped torsion wrench in the lock. He slid a half-diamond pick on top of it. Manipulated the tumblers. In less than a minute, he heard clicks as the mechanism aligned. Johnny rotated the knob. Held his breath, counted to three, nudged the door and eyeballed the place. He returned his tools to their case, stood and entered.

"Where'd you learn that?" Taylor's vision adapted to a forty-watt glow cast by a lamp. A 72-inch wall-mounted screen dominated the nine-by-twelve office. Wires and coax tethered the monitor to a computer tower, cable box and a combo DVD/Blu-Ray player on the floor. A hundred discs were stacked within reach of a stained, shit-brown sofa positioned for optimal viewing. "Nobody buys these things anymore. It's all streamed."

"Maybe he exports."

Taylor chose one. "*Amateur Nympho*? And we've hit the big time?"

"According to the owner of this fine establishment, yeah."

"What exactly you trying to track down?"

"Something featuring Emma. It'd help if we knew her porn name."

"Makes me wanna puke." Taylor rifled a mound of porno vids. "Enough silicon in those to bury the city. Or float it. Emma didn't need any artificial ingredients."

Johnny searched a cluttered desk in a corner opposite the giant TV. Uncovered a remote control. Pressed "on." A blue hue materialized and he joined the DVD hunt. " 'Entrance Exams,' 'College Daze,' d-a-z-e," he spelled. " 'Grad Knights' with a 'K'." Slid a disc in the player.

"Your boss called you Harvard," Taylor said as he inspected DVDs. "You go there?"

"Yeah."

"Rich kid?"

"So, so."

"Thought Harvard 'men,'" he packed it in sarcasm, "went to New York or DC."

"Some do, some don't."

"How'd you end up in 'don't?'"

"*Old Yeller.*" Johnny aimed the remote.

"Huh?"

"The film? Your mom and dad probably watched it with you when you were little? Definite multi-hanky flick."

"So?"

"Me, too. Momma treated me to a revival theater. Nothing's better than popcorn and a movie, she said. Sure was right, 'cept she split in the middle of it. She had to sneak a smoke. Hoped I'd understand. Didn't come back."

"For how long?"

"Forever."

Loud, cheesy music. Johnny muted the noise with the remote.

"You haven't seen her since?"

"No."

"Harsh. Why not?"

"Maybe she ran off with the pool boy. Or got flattened by a semi."

The porno rolled. A brass-band fanfare blared and gold, faux-Roman script on bright red, proclaimed, "Le Roux Productions International Presents." Johnny scoffed.

"Was she abducted?"

"Who?"

"Your mom."

"Never got any ransom demands."

"How old were you?"

"Almost ten."

The title *Dorm Daze* scrolled by. Slick, nude, nubile bodies groped, writhed and screwed.

"World-class free-style." Taylor Twisted and turned as he watched.

Johnny froze the picture. He considered five co-eds crammed on a twin bed in a dorm. Appendages intertwined, tongues grazed and probed. Difficult to discern if it was a sound stage or the real deal. Wall hangings were pixilated beyond recognition, probably to avoid copyright infringement, which tilted the answer to genuine. "Is Emma in it?"

"How do I know?"

"See her?"

Taylor glanced. "No. Don't you know what she looks like?"

"There's a bed full of them."

"What'd your old man do?"

"What? When?"

"After your mom."

"Didn't have one." Johnny corrected himself. "Didn't know one." He ejected the DVD. Slipped in another. A 70s disco tune played as a different ensemble of studs and babes earned their day rate.

"So you're an orphan."

"That's one way to put it."

"And after she disappeared?"

"Relatives. Boarding school. Harvard." Johnny fast-forwarded the porno. Triple-time nookie.

"And that was that?"

"No. Tried to figure where my mom got to. Never did, but burned a hole in my library card. Read 'em all - every mystery. Reckoned it'd teach me the how, then spent every spare minute on the why and loaded up a ton of questions. Along the line, it dawned on me reporters ask questions for a living, so here I am."

"At a rag like *True Crime*?"

"It's perfect."

"They pay by the question?" Taylor's attention was riveted to the monitor. "Slow it down."

Johnny pressed a button. Images resumed normal playback.

"No chance," Taylor said. A beautiful, naked blonde clasped a dude's large, hard manhood and led him to a kitchen island. She had a pouty mouth and azure eyes identical to the corpse in Whitley Heights. "Can't be."

"Sure it is."

"Millions of blondes in LA."

"Definitely your Emma."

On the TV a dog wagged its tail. Barked.

"Off," Taylor said.

"Woah. Intense."

"Turn it off."

"No wonder she couldn't shake Le Roux." Johnny was fascinated by the video. The dog barked again.

Taylor resisted but was drawn to the images of Emma's unthinkable, recent career. He punted a pile of DVDs and gripped the screen's bevel, ready to rip.

The television died. The room went dark. "Thanks."

"For what?" Johnny yanked the chain on the lamp. "Power's cut, and we need Emma's movie."

Taylor sniffed. "Better get it fast." A liquid oozed into Le Roux's office. Woosh. Fire erupted.

Taylor yanked open the door. Jumped the flames. Johnny followed into the hall. A bell clanged. Alarms screeched. "Stairs," yelled Taylor. They made a three-step dash towards the green glow of an exit sign on the backside of thick, smoky haze.

Two muscle-bound men, both over six feet tall, filled the width of the corridor.

"Damn." Taylor paused and shouted instructions. "Lower your head, cover your face with an arm and run." He demonstrated and spun a one-eighty. They bolted to the elevator. Taylor poked the down button. The blaze flashed. A barrier of flames separated them from the Hoods who marched through the inferno without a twitch or flinch.

"No way." Johnny was amazed and terrified.

Taylor searched for a weapon. Nothing handy. He shattered a fire extinguisher cabinet with an elbow.

Johnny grabbed the red tank, aimed the nozzle and squeezed the trigger. Empty. As a last resort, he lifted the tank to swing or throw.

Flames licked the ceiling. Fed on paint. Fixtures fragmented. The elevator opened. Taylor leaped in. Pushed L. Johnny heaved a hail Mary and lofted the cylinder in the general direction of the Hoods. Taylor dragged him in.

A Black hand separated the doors. Johnny snatched the emergency phone. Pounded the knuckles. It withdrew.

Taylor jabbed "L." The Otis closed and began its descent. "Come on, come on, come on." The numbers blinked 3. "You good?"

Johnny gave himself a quick frisk. Body inventory. Head, torso, legs. Everything worked. "Scorched sleeves is it."

Two flickered. "Any day..." Taylor said. One lit. Doors spread.

Johnny led through a foot-wide gap. Taylor was a yard behind. They charged across the lobby. Left a crowd of frightened people in their wake. Hit the sidewalk at a dead run.

Taylor sprinted the half-block to his car. Hollered, "Keep moving."

"Why?"

"No rubber." The Kia's tires were flat.

The bad guys advanced at a jog. Showed no sense of urgency as Silver Lake erupted.

Sirens wailed. Windows burst. A thousand shards of glass mixed with rain as yellow flames poured from the fourth story of Le Roux's building. Smoke billowed into the night. Red LAFD trucks arrived. Men, hoses and equipment deployed.

Johnny and Taylor ran.

CHAPTER 18

"Want a lift, big boy?" Heat shouted from a rusty, sky-blue 1965 Corvair Monza Coupe. She made a U-ie on Silver Lake, braked, opened the passenger side and lowered the seatback.

Johnny and Taylor raced to the mid-1960s, rear-engine Chevy classic. They praised higher powers, gods and providence. Swore promises they'd never keep. Johnny dived in the back, Taylor in front.

Heat rammed a four-on-the-floor into gear. Popped the clutch. Tires spun and caught traction. Her car shuddered forward. As it gained speed, she said, "Johnny. Check our six."

"Huh?"

"They following us?"

He looked. "No." The Hoods stopped in the wet and watched the taillights. "Owe you big time." Breathed a sigh of relief.

"Counting the ways, dude, counting the ways."

Taylor sucked air. "How'd Le Roux... How'd he know? Were you tailing us?"

"Would I do that?" She grinned.

"You go to The Baths and tell him?"

"Did I tell who, what?"

"Le Roux." Deep breath. " 'Bout us."

Heat stomped the brakes. Fishtailed. "Out."

Johnny breathed hard. "He's spit-balling theories."

Heat zeroed in on Taylor. "Get out."

"Pleasure." He unlatched the door and readied a leap. The street flowed by at about thirty miles per hour.

"She will call you on it and make your ass jump," Johnny said. "Say you're sorry. Seriously. You, too, Heat. He spends all his awake time with cops. He didn't mean it."

The Corvair was smacked in the ass-end. A bang and a rough jolt forced Taylor forward. The top of his forehead struck the windshield. That hurt, but was preferable to breaking his nose.

A black Cadillac sedan drew even. The guy riding shotgun leveled a shotgun - at Heat. She downshifted. Her car lurched and slid. Taylor's door swung.

Buckshot pierced the front left fender.

Johnny checked their six. "More incoming." The Caddy bashed the old Corvair again. He was knocked to the carpet.

Taylor gripped his seat cushion and leaned forward.

Johnny hollered, "Get your door." Taylor swiped at it. Missed. Almost fell out.

Heat ignored a red light. Disregarded a *Do Not Enter* sign. Zoomed on a one-way – the wrong way. Laid on the horn. Pedestrians scattered.

A red pickup drove straight at them. Johnny slammed a hand on the ceiling. Braced for impact. Traffic honked, the truck swerved, the driver freaked.

"Turn," Taylor yelled.

Heat threw her arms in the air. "You wanna do this?"

Seconds from impact, Taylor jerked the wheel. Escaped a meet-and-greet with his maker by inches.

Johnny's eyes bugged. "Thanks."

Heat shooed Taylor and seized control. "Cut me in on the piece, Johnny."

"Hell of a time for that discussion," Taylor said.

"Timing's not my strong suit."

"On your right," Johnny said. High beams closed fast.

"Cut me in."

Taylor braced. Prepared to jump. Always better to die in action.

Heat hung a left. Avoided a Harley by a fraction. The passenger door swung shut.

"Holy Jesus. Damn near pooped my drawers," Johnny said. "Okay. Contributor credit."

The old Corvair chugged up the steep part of Micheltorena, a peaceful, residential neighborhood. Engine and transmission strained to make the top. They crested a rise with an unobstructed view of the city that should have generated oohs and aahs. Not that trip.

Johnny had their rear. "Bogies up the ass."

Taylor twisted his torso and looked out the back window to judge speed and distance between them and death. "Gotta get off the hill."

Heat held the wheel with a thumb and finger. "Well, Johnny?"

Boom. Crunched again. Heat blasted the horn, dipped into a dizzying descent, blew another red light at full speed and launched. Went airborne.

"Okay! Full partner. But be care..."

The Chevy landed front-end first. Hammered everyone's teeth. The rear tires crashed to the pavement. Compressed spines.

"Glad we settled that," Heat said. The road bent, then S'd. The car skidded onto the Music Box Steps, a landmark made famous by Stan and Oli.

Taylor shouted, "What the...?" As they flopped, flailed and pogoed down the one-hundred forty-seven stairs.

Above, the Cadillac shot through a flimsy wood rail and over a cliff. Johnny tracked its flight. "Oh man, it's gonna smash on us." He lost sight of it.

The Corvair bounced to narrow Vendome Avenue.

The Caddy hit. Missed them by an instant. It rolled onto its roof, screeched and sprayed rainwater.

Heat wrenched the steering wheel. Came out of her seat and stood on the brake pedal. Tires locked. No traction. Her car hydro-planed, drifted and thudded to a stop against the curb at Laurel and Hardy Park.

Taylor pushed his door open and ran.

Heat scampered. Nailed her knee on the shifter. "Ow."

Johnny hurdled over the seat, out of the car and landed on all four.

The Caddy came to rest belly up on the wet pavement. Tires spun. Steam wafted and rose.

Taylor crouched and photographed the wreckage. Crab-walked to a less-obstructed angle. Remained focused on the Hoods. They crawled out of the pan-caked hulk and assisted each other to their feet. One of them fired a pistol at Heat. Clang. Punctured sheet metal. Thunk. A round chipped asphalt.

"We really gotta boogie." Johnny moved behind a boulder.

"Where're you going?" Taylor said.

"Anywhere but here."

"Safer to drive."

"You cracked?"

"Trust me on this."

Heat dropped into her seat and scrunched low. "You believe it? They lived?"

Johnny dove into the back. "Saw it, don't believe it."

Taylor vaulted into the front.

The rear windshield shattered. A slug punched a hole in the dashboard. Heat screamed.

"Pedal to the metal. U-turn and go," Taylor screamed. He scooted low. So did Heat. They had to pass the destroyed Cadillac and the two Hoods. No options. Heat peeked out the side window and gassed the Corvair. It sputtered along Vendome. No one bothered to kill them.

Johnny measured from the top of the seat to the crown of his skull. It was the width of his thumb. His hand trembled. "Close only counts in horseshoes and hand grenades," he said and brushed his scalp. Sprinkled bits of glass.

Taylor touched Heat's forearm. Fueled by the adrenalin spike, she jerked away. "Easy," he said. "It'll work out." He glanced at Johnny. "You good? Can you see 'em?"

Johnny looked out the back. "Yes and yes." The bad guys played besties out for an after-dinner stroll. "And that appears to be a wrap."

Taylor swirled a fingertip in the indented bullet hole. Exhaled. "Left at Sunset."

Heat white-knuckled and guided her wounded vehicle towards the cloud-shrouded towers of downtown Los Angeles.

CHAPTER 19

"Ten to one the little fucker killed Emma. Check that. Two to one," Taylor said.

"Maybe, maybe not," Johnny said.

Taylor rammed a key in a lock and leaned into a heavy door. Opened it, flipped a switch and lit a loft. He led Johnny and Heat inside. "It's Le Roux. Cocksucker."

Johnny, calm and contemplative, offered his take. "Okay, I agree a giant arrow's flashing at him, but there's no evidence he did it, which means we got no clue who did. We don't even know if there is an 'it.'"

"Who you shittin? We're wearing targets. Somebody sent those assholes. Aren't they the brothers that tried to kill us in Frog Town?"

"Could be." Johnny connected dots. "Yeah. Remember who else was there?"

"According to you, Baby Doll Getz."

"You saw her, too."

"Damn." Taylor hustled to an antique oak library table. Scooted and positioned a desk chair, sat at a keyboard and faced three monitors. A few keystrokes and an image of the Hoods popped up on the left screen. It captured them outside Emma's crime scene. One aimed a smartphone, the second stood watch. Taylor tapped keys. The shooters firing M-4s on the Frogtown loading dock filled the middle screen. "And tonight." Taylor pressed buttons on his Nikon. Showed Johnny the men as they emerged unscathed from the demolished Caddy.

"Yep. Same dudes. Would've helped if you'd spoken up."

"Didn't stitch it together 'til just now. What's Emma's line to Getz?"

"Skin trade. Getz runs it. All of it. Top to bottom. Le Roux has to pay her a tribute, a quarter of his action, or she shuts him down. Or sics the Russians on him. They pay her, too."

This was new info to Taylor. "Why?"

"It's kind of a business license."

"And if Le Roux doesn't pay?"

"Baby Doll snuffs Emma and shoots it. It'll go viral on the dark web. Huge bucks."

"That's, that's, a guess? Speculating?"

"No."

Taylor conjured a vision of Emma headlining her own demise. The notion devastated him.

Heat shrugged off her bomber jacket and let it fall. She hugged herself and inspected Taylor's loft. Sizeable. Gray concrete reinforced by a seismic retrofit of bolts and rods. A row of four, large, rain-streaked windows provided a diffused view of DTLA skyscrapers. Photography equipment. Cameras – video, digital, film – and all the accessories - lights, lenses, tripods. A tablet, desktop tower, scanner and printer were clustered on the oak table.

Large rectangles of mismatched carpet were scattered on the cement floor. Two well-used sofas – a plaid fabric and a cracked leather – took advantage of the urban vista. A stone-ware mug was on a clear-varnished, utility-cable spool, and sections of the morning paper encircled an old recliner and a vintage TV. Yellowish, foam-rubber padding leaked from the chair's arms.

Heat continued her appraisal. Chuckled at the bachelor kitchen. Functional came to mind. An industrial sink and faucet, a polished granite island, standard gas stove and a microwave. A do-it-yourself Scandinavian bookcase was a stand-in for cabinets – pots, pans and dishes neatly stacked on shelves. No dishwasher, so, by necessity, he cleaned and dried by hand. Points for that unless he ate nothing but carryout. And, of course, the basic starter fridge with a single magnet centered on the door. A red "1" on an olive-green, five-sided shield shaped like an elongated home plate. The Big Red One. First Infantry Division.

"Why the First ID patch?" She said.

"Souvenir."

"And behind the curtain?" She nodded at cobalt-blue drapes hung in the opposite end of the loft.

"The Wizard."

"Who plays Dorothy?" Heat flopped on a sofa, crossed her legs once, twice, sprang to her feet. Adrenalin surge. Noticed the backs of a dozen picture frames angled against the wall below the windows. Hurried to them. "What're all these?" Didn't get an answer.

Johnny paced. Contemplated developments. "Consider the deets. Give me a solid reason Le Roux torched his own building. Can't, can you? Logically, anyway, because he ain't the porno king he wants the world to take him for. He's small-time."

"Tiny time," Taylor said.

"Probably crapped his robe when we put the knock on him at The Baths. But Getz. There's a different kettle of fish. Especially if Le Roux stiffed her, which begs the question – how come you feel he's a killer?"

"Look at that porn he made Emma do."

"Think she did it for free?"

Taylor ignored the question, stepped to the refrigerator, removed a bottle of vodka from the freezer and poured shots. "Warm your innards?" Johnny waved him off. "Suit yourself." Taylor gulped his. Enjoyed the kick. "Fucker deserves everything that's coming to him." Splashed booze as he replenished.

"No. Le Roux deserves serious cogitation," Johnny said. "It's front page. Empty casket, missing teen porn star."

"She's not a teen."

"Be an even bigger story if we knew what he actually did to Emma."

"He broke her into the skin trade. That's enough for me."

"But he's so whipped. Bet he sits when he pees."

"Least he had a reaction. More'n I can say for you."

"I need to stay even-keeled. Cool."

"Cool? You're a cold SOB." Taylor tossed a swallow.

"Have to maintain. How else do I figure it?"

Taylor snatched color pics from the printer and flung them. "Curl up with these."

Johnny retrieved them. Dead Emma. "I was there, remember?" He hid a shudder as he placed the glossies alongside Taylor's photos of the coffin-lid serpent symbol.

Across the loft, Heat knelt by the picture frames. Tilted one. Appraised an image of gritty, exhausted combat soldiers. Examined another - female fighter pilots as they swaggered on the flight deck of an aircraft carrier. A third depicted refugees and all manner of collateral damage. "Wow. These yours?"

"Yeah," Taylor said.

A news magazine cover of haunted faces captivated her. Abandoned children sobbed and wandered among ravaged bodies of men and women. Parents? Relatives? The banner was *Mass Destruction*. It tore at her heart. She thought of her dad. Her eyes misted. Dabbed them with a pinkie.

Taylor joined her and lifted her hand from the picture. As he did, his fingers grazed hers. In the moment, Heat felt it. A spark. Connection. Did he? She tingled in critical zones and promised to bear his... Wait. No. Chill. Had to be an escaped-the-reaper adrenalin-rush. If she said it out loud, friends would commit her. Hell, she'd stipulate she was nuts and throw away the key, too. Life is not a movie.

Taylor rotated the frame, the children hidden once again. He ambled to the kitchen. She couldn't take her eyes off him. He turned, arched his brows, raised the vodka bottle and offered her a drink. Heat nodded, crossed the loft, eased close to him. Taylor poured. They raised a silent toast.

"All righty then," Johnny said. "We've got a ton of leads piling up." He passed the prints of the serpent symbol to Heat. "Can you work your magic?"

"Sure." But her eyes were on Taylor.

"Great. You can drop me at the rag."

"Uhhh... Corvair's on life-support."

Johnny snagged her jacket and lobbed it to her. Heat caught it, saluted Taylor and departed with Johnny. Oh well…

Taylor sighed and gazed at a color photo of Emma's body. A tear streaked his cheek.

CHAPTER 20

"'Nother suicide. Good," Bruno Morales said.

"Seriously?" Alita Walsh was surprised.

"Yeah. I'll get outta here and be home for dinner."

"That's a thing? What happened to abs day?"

"I should explain it to you yet again?" Morales grinned.

"Early 'old-timers.'" She pointed at her head.

"Think hard."

She scratched her scalp and eyed the ceiling. He hummed a popular game-show theme. "Oh yeah, now I remember," she said. "You got a new hostage. So - Stockholm Syndrome or the future fourth Mrs. M.?"

"Third." He gave her the bird but held the smile.

The Long and the Short of It were crammed inside an efficient, tidy kitchen. Portable illumination brightened faded turquoise walls and darkened every earthquake crack formed since 1950. Cops, criminalists and the other personnel heard the click, click, click of Taylor's camera and winced with each flash.

He snapped a picture of a window above the sink. It was chilly and gray outside. He photographed dishes drying in a rack on a ribbed porcelain drainboard. Shot dull, white, metal, post-World War II cabinets smudged with black fingerprint powder. Angled right and directed his lens at a red Formica table. Its chrome-plated legs were smog-pocked. Mail littered the top and shared space with laundry bundled in a plastic basket. Without a whiff he couldn't tell if it was dirty or clean and was thankful that was the detectives' job.

Walsh and Morales, two patrol officers and a criminalist stood in a semi-circle around the Deputy Medical Examiner, CC Rademaker. Bent at the waist, she probed a nude, well-developed male, early-twenties, on his knees, chest on a pristine oven door. The victim's brown hair was cut and styled. His arms dangled, but his knuckles didn't touch the worn, speckled linoleum.

Rademaker got to her feet. Stretched her back. "Studly corpse. Shame."

"Meet Vincent Parnelli," Walsh said. "A brother, son, and City College student." "Apparently, the deceased lived here with momma and big sister," Morales said.

"But mom ain't here to vouch or ID, and sis is in the Valley, trying to get over the hill."

"Traffic's a bitch," Rademaker said.

"Holidays."

"So who reported it?"

"Dead guy. Made a nine-one-one. Blabbed he was sorry, etc., etc. Dispatch center dug it up for us. Reminds me of your blonde AMW, T."

Taylor frowned at the memory.

Walsh nudged Rademaker. "Any ideas about the nakedness, doc?"

"Nope. Way above my paygrade. That's why you two get the big bucks. Don't see head-in-the-oven too much. Never did. It's a film and TV kind of deal."

"Didn't even get it inside," Taylor said as he composed images of that detail.

A cell phone rang. A dozen people reached for belts or pockets. "Mine." Walsh answered. "Go." Listened. "Copy that." Ended the call. "Fresh one." The text tone sounded. She checked an address. "East Hollywood. Round 'em up, Bruno."

"Ah, man. Why us?"

"Budget," Rademaker said.

"Nope," Walsh said. "It'll be number three with a similar look. Makes it a pattern. Means we get them all if there's additional."

"Or until the swinging dicks downtown decide to leave their brand-spanking-new abode and Sasquatch us," Morales said.

"That, too."

Taylor adjusted his lens. Framed the kitchen table again. Focused on a tabloid newspaper next to the mail. The front-page photo was the bottom half of a guy in a faux police uniform and black leather utility belt. He straddled a gorgeous female and aimed a pistol at her. Taylor saw a snippet of a headline – *SUBWAY SUR* - And a masthead grabbed his attention - *True Cri* - The latest issue. "What was in this dude's note?"

"No note," Walsh said. "Just the nine-one-one like your AMW. Slob went without a whimper."

CHAPTER 21

"Don't stall me, Harvard," Jolly Duncan said. He gripped a *Times* travel mug in one hand and rolled a lit stogie with the other as he supervised from his ergonomic executive chair.

Johnny peeked in the Editor's domain. The office reeked. "I'm guessing that's not a Cuban."

Duncan drew a deep drag and exhaled a retaliatory barrage of cigar smoke. He shook a fist at the red disc painted on the floor. "Got a biggie breaking in Perris."

"France?" Johnny marched through the haze and planted himself on the dot, a yard in front of Duncan. He hadn't changed clothes or bathed. Snuck a whiff. Borderline.

"Single E, double R. Perris, California. Sex, blackmail, even kidnapping. Principals all belong to a lodge for God's sake."

"Which one?"

"Deer. Antelope. Bear? Something that runs fast. Right up your alley, and it'll pop your cherry." Duncan sucked a lung-full.

"Sounds juicy, Chief. And I'll hop on it ASAP. But I need a little bit longer on the model murder. Not much."

"Murder?" Duncan hacked, opened a drawer, lowered his coffee mug out of sight and poured Scotland's finest into it. He sat up and sipped. Almost smacked his lips. "Thought it was suicide."

"So's the whole world. But my piece? It'll capture the town."

"How? Do pray tell."

Yeah. How? Everyone wondered. Heat kicked back, waited. Mass, Madam Speaker, Captain Showbiz and Panther didn't want to miss a syllable. Even Blitz was interested.

"Has big-city fix smeared like cream cheese on a bagel," Johnny said.

"Too thick."

"Okay. But trust me. Could be huge. Plenty of potential."

"Harvard," the Chief cautioned. "We've strapped in for this ride every damn deadline since I hired you. You realize that's once a week? What's different today?"

"It's big."

"How big?"

"Really big."

Duncan tracked his precision smoke rings as they rose.

"Pin this on." Johnny's words cascaded. "Last night we broke into a porn producer's private suite, barely escaped a burning building, had a car chase, a car crash and survived a gunfight. Actually, not a gunfight, per se. Baddies were shooting at us, but we didn't have weapons, so it was kinda lopsided." He paused for a breath.

"Save it for your screenplay."

TCLA staff turned to Heat for confirmation. A nod from her and "wows" all around. Their mission was to pitch the craziest stuff mined online and from inspirational source material. They'd land on the facts later, maybe. But Duncan rejected Johnny's best play, and it was the absolute truth.

"It's got weird whoop-tee-do, Chief. It's, It's..." Johnny revved his brain, searched for the winning word.

Mass, Panther and Showbiz scooted forward.

"Diabolical. Yeah. Diabolical. Might even hit the front page."

Heat fired a thumbs-up.

"You'd give your morning piss a 72-point banner on the cover if you could get away with it." Duncan scowled. "All of you would, which is why God invented editors."

Johnny pitched the perfect, high, hard one. Pulled his voice to a Serling-esque, "Imagine if you will… A hint of the occult."

"Oh yeah? Ritual sacrifice?"

Johnny played to Duncan's reaction. "Yeah. Seems we're sliding into that curve, Chief, and we'll cross the bridge when we come to it, but my old bones are vibrating and tell me it'll sell *beaucoup* copies."

Duncan contemplated. "Getting warmer. Your instincts are kicking in. Excellent. I knew you were a natural. Reminds me of early days at the *Herald-Ex*. Brand new to America, I was…"

"Oh no," Panther said, elbows on her desk, chin in her hands. "Not war-story time."

"I remember, Chief," Johnny said.

"Prime of me life, 'fore the wife nicked the rest."

"Pretty sure it was, yes sir."

"I recall a..."

"Better be crackin' on the model murder, Chief."

"Whoa..." Showbiz was impressed. "Kid's definitely sprouting a pair."

Duncan hated interruptions. "Throttle back, Harvard." The Chief rocked in his chair. "Okay, hotshot. Make you an offer. Seventy-two hours. Do the math. Three days, or it's howdy-ho Perris with an 'e'." He sipped again and hoisted his beverage in toast to seal the deal.

"Johnny done good," Captain Showbiz said to Heat.

"Yes, he did."

"*Merci*, Chief." Johnny hurried to Rookie Haven. On the way he flashed a thumb's up to Heat.

"Yo. Johnny. Incoming," Mass said. "Bloodthirsty. Hyphen?"

"No." Johnny's landline rang. He snagged it. "Lincoln." Listened, scribbled numbers and a street name. "Thanks." Hung up. Clapped once. "A third stiff." Headed to the door. "You coming?"

Heat gathered her things and dodged the 1999 stack of *TCLAs*.

"Where in bloody hell you think you're headed?" Duncan said as he scrambled out of his office.

Heat was halfway to the exit. Hoped she appeared chagrined enough to send a message. "Johnny and I partnered on the dead model."

"When?"

"Last night."

"Before or after the 'car chase?'"

"During."

"There's the first real news of the day, and I'm not loving it. You planning to inform me?"

"Did." She didn't appreciate his sarcastic tone. Slipped on her bomber jacket.

"You own a beat. Stick your arse down and work it."

"I am. Holiday Special is put to bed, and this week's is done and in."

"What's it about?"

"About a thousand words." Showbiz snark. Duncan ignored him.

"Same old shit," Heat said. "Cutie-pie in Texas catches hubs banging her cousin in the double-wide, or was it her sister? Yeah, sister. No... Doesn't matter. Double ditto result. She saws it off."

The males cringed. Duncan, Johnny, Blitz, Showbiz.

"Ouch," Duncan said. "See? Exactly what our readers crave."

"I for one am tired of the ho-hum shit."

"That ho-hum shit keeps the wolves at bay."

"In the spirit of the season, shouldn't that be ho, ho, hum shit?" Showbiz said.

Duncan sneered.

"My beat's managed, Chief," Heat said. "And suicide's got a claim to being the ultimate crime of passion. Remember 'Romeo and Juliet?'"

"Yeah, yeah, yeah. Knew 'em personally. But Harvard's convinced it's a homicide."

"Possible."

Johnny, in hat and coat said, "Is."

"Here's a concept. Speaking as your Editor…" Duncan paused, then bellowed, "You might bloody well want to sing the same sodding song."

"Yes, majesty." Heat threw a perfect salute and joined Johnny at the exit.

CHAPTER 22

"Whoever decided, 'the truth shall set you free,' was wrong," Johnny said.

"That'd be Jesus," Heat said.

"He never worked here."

"Welcome to the club."

They hustled to a filled, ten-space parking lot on the west side of the building.

"You'd think the Chief would be all in on my – sorry - our story."

"Like stink on a goat, right? Except to him, it sounds made up – too good to be true."

"As opposed to *Kinky Killer Clobbers Cult* or the other virtuoso captions you people conjure."

Heat settled into her battered Corvair, lifted her eyes to the old-car god, inserted the key and turned it. The engine caught. She shoved the shifter in reverse, eased out and ground gears as she jammed it into first and drove away. A pedestrian gawked at the crushed bumper, broken taillights and shotgun holes, not to mention the opaque, plastic sheet where the rear window used to be.

The sky spat mist. Wiper blades jerked across the windshield.

Johnny searched for a safety belt.

"Forget it. They were an option in the old days. Grandpa was cheap. Not even a padded dash. It was an option, too, in his time."

"When?"

"Nineteen sixty-five."

"Neanderthals." Johnny stuck a finger in the bullet hole.

"Aim us, Rook."

"Commonwealth Ave and Lexington." They chugged west on Sunset. "Last night. Scary, that. Guess we're battle buddies now."

Heat concentrated on the road. "Address?"

"Let me punch it into my GPS?"

"Just tell me."

Instead, Johnny wrote four numbers in his notebook and angled it so she could see. "That whole deal last night was amazing, yeah? Fire. Dodging bullets and bad guys. Lose your gunfight virginity, too? Probably not." He needed to commiserate. "An inch from pushing up daisies, right here, in this seat, only twelve hours ago."

"Taylor said it's his second suicide stiff today?" Heat was uninterested in sharing.

Johnny nodded.

"Didn't hear you."

"Yeah. And third in a week. All with a similar M-O. That a lot?"

"Yes."

"Even for LA?"

"Uh-huh. And the term is pattern."

Johnny watched her steer with her knees while she rummaged in her bag and took an occasional glance at traffic. Made him uncomfortable. "I'll excavate." He slid her purse onto his lap. "What am I digging for?"

She gripped the wheel with one hand. "Phone."

He found it, passed it to her, then traced the bullet hole's rough, round, indented edge.

A couple miles and twelve minutes later, they arrived at Commonwealth Avenue. It was a collection of modest, two-bedroom, one-bath stucco dwellings. They were protected by burglar bars and gated, iron perimeter fences that enclosed tiny plots, characteristic of the ethnic enclaves in East Hollywood - Russian, Armenian, Salvadoran.

Heat slowed at a light-brown house accented with green trim. It was early in the p.m. but parking was tough. She backed into the driveway, which killed the element of surprise. She wouldn't leave her banged-up Corvair in a red zone, or next to a hydrant, or anywhere else it might attract a visit from the authorities.

Johnny opened his door and moved towards an eight-foot fence.

"Hang on." She swung her feet to the pavement.

"Why?" He kept walking.

"Stop." Annoyed, he faced her. Heat drummed the roof of her car until he met her eyes. She fashioned a teachable moment. "Gated yard? Mandatory stop. No excuses. You wanna pay attention to your location. Scope it. Be sure it's all cool. Determine an escape route. What do you see?"

Johnny surveyed the street. Old junkers, no trees, kid clutter – toys and trikes. Puddles dotted muddy yards and a well-used swing set creaked as the seat swayed in the breeze. He wondered if her lecture was more about wild chases and gunfights because nothing on that stretch of Lex was out of place for the neighborhood. "All clear, boss." He took a step and pushed the gate.

"Halt."

"Geez…"

She joined him. "Each and every entry, make sure there's no dog. Best not to get chomped."

"No. Really? Thanks for the tip."

Heat turned an ear towards the yard. No barks or growls. She pronounced it safe. "Let's went." They walked along a short, flagstone path and ascended three cracked, concrete stairs. Remnants of yellow crime-scene tape fluttered against fissured, crumbling plaster.

"And it was," she said.

"Was what?"

"My first." She rang the bell before he could respond.

A matronly woman peered through the steel scrim of a security door. Saw Heat's wild, wind-blown, bright-red shock and 6'4" Johnny. "Don't want nothin'."

"Mrs...?" Heat didn't remember the name.

Peeved, Johnny rolled his eyes. "Mrs. Gaitan?"

"Yeah?"

"We're with Delta Life Insurance?" Heat said.

"Oh?" That caught Johnny by surprise.

Heat ignored him. "It concerns your daughter, ma'am, uh, uh…"

"Elvia," he said. "We're here for Elvia. May we have a moment and talk?" He raised his eyebrows at Heat.

Mrs. Gaitan slid a chain. Hinges creaked. She exposed chubby cheeks and brown eyes, allowed Heat and Johnny to enter as she wadded a dish towel. Used it to blot tears. She hadn't matured well. Looked fifty but was plump, which aged faces, and dressed too young. Or tried to. She puffed her jeans and popped a muffin-top under a snug T-shirt. So best guesstimate - forty.

Heat and Johnny observed a cramped dining area dominated by a stylized painting of a gaunt, bearded man meant to be Jesus. Large heart. Gold halo. The benevolent visage presided over six chairs and a veneered, oval table with lace runner and potted poinsettia. Sunday dishes were displayed in cabinets.

In the living room, furniture was worn but dusted. A decorated Christmas tree was bordered by the front window. Wrapped presents, piled on beige carpet under the tree, waited for the big day.

Heat eyed pictures of adults and children that filled a wall. She tapped an 8 x 10 of a raven-haired beauty in a cheerleader outfit. "Elvia?"

Mrs. Gaitan sobbed. Wiped her nose on her towel. "Junior year."

"Gorgeous. Where'd it happen?"

Gaitan led her visitors to a small, frilly bedroom. All pink. Curtains, pillows, rumpled sheets and blankets, a child-sized vanity and a variety of stuffed animals.

Wallet-size graduation portraits of seven girls were tucked between the frame and glass of an oval mirror. Top center was a group in prom formals.

"Teens still do this? Thought everything went straight to social media."

"She into classic. Even develops them herself."

"In a darkroom? Where do you find one of those?"

"Hollywood High. Photography her favorite class. She was on Yearbook."

Mementos of Senior Year were pinned to a corkboard. A graduation tassel, pompons, a dry, once-red rose.

A 5 x 7 of Elvia and a skinny, tattooed Cholo was on the nightstand. Shaved scalp and *EP 13* on his throat, he wore khaki chinos and an unbuttoned, flannel Pendleton. The top of Echo Park Lake peeked out from under a white wife beater.

Elvia had gone chola. Radical evolution from good girl to gangster. Her black tresses were drawn into a tight ponytail. Lips were blood-red with dark liner. Thin, arched, penciled-on brows furrowed, forming parallel, vertical tracks above the bridge of her nose. She showed off curves in her own snug wife beater. Elvia and the guy hugged and flashed gang signs but hadn't smiled.

"Who's the dude?" Heat said.

"Ricky. Enrique," Mrs. Gaitan said through sobs.

"Boyfriend?"

"Not so much."

"Gang banger?"

"Not really."

"Was Elvia?"

"What?"

"A banger."

"No. Never." Gaitan shook her head too hard. "She a sweet mija."

Heat resisted the urge to argue. Noticed a popular boy band poster tacked above the bed. Stepped over dirty clothes to an inexpensive chest of drawers below the mirror. Examined a dozen makeup containers. Foundation, concealer, blush and brushes were scattered in no particular order. "Kind of like me." She added, "When I was that age."

Johnny didn't buy it for a heartbeat.

Heat rummaged in a drawer. Elvia's bras and thongs. Pink and red. "Where'd you find her?"

Mrs. Gaitan wept. "Closet."

"Elvia wearing anything special? Jewelry that maybe meant something to her?"

"She didn't have nothing on."

"How 'bout a note?" Johnny said. "She leave one?" He felt huge and clumsy in the compact space.

"Five-oh say my baby ringed nine-one-one instead."

Johnny eyed a pile of gossip magazines, supermarket tabloids and a *True Crime LA*. They shared the tabletop with the image of Elvia and Ricky. The *TCLA* was opened to the classifieds. "Interesting reading for a kid."

"Not such a kid no more. She sixteen. Checks 'em out 'fore I bring 'em to the shop." She blinked tears.

"Shop?" He asked.

"Estetica."

Heat faked a cough, caught Johnny's eye and tilted her head a fraction of an inch. "We'll keep you posted with the definitive disposition regarding company policy." She led the way out.

Mrs. Gaitan folded her arms. "Policy?"

Johnny cradled her soft hands. "We're so sorry for your loss. God bless."

Heat hurried and plopped into her car. "Good interview."

Johnny sat and slammed his door. He was not happy. "Delta Life Insurance? Which hole you yank that from?"

"LAPD probably told her not to talk to us. To reporters."

"Makes sense. But down the road? In the future? Clue me."

"Won't need to, rookie. Now you know. So what'd you stick in your pocket?"

He was surprised. "Uh, the *True Crime*." He thumped it. "But I still don't *comprendre* why it was there, and how come they didn't bag and tag the rest of her crap."

"Because in their brilliance, the geniuses at LAPD recognized a pattern and made the call."

"Suicide."

CHAPTER 23

"Bodies in the box." A wizened news vendor with a salt and pepper flattop hawked his wears. "Famous bodies in the box." He held forth on the southeast corner of Cahuenga and Hollywood Boulevards. "Gitch yer annual *True Crime LA* Ghoul Pool. Who died. Who cried." Deep facial tan even in winter, he sported sunglasses, faded jeans, cheap running shoes, an orange, down-filled vest stained black at the pockets, and a gray sweatshirt. An enduring fixture and unofficial greeter to the *Walk of Fame,* he was the area's last outdoor purveyor of big-city papers from sea to shining sea and all the periodicals in between.

Getz's driver, the compact gym rat who tossed Johnny over the guard rail, selected a copy of the *True Crime LA* holiday special.

"Wheels. Darlin'," the old fart said. "What's shakin'?"

"Just my bacon, Ink, just my bacon." She offered a five-dollar bill.

"Put that away." Ink curled slick, grimy fingers and blew warmth on them.

"Thanks."

"Pleasure. Give a hey to the boss." For decades, Ink had witnessed every size, shape and color of the city's new arrivals. He preferred the spicy, petite exotics. "Dig the get-up."

"You're the greatest." Wheels wore cream-colored Jodhpurs, Aiken fox-hunt vest, black riding boots and silver English spurs, all topped by an Army-blue cavalry Stetson. She squeezed Ink's butt, left the shelter of a wet, maroon awning and swayed her ass to the limousine. She looked back at Ink and winked.

He sighed, lamented his loss of youth, and pitched a customer. "Bodies in the box. Gitch yer bodies in the box."

Inside the car, Wheels passed the tabloid to her boss in the back seat. Baby Doll Getz smoothed a taupe, micro-fiber raincoat, laid the weekly on her lap and perused the front page.

TCLA ANNUAL GHOUL POOL
WHO'S UP, WHO'S DOWN,
WHO'S PLANTED IN THE GROUND

She touched the flame from her Dunhill to a cigarette. Inhaled. Her lungs bubbled. Getz smudged the filter with ruby-red lip gloss and exhaled a thin thread of smoke. "You place bets?"

Wheels steered into moderate traffic. Glanced in the mirror. "Course. But with long odds. President. Pope. Prince Harry. So unless they croak by New Years, forget it."

"Me, too…" Baby Doll gazed at what she deemed her empire. It was mid-afternoon. The giant-sized strip-show barker stood post and hawked his wears. She knew he extolled the virtues of has-been hotties and liberated Jacksons from youngsters old enough to buy a lap-dance from a naked babe and die for their country but underage for a drink.

The superheroes, Marilyns and Wonder Women, began their day near the Chinese Theater hustling pasty-white tourists in town for the granddaddy of them all. Loiter even a minute at a cement handprint of Hollywood Past, and you'd have a caped-crusader or departed movie star slide up without warning. They'd hug, flirt and pose for a scene that wife, sis or cousin could shoot with a camera or smartphone. All for a suggested tip of ten dollars. The key words to avoid a citation and fine from the police were "suggested" and "tip."

"Check them out," Getz said.

"Who?"

"Across the street." A clutch of nervous teenage girls giggled their way past Kalessi into the *Gee Spot*. "Betchya it's a coming-of-age." Getz ruminated. "Eighteen. By then, I'd moved on to management. Had a string of four. But mine stayed in school. Money's *tres bon*, but education is the key. I insisted. You remember?"

"Never forget. My very first client was my sophomore geometry teacher. She still gave me a C."

Getz pressed a switch. An LED lit her *True Crime LA*. She laughed at a cover illustration of a dozen pine coffins under a Christmas tree, each wrapped with a black ribbon and bow. Headstones highlighted odds instead of dearly departed. 2-1, 4-3, 2-5, 20-1, and so on. She snorted. Later, she'd read the paper's prognostications for the Ghoul Pool and estimated payouts on a five-buck bet.

In the comfort of her cushy, leather seat, Getz bypassed ads for escorts, massages and Nevada brothels in favor of the "Personals" section of the Classifieds. She angled the page to catch the light and browsed tiny, agate font. Skimmed two columns, then, three-quarters down the third...

> Dear BDG – The better I know you, the more I desire to share you with the world. Soon. XOXO, JL

She smiled. "Can't have that."

CHAPTER 24

"You gents approve of my boobage?" Heat said to a pair of mid-watch detectives. "C-cup, free-range, no additives."

In the harsh, fluorescent glare of the squad room, the cops gawked as Heat leaned over Taylor's desktop. She studied glossies with him and Johnny and flaunted her cleavage.

Taylor appraised her killer bod. It held so many unexplored notions. He pondered what it might take, were he so inclined. "Show off. You're mean."

"Nah. They love it. They're titmatized." Heat's physical assets remained the center of attention as she perched on the desk and crossed her legs. Her skirt crept higher and bared thigh. She swung a foot. Grinned.

"Aren't you cold?"

"Yoga pants. They keep me cozy." She stuck her feet out and wiggled Purcell tennies. Solid Kelly green.

"Very seasonal," Johnny said. "Now throw some water on it." He drummed a stack of newspapers. "Got the time?"

Taylor aimed a thumb at a digital wall clock – 1915.

"In real-people time."

Heat translated. "Dinner time." Johnny gave her a look. "Seven-fifteen in the p.m."

"Thank you." His eyes darted to the elevator and the stairwell.

"Who're you expecting?" Taylor said.

"No one. So, me 'n Heat sussed the last location you gave us."

"The 'banger," Heat said. "Elvia."

Johnny dealt photos. Emma, Vincent Parnelli and Elvia Gaitan. "Any parallels between them?"

"They're all dead, and I shot them?" Taylor said.

Johnny bit his tongue.

"Might want to re-phrase. Especially here," Heat said as she re-arranged the pix. "Living, kitchen, bed. This a serial decorating a house? Dining and den, next?"

"Interesting theory." Johnny contemplated the images. "Has to be a connection."

"They're all nude," Taylor said.

"Yeah, got it, thank you."

Taylor turned Emma face down. Analyzed Vincent Parnelli instead. "No way Vinnie sucked gas in that oven. His head's not even in it."

"Maybe at the exact moment he expired, his muscles relaxed and he slid out," Heat said.

"Not a chance."

"It's a theory."

"First, there was no natural gas smell, which did not compute with the windows being shut. It was raining, remember?"

"Second?"

Taylor shrugged and shook his head.

"Come on. We all need to aim in the same direction," Johnny said. "We in agreement that Emma didn't off herself?" Nods all around. "That leaves the cheerleader-banger."

"Elvia," Heat said.

"ME believes OD," Taylor said. "Her findings go firm for sure tomorrow."

"But there's too much stink on her reports," Johnny said.

"Doctor Death?"

"Yeah. You trust her?"

"Never had a reason to speculate about it."

"You should." Johnny tapped each crime-scene photo for emphasis. "There's similarities in all of these, beyond being dead."

"Such as?"

"Where's it at?" Heat said.

"Where's what?" Taylor said.

"The head."

He held up Parnelli.

"The pisser? Convenience? Loo? Got the urge to spend a penny."

"End of the hall. Can't miss it. Has a girl on the door."

"Woman." Heat flashed both middle fingers. The gawkers thought it was meant for them and scurried. She laughed and ambled away.

Taylor viewed her hips. Magnificent. "How old you suppose those gams are?"

Johnny evaluated a picture. "Nineteen? Twenty?"

"Incredible curves."

"If you're into that kind of thing."

It dawned on Taylor that Johnny meant Vincent Parnelli. "You are pathetic."

"Why?"

"How old is she?"

"Her mom says sixteen." Johnny meant Elvia.

"Useless. Bet she's a Taurus, and that won't work. Not at all. I'm Aries."

"What're you yammering about?"

"Forget it." Taylor scrutinized Vinnie. "Okay. Onward and upward." He scanned the crime-scene pix. "They're all kids. And lookers."

"And it's a good bet Emma didn't have an autopsy. Double your money the other two didn't either."

"And none of 'em wrote a note, so what do you think of them apples?"

"LA ain't quite the place?"

The Brunette, in evening gown and Hepburn wig, strolled out of the elevator.

Johnny squatted, utilized Taylor as a shield. He tracked the Undercover and gathered his tabloids. "You sick of this paint?"

"What's with the papers?"

"*TCLAs*. Our DBs had copies."

"Not Emma."

"Yeah, she did. I nabbed it."

"Shhhh." Taylor glanced to see if anyone heard anything. Nope. He lowered his voice. "You're flirting with a big-time felony."

Johnny shrugged. "Whatever it takes." He changed the subject. "Victims flagged the Classifieds."

"Only jobs listed in your rag are 'massage therapists' and 'dinner companions.' " Taylor used air quotes,

"Then it's something else. There's a 323 number in the ads."

"Punch it up."

Instead, Johnny crouched. On full alert, he watched the Brunette sit and swivel his chair. Johnny rose halfway and crab-walked in the general direction of the green and white exit sign.

The Brunette yelled, "Freeze." He sprang up, hiked his dress above his knees and bolted like a running back. "You owe me."

Eight plainclothes cops jumped to their feet, drew their service weapons and assumed firing stances.

Johnny rushed to the stairs.

Heat returned and was startled as he scrambled past her. She saw the firepower aimed at her. Raised her hands. Grinned.

The Brunette stumbled in his high heels but maintained balance as he dashed across the linoleum and chased Johnny.

"Wow, what'd I miss?" Heat said.

"Nada," Taylor said.

"Sure?" Heat winked at the detectives. "That's an awful lot of nada pointed at me."

Her smile, ease of being and natural beauty took his breath away. He reached for his camera. Hadn't felt that itch in a while. Snapped photos. She preened.

Johnny hurdled steps to the lobby. He surprised the desk officer as he banged the bullet-proof, plexiglass entrance and sprinted towards Sunset.

The Brunette bounced on one foot, then the other as he slipped on sling-backs and spotted a Mercedes limo pull from the curb.

Johnny focused on the need to evade and avoid. He ran a block in a minute, slowed and peeked over his right shoulder. No Brunette.

From his left, Wheels head-butted his sternum. Decked him. Locked his throat in a chokehold, dragged him to the car, tossed him in the backseat and jogged to the driver's side.

Johnny didn't know who hit him until he recognized the Stetson. He put on a tough-guy snarl. "This better be damn crucial."

"It is, sweet meat. It is."

CHAPTER 25

"Three." Heat slammed an empty glass on a small, marred and scarred table. She shuddered as booze slid down and scorched her throat. "Mmmmm... Great burn. So how long you and the dead chick…"

"Emma," Taylor said.

Heat shrugged an apology. "Emma. You pour a lot of time into her?" She hollered above maximum noise generated by Gen Zs on the make. They were packed ass-to-elbow in a narrow, mahogany-and-leather, old-school watering hole. Seasoned by decades of martini lunches, red meat and cigarettes, the place had metamorphosed into an incubator for hipster hook-ups. That was the collective hope of the black-clad, manscaped dudes who grinned and pitched and the babes who flirted and caught.

"Two." Taylor meant drinks. About his ex he said, "A year or so." He sat on a padded bench, his back to a brick wall. Heat, trapped in a chair stuck in traffic, was jolted every few words by people shuffling from one end of the joint to the other. He shoved clutter, cleared space, and they leaned forward, eyes inches apart.

Heat scooted her ass, pushed her tummy against the edge of their table. She was jammed so tight her boobs rested on top. "You're a lap behind," she said. "Bottoms up."

Taylor was jostled by twenty-somethings on either side of him. They wore the tiniest of black dresses, crossed and uncrossed smooth, bare legs, spoke fluent body language, and transmitted signals to a knot of hovering, age-appropriate males. He winked at Heat and swigged his third. "Now we're even."

"So tell me."

" 'Bout Emma? Incredible lines. Camera loved her."

"Did you?"

"She was aces. You've been on that road."

"Not so much." Heat was knocked and rocked by the flow of customers. An icy wet splashed her neck. She jumped in her chair and scowled at a mess of bodies, but there was no way to ID the culprit.

"Me and Emma…" Memories struck. Taylor drifted for a bit, then hauled himself to the present. "We had our moment in the sun. Got the images to prove it."

"Get the T-shirt, too?" Heat licked her lips. Amped the temp. "So? Couldn't pull the trigger?"

Taylor locked eyes with her. "Sometimes you don't want to ruin a good thing."

"If you say so."

He broke contact and motioned for a waitress. The hotties beside him inched closer. He offered a round with a circular wave. They agreed. He hailed the help again and held up six fingers.

The delay annoyed Heat. "So who ditched who?"

"Who cares? Ancient history." He had to shout.

"Might crack the story."

"Solve the murder?"

"Potato, tomahto. So?"

"It was mutual."

"I call bullshit."

"Don't remember you bein' in the front row."

"Not blind. So why ever Emma kissed you bye-bye, my money says you weren't finished. Not by a long shot. No sir."

Taylor shredded a napkin and searched for their server. The women on either side bumped his thighs, brushed his arms and toyed with the ring of contenders. He considered Heat. She tossed down another mouthful and added to a collection of empties.

"Couple items about me and Emma. I wasn't gonna get her to the promised land."

"That's Hollywood."

"But…"

"Don't kick yourself."

Taylor lifted a hand to quiet her. "But when I put it together and understood what she wanted, how bad she wanted it, and what she'd do to get it, I broke it up. Ended it."

"Threw her to the curb."

"Hell no. Dumped her crap in the pool. Sunk her life in the deep end. And you know what? She left it there. Never even said a fair-thee-well. Next time I laid eyes on her was Whitley Heights."

"You went nuts 'cuz you figured Chatsworth."

"No."

"So why?"

Taylor self-debated. Shaped the bits and pieces of the destroyed napkin into a mound. "Me 'n Emma? We were expecting. You know, a baby. But she didn't want it because of stretch marks or prune belly." He made quotes. "Career damage."

Heat absorbed the info. "Was she jailbait?"

"Didn't think about it."

"B-S. You're straight and you've got a dangly between your legs."

"Yeah, okay. She just looked like jailbait. Emma's twenty-three."

The server dipped and deposited fresh ones. Taylor raised his glass, everyone clanked in a meaningless gesture and gulped ice-cold vodka.

"Four," Taylor said. "Here's to you."

"Yeah," Heat said with no enthusiasm. "Four."

CHAPTER 26

"Boss wishes you tides and greetings of the season." Wheels said as she eyed Johnny in the rear-view. A sprig of pine and a balsa-wood Santa dangled from the mirror.

Johnny clutched his *True Crimes*. He attempted a breath. "Ow. Oh God." Hugged his chest. She'd nailed him high and hard.

"Poor baby."

He straightened his shoulders. Intense pain racked his ribs. He grimaced but set his jaw and said, "What's the haps here, shorty?"

Wheels wagged a green envelope sealed by a blue flap. Flipped it. "Merry fucking happy." It floated to his lap.

Johnny snagged it by a corner, like someone's dirty undies. Wadded and flicked it. Landed on the floor.

She sighed, climbed over the seat and rammed his gut with a fist. The force of the blow knocked the wind out of him. She clamped a petite hand on his throat. "Would you disrespect your mother that way?" Straddled his lap.

"Probably. Yeah." Johnny gagged.

"Boss has something for you."

He ignored her.

She smashed his Adam's apple with a forearm. "Your name's on it. Pick it up."

Johnny labored. Managed quick gasps. Woozy, he trembled as he retrieved the paper ball and smoothed the crinkles. He slipped a pinky beneath the flap, ripped it and extracted a card. A simple rendition of a Christmas tree topped with a Star of David.

"Boss covers all the bases."

His lips moved as he read to himself.

"Out loud," she ordered and applied more pressure on his throat.

"Ahh..."

"No wimping."

Johnny squinted at precise cursive. "Dear JL." Pinched voice. "I'm afraid my family disapproves." He inhaled again.

Wheels smacked his nose. "Come on."

"Ow. Oh. I breathe through that." He strained but continued. "This must be *au revoir. Joyeuses Fetes.*"

"Nice froggy speak. I'm impressed. Finish."

"XOXO…"

" 'Love and kisses.' "

"BDG." Raspy. "Gee, I'm all broke up. Got a hanky?"

She grabbed his hair and jerked. Exposed his neck. Snapped open a switchblade. Dragged the razor-sharp tip across his throat and etched a five-inch cut.

He screamed. "Ahhhhh..."

She giggled. "Three, four minutes max. Your heart's pounding. Who knows? Maybe sooner." Unlatched the car door.

Panicked, Johnny gasped. He was frantic. Prodded his neck and throat to locate and plug the bleeding.

Wheels hopped off him. Bounced her butt on the cushion and shot her legs forward. Kicked him in the ribcage and out of the car. "Buh-bye."

Johnny crashed, sprawled on the sidewalk.

She flew from the limo and landed on him, full cowgirl. Spurred his torso. Slapped his face. Flung his *TCLAs*. "I'm just funnin' with ya. You'll live. Told you it'd be damn good." Wheels laughed, jumped in the Benz and stomped the accelerator. Tires spun. Left a month's worth of rubber on the asphalt as newsprint churned in the vortex.

Johnny felt his pulse race. Heard a shrill ring in his ears. He struggled to his knees. Grasped his throat. How much life until he dropped? A minute? He didn't see a fountain arcing from his carotid or spatter on the ground.

CHAPTER 27

"Dos additional, see-voo-play," Taylor said as he tried to flag somebody. Anybody. He was on the backstretch too hammered but did his absolute best to pretend otherwise.

The Gen Z-ers in little black dresses scooted their asses to make room for new, thin friends. Booze beauties? Taylor peeked at cleavage. Nah, he wasn't that far gone. Those babes didn't require vodka vision. He made every effort to be a gentleman and adhere to the three-second rule but frequently failed. Mostly failed.

Heat's arms formed an inverted V. Her hands cradled her chin. She stared at Taylor, but her elbows slid farther and farther apart. Her head slumped and chin hit the rim of a glass before she caught herself and shook some sober into her brain. "So Emma went and got rid of it?"

"Yeah." Taylor swayed against a blonde. "Oops. Sorry."

The woman flashed her pearly whites. Apparently, no harm, no foul.

"That's career planning to the extreme," Heat said. "Usually, it's stars. I used to think those stories were Tinsel Town BS 'til I got here. In my gig, I get clued about that stuff all the time. Like every week. Celebs avoiding stretch marks. Making sure not to screw up their bodies, pardon the pun, so they offer a ton of bucks to recruit secret surrogates and such, and I believe just about everything I hear. Especially the stars claiming to be camera-ready and back to work in a minute-and-a-half. But a wanna-be? Never stumbled across that before. Technically, guess I still haven't, Emma being a goner, and I'm hearing it from you, and your credibility isn't exactly neutral, being the ex-squeeze and all." She sipped her vodka. Dribbled. Wiped. "What went down next?"

"No next. The end."

Shook her head. "Not even the beginning."

Taylor gripped the sides of the table. Steadied himself. Over-enunciated. "So, what's the skinny on him?"

"Him who?"

"Johnny."

"Finish Emma."

"Did. So?"

"Plenty. Got bupkis on you, though."

"Nothing there."

"And he's modest, too, Mom. So – Emma."

Taylor gulped his vodka. Winced.

Heat was vexed. "New category. How'd you get to the war and shoot all the magazine covers?"

"Airplane."

She raised both middle fingers.

Taylor fired his at her.

"Ohh-kay, try this. I tell you, you tell me. I'm an Army Brat."

"Knew that."

"Now you give me something. Has to be garden-fresh, though."

"I'm black."

Heat placed her right arm against Taylor's left and compared them. Her skin was lighter, but not much. "You're a quart low."

"Dad's Caucasian." Taylor was drunk-serious.

"Old news."

"Yours?"

"Told you already."

He saluted. "And your mom? Mine's black. Yours a sistah, sistah?"

"Look deep into my eyes." She opened them wide. But Taylor wanted to get lost in her boobs. Lowered his gaze to her cleavage. "Up here. My baby browns." She pointed. "Imagine the islands of Japan. Japanese?"

"Ohhh… Your mamacita… is a mama-san?"

"That's a tad racist, but give the man a prize anyway."

"Mine's black."

"Said that."

"Yours from Tokyo or where?"

"San Diego. So, let's give it another shot. How'd you land in the Army and the war?"

"Anything's better than being the 'afro' kid," air quotes, "in a famous Idaho ski town."

"Sun Valley?"

"Not that famous."

"Going to answer my question?".

"Didn't take this for an interview."

Pissed, she crossed her arms.

"Don't go all hissy on me. College in Moscow."

"Russia?" She smiled.

"Idaho. Did ROT-Cee. Commissioned. Infantry basic branch. I-Rack. OEF."

"You're Army?" She brightened. "You be holding out on me."

"You saw the First ID patch."

"You said souvenir. Took you at your word. How long were you in?"

"Long enough."

"And then?"

"Got out."

"Why?" Drunks bumped her. "Geesh… Watch it."

"Five years, three deployments." Taylor took a taste of vodka. Swirled it in his mouth. Swallowed.

"Don't quit now. Story's getting' good."

"J-school at CoMo on the Bill."

"And you went back to the war?"

"Sure."

"Crazy."

"Probably. But I loved it."

Her skepticism surfaced. "Of course you did."

"Action. Loved the action. Army part – take it or leave it."

"Next?"

"Freelance embed in the sandbox for a year, then actually got hired and sent to Kabul. Stayed way past my expiration date. Get what you need?"

"Never."

"And you?"

"Same." They laughed. Broke the tension. "Moved a bunch. Went to seven or eight schools. Spent more years living overseas than in the States."

"Where?"

"Germany, Belgium, Japan. And F-ing Texas."

"Must've been tough."

"Didn't know any other life. A year here, couple years there. Lots of hellos and see-ya-laters. Make friends fast so you can party, but don't get too close because you'll leave or they will. You were in."

"It's different. Not like being a dependent."

"Yeah. No shit. We can't get out."

"Your dad still in?"

"Yep." Heat dipped a finger in her drink. Licked it.

The meter stirred inside Taylor's jeans. It'd been a while. "Uhh... Where's he stationed?"

"Germany, again."

"He push troops or paper?"

"Both. He's EuCom commander."

"Seriously?"

"Seriously."

A memory clicked. "The four-star? Jack O'Leary? Wow." That was difficult for him to digest. "He was my Colonel. My brigade commander when I was a butter bar," military slang for second lieutenant.

"Ever meet him?"

"Yeah. Sure. He's your dad?"

"Remember meeting me?"

"You?"

"In Vilseck? Right before you deployed to the war?"

Taylor searched for a recollection. "Oh yeah. All officers and NCOs in the post theater. Colonel brought his wife and daughters. Said this is what we're fighting for. That was you?"

She nodded.

"How old were you?"

"High school. Then he made me 'n my mom and sister meet the entire brigade."

"You shook five thousand hands?"

"No. My job was to be nice and sweet to five thousand soldiers, most of them not much older than me, all of 'em looking down my top."

His eyes drifted to her boobs. "Now I recognize those."

Again, Heat's middle digits rose to the occasion and she stuck out her tongue.

"Wow. Hot Bod in the flesh."

"Excuse me?"

"Never mind. Sorry I brought it up."

"Hot Bod?" He nodded. "How'd you even know about me?"

"The Colonel's daughter? We'd watch you and your posse walk from the post school to the snack bar in the HQ building almost every afternoon."

"What'd you call the rest of the girls?"

"Don't recall."

"Liar."

Taylor was anxious to change the subject. "How'd you get here? In all of this?"

"LA here?"

"Yeah."

"Why's anyone come to La La Land?"

"Weather?"

"You fall off the boat last night or this morning? To be a star, numb nuts. That didn't happen, so decided I'd be a writer."

"Just like that?"

"I'm stunningly brilliant. What can I say? You're up."

"Drove."

"And you were on a roll."

"I'm supposed to pour it all out to you?"

"Have someone better in mind?"

He didn't. "Got tired of bullets and bodies."

"Isn't that kind of your job for the PD?"

"No lead flying by the time I show, and the stiffs are strangers. So far. Until Em…"

"But..."

"My ask." All he could manage was a gaze. "Wow. General Jack's kid."

"Come on, now. Daddy wears the stars. Me? I'm your basic, all-American girl." Wide, phony grin.

An overload of unexpected info flash-flooded Taylor's conscience.

"Ten ticks to spit out your next question or forfeit. Eight, seven," Heat said.

"You forget ten and nine?"

"Six."

"So. Johnny."

"Finish Emma."

He glowered at her.

Heat relented. "Okay. Johnny's special."

The waitress delivered a round. Taylor lifted his ass and slid his wallet from a pocket. The honey on his right giggled as his wrist brushed her boob. He found four twenties, passed them to the server and waved thanks. She patted her heart. Taylor flipped a shot glass, balanced his billfold on it and re-focused on Heat. "You stopped at special."

"There are facets to him." She toyed with the wallet. "Nice. Dad has one. Cobra skin." Light and dark scales melded into thin, diamond shapes. "Been to Vietnam?"

"Friend went. She bought it for me. Tell me 'bout Johnny Lincoln. He wants us to work together."

"Don't know you well enough to spill."

"Sure you do. Bet you're marking up a Taylor checklist as we speak."

Heat blushed. She was. And she'd zoomed through the YES boxes, vodka-fast.

"Allow me. Handsome." He held a pose. "Hot. With a bod to die for." Flexed his pecs. "Smart." Frowned. "Funny." Smiled.

"Excellent teeth, too. He's a keeper, mom." She sipped. "Oh, hell with it." Heat tilted forward, vodka-serious. "Can't repeat this. Not to anyone."

Taylor raised a hand in solemn oath.

Heat gulped and fueled. "Johnny claims he's a Blue Blood? Boston Brahmin? Nope." She popped the p. "His old man was a junkie. OD'd in New Orleans, and his mother split when he was three or four. Spent his growing-up years in group homes and an occasional foster family."

"In NOLA."

"Yep."

"No Harvard? No 'Old Yeller?'"

"Definitely no Harvard. Got zilch on 'Old Yeller.' You mean the movie?"

"Yeah. So where's he rustle up all that cash?"

Heat ruminated. "In for a penny?"

"Sure."

"Color laser printer."

Taylor damn near choked.

"Johnny bleaches singles and prints old-style twenties on them. They feel right to the touch, so nobody pays attention."

Taylor chuckled. "How do you know all that?"

"You think I'm just another pretty face? Johnny and I share a special relationship."

"Is it gonna be a problem with us?"

She blinked. "What us? There's no us."

"Too bad. The meter was moving."

Heat wasn't sure whether to gag or smile.

"So where's he do his bleaching?"

Heat sipped.

"He live around here?"

She shrugged.

"Some kind of special."

Heat glared at him. Tried to scoot back. Impossible in the crush of bodies, so she shimmied up, thighs jammed against the table, and squirmed into her bomber jacket. She slipped fingers under her top, between bra and boob, and extracted folded, damp Jacksons. Tossed two on the empties. "These are real."

"Hey… Why're you pissed?"

Heat attracted booze leers and bar gawks as she shoved past the throng. She scowled, muttered several get-your-ass-outta-the-ways and elbowed a path to the exit.

It was a moment before Taylor realized she was headed to the door. "Sayonara, ladies," he said to the hotties on his flanks. He wobbled to his feet. Listed right. Corrected left. Stabilized, climbed over them and stumbled into the wet night.

On the sidewalk, Heat zipped up.

Taylor reached for her.

She twisted away. "I'm late."

"For dinner with your cats?"

"Cat. He's hairy, but he purrs."

"Why you so hot for me? My bod? Mug? Oh… It's 'cuz your dad was my CO."

"You are the reason I do not carry a gun."

"Ha. Ha. Good one. But I got you figured out. Your toes are curling. Yes, they are. I'm an expert. I know about this." He swayed.

Heat almost hooted but eye-fucked him instead. A foot separated them. She narrowed the gap. Stood as close as possible without contact. Damn. Her Purcells didn't cut it. Six more inches to go nose-to-nose. High heels would have put her close. Did she even own any? Didn't remember. Heat set her jaw. Hoped she was fierce and scary. But down deep, tingles spawned. Laughter bubbled. She had no idea how long, if at all, she could stifle it. Marched off.

"Why the rush?" Taylor threw his hands in the air. "We're just gettin' intimate here."

Across the street, Michael Le Roux, all washed and combed, was huddled in the entry of a candle shop, protected from the drizzle.

CHAPTER 28

"It's your wake-up call," Johnny said. Hoarse. White gauze wrapped his throat. A thin, horizontal line of blood leaked from ear lobe to ear lobe. He removed his lock picks from a deadbolt, cracked open Taylor's loft, and entered.

In the quiet gloom of a soggy morning, Johnny clenched a rolled *True Crime LA* and limped past the sofas. He coughed. Grimaced. Sharp rib pain forced him to lean against Taylor's kitchen island. He paused for the ow to ebb. Managed a shaky stride. And another. Progress helped. Coughed again. A nasty ouch, but he pressed on, beyond the TV and picture frames. He arrived at the green curtains that hung in the rear of the loft. Snuck a peek between them.

Taylor and Heat were forehead-to-forehead, entwined on a king-size mattress, a big lump beneath a glen plaid comforter.

"Rise and shine." A whisper. Johnny sucked a breath. "Hey, hey," He was loud enough that they heard and flew apart as if busted by an angry parent.

Heat spotted Johnny, yanked the covers to her chin and slammed her eyes shut. Taylor yawned, sat up, but groaned and fell to his pillow.

Johnny did a double-take. Heat and Taylor? An item? That hadn't occurred to him. Not once. "Uhhh... Sorry."

"It's cool," Taylor said.

Heat flared a no-it-is-not, but he didn't catch it.

Taylor did, however, see Johnny's bandage. Pointed at his throat. "Should I even ask?"

Johnny was speechless as he eyed Taylor and Heat, Taylor, Heat, Heat, Taylor.

She wasn't much better. Wanted to die. Or dig a hole and crawl in. Tugged the duvet and shimmied deeper in bed. All Johnny saw were brown eyes and red bangs.

Taylor propped himself on an elbow. Jagged, keloid scars blemished his upper body. "How'd you get in?"

Johnny showed him his picks.

"Learn to knock."

"Did."

"Or phone."

"Uh-huh." Johnny stared at Heat. Hated the sight of her snuggled in Taylor's bed. He'd never given it a thought until a minute earlier, but it bashed him like a 2x4 to the noggin. He was a jumble of unexpected, latent passions. Brand-new, uncomfortable stuff burst free, and it was all about her.

"What's so important?"

Johnny waved his *True Crime*. The arm motion generated a piercing pain. He cringed. "Uh... the uh..."

"Spit it out, Scoop."

"The uh, victims. Suicides. All tracked the *TCLA* classifieds. 'Cept they weren't hunting jobs."

Taylor sat back and held his hand out for the paper.

Johnny presented a page of ads and tapped one he'd circled. "Hey," he said to Heat.

"Hi." She averted her eyes.

Cut, battered and bruised, Johnny would've loved to take a load off, but there was no chair or sofa in the immediate vicinity and for him, the bed was radio-active. He scrutinized a smudge on a rug.

Taylor read the ad. "Interesting. Says, The Way. In caps and bold. 'The Way – out of debt, psychic barricades, your distressing existence, a life that won't leave you in peace. Three-two-three yada yada, or visit our website, www dot, etc., etc. Success guaranteed.'" He waited for Johnny to spout the connections. Instead, Johnny studied the carpet. "Scoop?"

"Hmmm? Oh. Yeah. It, uh, clicks." He contemplated Heat. Was she naked under the quilt? Panties? Panties and a T-shirt? No. Probably not. All the new brain blasts messed with him. Johnny struggled to concentrate on the reasons he was in Taylor's loft with Heat. And Taylor. "It uh..." He needed to move beyond this, this, distraction. Yeah, a distraction. "The, uh, ad…" He focused on the issue at hand. "The ad links the suicides. They all had shit doggin' 'em. Vinnie owed big bucks. Elvia couldn't shake her cholo boyfriend and the gang. Emma's pornos."

"Sounds about right. It hit you the same, babe?"

Embarrassed, Heat gazed outside and counted raindrops.

"Wanna stay for breakfast, Scoop?"

Johnny mustered fake cheer. "Oh, no, you kids go on and enjoy yourselves."

He limped from Taylor's and navigated the two flights to the street one slow step at a time, grumbling and berating himself. "I missed it? How in God's name did I not see her?" At ground level, he shoved a heavy fire door and was outside in the fog. "She's at her desk, next to me for months." Angry, he place-kicked a fluted column. "Ow. Oh." Doubled over.

"Scoop," Taylor said. Bare-chested, only jeans and no shoes, his scars were ragged and severe in the chill. "We do something wrong? Neither of you mentioned anything. Not you, not her."

Johnny didn't respond. He fought to maintain his dignity as he battled the throbbing and hobbled away.

Down the block, Michael Le Roux, in a sport coat, observed from behind the wheel of a faded, red, '91 Beemer 3-series as he stubbed a cigarette in a loaded ashtray.

Taylor noticed the car, didn't recognize the driver, and climbed upstairs.

CHAPTER 29

"When did I become the meat in the sandwich," Heat murmured. Stuck between Taylor and Johnny a dozen bodies deep in a Red Rapid, she hugged a shiny pole. Her ass rocked into Taylor. Yuck. She edged towards Johnny who hung onto a grab handle.

"Get a prognosis for your Corvair?" Taylor said. He gripped a handhold and admired the curvature of Heat's mini skirt.

"Yeah. Not great. Bullets in the butt and the oil pan. That's why we're on Metro's finest. Yours?"

"In the PD impound. Evidence."

"So here we are."

"Here we are."

Tires bounced in and out of a pothole. Heat bumped Taylor again. He whispered in her ear. "A little higher, please." Winked.

She butt-banged his balls. Sort of. And hung on the pole, so the bang was more implied than adamant.

"I'm kidding. Come on… Where'd you stash all the warm and fuzzies?"

Heat closed her eyes and counted from a hundred. Ninety-nine, ninety-eight…

To Taylor's left, a bearded guy raised the hem of a frayed kilt a couple inches. With a thick Glaswegian accent he said, "Ever wonder if it's veritable?"

"What?"

"The Scottish Secret." Kilt Man lifted his hem, exposed skinny, hairy thighs.

Disgusted, Taylor wrinkled his nose. "Leave a little mystery." He was wedged against a seatback, and the secret was seconds from reveal unless Heat thawed and allowed him to spoon. Snowballs in Hell came to mind. But good tidings prevailed, and the drifters, normies, even crazies, tucked elbows and attempted to obey the unwritten rules of bus Karma. Thank God a majority had bathed.

"Ya sure?" Kilt Man said. He leered.

Two hippie chicks strummed guitars and sang carols. Tourists. They wore cut-offs and sandals in December. They decked the halls and fa-la-la-ed. Folks joined in, some in themed outfits that brightened the trip - Santa and elf hats, antlers and ornaments.

A stop. Passengers boarded, the sing-along faded and Heat's butt was packed tight into Taylor. He wiggled his pelvis. She jabbed his ribs. He scooted into the Kilt.

The bus rejoined heavy traffic, jerked, braked, banged riders together. Johnny groaned. Each jolt was an adventure in pain. He hurt from the beatdown but sucked it up and gritted his teeth.

The automated voice announced, "Vine Street." Air brakes whooshed. Momentum crammed everyone tighter. There were grins and flinches.

"Miss Edna'd definitely get a kick out of this," Johnny said to Heat. "Let's buy her a ninety-day pass for Christmas."

Additional folks squeezed in. Before all the new arrivals paid, the engine revved. A woman lugging packages lost her balance and knocked Heat into Taylor. Heat blamed it on him. "How much longer, Johnny?"

"Not too far. H and H."

Someone pulled the cord. "Stop requested."

"That's us," Johnny said.

Heat pushed through to the middle exit. A few minutes and several ruts and dips later, the giant vehicle shuddered to a halt. She jumped to the sidewalk, happy to escape.

Taylor was next, followed by Johnny. There they were at Hollywood and Highland, the heart of moviedom, spiritual birthplace of the most prestigious award in the world. Not the Nobel Peace Prize, the other one - the one that compels delivery of an acceptance speech to a steamy bathroom mirror at least once.

The Rapid's compressed natural gas engine whined as Johnny, Heat and Taylor found their way to the legendary crossroads. They ignored the drizzle and plowed through a swarm of visitors gawking at golden statues identical to the trophy. The sightseers aimed cameras and phones and shot photos and video for the folks back home.

A hundred yards west, all the superheroes and Marilyns paraded back and forth in front of the historic Chinese Theater and geared up for an evening of poses and tips.

Johnny watched a rotating restaurant atop a hotel a block-and-a-half north. It resembled a flying saucer on final approach. He'd been for the ride. Sipped a nineteen-dollar drink on the twentieth floor. Fantastic vibe as he'd relaxed and enjoyed a slow circuit around the heavens, if heaven were the LA basin. And who knew? It might be. He turned and laid eyes on First National rising on the opposite side. "Thar she blows." He poked the "walk" button on the pole. Once, twice, three times.

Heat grabbed his sleeve. "What's with you?"

"Besides the sliced neck?" Johnny pulled his arm from her and stepped to the pavement.

A cop on a horse scolded him with a frown. Holidays. Police flooded the zone in cars, on foot and with the mounted patrol. A fine of a hundred and ninety-six bills was too rich to risk, but Johnny projected defiance. He glared a challenge at the officer. Before any repercussions, the signal changed. Legal, Johnny marched six lanes in the cross-walk, avoiding an assortment of whackos. Costumed hustlers, panhandlers and buskers worked out-of-towners for a buck. Johnny evaded vacationers clumped for mutual safety. "Rubes," he said.

"And you're not?" Heat said.

"Nope." Johnny had dived into La La Land and adapted to Tinsel Town life in four short months. He loved everything about it.

At the center-divider, Johnny glanced over his right shoulder at the lime-green Gee Spot sign. To his left, he noticed the rainbow awning at the Guess Who? Club. He reached the curb, leaped over the gutter and landed in history - the First National Building. Heat and Taylor flanked him.

The elegant, art-deco and Gothic edifice straddled the corner. Wings, one north on Highland, the other east on the boulevard, emanated from a grand entrance of bronze doors, eight feet wide. A discreet brass plaque bolted to the wall announced, "The Way." It was the only indication of the old bank's current function. A tower rose above the entry and dominated the intersection. Johnny counted floors. Twelve. Red and green lights that celebrated the season lit windows. Spotlights illuminated stone eagles perched on the terrace of the hexagonal penthouse.

"Let's check comings and goings," Heat said.

Enthusiastic, attractive people in their twenties and thirties entered. They blended banter, nervous giggles and laughter, broad gestures and swagger. There was no evidence of crazies – significant in that part of town.

"Aaannnd action." Johnny took a stride.

Heat yanked his collar. "Plan."

"We hashed this out a thousand different ways."

"Give me the plan." Firm. Not interested in crap.

"Yeah, yeah, yeah. Talk, ask questions, snag blurbs. Find why Emma, Vinnie and Elvia gave it all up, then we boogie."

"Need a rendezvous location," Taylor said. "In case we're disconnected."

Johnny agreed. So did Heat, but she wasn't about to bestow credit.

"H and H Metro station. Ticket machines. Got phones and numbers?"

Heat rolled her eyes.

"Yeah," Johnny said. He looked skyward, uttered a mantra, "Cover story, cover story, cover story," and hurried towards the former bank.

He led Heat and Taylor beneath an alabaster archway into LA's glamorous once-upon-a-time. They joined a hundred-fifty Millennials and Gen-Zs who mingled, chatted and chortled in an opulent lobby. Four crystal chandeliers sparkled. Gold-leaf fixtures and sconces glistened. The place was living proof that a couple years after Jolson's "Jazz Singer," as Hoover, Republicans and the Great Depression clobbered the country, First National had been the film industry's premier financial institution when movies were the only business in town.

The wait-staff, actor-hunk males and model-gorgeous females, typical of a Los Angeles social occasion, glided across polished, pink marble in black tops, pants and aprons. They balanced trays of hors d'oeuvres or bubbly on fingertips and slalomed around a dozen potted weeping figs. A server offered Johnny a beverage. He declined. Taylor didn't.

Clusters of guests browsed DVDs and Blue Rays or books and pamphlets exhibited on lacquer tables. Heat scanned a hardback. Read cover kudos touting "The Way" and a fresh dawn for YOU. "Gobs to digest," she said. "I'll take one."

Johnny pocketed a freebie and nodded at an energetic, thirty-ish woman in a flowing, indigo frock. She danced in place and displayed a DVD. "Suggested donation of thirty. But only if you can afford it." She twirled. "And the proceeds go to a worthy cause." He thumbed bills and made the purchase.

Champaign fueled a festive mood. Pronounced dings penetrated loud voices and laughter. Three copper-colored elevators on the far side opened. Five people emerged from each. Males and females dressed in identical white shirts, thin, red ties, white slacks and white Oxford bucks. As they deployed, Johnny noticed the fifteen wore red socks. Odd.

Grins were pasted on, welcoming, but not too forward. There wasn't a strand of errant hair. They hailed invitees and presented brochures. One bee-lined to Johnny who stood a head above the pack. "Hi, I'm Dennis." He switched on a thousand-watt smile, pumped Johnny's hand, shook Taylor's and clasped Heat's with both of his. "You have to be virgins."

"Uh, yeah... once," Heat said. That was unexpected.

"This your first event? Here? At The Way?"

"Uh, yes."

"Yeah," Taylor said.

Dennis beamed. "Then you are Virgins. So exciting." He mimed clapping. "Peruse our literature, partake of the munchies, sip some bubbly, make new friends. Any queries? Don't hesitate to ask." He blew kisses, trotted off, redirected his robust persona and welcomed more visitors.

"Born-again virgins. Who knew?" Heat said.

Johnny meandered among the throng. Exchanged hellos, bumped fists. Heat selected a flyer. Taylor palmed his smartphone and photographed the gathering on the down-low. Johnny wound his way to heavy double doors that dominated one side of the lobby. He faced the festivities, shifted, felt a knob behind his back. Not locked. Leaned into a door. It opened. "Kids?" He slipped out of sight.

Taylor and Heat scoped nearby partiers. They were in the clear and trailed Johnny into a spacious, sixty-by-forty art-deco room lit by recessed LED bulbs and filled with thick, vinyl gym mats. "What do you suppose goes on in here?" Taylor said.

Heat performed a cartwheel.

"This is our Relaxorium," Dennis said.

Busted.

"Explains everything," Johnny said.

Dennis held the smile, but his arms were folded, and his posture screamed suspicion.

Heat regained her poise. "Relaxorium?"

Dennis threw the doors wide open, clapped twice and addressed the attendees jamming the lobby. "Ladies and gentlemen." Clapped again. "Ladies and gentlemen. Please." Conversations petered and died. Dennis waited as drinks were drained and the assembled settled. At that point, he possessed their attention and bowed. "Join me."

The meeters and greeters sporting the red ties and socks, separated certain party-goers from the crowd. Heat observed them cut and herd a hundred to the exit. Fifty were led to the Relaxorium. They were youthful and stylish. A few recognizable from TV or film. At first glance they were the type who paid attention to fashion and could afford to keep up. Impeccable makeup and haircuts. Perfect shoes and apparel.

Inside, some toed the gym pads, a handful bounced, and a few were still and silent. The doors latched. A murmur of long-term, post 9-11 anxiety ignited.

"Joyous salutations," Dennis said. Upbeat and cheery, he motioned to his audience, an even mix of men and women. "Sit. Be comfortable. As the name implies, this space is devoted to our stress-easing exercises."

Heat accepted the invitation and studied Dennis. Five-ten, well-groomed, easy on the eyes, but bland. No distinguishing characteristics. She'd be hard-pressed to describe him beyond the basics.

Dennis continued his pitch. "The Way promises self-awareness by specific goal identification achieved with body work, collective therapy, positive imagery and traditional gestalt encounter."

Next to Heat, Taylor whispered, "Any idea what he means?"

"Of course."

"Limbs straight," Dennis said. Half the people complied. "Excellent." The remainder wavered or didn't play. "Now, rest on your elbows."

Heat did.

"When can we register?" Johnny said. He was the last one standing. The interruption caught Dennis off guard, but not enough to rattle him. It did, however, surprise Heat and Taylor.

"We hope tonight." Dennis smiled and continued. "Extend your legs. Chop, chop." He allowed the holdouts a moment to conform. "Comfy? Tilt your cranium." Some dropped their chins to chests. "No, no, no. The opposite. Stretch that throat." He demonstrated. "Yeah. Now rotate. Clockwise. Let's do it."

Taylor followed instructions. "Oh… ouch."

"Tension," Heat said.

"Slept crooked." He smirked. "Or twisted a muscle."

Disgusted, she ignored him.

"And – counter-clock-wise," Dennis led.

Heat heard Taylor's spinal column snap and crack. "Ow…"

"Rice Crispy neck. I, however…" Heat did an unhurried swivel of her head. Not a sound.

Johnny didn't participate. He remained on his feet. It amazed him that strangers obeyed the commands of a stranger without question.

"Young man? Care to join?" Dennis said to Johnny.

"I'm good." He touched his bandage.

CHAPTER 30

"Can't do it, Johnny. Your Libra's in the wrong house," Heat said. She dogged him as they hustled out of The Way.

"Gee, you forgot that, Scoop?" Taylor led as they jogged across rain-wet Hollywood Boulevard.

"Shut up," she said. "I'll enlist."

"No." Johnny was adamant. "I'll do it. Three souls walked in there and all of 'em came out wearing a box."

"Technically, two," Taylor said.

"Two, ten, who gives a rat's ass?" Heat said.

"Two and a mystery, all right?" Johnny said.

"Or three, or three-hundred. We haven't figured it yet. Not for sure."

They dashed through the mist to the south side of the street and into the bus-stop shelter. Heat invaded Johnny's personal space. "I'll do it. End of discussion."

"You do own a pair, sister." He admired her.

She advanced. Breached his comfort zone. He shuffled backward. She dogged him.

Bus brakes phussed and doors opened. Heat didn't budge, nor did Johnny. Taylor waved the driver on.

Fists on hips, she was tits-to-ribs with Johnny. "I've run the gamut of self-help seminars. Done them all."

"Not The Way, and in addition to that, we don't understand anything about it."

"They're all the same."

"Nope. Too dangerous."

"Second that," Taylor said.

"Those dudes," Heat said, "who tried to knock you off? At Le Roux's? Then in my car? If they're involved, you're burned toast."

"Might've been random," Johnny said. "Road rage."

"Even you don't buy that. They know who you are. They never made me."

"You were driving," Taylor said.

"This does not concern you."

"Like hell."

She turned to Johnny. "Those guys were gunning for you. Camera boy's probably on their hit list now, too. Guilt by association. But most definitely you're the target, and they're hunting."

Not a pleasant notion, but she had him - packaged, sealed and out of options. "Okay."

"Okay." Heat folded her arms. End of discussion.

"Chill, babe. You too, Scoop. Rein it in," Taylor said. "I have a right to say something."

"Babe?"

"Oh?" Johnny said.

"Yeah. I mean, last night and all."

"Let me tell you something, *babe*." Heat seemed to spit the word and grind it into the sidewalk. She flashed a scary look, a combination sneer and mock Johnny had witnessed twice at *TCLA*. His instinct was to duck and cover, but instead, he moved a step to avoid the line of fire as Heat stabbed Taylor's chest with an index finger. "So listen up. Our romp? Maximal, it got you *hasta la vista* after breakfast."

"But..."

She jabbed him with each syllable. "Just 'cuz I said 'go deeper' and you could, does not mean we're getting married."

Johnny plugged his ears. "TMI. Put a muzzle on it."

"You can't let her do it," Taylor said.

"Ain't my call."

"And don't forget it," Heat said.

"But why not let her?" Johnny said. "We're zeroing in on a big story." He gripped Heat's shoulders. "Huge."

"It's not about that." She slumped.

He turned to Taylor. "Front page, *mon ami.* It's obvious you miss the game. Here's your ticket."

A Rapid arrived. Johnny boarded.

"I'll go along with it, but..." Taylor said.

Heat punched his pecs and drove him to the bench. "No buts. You don't have fuck-all to say."

Johnny hopped to the curb. "Dial it down."

Taylor threw his hands above his head. "Uncle. Things get too heavy, we go to the police. Deal?"

CHAPTER 31

"Home sweet home for the duration," Johnny said. He wrenched a storm-soaked For Rent sign out of soft ground. "Ta da. Furnished and ready for you."

Heat peered from under the bill of a blue baseball cap. She inspected a shabby, pre-war building on Merwin Avenue in Echo Park, between the 101 Freeway and Sunset, west of Alvarado. It was a disaster. Gang tags and assorted, sordid graffiti smeared the stucco. A 'banger had spray-painted an ominous skull and crossbones on the sidewalk. Pairs of sneakers, laces tied, hung on utility wires. Those symbols were the human equivalent of a dog taking a whiz on a hydrant to mark its territory.

"This is it? This is your plan?" Heat said. "Our deadline's today."

"Not if the Chief doesn't see us."

There was a rectangular void instead of a door and no fire escape. She'd have to fly to save herself. "I get it. Fake name, different address. You think they'll check?"

"Why chance it?"

A short block away, Michael Le Roux sat in his red Beemer and inserted cartridges into a six-shooter. He eyeballed Johnny and Heat, in the wet, arguing. Saw a second guy balancing boxes and stuff, but couldn't see his face. Crazy people.

Le Roux slapped the cylinder, spun it, sighted the redhead and took an imaginary shot. "Ka-blewie. Splat."

Taylor juggled sacks packed with department-store purchases. "Debate it inside."

Johnny kicked a crumpled beer can and led them past ripped, filled trash bags and a burned, water-logged futon. At the entrance, he paused, eyed the interior and walked in. Newspapers shrouded a five-foot lump. Yesterday's captions shifted. A dark, oily, tangled mess crowned one end of the heap. A filthy ankle and muddy shoe stuck out from the other. Couldn't discern male or female without closer examination. There were no volunteers.

Heat sniffed. "Fish. Cabbage. Curry. And the ever-classic, Eau du Pee. Unh unh. No way. Not a chance."

"C'mon, doll. Bet you've seen worse."

"Seen, but not slept."

Johnny jogged up a flight. Heat tested her weight on a splintered tread. Taylor juggled his cargo and climbed past her.

Johnny slid a key in a knob, turned it and pushed. "Tah-daaah." He swept his arm and invited Heat and Taylor into her new abode.

She stood on her toes. Scanned the place. "It's a fucking… I don't know… Shit-hole?"

"I know. It's perfect. Defines rock bottom. Hunting for a fresh start."

She laid a dead-man stare on him.

"C'mon. It's a studio." A landlord's enhanced description of 300 square feet posing as a one-room apartment.

Heat spotted a bent folding chair and a small, three-drawer dresser. She entered. Probed the cushion of a lumpy, two-butt sofa below the only window. Decided it was safe to sit. Wiggled her ass and laced her fingers behind her neck. She put her tennies on a kidney-shaped, plastic-laminate coffee table blemished by decades of cigarette burns. Jutted her chin. "Where, exactly, do you expect me to sleep?"

Taylor dropped his load and unlatched a Murphy Bed built into a wall. "Incoming…" He jumped back as the steel frame crashed to the carpet.

"Scored you a DTLA view," Johnny said.

Heat gazed through the grimy pane. "Not seeing it."

"Lift. The window."

Her expression leaped between "duh," and "got it, bitch." She kneeled on the couch. Clenched the handle. Pulled. The window didn't move. She re-gripped, yanked, pounded and rattled the casement. Put everything into it. The wood frame shrieked as she raised it about a foot. Heat poked her head out and deflected rain with an arm. Glanced side-to-side. "Vista del dumpsters."

"To your right."

Peered that direction. "Nope."

Taylor crowded next to her. "Sure. There it is." He pointed.

"Of course. Gee, how'd I miss it?" Disgusted, she said to Johnny, "Pony Boy."

Heat held her hands away from her body and searched for a towel. Settled for Johnny's coat.

"Hey. That's brand new."

"The tippy-top of one skyscraper? You are such a freakin' optimist."

"It counts. Downtown building, downtown view."

"Pony Boy." She tossed his coat.

"Am not.

"Sure you are.

"No. I'm. Not." Johnny insisted.

"Any idea what it even means?"

He didn't react.

"Wanna learn?"

No answer.

"Of course you do, but we won't let anybody in on it, fair enough? So here goes. Say someone, for example, *moi*, delivered you a pile of warm horse poop. You'd get with your dumb-ass grin and ask, 'where's the pony? Can I go for a ride?' Hence, Pony Boy."

"So?"

"You're a reporter." She yelled, "We don't do optimism," and lowered herself to the Murphy's thin mattress. It sagged. She snagged a canvass tote, rummaged in it, found an aerosol can and sprayed. "Be useful," she said to Taylor. They flipped the bed. She de-bugged the underside.

"Let's try on the new things," Johnny said.

"Let's? As in, 'let us?' You first, Pony Boy." Heat dug in a shopping bag and extracted a cellophane packet of red and green tights. "You'd be extra spicy in these. Giving you dibs, Johnny."

He had the smarts to keep his mouth shut.

Heat stepped to the opposite side of the room. "This the bath?" She toed open a door. Crinkled her nose. "Gross. What're you smokin'?"

"Remember. Byline," Johnny said.

"I get at least one of those every week."

"Cover story."

"Fair enough. You got my six? You moving in across the hall?"

"Uhhh..."

Neither guy looked at her.

"I'm here all by my lonesome?" Heat's eyes and mouth hardened as she regarded a rusty-brown tub, corroded fixtures, dusty sink, and a toilet bowl stained yellow. Years of neglect and a lack of basic hygiene. "I get top billing."

She flapped a shower curtain. Black mold grew on the lowest inch. "Hell with that. Solo credit."

"Mirror's okay," Johnny said with a hint of optimism.

"Out." She shoved him, slammed the door in his face and tugged a string dangling from a light socket. A 40-watt bulb lit but wasn't a help.

She looked into the mirror and removed her cap. Her hair fell into a new cut and style. Heat was accustomed to the frizz caused by too much dye. She stroked her locks. Wow. Soft and smooth. Scrutinized her reflection and approved. At least a part of her day hadn't been wasted.

She scanned the bathroom. "Where's the damn paper towel?" She shouted.

"We'll get some."

Nothing to wipe the edge of the tub. She leaned forward, careful not to touch her legs on anything. With the tips of her right thumb and index finger Heat turned an old, fluted, plastic handle. Water spurted then flowed. At least it wasn't dirty. She hoped nothing crawled out the drain or faucet and bit her. She'd read too many urban legends and watched too many horror movies. Remembered one film where the blonde bought the farm. Naked and relaxed in a hot bath, a snake slithered from the spigot and sunk its fangs into her. It was somebody famous. She couldn't remember who.

In the main room, Johnny lounged on the sofa and toyed with his phone. Taylor plopped on the mattress.

They heard Heat. "Fuck," she said. Not an angry fuck, but a fuck of surprise and awe. A lot of "U's." Repeated it. "Fuuuuuck."

Johnny and Taylor gazed at the lav. Heard, "Wow." Then, "Oh?" Followed by, "Ohhhh. Geez." And an amazed, "O-kay."

They glimpsed a new, ruby-red shoe as it peeked out of the bath. Shot silent questions at each other.

Heat retreated. Examined herself closer. Didn't trust the image she saw in the mirror. Sure didn't trust Johnny's and Taylor's opinions. There was no choice. It was for the story. Yeah, sure… She drummed up enough confidence for a tentative step.

Johnny saw her. "Va-va-voom."

Heat wore a modest, black skirt. Modest for her, anyway. Longer than usual. It was the red, laced corset topped by a matching, waist-length leather jacket that launched her to a new orbit. The ensemble emphasized Heat's classic hourglass figure. Rounded breasts nudged into deep cleavage, and her hips flared. She presented the new outfit with a wobbly pirouette. Glimpsed herself in a cheap, full-length mirror nailed to the closet. "Holy moly. If I didn't know, I wouldn't know." She stumbled. "Damn heels." Recovered her equilibrium and explored her image. "Holy fuckin' wow." Heat was astonished by the transformation. The bombshell in need of a tune-up finally had one. She resumed the three-sixty.

Taylor bowed and bequeathed a box. “Does Mademoiselle wish to slip into her new pumps?”

“Got a death wish?” But she curtsied and accepted it. “Can’t remember when I... Heidelberg? Junior prom in the castle?”

Johnny cleared his throat. Her hotness was an unexpected distraction. “So, uh, where’s home?”

“PCSd constantly. Fort Hood, Bamberg, Vilseck, Heidelberg.”

“Not you, you.”

“Yeah, sorry.” Heat poured butter and syrup on grits with a thick, Texas accent. “Waxahachie, sugar. And straight to UT after graduation. Notched my ‘M-R-S.’, eventually a B-T-D-T in di-vorce.” Pronounced it dye-vorce.

“What’s…”

“Been there, done that, darlin’. And no rug rats. Lucky me. Now I’m here, dreamin’ big, hopin’ bigger. Hot damn howdy.”

CHAPTER 32

"Goddamn, Sam, even my teeth are numb," Heat said. Her jaw chattered in the chill as she huddled with Johnny and Taylor at the bus stop on the northwest corner of H and H. She reached behind, grabbed Johnny's belt and pulled him against her backside. Taylor scooted forward. She scowled. He withdrew.

Legs together, arms and elbows pressed to her sides, Heat cradled a to-go cup and sipped. Her new threads and "do" exposed more of her to the elements than normal. The jacket didn't begin to cover her décolletage, and the new tights provided minimal protection. She shivered, exhaled on her palms and relented. Wrapped Taylor's buckle with a hand and drew him close.

Taylor ogled her boobs.

"Use your imagination."

"Don't have to."

Johnny wanted to steal a peek but instead said, "It's go time."

"We got your six," Taylor said. "Situation crashes, bolt."

"Easy for you to say." Heat swallowed the last of her coffee. She pitched the empty in a trash can and bussed Johnny on the cheek. Eyed Taylor. "Wish me luck." Kissed him on the lips. "Here goes anything." Her new "do" bobbed as she crossed Highland.

"Hey," Johnny said. "Where're you from?"

"Waxahachie, sugar."

Johnny and Taylor were as proud and anxious as parents on back-to-school day. Taylor paced and Johnny fiddled with his belt as Heat joined a collection of people gathered at The Way's entry. She greeted and air-kissed all of them and fired up a conversation with a petite, blonde woman.

"Wish we could go," Taylor said.

"She's tough. A trooper. All the clichés, and a lot she's never shown us," Johnny said. "Come on. Walking's warmer." It wasn't freeze-your-ass cold, just SoCal see-your-breath cold. Johnny skidded on the wet sidewalk. Taylor caught him. They had the town to themselves - no pedestrians, no vehicles - as the first hint of dawn erased the reflection of Christmas on damp pavement. They marched east, in silence, past the *Guess Who?* and turned at Wilcox.

Five minutes and three long blocks south, Taylor punched in the code at the cop shop employee entrance. "Stay here. Cedar Tree's tightening the lid. No civilians."

"I'm not unfamiliar with the hallowed halls of Hollywood Homicide."

"Catchy."

"Which is how we met, you and me." Johnny stabbed the elevator button.

"And it's baked into my brain, you creeping around. However, today's Saturday. Energy conservation. Wait in the lobby." Taylor enjoyed Johnny's frustration. He tapped four digits on the stairwell security keypad, opened the door, climbed to the second floor and traversed the linoleum vestibule to the squad room. It was still tucked in for the night. He flicked a switch. The fluorescents blinked to life. Taylor sat at his desk and wiggled the computer mouse. The LAPD logo popped on the screen. He typed a password and eleven asterisks appeared. He clicked on a new page. It demanded keywords and search parameters. He sounded out, "Su-i-cide." Did a two-finger hunt and peck. Next, he typed, "no note."

"Don't forget nude," Johnny said.

Surprised, Taylor flinched. "What is it with you?"

"We're a team. No 'I,' two heads and all."

Taylor didn't bother to argue and entered n-u-d-e. "Anything else, boss?"

"Try 'at home.'"

CHAPTER 33

"Good Morning, Virgins," Dennis said at 7:15 a.m. sharp.

"That'd make mom's day," Heat said as she slipped into a queue of fourteen persons. She held her jacket closed, bounced on the balls of her feet and took a survey.

Eight babes - four white, two black, one Hispanic, and Heat's fifty-percent Japanese. Diversity plus. Each clutched a caffeinated drink – brewed or cola – and a phone. They used forearms or fists to hide yawns and discreetly stretched, awake too early. But even at zero-dark-thirty, they were chic and coifed, makeup expertly applied. Several sported trendy earrings and necklaces. All wore pricey, fitted attire and designer footwear. To a one, they were young and gorgeous – cheerleader-cute to super-model perfect. Heat doubted she was suited for this group, not convinced Johnny and Taylor told her the truth.

And the dudes. Hunks. Heat's chemical reaction was, WOW. Handsome and wholesome in conservative or trendy. Physique dictated brand and style - tailored blazers or sport coats. Two sported silk, French-cuff shirts, three, cotton. But expensive cotton, and monogrammed. Same with the bottom half. Five were in jeans, one, slacks. Hard to tell what was happening beneath their clothes, but Heat sensed splendid, concealed bulges, rock-solid biceps and six-pack abs. She'd love to find out. The African-Americans and the Latino shaved their skulls, which she'd never appreciated. No need to hurry it. Bald will bite you soon enough. The Anglo guys had hair and the obligatory hipster beard growth. A nice look, but in practice, she hated the feel of it. Too scratchy. Chewed up her face and thighs. Thighs if she was lucky.

"On me," Dennis said.

The bronze portal opened. He led the Virgins single-file into The Way, across the polished marble to the Relaxorium. They gawked at the décor and architecture and were met by an equal number of bright-eyed and bushy-tailed men and women, seven on either side of the entrance. It was the bunch Heat had encountered at the recruiting reception. White button-downs, trousers and shoes, red socks and ties, all five-ten. So-so for the males, but Amazonian for the females.

"Billfolds, watches, jewelry, cells, purses, everything, in a pile." Dennis ordered.

"But…" a female newbie said.

"Absolutely no distractions."

"I'm expecting…"

"Then leave."

She set her bag on the floor.

Dennis shifted gears. Clapped twice. "Time for Coupling."

Coupling? Experience taught Heat that new members were matched with mentors. Basic, self-help SOP - standard operating procedure. She'd never heard it put that way, but since they were "Virgins," it made sense.

Dennis scurried to a perky girl with a pixie cut whose previous gig was probably high school cheerleader - the 95-pounder they tossed to the sky. Wrap-around skirt, snug sweater, she swayed. Dennis laid his hands on her shoulders. Kneaded her muscles. "Air in. In… Hold it. Hold it. And, liberate…"

Her eyes widened and she shook her head. Had no clue.

"Exhale. Slowly. And, again." She obeyed and offered a hint of a grin in a quest for approval. Dennis was happy to oblige. "Excellent." He urged her on. She stepped away from her possessions. Felt a rush of separation anxiety, paused and hugged herself. Dennis positioned her in front of a male associate, then stationed each Virgin facing a Way member of the opposite sex.

Must be part of the welcome ritual, thought Heat. She judged her assigned male. Not bad. Brown over brown, in Johnny's age range. She preferred taller but wouldn't kick him out of bed for eating crackers. Covered her mouth and coughed. Hoped it camouflaged her exploration of his features for distinctive characteristics. She didn't identify any.

"Say hello to your First," Dennis said.

The newbs mingled. "Hi," "Hello," "Hey."

The Firsts remained silent.

"Howdy," Heat said to her First. He leaned in. Prelude to a kiss? Sure seemed like it. She resisted the urge to dodge his lips. Knowledge and experience kicked in. She stood her ground. The other Virgins bent backward and avoided contact.

Dennis noticed her stance. He gestured at the fourteen people flanking the doors. They advanced towards the Virgins, drew them forward, embraced, and kissed. Neither tentative nor a peck, or intense and soulful. Somewhere in the acceptable middle, but they did manage to percolate a bubble or two.

Dennis sighed and said, "You'll remember your First forever." He allowed ample opportunity for the uneven line of novices to fidget and blush, then ordered, "Forward march."

Heat came chest-to-chest with her First. Her boobs brushed him when she inhaled. She was uncomfortable with the intrusion but knew the reason - begin the process of molting convention and decorum. She was the only Virgin who moved.

"Vestals…" Dennis admonished.

Half complied.

"Pronto. Chop chop." He clapped twice.

The balance of newcomers, nervous and unsure, acquiesced. They tested the limits of peripheral vision as Dennis stalked them. He moved behind Heat, gripped her upper arms and spoke into her left ear. "See him? Your First?" His low, resonant delivery drilled deep. "He'll adore you, pull you, push you beyond horizons never envisioned, to destinations never imagined. Gently, firmly, totally, you will surrender and submit and embrace the moment of present and the promise of future. Completely. And there you will be and stay, because," Dennis sucked a breath, "because there is no past, therefore, there is no pain."

Such crapola, Heat thought. And too many adverbs. But she maintained. Didn't mock or pooh-pooh. However, her knees fluttered as chills ran wild. It was Dennis's timbre that wobbled her and tingled, not the touchy-feely BS. She'd been subjected to the message before – it didn't change much from one cult to the next. The differences were labels and slogans – how the guru peddling a new salvation referred to people, places and things. But Dennis weaponized *blow in my ear and I'll follow you anywhere* into a float-your-boat intensity. She resisted, but her mouth twitched.

Dennis saw it. His brow arched a bit. He released her and trotted inside the Relaxorium as he cheered, "Hey. Hey. Hey. Let's go. Let's go. Let's go," and skipped across the gym mats.

The Firsts clapped and chanted, "We're here. We're here. We're here."

The beginners watched and wondered.

Heat knew confusion was the objective and applauded. Shouted, "Yeeeeaaaaahhhh…" and dashed in. The Virgins lumbered after her with no energy and apathetic hollers.

Dennis focused on Heat. "What does the world call you?"

"Heather."

"Get their asses out of here, Heather."

She had a flash of confusion about the instructions, then clarity. "Come on. On me. Now," and shepherded the Virgins to the lobby.

The Relaxorium doors closed with a bang.

The recruits were willing, but confused and anxious. They huddled and gazed at Heather, their new leader. The Cheerleader dribbled a tear. Heat hugged her. "Who are you, baby?"

"Cami. One 'm.' Short for Cameron."

Of course it is. Heat would bet big all the Caucasian chicks were Morgan, Carter, Cody and Riley, or similar names once given to boys.

"Up their's," A robust Latino said. He found his pile, scooped up his phone and dropped his wallet in a pocket.

"And you are…?" Heat said.

"Steve."

"Oh?"

"Heather?"

"Dad's choice. Mom gave me my middle initial."

He waited for her to say it.

"Okay. Y."

"And that stands for…?"

She fostered an ounce of trust. "Yoniko."

"Yo! Yo…"

Heat cringed. "And now you know."

"Esteban." He powered up his phone.

She plunged in. "Put your stuff down – Steve. It's all copacetic." She occupied Dennis's spot. "You're not getting the boot. None of us are. And believe me, Cami, they want you. They really, really want you. Stick to my lead. We'll all be adored forever."

Doubt lingered, but in less than a minute, the Virgins' angst eased. Heat jogged in a circle. Yelled. Hollered. An attractive, mid-twenties Black man joined her. Soon, Steve and Cami did.

A striking model-type flexed her arms and said, "Well hell."

One-by-one they hopped, flailed and shouted.

"Ready?" Heat said.

"Yes."

"Are you ready?" Emphatic.

A loud chorus of, "Yes."

Heat threw open the doors and charged into the Relaxorium. She whopped it up. Bounced on the vinyl pads. The newbies howled and trotted.

Dennis applauded. It was difficult to gauge his sincerity.

The Firsts joined in. "One group, one heart. One group, one heart," over and over. "One group, one heart."

Heat joined the chant. "One group, one heart."

So did the Virgins. "One group, one heart. One group, one heart."

"Great work. Great work," Dennis said.

The Firsts jumped to attention.

The novices recitation petered out with a couple weak, "One heart." They eyed Heat for cues. She stood at parade rest.

"On me," Dennis said.

Led by Heat, they trudged into a ragged circle and looked at her for approval. Did we do okay? Is it correct? The Firsts formed a second, larger ring and surrounded them.

"Be seated," Dennis said. The recruits were slow to react. "Sit!"

Heat lowered herself as the Firsts trooped to the four corners of the room and retrieved file folders. They distributed stapled, printed papers and yellow, Number 2 pencils. She scanned a comprehensive, seven-page survey. It asked for a biography - date and location of birth, schools attended, jobs, relatives, neighbors, teachers, relationships. She reviewed the personal history Johnny and Taylor had conjured. If that didn't cut it, she'd embellish. Easy enough - it's kind of how she earned a buck.

"Your answers are critical and will reveal the way you are at this precise instant," Dennis said. He enjoyed his pun. "When you've lost it and are no longer a Virgin, we'll revisit and ask the core question." They were anxious to hear it. I hung on every word. "Okie-dokie. At the top of the page? Where it says name?"

CHAPTER 34

"We absolutely have to talk about it," Taylor said. He grasped a shiny pole near the center exit of a Rapid. The bus rocked as tires thumped rough pavement.

"Why? It's all good," Johnny said. His knees absorbed the bumps as he held on with two fingers and a thumb.

"Not exactly."

"Believe me, it's cool. You called heads, I got tails. You won."

"Huh?"

"You won."

"What?"

"Who."

"You lost me."

"Want me to spell it out?"

"Suppose so, yeah."

"Then pay attention. Back in the day, it would've been a love triangle."

"Only a triangle if it has three sides."

The almost-empty bus jolted to a halt. Johnny and Taylor disembarked in East Hollywood. Johnny checked the GPS map on his phone. "Next corner, left, and up the hill a bit." He hurried to a residential street.

Taylor kept pace. "Something weird's rattling around your brain and there's no hint to what it is," he said. "We ought to strategize." He removed a creased sheet of white copy paper from his camera bag. "Because this changes things."

"How?" Johnny glanced at his map app. They hiked another block. "Here we be."

Morning sun lit cracked, puke-green stucco. A house of a thousand square feet boasted all the amenities – rusted iron fence and gate, cement yard, scattered toys. It also featured burglar bars over the windows.

Taylor waved the paper. "The system coughed up more could-be suicides. Total's six. Five's a serial."

"But there's no clue to any linkage."

"RHD ghouls don't give a flying fart. They're gonna be sniffing our asses, and if they decide to play, it'll be their ball and their game, which leaves you, me and Heat on the fringes, and Emma..." Taylor let the notion linger as he pushed the gate. It creaked.

Johnny grabbed his sleeve. "Cool your jets. Verify there's no dog."

"You shitting me?" But Taylor, the combat veteran, cocked his head and listened. No growls or barks. "Any other instructions?" He didn't linger for an answer and marched to the porch. Stood to the side of a heavy, rusty, steel-mesh door, on his toes, prepared to leap.

Johnny pressed the bell button. No reply. Knocked.

"Ain't buying nothing." A woman said. She was unseen behind the mesh.

"We at the Francisco Gabaldon residence?"

"Who asking?"

Johnny slapped a business card against the steel screen and announced, "Mutual Life Assurance, ma'am."

"Ain't buying no 'surance. He dead."

"We're not selling. We need to confer with you concerning his policy?"

"Frankie?" She shrieked. "Frankie had life 'surance? How much?"

"A million," Taylor said.

"Dollars?"

"Uh, not exactly," Johnny said. He shot Taylor a look as the security door flew open. Damn near hammered him on the jaw.

"Fucking Frankie?" A pretty Latina in her twenties wore a fitted, cream-colored v-neck blouse tucked into black skinny jeans and wore it well. "Where I sign? Where I sign?" She squealed. Two little girls cuddled her legs. One child was taller. Johnny guessed she was older.

He stepped to a small living/dining combo. Noticed a Christmas tree, three, maybe four feet tall. Generic ornaments mixed with a string of lights. Felt like an after-thought.

"For my mija," she said. "They wan' make sure Santa finds 'em."

"Mrs. Gabaldon…"

"Consuela. Connie."

"Consuela, this is my colleague, Mr..."

"Jones," Taylor said.

"Yeah, yeah, nice to meet you. I get it all today? The money? Or I gotta wait on it? A million bucks?"

Taylor decided to leave the answers to Johnny. He stepped away and saw a worn, brown, cloth-covered sectional sofa, maple coffee table, a new, flat-screen TV and three, bare, beige walls. On the fourth was a framed, 18 x 24 color photo. A recent family portrait. Mom, Dad - Taylor presumed it was Frankie - and his daughters, scrubbed, combed, in their Sunday best. The big sister was in a frilly, white, ankle-length dress with a lace doily on top of her head. She beamed a huge smile. "Easter?" Asked Taylor.

"Ain't a Catholic, are you?"

"Kind of. Sort of, maybe. Never did the initiation."

"First Holy Communion?" Johnny said.

"Clemencia's."

"When?"

"October," the taller girl said.

"You're Clemencia?"

She nodded. Wasn't sure if she should smile.

Johnny admired the family picture. Francisco/Frankie was movie-star-handsome in a south-of-the-border way. He'd been the proud papa of beautiful daughters, husband of a gorgeous wife, but punched out before thirty.

"Your seventh birthday?"

She nodded again.

"Bet you miss your daddy," Taylor said.

Clemencia hugged momma's thigh.

"Where'd you, ah, come across him?" Johnny said.

"Frankie? Bedroom," Consuela said.

"How'd you find him?"

"Dead."

"No. I mean, did he…? Was he…?" Johnny hesitated. Didn't want to go into details in front of her children. "Clothed?"

"Frankie? No."

"So he was…?"

"Nekkid? Yeah."

The girls buried their faces in their mother's jeans. Broke Johnny's heart. "We appreciate you seeing us." He gave her a solemn, two-hand shake.

"Hang on a minute." She touched the thermo-engraved letters on the Mutual Life card. "Classy. He had 'surance? I get the check now?"

"The police reported he expired as the result of suicide." Johnny didn't address her question. "Sadly, the company doesn't pay on self-inflicted passing."

It took an instant to register and another for her cheeks to flush. "So why you here, cranking me up?" She screamed.

"Cross a T, dot an I."

"Que?"

"Knot the loose ends."

"Least give me the cash he paid in. Don't seem right, him paying and all, and me 'n my kids gettin' nada."

"No it doesn't," Taylor said. "We'll do what we can, won't we, Mr. Smith?"

CHAPTER 35

"Cynical," Heat's First said. She sat opposite him in the Relaxorium. They held hands. He peered into her eyes.

"*Moi?*" She said.

He squeezed. Collapsed her knuckles.

Damn. That hurt. But Heat never blinked. The pain kept her alert and "on mission," as her dad always said. She focused a half-inch above the bridge of her First's nose. Dad taught her to lock in on that spot. She wouldn't have to fight the stare, and they'd never know, even if she was a foot away. Heat concentrated. Breathed evenly. Accepted the challenge.

Dennis walked to her. The gym mats absorbed the sound of his movement. He hauled Heat to her feet, placed his thin lips a dime's distance from her left ear and whispered, "Be right? Or be happy?"

The novices, paired and dispersed, saw Heat sag, then recover. She stood straighter, more determined. Dennis kissed her ear. "We can stand here all day. It's been four hours? Five? Only four or five to go?" The resonance quivered her spine and radiated to her toes. "And do not forget. What happens to you..." Paused. "Happens to them." Heat tried to suppress a gasp, but couldn't defy the tingle. It spread. Sought her natural weaknesses. She trembled.

A sense of fear rippled Virgin to Virgin. Oh no... She was their crystal ball.

Cami swayed.

The model sank to her ass. A First clasped her throat and flashed a wicked grin. "Please me," he said. She opened her mouth to talk. The First roared, "Please me." She rolled to her knees and tugged his zipper.

Dennis yanked her up. She dripped tears. Looked at the others for an ally.

Silence. Down-cast eyes from the Virgins. A couple of them peeked.

The model burst into sobs. Dennis tossed her and strolled to a nascent Coupling. He sneered at a hipster with a man-bun and fixed his attention on the partner. Caressed her cheeks. Leaned forward and whispered in her ear. "Ready to elevate?" Nervous, she ran three-hundred-dollar fingernails through wilted, thousand-dollar hair.

"Don't," a tall female First said to Steve. "Don't do that."

"What?" He was so frustrated.

"That!"

Steve was clueless.

"He's stubborn."

"They all are," Dennis said. "Until..." He let the comment drift.

Steve's First said, "I'm telling you, do not do it."

"Okay." Steve was more confused.

Heat had dived into similar rabbit holes on previous self-help weekends. Poor ol' Esteban. His tall First compressed his knuckles. He cringed. She flattened her boobs against him. Rubbed her body up and down. Cooed. "Requests?"

"You name it, you got it," he said, teeth clenched, breaths short and fast.

She stroked his hands. Licked his ear lobes. "No, no, baby, you tell me."

Flummoxed, Steve trusted a vague response might do the trick. "This?" He bared his teeth. Hoped it resembled a smile. His expression begged for answers.

The First traced his chin. Whispered, "Tell me." Tilted closer. "About." Put her mouth to his ear. Cupped his package. Caressed it, squeezed and yelled, "This." Steve jumped.

Heat eyed the furrows between her First's brows.

CHAPTER 36

"So the widow's a winner for a minute. It's Christmas. Is that so wrong?" Taylor said. He rode bumps and potholes in a bus, knees bent, hands free. Trusted his balance.

"It's unethical," Johnny said.

"From you, that's funny. Don't make me laugh." The bus bounced. So did Taylor.

"At the very least, it's mean to get someone's hopes up. With Francisco/Frankie getting offed, she reckons her future's on empty, which is probably accurate. Then ka-bam, we knock, and you blab some shit about her hitting the jackpot? Bet she conjured a wish list and had it all spent by the time we boogied. That's why I told her no pay on suicide."

"Point taken." Taylor watched East Hollywood glide by. Sun-faded storefronts needed fresh paint. Homemade signs advertised sales and discounts. None of it interested him. "Wonder how Heat's doing?"

"No news is good news."

"She'd get word to us if it starts to go sideways, wouldn't she?"

"That's the plan."

"We should've enlisted, too." Taylor grabbed a pole as the bus slammed to an unexpected stop, then accelerated.

"We parleyed about it. The three of us. Lots."

"We oughtta at least be close-by. On the corner or in an alley. If we don't, nobody has her six, and we promised her. The PD would never do that – leave their peeps hanging."

"She'll be okay. She's got a cast-iron set."

"But they're useless if they figure her."

Johnny was worried, too, but accepted reality. "We gave her the over-under. She's up to speed. If it makes you feel any better, go hang at H and H, but don't let them put eyes on you. I'll scope the new cases."

A tri-tone text alert rang in Taylor's pocket. He palmed his phone and scanned the message. "Duty calls."

"New suicide?" Johnny said it too loud. Passengers and the driver flashed eyes at him, but other than that didn't react. A typical day in Hollyweird.

"We'll know soon." Taylor pulled the cord.

"Wilcox Avenue," the automated conductor announced. A pump of the brakes and they arrived. Taylor jumped to the sidewalk.

"Can I come?" Johnny said.

"You got a death wish?"

"Cops aren't wise to me."

"Not your best idea. You under-estimate the LAPD at your own peril. What about Heat?"

"Gentlemen?" The driver said.

Johnny smiled at her – an appeal for a couple seconds. "I'll go to H and H, a-sap. You wrap the new one, then we'll hook up with her as soon as she's done."

"And if we're too late?"

"Won't be. It's all hunky-dory." Johnny said it with a bit of Pony Boy optimism.

Not convinced, Taylor handed him the printout of possible suicides and hustled south.

"Send me the pertinents on the new body?"

Taylor waved.

Johnny examined the list. Didn't notice the red, primer-pocked Beemer and Michael Le Roux.

Bathed and groomed, Le Roux drummed the steering wheel. He tweaked the rear-view and arched his back for a better look-see as Taylor passed a building and disappeared. "Damnditty, damn, damn, damn." He pounded the dash as the Rapid rumbled into traffic. "Where'd the big one go to?" He couldn't locate Johnny. Smacked the side of his head. "Drive, dude." He shot across lanes and skidded a left at Wilcox. The BMW still had game. Le Roux hit the brakes in front of the bail bonds shop as Taylor drove the Photographic Unit out of the station parking lot.

CHAPTER 37

"Little girl's room?" Heat said with the sweetest Texas drawl.

"You're trapped," Dennis said. Not a glimmer of sympathy.

"I really, really have to go. I'm serious." Heat squirmed in a sunspot. A bright, afternoon swath of natural light shone through a window in the upper reaches of the Relaxorium. It lit a sheen of sweat and an angry frown. She gritted her teeth. Her entire being focused on holding it in.

Dennis made a circular gesture. Firsts and Virgins formed a ring. "We are your roadblocks, Heather," he said. "Your obstacles. Everyone and everything that's kept you from growing up. You wanna be a grownup, don't you?"

Heat hitched her skirt. "Swear on momma's grave I'll rip my drawers off and piddle right here."

Dennis orbited her. Taunted. Used a phony southern accent. "I'm your daddy, Heather." Insulted and demeaned. "Wanted me an heir, not you."

She dipped at the knees. Shimmied.

He poked. "Get yourself a stud. Birth a litter of rug rats. Don't even need to hurry down the aisle."

"Sure Daddy, but let me go tinkle. If you love 'em, let 'em go?"

Heat turned to the exit. Her First blocked her. She shifted. So did he. She skipped left. He mirrored her. Heat squatted. The First grabbed her. She twisted. Uh-oh. A leak? Clenched.

"I'm your job," he said. "And like it or not, you can't live without me. Stay."

Heat bobbed and weaved. Had to keep it in.

An Asian First smirked and pranced to her. "I'm your credit-card bills, Heather. I say stay."

Heat shoved her. The Asian didn't budge. Heat pushed harder, which generated a sneer from the First.

"I know you know," Dennis said. Again.

What'd that mean? She clamped her legs.

"I knew you weren't gonna amount to crap. Zero. Zip. Nada. Not a goddamn thing. Just a jiggly ass with so-so tits."

Heat glared at him, her lips twin lines of anger. "Wrong. I'm a writer, daddy. A fine one."

Dennis approached her with a swagger. Cock of the walk. "Do tell."

"I, uh, I write journals, daddy." She realized her grade-A-super-size cock-up. Monumental and colossal also came to mind. "And poems and such." Delivered a solid Texas pronunciation - *poims*. "Never show anybody."

Dennis paused less than a foot from her. Held the stare. "You lying to me, Heather?" His tone was ominous.

Heat shook "no" as she pressed her thighs together.

A female First, a spectacular blonde, strutted to Heat and tickled her ribs.

"Bitch," Heat said. Waist bent, she rallied for a few jerky, contorted steps.

The big blonde mocked her with a German accent. *"Shtay, baby. Ve'll make fun."*

A dazzling Latina pinched Heat's cheek. "Fuug-ly. You'd be nothing but a Glory Fuck."

Hours earlier, Heat might have agreed to go along and get along. She knew the tease and taunt accomplished submission and acquiescence. However, in the moment, the head and tail of her being was to pee but not to pee. Period. No amount of brain-washing permeated that. She chicken-walked towards relief.

A male barred her way. "I'm the car you can't afford."

The Latina First said, "I'm the collection agency." Faked a tickle.

Heat flinched. Uh oh. Another leak?

The Latina got up in Heat's grill. "You're so easy. I be all them new outfits and shit you keep buying so you can scratch the itch, baby."

That was breaking news, and Heat damn near cheered. They hadn't broken her cover. Splurge on clothes? Not in this realm. She chuckled, which jacked the urge to pee,

"What's funny, Heather?" Dennis said. "Share."

"Nada, Daddy."

Dennis signaled the Firsts. They tightened the circle. "We're all a part of you, Heather, and we ain't movin' darlin'."

Heat snarled, pivoted and threw a punch. Smashed Dennis's jaw.

The Virgins gasped.

The Firsts were shocked.

Dennis crumpled.

Heat straddled him. Shook her fist. Damn that hurt. Defiant, she slapped her hands on her hips and thrust her pelvis at his chin.

He scooted downrange, leveled a fierce look on her. Rose to his knees. Six Firsts rushed to help. He sluffed them off and stood. "Great work, Heather. I knew you had it."

Heat almost peed, she was so astonished.

The Firsts gathered their composure, surrounded and embraced her.

Leaderless, the newcomers didn't know how to act. They floundered.

"Do the rest of you possess Heather's substance?" Dennis said.

"Yes." About half responded.

"Really?"

Group indecision bloomed for several seconds until Cami broke ranks and joined the hug. The model was next. Steve followed.

"Do you stand charged to slay your demons? Do you?" Dennis eyed them. "Do you seek a new beginning? A challenging opportunity?"

A couple Virgins stepped towards Heat.

"Do you?"

"Yes!" Ecstatic, the remainder of the group hugged and smooched her.

She craved the kudos, but the bathroom beckoned.

"Let's take a break. You've earned it," Dennis said. Heat ran.

CHAPTER 38

"Did the Medical Examiner perform an autopsy on your daughter?" Johnny said. Shadows were long at Hollywood Forever.

"Excuse me?" A woman in her late forties dabbed her cheeks.

Johnny was ten feet and a green, tarp-covered mound from thirty African-Americans. Multiple generations. Parent-types, kids, even a granny, were bundled in heavy coats and scarves. They sat in white plastic chairs. Some cried. Others gazed at a deluxe casket. Burnished mahogany and polished brass handles glinted beneath a blanket of flowers. Black bunting draped a poster-sized, college-graduation portrait of an attractive co-ed in cardinal-red cap and gown, her anxious eyes filled with the burden of an entire family's expectation.

A solemn, slot-collared preacher clutched a Bible and led the mourners. "We pray for her everlasting…" He spotted Johnny. The minister brandished his Holy book to ward off the intrusion.

Johnny avoided the mound and targeted the memorial. Distressed family members watched. One snorted awake.

"Hi. Johnny Lincoln. *True Crime LA*." He dealt business cards to the bereaved. "Beautiful day for a funeral." It was a crisp fifty-three under a blue sky, according to his weather app. Johnny saw his breath. "Happen to know if the ME did a post-mortem on, uh…" located a name on his printout. "On Chantal?"

"My son," the Pastor admonished.

"You folks could play a starring role in me breaking an important story."

The bereaved read his *TCLA* business card.

"Never heard of it," a deep-voiced man said.

"Cable channel?" Somebody else said.

Undaunted, Johnny persisted. "This the service for Chantal Harris?"

An elderly gray-hair sobbed. Grandma? Johnny wondered.

"Lord Jesus, see what you gone and did?" Deep Voice. He was middle-aged but muscled. Looked as if he could hold his own in a brawl. He cuddled and patted the old dear. "Where's your respect?"

"I'm... Every once in a while I get... Sorry. I'm on a huge... Don't aim to waste... Any of your time. Am I at the right grave? The Harris burial?"

"I'm Chantal's dad." Deep Voice again, ill at ease in an off-the-rack suit. He tugged at the collar of a white, perma-press shirt, rotated his head and rolled his shoulders in an effort to be comfortable. Made it worse. He went for his necktie. Loosened it. Scrutinized Johnny. "Best be explaining yourself."

"The LA County Coroner, the Medical Examiner, give you a written report determining Ms. Harris's COD? Or MOD?"

"What's that mean?"

"Sorry. Cause of death or manner of death."

"They told us how she died."

He waited. Looked from dad to a middle-aged woman dressed in black. "Which was…?"

"Bee stings," she said.

Johnny assumed she was Chantal's mother. "In winter? You receive anything official?"

"A death certificate."

"You have a closed casket at the church?"

"How's that any of your business?" Dad said.

"No," Chantal's mother said.

"Really? No?" Perplexed, he double-checked a printout. "Harris family? Chantal? Suicide?"

Many of the Harrises burst into tears. Johnny wanted to feel terrible. Hoped later he would but pointed at the coffin. "You consider opening it for me? Confirm it's her?"

Uh oh.

CHAPTER 39

"Bullshit, Andre, you meant to." Dennis screamed at a tall, handsome man. "No way. She's the one's getting freaked. Threatening to snitch to my wife." Andre slouched. Fought a yawn.

"You bored?"

On the opposite side of the room, Heat couldn't decide if Dennis was disgusted or disappointed.

"No, sir." Andre and his First, the gorgeous Asian, occupied a shaft of winter sun that cast a harsh luster.

"You thirty yet?" Andre's First said.

"No."

"How old, then?"

"Twenty-six."

"And you're married?"

Andre shrugged.

"That's it? That's all you got?"

Andre started to shrug again. Caught himself.

She swirled a glittery fingernail on his chest. "Studly brotha went and got himself hitched? That's big love, baby."

Ashamed, he lowered his head. "Had to."

"Oh yeah? Hey, y'all, he's a breeder. Boy or girl?" She toyed with his belt buckle.

"Girl."

"Better pray she don't grow up and meet a swinging dick like her daddy." She clapped twice. Shouted to the group. "Let's take inventory. Shall we?" She pretended to unfurl a scroll. "Ta Da… One wife. Hang on. Only one? Not hiding a second family up in Bakersfield, are you?"

Andre whispered, "No." Tried to smooth crotch wrinkles in his slacks.

The First wagged her left index finger. "A wife." Wiggled her middle finger. "And a squeeze. Any more?"

Andre contemplated the floor. Sweat beads popped on his shiny, shaved pate.

"Don't let me slow you down. C'mon, now."

Andre held up a couple fingers.

"We're not freakin' deaf."

"Two."

"A play-ah. So, to recap. One wifey and THA-REE squeezes. Count 'em." She raised three fingers. "THA-REE squeezes. Correct, Andre?"

He blinked.

"Eh?" She cupped her ear.

"Yes." Sweat stains soaked his shirt.

"I salute you, sir. So, who are they?"

"Huh?"

"Tell us their vitals."

"Uhh…"

"Name, age, height, weight. Special kinks. You know, the good stuff."

"Azah."

"And…?"

"Monique."

"That's two. Number three?"

"Bonnie."

"Bonnie? What's a 'Bonnie'?"

"A ginger."

"Redhead?"

He nodded.

"A real one? Freckles? She the one ready to blow a hole in your bed?"

"Yeah."

"You rich?"

"No."

"Shut up."

"Huh?"

"Answer."

"What?"

"Why you?"

"Says I'm her first BBC."

"Ooohhh..." His First circled him. "BBC?" She smelled blood in the water. "A BBC?"

Andre cringed and silently begged her to let it go.

"What's a BBC?"

Andre muttered something.

"Heather," Dennis said.

"Sir."

"You hear that?"

"No, sir." Heat and her First were by the far wall, ten yards away.

"Me, either."

"The fuck is a BBC?" Andre's First demanded. She grinned. She knew.

Embarrassed but proud, he said, "Big Black Cock."

Snickers and stifled laughter. From Firsts or Virgins? Heat guessed Virgins. She eyed them.

Her guys dripped sweat, clothes plastered to their bodies. Her gals were worn and wrung, hair damp and stringy, makeup smeared, tops untucked or unbuttoned. Several women swayed, but Heat remained steady and jabbed fingernails into her palms to generate a little pain.

The Latina recruit collapsed. Dark tendrils stuck to her pale brow. Smudged eyeshadow streaked her cheeks. She planted her face in the mat. A First grabbed an arm and pulled. The Latina staggered upright.

Heat wondered if she was that ragged. Dog-tired, she concentrated on isometric exercises to maintain clarity and focus. She stretched calves as she observed Dennis, Andre and his First.

Andre whined, "Bitch is gonna rat me out."

"Bonnie?" His First said.

"Yeah. Skank. Jammed me up in this suck. Can't shut her up. Not even sure I care."

"Oh hooey," Dennis said. "Own it, Andre. Chaos. Magnificent, erratic, unmanageable chaos. It's your heart's desire. It wants the whole enchilada to go ka-bam, and Bangin' Bonnie Spinner is your stick of dynamite."

"No."

"Sure she is," his First said. "Bonnie baby's fuse is burning, and you lit it." She pressed against him. Licked his right ear. "Boom, Boom, Boom!"

Andre shuddered. "Got nothing to give."

"For wifey or Bonnie?"

"No one." He slumped.

Dennis tapped his Rolex. "How long since we commenced?"

"Uhhhh..."

A First screamed, "Do the math."

Andre peeked at the others for a hint, but they'd surrendered their watches hours ago.

"Nine hours and eleven minutes," Dennis said. He studied Andre and summoned his First. She handed him a completed questionnaire. Dennis skimmed pages. Nodded. "You're done."

Andre strained to process and understand. "Huh?" It dawned on him. "Why?" He struggled to stand. Slipped. Crashed. Cried. His torso heaved.

Dennis signaled two male Firsts. They dragged Andre over the gym mats to the exit. Stunned, he pleaded, "No, no, no."

"You lied," Dennis said.

"Left some blanks, is all."

"You think?" Dennis waved Andre's answers.

The men dropped him. Fake-kicked his ribs. Andre flinched. Curled into a ball. His First sneered and stomped his ass. He crawled in a futile attempt to evade her. They herded him to the lobby, slammed the doors and turned the deadbolt.

"Please." Andre pounded. Begged, "Please." Rattled the knobs. "Come on." A weak knock. A desperate, "Pleeeeease…" Silence.

Heat was shocked by the degree of cruelty but not surprised. She knew Andre's expulsion lit the rocket. Fatigue-enhanced fear of similar treatment would force group submission leading to, "the planting of the seed of salvation," or whatever tag The Way slapped on it.

Dennis scowled a non-verbal challenge.

Steve thanked his lucky stars. Cami snuffed. The Latina rubbed her temples, relieved to be an insider, grateful for a glimpse of failure.

Heat surreptitiously flexed one muscle at a time to repel the mass hypnosis. She occupied her mind crafting the lede for her next story. "They, they, the…"

CHAPTER 40

"This one's NHI," Bruno Morales said. He and Alita Walsh eased into a small, crowded bedroom. They flanked a body. A young, nude Latina was face-up across an unmade twin bed at a forty-five-degree angle. Her head and shoulders hung over one side. The girl's legs were spread, and tattooed arms dangled off the edge. Mouth open, eyes glazed, her thick, brown hair cascaded towards the floor.

"Cold, Bruno. Even for you," Walsh said. "She's a kid. Sixteen? Seventeen?"

"How can you tell?" Taylor said. His camera captured a slender adolescent with firm breasts, prominent hip bones and no pubes – a full Brazilian.

"No wrinkles, sags or stretch marks. So you look at nipple development. Or lack thereof."

"I repeat - no humans involved." Morales tapped the tip of his pen on the base of her throat.

"Easy, shorty," the Medical Examiner scolded.

"She's Echo Park 13s." Gothic script, *EP 13*, inked the front of the victim's neck. Full-sleeve tats extolled her 'hood with a depiction of a lake, lily pads and a 'banger named "Hector."

"Her quinceanera was probably the night she was jumped in," Walsh said.

"So I can recommend to Robbery-Homicide that they can shove it where the sun don't shine?" Cedar Tree Hoffman said. He stood in the entry.

"L-T?" Morales couldn't hide his surprise.

"Boss? What brings you out of your cave?" Walsh said.

"Sightseeing, in case she might be part of your series. Don't run into those very often."

" 'Bout as often as we're honored by your presence outside the confines," CC Rademaker said.

As a Lieutenant, Hoffman had no reason to be at any crime scene. If his people required a supervisor, they'd summon a Detective-Sergeant or a Detective III, but never him. "Well?"

"Doesn't fit the pattern," Walsh said. "This one left a note and momma called it in."

SID personnel resumed work. They dusted, swabbed, tweezed, tagged and bagged.

Taylor shot stuffed animals. Changed angles and took pics of a pic tacked to a bulletin board - teens in demure, plaid, school uniforms, smiling, flashing gang signs.

Rademaker tugged off her latex gloves. "T, you shoot the glossies?"

"Yes, ma'am."

The ME checked her watch. "Get her wrapped and under the tree. Time's a waistin'."

Taylor photographed piles of jeans, tops, plaid flannel shirts, bras and thongs. Aimed at a closet filled with the deceased's former wardrobe – real Catholic school-girl outfits and white, cotton blouses. They were coated with a thin layer of dust. He re-focused on used condoms that littered the carpet beneath the bed, then noticed a tabloid newspaper between a pillow and the wall. He wanted a closer inspection but wasn't authorized to touch the paper or remove it. Evidence techs did that. No one else.

Taylor switched lenses and framed an image of a page visible above the soiled sheet. A red arch drawn on the newsprint bordered agate type too tiny to read. Classified ads. He'd enlarge it later.

"Swingin' dicks from RHD are hollering for their summary," Hoffman said. "Anything in particular I should impart to their eminences?" He shifted his weight to his heels. Clasped hands behind his back.

"Bruno nailed it." For emphasis, the Medical Examiner pointed her liver thermometer at Morales. "NHI suicide. She breaks the mold."

"See?" Bruno smiled. "Even doctor death agrees."

"Not sold," Walsh said. "This body resembles the others. No obvious wounds, and even though she's showing a ton of gang tats, she's no junkie. Aren't any tracks."

CHAPTER 41

"Drop, Heather, drop," Dennis said. He was excited. Full of energy.

Heat was at rigid attention on a squishy mat in the center of the Relaxorium. Her fists were balled, toes clenched.

"Relinquish and trust."

She didn't move.

The Firsts clustered.

Virgins sat on the mats, fixated.

Dennis was irritated and impatient. "Heather?"

"Sir."

"Where do you suppose we are?"

"The Way."

"Congratulations..." Condescending. "Now that wasn't so hard, was it? The Way. The Way out of your past. You're here for a new – Way - aren't you, Heather?" Nasty. "The Way out of your crappy debts, all your crappy relationships with crappy boys. Or crappy babes. Your crappy job. You crave escape, don't you, Heather?"

Heat whispered, "Yes."

"And this beautiful place?" Dennis gestured. "Is...?

"Relaxorium?"

"Did not hear you."

Louder. "The Relaxorium."

"Well?"

Heat drooped.

"Heather."

She straightened. "Sir."

"Tell us the heart and soul of losing your virginity."

Previous "self-help" weekends taught her that she'd reached the critical moment of the "buy-in." She played the supplicant. Avoided his eyes. "Trust?"

"Excellent. Otherwise, it's just...?" The question hung.

"A fuck." Heat fell backward. Her First scrambled and snared her six inches from a crash-landing on her tail bone. "Whew." She was pudding. Trembled as he raised her.

"And again?"

Heat crossed her wrists over her boobs and fell back again. Her First was prepared the second time and caught her a yard above the floor. He held her in that position as the remaining thirteen Firsts ringed them.

Heat's extremities tingled. Wow… as terrific as an orgasm, but different. Nookie? Her head went there in the middle of this? Comparative cums? Why not? She had a specific mission, so any brain activity was a plus. She needed to run a list. Item Number One - orgasm. An anticipation, not a reality. Okay, so maybe it was the twin of an "O." But fraternal, not identical. She presumed someone would catch her before she hit. By definition, an expectation with an undetermined conclusion. Same as sex. Aim high, hope, but you won't know 'til the end. She'd never dissected the metaphysics of orgasms. Was it a random thought or deep-seeded issue? She didn't care. Goal was to keep her mind active. Could have been dull, dry, stock market quotes. Prior self-help emersion taught her she'd be fine. Heat decided the sensations spawned by the fall, not knowing if she'd crash or not, were similar to the ascent to an "O," but impacted different erogenous zones. Did they ever. With an attentive lover, Heat felt she dissolved into an orgasm, absorbed by her partner. The fall melted her to a different state—whole, but diffused and dispersed. Big difference.

She was face-to-face with a female First. Labored to take mental notes. A doll. Johnny would call her that. Hell with PC. He'd say tall doll. Better yet, Stretch. But they're all tall. She was Asian, so Stretch-A. Oh yeah, the black dude's First. The guy they booted. Andre. She remembered. She must be okay. Heat had liquified once or twice for other gurus. Always a temporary form. She'd solidify. Eventually. No problem. Always did.

Heat's First shoved her forward. "Oh…" She plunged into the arms of the Asian who spun her tits up to another First. In mid-air, Heat rotated and gasped. "Whoa." She was lobbed from one to the next, flipped up then down until she was returned to her First. Limp. Her chin quivered. She couldn't remember a comparable experience, not even close. At that moment, she was foggy-brained, struggling to keep her mind sharp. Run a list? Of? Began at the bottom. Ten of those. Two… two… The curtain lowered. Uh oh. She concentrated. Got it. Ankle. No, missed something… What'd she forget? Oh yeah, foot. Feet. God, the circle toss wasn't necessarily better than screwing, but it ranked a lot higher than the night her dad's Colonel's son deflowered her after a teen club dance when they were stationed in Heidelberg in the eleventh grade.

Dennis lifted her.

"Oh... don't stop." To her own ears, Heat sounded hoarse. Spent. In the throes. Her jaw sagged. Near collapse, her thighs shivered. Breaths ragged, eyes unfocused, her thoughts idled in neutral. Then a residual tingle more intense than any she'd experienced arced through her body. Heat looked from First to First for support. They turned away. Dennis, too. She wobbled but did not wilt.

The Virgins wrung their hands. Cast apprehensive glimpses at each other. They were on deck.

Dennis allowed Heat's buzz to permeate for several seconds. His warm breath coated her neck. She smelled it. Minty. Beyond that, her mind was silent.

"Go," he said.

Heat's First gripped her arm.

She erased a tear and followed.

CHAPTER 42

"Pssssst. Psssssst." Johnny waved at Heat as she crossed the Boulevard. No response. Instead, she clasped her jacket and hunched to block a steady wind.

Johnny, collar up, hat brim low, leaned against the plum-colored *Ripley's Believe It Or Not* building on the southeast corner of H and H. He wanted to blend, but his height didn't lend itself to nonchalant.

"Psssssssst." Insistent, and still no reply. Johnny cleared his throat. No reaction. Give me a break, he thought. He saw her, so he knew she saw him.

Heat and three Virgins huddled under the bus shelter roof. It wasn't dark, not at Hollywood and Highland. Streetlamps, giant digital displays and holiday decorations lit the intersection like a movie set. Heat embraced a young man. A small woman hugged them both. "I'm so buzzed." It was Cami. The Latina joined.

"Me, too," the guy said. Esteban. Steve.

"For sure I thought you'd pee on him," The Latina said.

Heat laughed. "Almost. A couple more seconds."

Johnny wondered what that meant.

"Bet he's a wet freak. Kind of dude who'd lick his own self clean." The Latina giggled.

"Ewww. Gross," Cami said.

Heat hugged them again. "Don't tell, but I was ready to cum if they'd kept throwing me."

"I did," the Latina said.

"Me, too," Cami said.

"For real?"

"Oh, God yes. Multiples."

"Now we know you're not a moaner."

Johnny saw the male blush. Tried again. "Pssssst." A passerby or tourist might have mistaken him for a john on the troll - somewhat expected in that neck of the woods.

Heat offered him a dreamy gaze.

"Not good," Taylor said as he joined Johnny.

"Nope. But she seems okay."

Taylor shot candids of Heat and her giddy co-Virgins as they smooched bye-bye and scattered.

Alone, Heat stomped away the chill until a Metro Orange arrived.

"I'll go de-brief her," Taylor said.

"No need. She's got game. Let's you 'n me hop to it."

Heat boarded. As the bus accelerated, Johnny pondered The Way. Tower windows were again lit red and green to celebrate the season. "Let's hit it." He took a stride. Taylor snagged his sleeve.

The Firsts, ushered by Dennis, departed the First National Building. He secured the bronze entry, executed a precise about-face and snapped his fingers. The fifteen fell in. He led them single-file towards Johnny and Taylor.

Johnny compiled a list of options. Run and be recognized, which could put Heat's ass in the fire. Or...

He grabbed Taylor's head and performed a stage smooch.

Taylor jerked his head away. "The hell...?"

"Give me a better idea." Johnny massaged Taylor's shoulders. Taylor tried to shrug him off. "But if you can't, you really gotta sell it."

Taylor puckered up and leaned in. "For Heat." He laid on the snog, opened an eye and scrutinized Dennis and the Firsts as they trooped by without a glance. Two dudes in a lip lock? Not news. They entered the greasy-spoon diner adjacent to Ripley's.

Taylor pinched Johnny's butt.

"Don't."

"You started it."

Johnny cleared his throat, took a step and eyed the penthouse. "Imagine if Baby Doll's up there. That'd be so cool."

"Pop in for a drink? A quick interview?" Taylor cleared his throat. "Now, Miss Doll, about those murders."

Johnny scowled and tugged his hat. "Elvis time."

Neither moved.

"You know this is three Os stupid, don't you?" Taylor said.

"Huh?"

"Stooopid. Going inside."

"Got an alternative?"

"For me or for you?"

"For all of us. We figure Emma, you're on the comeback trail. I... We, land a story and the cops close cases. Win, win, win."

"Like I said–stooopid." Taylor loathed stress but craved the rush. Chicken and egg. Can't have one and not the other. He'd been an adrenalin junkie since his earliest runs down a mountain on skis. In kindergarten.

"Cold feet?"

"Not in this lifetime, or the next. No bullets here."

"Not yet, but it is Hollywood."

Taylor responded with a sprint across the Boulevard against traffic.

Johnny watched him, then dodged cars to the opposite side. They marched north, past The Way's main entrance, to an alley. Murky and fragrant – trash and cat pee. They jogged twelve yards to the rear of the building. Johnny spotted a security camera. Tilted his fedora to hide his features.

"Smile and wave. It's the third I've seen."

Johnny crouched at a door. Selected a torsion wrench and a pick from their trifold wallet.

"You take B and E 101 at Harvard?"

"Junior year. As an elective."

Bang. Clang. Pulse-rates soared. They fell to their knees and hunkered in shadows. Heard a loud yawn. Sounded male. A filthy, scruffy person rose from a dumpster. Noticed Johnny and Taylor. Burped. "Well. *Escuse em moi.*" A scratchy booze-and-cigarette voice. He climbed up and over, dropped to the pavement and wandered off. Too dark to determine if he was a geezer or not as he coughed and hacked.

Johnny trained his tool on the lock but trembled and missed the keyhole.

"Breathe," Taylor said.

Johnny sucked air.

"Hold it."

"How long?"

"Don't talk. Count to ten."

Johnny inhaled and steadied himself. Inserted his picks. Exhaled. Repeated. His heart rate slowed, but he was shaky. After a few false starts, the tumblers clicked.

"Alarms?"

"Oops." Johnny shrugged and smiled.

They slipped inside The Way. A trace of moonlight penetrated opaque, industrial-grade panes but wasn't enough to help navigate. Taylor aimed his phone and followed the thin beam. His knuckles brushed a knob. He twisted it. Pushed. Janitorial supplies - brooms, mops, buckets.

Johnny bent his waist to create a smaller profile. He grazed the wall with an elbow and frog-walked to the end of the corridor. Metal, four-drawer filing cabinets filled the space; nine to his left, nine on the right and eight straight-ahead – four on either side of a closed door. Johnny did the math and crept to the first cabinet on his left. "A" was printed above the top handle. He lit "B," then the third, labeled "C."

Taylor recited the alphabet. Hustled to "M." Found dozens of files, names written on the tabs. "Old school. All hard copies." He lifted one. Examined a photograph. "Emma."

"Not a shocker." Johnny scooted to the "P" cabinet. Pulled the top drawer. Also crammed. Slid out a dossier and an 8-by-10. "There's skinny on poor Vinnie Parnelli goes all the way back to bed-wetting." Turned the page. "Wow… And he volunteered it. Questionnaire."

"Yeah. Emma, too." Taylor stepped to "Q." Only a single record under his letter. He removed a picture of himself working a scene. "Uh oh. I'm in here."

"Makes sense. Emma and all."

Taylor slammed it shut. "Doesn't lower the creep factor."

"Shhhh…" Johnny searched "L." "I'm not in here."

"Yet." Taylor opened the door that divided M and N. An eerie glow lit him.

CHAPTER 43

"He's where?" Baby Doll Getz said. She was on the telephone. A landline with a kinked cord. The answer surprised her. She hacked. Phlegm rattled. She sat in a tan executive chair, scanned a copy of *True Crime LA* and rubbed her pearls. "Okay, stick with it. No changes." Getz hung up and wiggled her bare toes against the polished edge of an antique desk. It resembled the President's in the Oval. "Stupid kid." She smiled.

Her huge desk did not dominate an elegant office. A trio of museum-quality paintings did. They represented the evolution of Western culture. Behind her was a Rembrandt. Opposite, thirty feet away, a Pollack reigned over a black, leather sofa. Midway, above polished teak bookshelves, was a Remington. Abstract modern, wild west and old master. They combined well, complimenting a talented decorator or Getz herself. She'd never tell.

Below the vibrant abstractions of the Pollack, the tufted couch and a matching wing-back recliner formed a power corner. From there, or anywhere in her domain, Getz could peer out a row of windows that framed jetliner views of the LA Basin.

Baby Doll mulled over the call. She tapped a foot in time to the faint throb of a bass guitar. Shook a pack of imported Turkish Yeni Harman cigarettes, extracted one and stuck the filter between her thin lips. She sparked her Dunhill and touched the flame to the tobacco. The tip flared. She choked a cough. Managed to utter, "*Prochaine.*" Next.

Louder music wafted in. Her Chauffeur entered. Wheels, Stetson atop her mound of hair, wore a white, scoop-neck tee, tan riding breeches, polished black boots and the silver English spurs.

Baby Doll admired her driver's exquisite curves and muscle tone. She approved. "*Coo wee.*"

Wheels curtsied her thanks. "Picture's up." The Guess Who? Maitre d' and Bouncer shuffled in. Both were in civilian clothes. The Maitre d' in ironed jeans, expensive Italian loafers, no socks, and a blue body shirt. Red sweats and a rainbow, tie-dyed wife-beater for the Bouncer. Minus the purple makeup and tights, he was nothing more than a frightened fatty.

She prodded them with a riding crop. They stumbled and slouched in front of Getz. Wheels spanked their thighs with the whip. Painful smacks. The Maitre d' winced. The Bouncer whimpered.

"Do better." Wheels maintained her attack stance, crop at the ready. "Hows about a little self-respect?"

Getz soaked up their terror. Feasted on it. "Relax." They didn't, and she knew they wouldn't. "Okay." She clapped once. "So sorry I delayed discussing your encounter. What'd you say to him?"

"Wh', who?" The Maitre d' said. Perspiration coated his forehead.

Wheels grabbed the Bouncer's crotch. Wrung his nut sack. He squealed.

"The reporter," Getz said.

"N' Nothing," the Bouncer said.

"Sure?"

"Ye', Yes ma'am." The Maitre d' analyzed the tops of his shoes.

"Absolutely, positively? No doubts?"

Wheels squeezed. The Bouncer squealed again. "Yes, ma'am."

The Maitre d' snuck a peek. Saw a squinched face.

Wheels loved it.

"Tell me what he wanted to know," Getz said.

"He, uh, demanded info about Sullivan."

"And you told him what?"

The Bouncer yelped.

The Maitre d' cringed. "Nothing. Absolutely nothing. We, we disengaged, per your instructions."

"Ran," shrieked the Bouncer. "We ran." He sobbed. His blubber jiggled.

"Aah-hah…" Getz was disappointed.

Wheels squeezed harder.

"Her name. We told him her name." The Bouncer sniveled.

"Whose?"

"Sullivan's," the Maitre d' said. He hoped they'd show his friend mercy.

Getz mused. Stubbed her half-smoked cigarette. "That ain't such a strain, no? 'Cuz you know? I'm re-assigning you. New challenges. Fresh settings does a soul wonders. Re-charges the batteries." She slapped the gold-leafed desktop. "Paul and Marcel will escort you tomorrow."

"No…" the Maitre d' forced the word as his throat constricted. He retreated.

The Bouncer's knees buckled. Three hundred jiggly pounds collapsed in a mound.

Getz understood fear. Welcomed it. But cowardice? She dismissed them with a wave.

Wheels kicked the Bouncer into a crawl. Jabbed the Maitre d' in the kidneys with her crop and drove them out.

The Brunette glided in, resplendent in a teal, floor-length gown and the Hepburn wig. He was troubled to see the Guess Who management.

Getz appraised him. Allowed the silence to build.

The Brunette displayed no outward hints of concern, but wire him up, he'd peg the meter on a lie detector.

"I forgive you," Getz said.

The Brunette wasn't sure why. "Appreciate it."

A corner of Getz's mouth twitched. Big *couillon*, she thought. "The reporter. He's, what we say..." she hunted for a term. "Resourceful. And you..." No matter the insolence, she approved. "You are dazzling."

"I aim to please."

"Stay available. We'll definitely throw gigs your way." She swiveled and rocked. "Next."

The Brunette bowed and backed away.

Wheels returned with the Gee Spot Manager. She danced a two-step on bright-red fuck-me pumps and wore a stretched, black bandage dress that accentuated a yard of legs and superb DNA. "Merry, merry, boss."

"You, too, cher. You're free to be, Wheels."

She hugged and air-kissed the Manager.

Baby Doll patted her lap.

CHAPTER 44

"This is so cool,"Taylor said. He peered into a radiance cast by aquariums. Ten were on waist-high benches that lined three walls. Six more filled tables bunched in the center of a room. The tanks were five feet wide, two high and two feet front-to-rear. Was it a lab?

Exotic fish, one per tank, swam lazy circles, ruffled faux seagrass, or hid in tiny castles. Bubbles floated to the surface. Johnny approached one. Fascinated, he placed a couple fingers on the glass. A roundish, seven-incher dotted with spots and spikes swam to him. "Wow. It's checking me out." He studied a second fish. It was smaller, also had barbs and was shaped the same. Its markings resembled figure eights.

An ugly creature at least a foot long swam to Taylor. It blew into an enormous ball with eyes and a thousand spikes. "Whoa." Taylor recoiled. "Almost pissed my pants. You see that?" It deflated and resumed a lazy swim.

"Shhhhh. No."

Taylor absorbed the adrenalin and stepped to a bench in the middle of the lab. It held an empty aquarium, Bunsen burner and microscope. Below was a drawer. Taylor pulled it out and rummaged through the contents. Discovered plastic sandwich bags containing minor amounts of white, flaky powder.

Johnny moved tank-to-tank. Each fish, regardless of colorization or size, swam to him. "Interesting. Only one per."

"Got something."Taylor dipped a pinkie in a baggie. Raised it for a taste.

"Don't! You watch too damn much TV."

"It's copacetic. I work for the cops."

"No. We'll take it with."

"Yeah, yeah, yeah…" Taylor cleaned his hand on his jeans and appropriated the powder. He photographed the lab and its gilled occupants. Every exposure cast a brief, intense light.

Johnny rifled cabinets. Loaded additional documents in his coat pockets.

Taylor's synapsis snapped to red alert. He froze. A Smith and Wesson .38 corked his right ear.

"Peace on ya, comrade," Michael Le Roux said. "Rotate, but go slow."

Taylor did as ordered, completed a one-eighty, and tracked the snub-nosed barrel of death as it came to rest on his sternum.

Le Roux located Johnny. "Gimme, comrade."

Johnny calculated odds. There weren't any. He fanned files. "Pick a card, any card. 'V.' Or 'E.' 'F?' Choose."

"All of it. And you, shutterbug, the camera and whatever else you're carrying."

Taylor removed the strap and lifted his Nikon an inch from Le Roux's face. Click. Flashed the strobe.

Blinded, Le Roux threw his arms up. "Ahhh."

Taylor launched a left hook. Connected. Jawbone crunched.

Le Roux squealed. Flailed.

Taylor dived.

Johnny froze.

Le Roux tottered. Discharged his revolver at a memory. Bang. Nailed the floor. Bang. A bullet shattered an aquarium.

A hundred-twenty gallons of water poured over Taylor. A fish puffed into a sphere and rebounded off his shoulders.

"Missed," Johnny said as he squatted.

Le Roux whirled and fired. A tank exploded.

Johnny crab-walked to Taylor.

Le Roux tripped on wet tile. Jerked the trigger as he crashed. Plugged the ceiling.

Johnny and Taylor sprinted to the hall. Shoved open the last door and tore into the alley.

Moments later, Le Roux lurched outside. Tried to blink some vision as he waved his gun. Wanted a clear shot. Bellowed, "Ahhhhhh…" Johnny and Taylor had vanished.

A Metro Orange stopped at Hollywood and Highland. Johnny hopped on and tapped his fare card twice. Taylor, drenched, was a pace behind. Passengers were jam-packed but scooted back. Taylor wiped a trickle from his chin. Tasted it. "Salty." Inspected his equipment. It passed muster.

"I'll scope these files," Johnny said. "You make nice with the crime lab. Get 'em to run a test and give you the particulars on that powder."

"How am I supposed to get there?"

"This bus'll take you."

"You expect me to go halfway to Kansas at one-thirty in the A.M.?"

"It's only East LA. Lab's at the college. Not far. And it's a round-the-clock operation. You can uber home."

"Appreciate the enlightenment, yes I do." Taylor scowled and dribbled.

"Cheer up. We did decent."

If looks could kill…

CHAPTER 45

"Aren't you a pretty kitty? Yes, you are. Grenade's a good boy," Heat said. A chubby orange tabby purred as she scratched behind his ears. "Need to put you on a diet." She sat on a braided, Army-green and khaki oval rug and leaned against a king-size bed. No frame, box-springs on the floor, it was the single piece of furniture in a well-kept studio apartment. Books filled half the mattress, the other side was prepped for sleep, blankets turned down, pillows fluffed.

Grenade the Cat nuzzled as Heat covered her legs with an extra-large, plain-white T-shirt. She was ready to burrow into crisp, mauve sheets, but her synapses zapped too fast.

Hair toweled, she set up her laptop, cracked her knuckles, attempted to concentrate but couldn't. The marathon day at The Way had left her exhausted but buzzed, body done in, brain ablaze. She yawned, bent, touched her toes. Hung for a ten-count, straightened, tossed her computer on a pillow and moved to homemade, cinderblock-and-board shelves. Unpainted 2 x 10s, eight feet long, were stacked six high. Hundreds of volumes were jammed between the blocks.

She studied a photo taped to a shelf at eye level. It was the serpent symbol on Emma's coffin. Or would have been Emma's had Johnny found her in it. Kudos to him - big balls on that one. So far, she'd researched a ton of "symbols" and "serpents" online. Tried dozens of different phrases and keywords in a variety of combinations, with zip luck. She flicked the bottom edge of the picture and gazed out the window. A traffic signal changed from red to green and a delivery truck traveled west on Sunset Boulevard. At the intersection, yellow neon lit damp pavement and announced, "Café Tropical."

Heat ducked. Eyes like saucers, heart pounding, she fought panic. Crawled to her door. Reached for the light switch.

On the street, the Black Hoods straddled the front fenders of a vintage Cadillac and observed Heat's place go dark.

Her back against the wall, clasping thighs to chest, she rocked. "Fuck, fuck, fuck." How'd they know she wasn't in the furnished flop?

CHAPTER 46

"Super-duper mean, yeah. A taste of this stuff and bam," a woman on a stool said. She smiled at Taylor. "How'd you get all soaked? Singin' in the rain?"

"I wish."

"No honey to rub you dry?"

"You be otherwise engaged, Doctor Clarke."

Embroidered on the left breast pocket of a standard, starched white lab coat was *Caroline "Crazy" Clarke, PhD.* "Oh, T, running again with the sweet nothings. Shame on you." She winked.

Alert and peppy, no furrows or blotches on her smooth skin, she was one of twelve people seated at workstations in the well-lit LA County Crime Lab. At two-ish in the middle of the night, most who slogged through the graveyard shift exhibited wear and tear. Not her. Impressive. Taylor knew her age. Same as his.

Her ponytail swung as she swiveled, adjusted stylish glasses and squinted at an array of sophisticated machines, monitors and microscopes. "Yeah. Look here." Dr. Clarke tapped a graph on the screen. "Know what happens? Your ticker slams on the brakes to about nada, you get cyanotic – kind of blueish around the eyes and lips - then it's Sand Man time into a deep-ass coma."

Taylor remembered the lab and blanched. "Grim, Crazy."

"Worse. A grain extra, and it's auf-good-bye-bye, sayonara baby." She slanted her torso towards the computer console. Her lab jacket fell open, uncovering blue jeans and a scarlet blouse. A distinct contrast to her pale complexion. She pressed a button. A printer spit a tape similar to a receipt. Crazy gave it to Taylor, played with the ends of her hair and aimed her knees at him as he read. Flirty.

He didn't notice as he sounded out a difficult word. "Tetro-do-toxin. I understand the toxin part." He strung the syllables together as a question. "Tetrodotoxin?"

"Yeah. Comes from the puffer fish."

"Can you trace or track?"

"Totally impossible to ID individual DNA, but we can determine where in the deep blue it lived." She reached for a clipboard, attached a form, clicked a pen and wrote his name.

Taylor snatched the document, wadded it and scooped the bag of powder. "Glad you were here."

Her expression quizzed him, but he didn't reveal a thing. "Oh-kay. Vampire crew at your service. Don't see enough of you."

As he ambled to the exit, Taylor stopped and turned. "Why they call you Crazy?"

She offered a coquettish grin.

CHAPTER 47

"Learn the secret handshake?" Johnny said. His clothes were fresh and he slid a pen in a pocket.

"Soon," Heat said. At her desk, nose buried in the newspaper, she couldn't look at him. Didn't want an errant glance or averted eyes to divulge anything, and on threat of death wouldn't tell him she'd spent the night at home. She had a pile of guilt about that. "One final session."

"Then graduation?"

"Something like that."

"When?"

"They'll text us."

Johnny, coffeed up, a bundle of energy, bounced on his toes, ready for the day. "C'mon. We ought to boogie in case His Chiefness shows."

Heat ruffled pages. "It's Sunday."

"Wanna chance it?" He dropped three files in front of her.

She lowered the paper. "And these are?"

"Yikes, doll." Johnny reacted to her appearance.

Dazed and groggy. Bad bed head. Croissant-shaped bags below bloodshot eyes. She hadn't bothered with the new makeup scheme. All evidence of her overhaul had vaporized.

She skimmed the top file. "What's this?"

"Our story. And Taylor checked in from the lab."

Heat sipped caffeine. Traffic noise wafted into the newsroom as Mass stepped inside. "You? On a Sunday?" She said.

"And howdy to you, too, at ten in the a.m." Mass closed the door. His wrinkled polyester shirt and shapeless trousers had lost their creases long before the new millennium, and his shoes needed a shine. He waddled around the stacks of back issues and lobbed a loose-leaf notebook at Johnny. "Here you go, teach. Lucky the dog didn't barf on it."

"Don't have a dog," Panther said as she wandered in.

"Details, details."

Heat was puzzled. "Why're they..."

"Holy crapoly," Johnny said from his desk in Rookie Haven. He was engrossed in a file.

"I concur," Captain Showbiz said as he and Madam Speaker entered. "Girly, I hope it was worth it." He meant Heat.

"You two, too?" She said. "Somebody explain."

"Just following orders."

The staff, minus Blitz, assembled on a blustery morning.

"We're here to help," Speaker said.

Heat thought about that. "Ummm—not buying it. I mean, I am, but there's gotta be a catch."

"Cynic."

"I asked them to lend a hand," Johnny said.

"Apparently, you landed a whopper and could use backup," Panther said.

"Support," Speaker said.

"Hel-lo-o. Someone want to fill in the blanks?" Showbiz said.

"They fell into a barrel of shit," Mass said.

"More like an empty grave," Heat said.

"So which is it?" Showbiz said.

"It's The Way." Mass waved a file folder.

"That new do-over set-up?" Showbiz yawned and strolled to the coffee pot.

"You heard of them?"

"Sure."

"How?"

"It's my job?" Showbiz poured a cup.

"Ain't so new, though. The Way's actually been in business thirty years. Got going in the South. Louisiana. NOLA."

"New Orleans?" Heat said.

"Yeah. Before there, the Caribbean. A definite guru-based scam with bucks."

"Whose?" Speaker said.

"Ask Harvard. It's his gig. Miles above my pay grade."

"Who's the guru?"

"That's the mystery."

"Keep digging. It didn't invent itself."

"How about magic?" Showbiz said. "Or divinely created?"

"Caribbean?" Heat said.

"Yep. It's all in the file." Mass emptied his ashtray in a trash basket and lit another smoke.

"Great balls o' fire," Johnny said as he scanned Mass's report. Excited, he searched his notes.

Heat had suspicions regarding her cohorts. Lots. She loved them, and they loved her, so they claimed, but they'd rob a by-line in a heartbeat. "Isn't it Sunday?" She checked the newspaper.

"All day, sweetie," Showbiz said. He plopped five sugar cubes, one at a time, in the steamy brew. Stirred. Extended his right pinkie, puckered, blew, and slurped. An obnoxious noise. So unpleasant that Miss Edna, in the shadows, plugged her ears. He slurped again.

Madam Speaker despised the noise, too. It was worse than the sound of a cat puking, and the Captain nursed a full cup.

"Let's motor, doll," Johnny said.

Heat cradled her mug.

"C'mon." He dragged her out of her chair. She stumbled. Spilled her beverage.

"Hey."

"Sorry. I… We, I mean we, scored a lead."

"What?"

"Fish."

"You lost me." Heat chugged the last inch of caffeine and put on her bomber jacket.

The public-address system squelched. "Heat and Harvard. Both of you," roared Jolly Duncan. "On the dot."

"Uh oh. Beam me up," cackled Miss Edna.

"What cave he crawl out of?" Mass said.

"I can hear you," Duncan said.

With a look, Heat questioned Madam Speaker who shook her head. Johnny queried his colleagues with arched brows. Nobody knew.

Duncan hollered, "Now," punctuated by an electronic screech.

Heat didn't move. She'd never experienced the Chief yell. Get pissed off? Sure. Shout? Yeah. But angry screaming?

"Not much choice," Johnny said.

Duncan's phone rang. He answered with a pretend-nice, "City Desk, how may I direct your inquiry?" His neck, cheeks, then baldness, flushed red. "Yeah. Uh-huh." Glared at his reporters.

Heat possessed no desire to walk in there. None. Held back.

"He signs our paychecks," Johnny whispered. He faced the Editor in Chief's office and its angry occupant.

"Don't remind me." She stepped forward. Together, they passed through Duncan's portal.

Madam Speaker, Mass, Captain Showbiz, Panther and Miss Edna watched. Panther drummed her fingers. Speaker crossed her legs and swung a foot. Mass and the Captain were, "Meh," and projected idle curiosity.

"T'ain't no biggie," Miss Edna said. As far as she was concerned, she'd covered and reported it all. This was a re-run.

"Copy that." Duncan parked his phone it in its cradle.

"If you like, we can parley over a brew, Chief," Johnny said. He made a half-turn to exit.

"Not so fast, Harvard. Model piece." Duncan pointed to the spot on the floor.

Johnny stood on the circle. Heat was beside him. She said, "Deadline's not 'til…"

"What the bloody 'ell happened to Friday?" The Chief shrieked. "You blew your deadline. Made me be here since zero-dark on my damn day of leisure. Where've you been?"

Heat backed up a step.

Johnny was unflustered. "Doing everything you taught me. Work the story. Hunt leads. We started at a Hollywood party. Later, broke into..."

"Beep, beep. Time's up. Deal's a deal."

"*Deux* days and the Pulitzer's yours."

"Already won one. Team prize, but obituary worthy." He gestured at his credenza. Centered in a place of honor was, indeed, a pentagon-shaped, crystal Pulitzer Prize.

"Forty-eight hours, Chief. Trust us."

"Pasadena, kiddo. We soldier on. You forget that breaker in Perris?"

"France?" Heat said. "Cool."

In unison, Johnny and Duncan said, "Single 'e' double 'r.' Perris, California."

She squared her shoulders. "Six p.m. Tuesday, Chief. It makes this week's issue. You're happy, we're happy."

"Not our agreement. You will do the work I pay you for."

"Can't, Chief. Sorry," Johnny said.

"Oh?" A vein pulsed on Duncan's left temple. "Read my lips. All a you. Listen and listen good." He zeroed in on Heat. "You are sacked. Done. Terminated. History."

No one uttered a sound. Heat had no idea what to do. Five seconds later, Johnny marched out.

Duncan pushed "announce" on his PA mic. "Get security. These traitors aren't stealing the stationary. They're finito. Surrender your keys to the lav. I mean it."

"Don't have stationary, Chief," Mass said.

Johnny dumped his few personal items and files in a banker's box.

Heat staggered to her seat and collapsed. Retrieved two, silver, 5-point stars from a drawer. Once worn by her father, she clutched them to her heart. She was so proud of her daddy when they were pinned on his shoulders. Bawled like a baby when he presented them to her. She dropped the stars in her bowling shirt pocket and salvaged the cheap, framed certificate that sat next to her nameplate.

Heat O'Leary
True Crime LA
Writer of the Year

Recalled with a smile that the award included a hundred-dollar bonus.

Johnny fidgeted as Heat rested an Army rucksack on her lap. She unzipped it. Slipped in her possessions. Fought tears.

"He'll change his mind before you even get to the curb," Mass said. "Always does."

"It's Christmas." Showbiz said. "Even Chiefie has a modicum of seasonal spirit."

Heat snuffed and wiped her eyes. Her chin quivered.

Johnny bundled his hat and coat, stuffed notes, *TCLAs* and assorted papers in the box, and stalked to the exit.

Speaker, Panther, the Captain, Mass and Miss Edna rose to their feet. Each mouthed "bye." Heat tossed a half-hearted wave.

Duncan hunkered at his desk, rattled "*Manhattan Murder*," tried to concentrate, but peeked.

Heat reached Johnny. He opened the front door to sunshine. She heaved a sigh, came to attention and marched out.

CHAPTER 48

"Yo. Picture Boy," the Brunette said. Alone in the vacant squad room, he leaped to his feet and rushed to the elevator. Floundered in his high heels.

Taylor, exhausted, ignored the Brunette. ID badge clipped to a yellow collar, camera strapped around his neck, he joined Walsh and Morales.

"I'm talking to you." The Brunette shoved the photographer, spun him, slammed a forearm against the base of his throat and pinned him to the wall.

It took a couple breaths for the shock to dissipate. Then Taylor smashed an elbow into the Brunette's gut. They clenched and skidded on the slick, buffed linoleum.

"Hey, Cinderella," Walsh said. She laughed at the sight of one of their own in a wig, royal-blue gown and pumps, as he struggled to take down Taylor. "Let's git, T. Stiff's getting' cold." She moved to separate them, but Morales gripped her blazer.

The Brunette was too short to go nose-to-nose with Taylor but angry enough to continue the scuffle. "Tell your punk pal things're hot and wet and I want all the scraps he has. All the info."

"Bet you do," Taylor said. "Tall stud like that? Um, um, um."

"You tell him."

"I resemble a delivery service?"

The Brunette grabbed Taylor's sleeve. "I get, or he ends up..." he stopped shy of the threat.

"Or he ends up what?" Taylor thumped the Brunette on his head. "Say it."

The Brunette didn't budge. "Your wanna-be crime dog gives me the whole kit and kaboodle on our Baby Doll by end of watch tomorrow."

"Or?"

"Screw you."

"In your dreams, white boy." Taylor forced him to retreat.

"Enough. Finito," Walsh said.

Morales was less conciliatory. "Let 'em kill each other."

Taylor pinched and patted the Brunette's cheek. "Adorbs. You wax or shave?"

The Brunette lunged. Walsh locked him in a chokehold.

"You need to decide whether you're the pin or the cushion," Taylor said. "You'll be way happier."

"Cocksucker," growled the Brunette as he grappled with Walsh. Taylor disappeared into the stairwell.

"Easy there, gorgeous," Walsh said.

The Brunette threw her off.

Before Walsh retaliated, the elevator dinged. Morales pulled her inside.

Cedar Tree Hoffman was more curious than angry as he paced his office and shot the Brunette a silent, "So?"

CHAPTER 49

"I really want to know," Heat said. She and Johnny lugged her pack and his gear along Sunset Boulevard. It was overcast but dry. Light Sunday traffic zoomed by. They'd trudged half a block in half an hour. At that pace, they'd hit Murder Burger by dinner, which was okay. She thought it best to stay near headquarters on the off chance the Chief told them to return. Or, to save face, sent an emissary to make an offer.

Heat adjusted her load. Gazed at the *TCLA* building. "Someone please tell me. What's it take? Livin' the dream one minute, out on my ass the next." She eyed the heavens. Smeared snot on a sleeve. "Can you answer me that? What does it goddamn take?" Sighed. Took another yard of sidewalk contemplation. "Suppose I could follow dear old dad and join up. Officer Candidate School. A commission. Can you imagine? Second-looey Heat? Butter Bar O'Leary? Haven't aged out. Got five years, or close to it. And women are allowed to dodge bullets. Whoop-de-fuckin'-do..." She saluted. "Or I could go with complete and total surrender. Hook up with dad's Colonel's son. Wonder if he's footloose? Dude had the hots for me, big-time. Worshipped me. And he was kinda cute. Be set now if I'd blinked my lashes and said yes. He didn't really ask. We were too young. But he hinted around at me being his one-and-only when he went to West Point and that we'd do the ceremony – that's what he said instead of a wedding – do the ceremony with the swords and all the trimmings after graduation. He'd almost be a major, now. I'd be Mrs. almost-a-major. Probably would've popped out a Junior almost-a-major. Maybe one of each. But no, I landed in the nut bowl and chased my passion." She dripped sarcasm and kicked a crack in the cement. "Why'd I ever wanna come here? Freakin' La La Land. Tinsel Town. Hollyweird. Why?" She scowled at Johnny. "Got an answer for me?"

"Sorry."

"Lotta help you are." She slumped. Dabbed tears.

Johnny considered himself a gentleman and offered her a piece of paper towel.

Butt on the curb, shoes in the gutter, Heat paid no never-mind to him or the cars. "You fork over body and soul. Every last ounce. Live for the job." She squinted at Johnny. "You don't give a rat's ass. I didn't even register on your scope 'til a week ago."

He knew enough to keep his mouth shut.

Heat beseeched the sky again. "Desire, baby. Had it. Yes, I did. Full tank and then some." Laid her eyes on Johnny, "Definitely might have shared the extra, but big surprise – it's too late. Too damn late. I'm dry. Tapped out." She drew her knees to her chin and buried deep weeps in her skirt. The flood gates parted.

It was the first female meltdown Johnny'd ever been through. Rephrase that - witnessed. And he felt for her, consumed by her career.

Neither noticed the two hoods relaxing in their Cadillac land yacht on the other side of the street.

CHAPTER 50

"This one's same old, same old," CC Rademaker said. So was she. Faded jeans ten pounds too tight, flat curls, Kelly-green polo shirt, hiking boots and official Deputy ME wind-breaker.

"'Cept he's Black," Walsh said.

"There is that." Rademaker examined the corpse of a male black. It lay supine in the middle of a queen-sized bed, sunk in a puffy, beige duvet, face obscured by a matching pillow.

Taylor recognized the MO. "Too bad."

All personnel in the en-suite master glanced at him – ME, criminalists, Coroner's people, uniforms, detectives.

"Friends with him, too?" Morales said.

"Unh unh. Don't enjoy seeing you lose one to the ghoul squad."

"Better them than us. Crap case has gone boring."

"Morales," Cedar Tree Hoffman said. "You require a refresher? About who we work for?" The boss filled the doorway.

"Uhhh, no, L-T. The victim." Morales shrugged an apology but didn't mean it.

"So? What's what?" Hoffman said to no one in particular.

"Fits the pattern," the ME said.

"Well…" Walsh was skeptical.

"Yeah, I get it. Black."

"Not exactly what I was going for. A key box doesn't check. Wifey swears it's a joyful and fruitful marriage."

"Hope so. Hubby's hung like a horse. Sure can absolve a ton of sins."

"That a medical term, doctor?" LT Hoffman said. "A little respect. A representative from Homicide Special has requested a word."

Everyone quieted as a diminutive woman emerged from behind Cedar Tree's bulk and entered the crammed space. Olive complexion, bottle-blonde hair cut in a utilitarian wash-n-dry, a different shade where she'd touched up the roots. She used no makeup except on thin, plum-colored lips above a square jaw. There were no earrings, rings or bracelets, but gold, military-style dog tags dangled around her neck on a thick, fourteen-carat chain. She tugged on a smooth, navy-blue pants-suit jacket and strode in four-inch heels - two inches taller than regulations permitted.

"Hand Job's here?" Morales whispered to Walsh.

"Not good. Not good at all," she said.

D-III Alberta "Birdy" Hand had served as a Marine MP for five years, and it showed. She held herself straight and stiff, thumbs against the seams of her slacks. Behind her back, LAPD rank-and-file, male and female, referred to her as "Hand Job" due to her frequent promotions and the persistent rumors that accompanied them. She'd rocketed from the Academy all the way to RHD in six years. Many in the Department deemed it the modern-era record, which dated to 1950 when Chief Parker ascended.

Hand Job fixed hazel eyes and a smirk on Walsh and Morales as she paraded across the carpet, passed a wood veneer dresser, and arrived at the Cal-King mattress.

"You." She waved a fist at Long and Short. "Deliver all the murder books for this series by end of watch. Get my e-mail from your Lieutenant." Not pleasant or user-friendly, Hand deemed the Hollywood Ds amateurs, pretend investigators, trapped at division, not smart enough for advancement.

"They're all hard copies," Walsh said.

"Doesn't change my order." Hand Job trained a warm smile of tiny, bright teeth at Taylor. "T."

"Hey there." He winked.

She blushed and joined Rademaker. Viewed the body toes to throat. Lingered on its tumescence. "You are accurate, doctor. Impressive. Anything else?"

Rademaker rattled a prescription pill bottle. "Hillbilly heroin. Oxycontin."

Detective Hand fired a glare at Walsh and Morales that demanded they surrender information.

"No suicide note," Walsh said. "That's consistent."

"And, a nine-one-one selfie before the pills hit," Morales said.

"Wife found him. I suspect she screamed."

Morales choked back a laugh.

Hand ignored him. "Shoot the glossies, yet, T.?"

"No ma'am."

"Can we, doctor?"

"Can we what?"

"Flip him."

"Yes ma'am."

"S-I-D? You ready to transfer the scene to me?"

A mature, plump techie in a lab coat said, "Sure."

Detective Hand frowned displeasure.

The SID technician grasped the gist and peeled off her latex gloves. "Yes, ma'am."

"Detective."

The Tech folded her arms in a huff. "Yes, Detective ma'am, it's all yours."

Hand Job seized possession of the case, the scene and all that came with them. She also owned the outcome, a responsibility she embraced. She lifted the pillow, lobbed it to a criminalist and snapped her fingers. "Decedent's name?"

Morales took his sweet time. Ran a pen down a page. Moistened a thumb and turned to the next. Deciphered his scrawl.

Drove D-III Hand nuts. She folded her arms, tapped her foot.

"Got it. Yep. Here we go," he said. "There it is. Swopes. Andre. Married. Twenty-six."

Taylor focused his camera. The guy appeared asleep rather than dead. Race aside, there was nothing new.

"Actor-model-hunk," Walsh said. "Not sure if he was still a wanna-be." Checked her phone. "Has an IMDB page and a few credits, but no bio posted."

"Any clues from the spouse?" Hand said.

"Nope. He came home early from a weekend retreat and refused to confide as to the reasons."

CHAPTER 51

"One more for the road," Johnny sang. He tried to croon at the top of his voice. "And one more for my..." He was tone-deaf. "For my..." Paused. "For my..." Sucked in his cheeks. Made a fish face. "For my what?"

"You got it reversed," Heat said.

His off-key efforts at a solo provoked nasty glances from the four customers.

Heat and Johnny occupied spots in the staff booth at the Mongol Horde. Box, backpack, trench coat and bomber jacket filled the others. She fidgeted. Johnny hummed, sort of. "Reversed?" He said.

Heat chugged the remainder of a cloudy liquid and raised her glass. Genghis, in his mock-Mongol sheepskin vest, poured a refill of Kumis and parked a fresh bottle in front of her.

"Allow me," Johnny said. He concentrated on his fingers. They were so heavy. Mini lead pipes. He fumbled with his cash.

"No, no, no. My treat." Whispered, "Tab?" to Genghis. No way she'd pass bad bills and commit a federal felony. Especially on a friend.

Genghis topped their drinks.

Johnny sipped. "Yuck..." He was smashed, and it tasted terrible. He angled the amber bottle at a ceiling light and contemplated the label. It was an idyllic depiction of a Mongol herder on a horse, snow-capped mountains in the distance under blue skies. He studied the list of ingredients. "Mare's milk?"

"Fermented," Genghis said. "Mongol Tradition."

Johnny paled.

"Get him a bucket," Heat said.

"Jush fine." He tore a chunk of bread, stuffed it in his mouth and chewed.

Genghis clapped twice and summoned an attractive, college-age waitress who strained the limits of her vest. She presented a platter of food and he announced, "Mongol Bee Bee Que specialty. Spicy."

Johnny eyed a steamy mound of shiny, diced meat garnished with green bits and slathered with an exotic sauce or something. The "or something" worried him. He swallowed. "Not the mare, is it?"

"Tradition." Genghis chuckled.

Johnny's stomach lurched. He pushed the platter to the center of the table. Listed left into Heat. Tried to snuggle. She sloughed him off. He slurred, "Don't hafta quit the story. Chief'll beg us for it."

"Your lips to the Devil's playground."

Johnny sat up straight and looked out the window. "Dark?" Then fell to the seat cushion.

"Been here all day." She poked his ribs. "C'mon." He didn't move. Heat dribbled a wake-up call on his face with her water.

Johnny jumped. "My respon-sha-billy. Take full."

She tugged and twisted his ear. "Come on."

"Ow." He swayed, caught the top of the banquette and pushed. Stood, reached for his coat and tripped. He recovered and rammed a fist in a sleeve. Groped for the belt. Wasn't there. The coat hung from one shoulder. He stabbed air and remembered he owned a second arm. London Fog on, Johnny rotated his head and neck. "Okie doke."

"Don't forget your junk."

He grabbed his crotch. "Got 'em."

"Your other junk."

Johnny took a couple stabs at gathering his box. On the third try, he discovered the hand holes. "Wow."

Heat put on her pack and held Johnny's collar. She nodded apologies to the diners and guided him into the night. A foot shorter and a hundred pounds smaller, she labored to keep him upright. He banged his shins on a chrome bumper. "Ouch…" and hobbled across the parking lot to the Sunset sidewalk. Went right.

Heat used elbows and prodded him in the opposite direction. Johnny slurred, "re-calculating," and staggered towards *True Crime HQ*.

She had no desire to be Johnny's keeper, but he was, as he put it, her battle buddy. She could not leave him alone. Not hammered and unemployed. She aimed him at the *TCLA* building. Their size difference forced her to walk too close. She clipped his heels.

Johnny stumbled. His carton hit the cement. He crashed on it. Heat belly-flopped on his back. Knocked the breath out of him, but he felt no pain. She struggled to her full height, all five feet four, pulled his collar until he was vertical, and steered him to the brick building. At a side entrance, she reined him to a stop.

He clucked his tongue. "Whoa there, fella." Giggled. "My own sound effects. Cool, huh?"

Heat propped him against the wall with a hip. Swung her ruck off her back and hunted for keys.

Johnny drawled, "We're at the paper?" His knees hinged, and he slid a few inches. Flapped his arms. Regained balance.

"Careful. C'mon. Use those legs. Participate. I can't keep you up all by my lonesome."

"Bet you can." He leered and clenched Heat high on a thigh and giggled. "This happen to Marlowe? Sam Spade? No way, Jose. Jose-ette. Jose-nita." His hands crept up. He snickered.

"Down, boy…" Heat unlocked a door, propped it open, gripped Johnny's lapels and maneuvered him inside. They confronted a flight of stairs. Eighteen of them. A banister on the left led to a second-floor landing.

He squinted through booze haze. The ascent was formidable. "Climbing Aconcagua."

"You can drop and curl here. It'll be base camp."

"Nah. Easy-peezy."

She hoped he'd collapse. It'd make life easier.

"Doll. Full disclosure. Mighta stretched the truth 'bout myself."

"You think?"

He burped long and loud. Hugged the banister. Steadied himself and resumed the climb. Halfway, he peeked behind. "Doll?" Didn't see her. Vertigo kicked in. He panicked. "Heat?"

"I'm here."

He glanced. Teetered. Plopped his butt on a step. Embraced the banister.

She prodded his ass. "Up or down."

Johnny eyeballed the top, lumbered to his feet and scaled the last nine treads.

They made the summit. Heat leaned him face-first into a wall and braced his back and hips. A fall would kill him. A viable option, considering her mood. Problem was, she had no clue how she'd explain it to Homicide.

Heat jabbed a key in a lock and turned the knob. Reached in, flipped the switch and nudged him. "Sit."

"Where?" There was no place to settle. Her bed was loaded with books. Grenade the Cat, curled on a pillow, watched and switched his tail. "Nice kitty… You live at work?"

"For now."

"Pay the Chief rent?"

"Miss Edna."

"Yeah? It's bona fide?"

"What?"

"She owns our rag?"

"I'll never tell." She smiled

Johnny missed it. Folded his arms and rocked. "Need an Xmas tree. We'll get you one. Decorate it. Hang stockings. Three. You, me and kit-tee." He recognized the serpent symbol taped to the shelves. "Wish we could figure that."

"Yeah." Heat scooted a stride-and-a-half to a kitchenette outfitted with all the comforts – sink, faucet, counter, hot plate, microwave and mini-fridge,

"Oh wow." Excited, Johnny recited members of the Pantheon of mystery writers. "Dash. Chandler. Connelly 'cuz we're in LA. MacDonald. Oh, Karin Slaughter. Laura Lippman. My homie, Burke. The Whodunnit Canon. How'd y'all get my stuff?"

Heat ran the tap.

Johnny slipped a volume off a shelf.

She filled a mug, scooped in a heavy dose of instant and stuck it in the microwave. The machine whirred.

He cradled the paperback as if it were a rare piece of art. " '*Galton Case.*' Kinda my primer. Learned it all from this puppy." He fell on the mattress and stared at a lamp. "Saw me around all kinds of poo. Read it so much it frayed and fell apart. Sorta like a favorite Teddy Bear, 'cept never had me one a dem."

Ding. Heat removed her coffee, stirred and sipped.

Johnny seemed sad. The booze? "Then there was that day. That dark, dark day. Can't find ol' Galton. Nowhere around. Group Home. Sorry, new maid. She tossed him."

Heat listened as she prepared a mug for him.

"Me, I be crazy mad." Upset, Johnny's accent drifted. "Gotta have him. Too old and ratty, she say. She'll get me a new one, cher. But I want me my Galton."

It was the first she'd heard of his NOLA patois. Booze let loose the truth of birth and pedigree, but she was amazed by its heft.

"Rip tru da ward. Dived all da dumpsters, but ol' Galton, he gone." Snuffed. Wiped.

"I'm so sorry. Take that one. Early Christmas." Another ding, but she didn't bother. Johnny was curled, *Galton* clutched to his chest as Grenade kneaded his hair. "Oh well…"

"Knock, knock. You decent?"

Startled, Heat slopped hot coffee on her hand. “Ow. Damn. Whoever you are don’t sneak up on me.”

Her door cracked open. “We caught a fresh stiff.” Taylor presented a fifth of vodka.

“Not tonight.”

Johnny mumbled and rolled over.

Taylor spotted him. “Ah.”

Heat eased out of her apartment and joined him on the landing. “How’d you track me?”

“Kidding?”

“No.” The obvious struck her. She was embarrassed. “Cops.”

“We have a winner.” Taylor raised the bottle in invitation.

“Can’t.”

“Because of him?” He jutted his chin at Johnny.

“Shush. It’s…”

“Complicated. Yeah, yeah, yeah.”

“Don’t get all pissy. You’re the one who went silent. A text would’ve been nice. Or smoke signals. Semaphores. Anything. But what do I get? Ghosted.” A straight, single woman’s number-one man-issue.

“You’re tough to locate.”

“Am not.”

“You’re getting shrinkage at The Way. Got canned.”

“How’d you know that?” She was chagrined. “It’s more ‘cuz of him than me.”

“And you’re not at the flop where you’re supposed to be.”

“I can explain.”

“And what’s the point of having a phone if the damn thing isn’t on?”

“We’re here now.”

Johnny snored. Taylor looked at him, then Heat. Thought about it. Headed out.

“Cut and run your only trick?”

He had a choice retort on the tip of his tongue. Was ready to fire it. Instead, set the booze on a step and took the remaining stairs two at a time.

Heat dripped a tear as Grenade nuzzled her ankles.

Johnny shifted but didn’t wake.

CHAPTER 52

"Ice Bitch. I'll melt her. Sure you will. With a blow torch," Taylor said. He ranted as he trudged past the window displays of The Last Book Store. A downtown-LA Mecca for lit lovers, it occupied the bottom floor of a century-old former bank. A hundred thousand tomes had saved the historic structure from the wrecking ball. Inside, the hands of a round, yard-wide clock mounted above a sculpture of a reader passed midnight and edged into tomorrow.

Taylor crossed Spring Street at Fourth. His neighborhood, The Old Bank District, was rolled up and tucked in. Not a sound. No vehicles or pedestrians. Green, yellow and red traffic signals played to an empty house, and El Nino was on hiatus.

He entered his building, also once a bank, with majestic columns and angry gargoyles. His diatribe slowed to a self-debate of the merits and flaws of one Heather "Heat" O'Leary. "Compared to Emma? She won't puddle fast." He hauled his ass upstairs to home sweet home, draped his field jacket on a chair and canvas bag on the oak table.

A thousand watts of bright burst into Taylor's vision. He ducked. Covered his face with an arm. "The hell? Who's here?" He attempted to discern the intruder's position, but the intensity blinded him. "C'mon, whoever you are, talk to me. We'll deal."

"Get your pals on the line, comrade. No tricks. We're gonna trade."

"Le Roux?"

"Surprise, surprise, Sergeant Carter. In the flesh. Look at this place. Sure do got a boner for lights, camera, action."

"Fuck you."

"Or die tryin'."

"Where'd you come from?"

"Ain't the question." Le Roux waited. Couldn't endure the silence. Yelled, "Ask."

"Ask what?" Taylor was pissed, not afraid, but unable to see Le Roux.

"Ask, muthafucka!"

Taylor was silent.

"Geesh. Worse than yanking goddamn teeth. Ask."

No answer.

"Trade me the crap you found on Emma, 'cuz I'm not taking the tumble."

"Or?"

Le Roux cocked his revolver. "How's that for 'or?' Give me all you got on her murder. And all the shit you lifted out of that fish farm."

"Murder? Detectives say suicide."

"Who cares? She's dead." Le Roux spent his limited supply of patience, charged Taylor and smashed him between the eyes.

Taylor cocked his arms to throw a punch but froze when the gun barrel met his chin. "I got zip."

"How about the tall fuck?"

"He doesn't, either."

"Somebody does!" Le Roux needed to explode brains and splatter blood. Instead, he screamed, "Call him."

Taylor's instincts, honed by years dodging hostile fire in combat zones, were a hundred percent operational. On alert, he calculated odds and options. "It's in here." He patted the front of his jeans.

Le Roux waived his pistol, granted permission.

Taylor used a thumb and finger to extract his phone. Showed it. Touched the screen. Held it at his left ear.

"Speaker." Le Roux waved his gun.

Taylor did not want to take his eyes off the Smith and Wesson but had to as he tapped. He and Le Roux listened to each other's ragged breaths and the tinny sound of four rings then Heat's outgoing recording. "Leave a message." Beep.

"Miss O'Leary, this is T.N. Quigley the third, Los Angeles Police Department. Contact me ASAP. Thank…" Le Roux whacked Taylor's nose. "Ahhh."

"The guy, not the girl!"

"He's with her. Two for one."

"The dude, dude."

Taylor did as he was told. "You've reached Johnny Lincoln. At the tone, leave your..."

Le Roux grabbed the device. Killed the connection. Dragged his own from a pocket and pitched it to Taylor. "Her."

"If she can't answer, she can't answer."

Le Roux thumped Taylor's scalp.

"Okay." He pressed Heat's digits.

"Speaker," demanded Le Roux.

Taylor obeyed. Heat's number rang again. Once, twice.

"Hello?" She said.

CHAPTER 53

"There it is." Heat peered out the windows of a Sunset Boulevard bus, then verified hand-written info on a half sheet of legal-pad paper for the umpteenth time. She pulled the cord.

"Stop requested." The automated voice was male.

"Up and at 'em," Heat said.

Johnny was sprawled on the bench seat. Asleep or unconscious, whichever, he was down for the count. Mouth agape, legs in the aisle, he cuddled her pack on his lap. She elbowed him. "C'mon. Get it together."

He moaned. "Working on it." Burped long and loud.

"Don't you dare barf in my vehicle," the driver warned.

"Yeah, yeah, yeah." Johnny struggled to put on Heat's pack. The straps were sized for her, not him. He slung it on a shoulder.

"Portia Street," the driver said.

Johnny yucked. "Shakespear Portia. With a T. Not the car." Thought it was funny.

"Gag it," Heat said.

Air brakes hissed and doors folded open. They exited and ventured into the heart of Echo Park. A mile east of *TCLA HQ*, a collection of gangs, mom and pop shops, and chic hangouts brawled and killed for supremacy over a dozen square blocks. At least the 'bangers did. Dusk to dawn, shots reverberated, and bullets struck bodies and buildings a couple freeway exits west and north of the DTLA skyline. Dangerous or trendy, nightmare or wet dream, it was an urban dweller's theme park.

Heat hopped to the sidewalk. She tugged her yoga pants and shimmied, stuffed her hands in the pouch of a hoodie and crossed the deserted Boulevard. Johnny moaned and groaned but kept pace. The decrepit Little Joy Cocktail Lounge inhabited the northwest corner of the intersection with Portia. A partial neon sign winked - Lit Jo Cock Lo -producing an unintentional rhythm and rhyme. Johnny belched again to quash a compulsion to puke.

Heat hurried west of the bar to a vacant parking lot and a large, mid-century structure with an arched roof fronted by a moon-lit billboard.

STICKY WICKET STAGES

"This was a supermarket when I got to town."

Johnny hugged his gut, but didn't throw up. "Must've been eons ago."

"Six eons." She dashed to the old store's main entrance. Gripped the handles and shook. Made a racket. Locked.

"Quiet."

"We're expected." Heat knocked a knuckle on an aluminum-framed directory. Read the single listing. "Le Roux International Studios?"

"Fantasy. Anyone else listed?"

"Nope."

"Ring the bell?"

She laid a fist on a button next to the registry. They heard a faint buzz as Johnny chose picks.

"Fuck it." Heat jogged along the building wall until it ended. She turned right, out of sight.

Annoyed, Johnny secured his tools and trailed her to an alley.

Heat was on a loading dock, grunting and groaning as she wrenched the handle of a closed, twelve-by-twelve freight door. It wouldn't slide. Discouraged but determined, she tried again. Not even an inch. "God-DAMN."

Johnny stretched an arm around her, lifted a shield on the mechanism and eased her out of the way. He slid a latch and pulled. The strain forced him to resist an upchuck. Stomach acid burned his throat, but he continued. Steel-on-steel screeched long enough to create a gap. Heat slipped through. He was miffed by her lack of caution. "Hold up." But she jogged into an unlighted, cavernous interior. He pushed inside and shined his phone on her.

She ducked from the beam and whispered, "Don't."

Skittish, on alert, he scooted to her and moved the light in an arc. Beyond ten feet, it didn't help. He stepped deeper into the darkness. Saw coiled power cables, wood tripods, a mic boom, even a nested stack of full, half, and quarter apple boxes.

"Sound stage?" She said.

"You're practically an LA native. You tell me."

"Has the crap."

Johnny swallowed an acidic eruption of nausea, eyed ropes lashed to studs and followed their paths upwards, into shadows, near the ceiling. Bulky items, sets and scenery, hung on a lattice of rails accessible by catwalks.

Thirty yards away, a low-watt bulb backlit a small woman with big hair at the far end of the building. She cocked a short-barrel Mossberg, rested it on her hip and advanced.

Heat was familiar with the ominous sound due to years spent at shooting ranges with her dad. She grasped Johnny's arm.

"Who..." Johnny cleared his throat. "Who dat?"

The silhouette of a second, taller person appeared. The staccato of spike heels on concrete echoed as taller joined smaller. They marched towards Johnny and Heat. "Johnny Lincoln. Get your butt in gear, son." She coughed. A smoker's hack.

"Awesome. Baby Doll Getz." Johnny was starstruck.

"In the flesh, cher." She halted a foot from him and primped. "About time me and you said hey."

In the dimness, it was difficult for him to peg an age, but, wow. Baby Doll looked younger than he imagined, considering cigarettes were horrendous on complexion. Even better, he now had his lede. She lived up to her moniker. There she was, black dress and pearl necklace under a belted, micro-fiber raincoat with a sexy bodyguard-sidekick.

"Check you, all gussied up in the wee hours. You do that for me? Or you been out and about, Baby Doll?"

"You get lucky enough to write about me, maybe I'll fill you in on the details. And it's Beatrice Dolores."

"Yes, ma'am."

Heat clutched Johnny's sleeve. The Chauffeur leveled the 12-gauge at her and racked a second shell.

Johnny and Heat stood their ground.

"And you've met Wheels." Getz patted her driver's butt. "Now okay."

Wheels pivoted and strutted into the dark.

"How'd you know we'd be here?" Johnny couldn't decide if he'd won the lottery or received a death sentence.

"Please," Getz said, as if Johnny needed to ask. She removed a compact Walther PPK, the size of her hand, from a black, satin clutch. Perfect for an evening out. Chambered a round.

Heat gasped again. This was it? Curtains? The finale? Always the General's daughter, she clenched her fists and stepped forward to fight for her life.

"Don't jump the shark, Cher. I took it upon myself to assist you. Let's keep it like that, yes?"

"Whatever floats your boat," Heat said.

Getz glared but tolerated the insolence.

Wheels returned. Used her shotgun to herd Taylor. Red gaffer's tape covered his mouth. His arms were bound behind his back with zip ties.

"Found him already trussed," Getz said.

Taylor confirmed with a nod.

Wheels snapped her switchblade. Johnny and Heat tensed.

"Relax."

The Chauffeur ripped the adhesive off Taylor's face. She enjoyed the sound and his cringe. "Poor baby." Licked her lips and traced his with the tip of her knife. He tracked it as she etched a scratch down his chest to his waist. A flick of her wrist freed his hands. She shoved him. He stumbled to Johnny and Heat. Regained his balance and flexed, prepared to take a blast.

"Y'all got almost killed," Getz said. "But not by me. No, no." She signaled Wheels, who sliced a taught rope anchored to a floor cleat. The line whipped from its mooring. An object crashed inches in front of them.

Heat screamed. Johnny and Taylor raised their fists.

A moan broke the silence. A human dangled at the end of the rope, head jerking above the concrete, elbows and wrists cinched.

"Boy here was hell-bent on making you chum."

Wheels rotated a battered, bruised, but recognizable figure. Johnny, Heat and Taylor watched spit, snot and blood mix and drip.

Taylor had seen worse. Heat fought the urge to puke and run.

"Le Roux," Johnny said.

At the sound of his name, Le Roux parted two swollen slits. Eyes. Moaned again. Did he recognize Johnny? Another groan. A plea?

Baby Doll patted Johnny's cheek. "Clock's run out. Our game's done, cher. I do you a favor, I require tit for tat."

"Yes, ma'am."

" 'Cuz dis should not happen to you and yours." She placed the muzzle of her pistol against Le Roux's brow and fired. Bang. Shot him.

Heat recoiled. Gore, jagged shards of skull, and warm, wet scraps of brain splattered her. Johnny and Taylor, too.

Getz slid the PPK into her purse. "You good, son?" She turned a one-eighty. Her heels clacked as she disappeared.

Johnny was petrified. His response was a glance at Le Roux.

Wheels blew a kiss. "Buh-bye."

Le Roux drained. Fluids pooled below the remnants of his skull.

Johnny, Heat and Taylor were horrified, motionless.

Through his fright, Taylor managed a hushed, "Go." Nudged Heat. She made a dash. He had her six.

Johnny scuttled backward, the rear guard, facing Le Roux and any attack that might arise from his killers.

They jammed the narrow opening, squeezed through to the dock outside, scrambled towards the parking lot and ran left. Reached the sidewalk. Sprinted right. Slowed at the next intersection. Pulses pounded. They gulped air. Taylor positioned himself between Heat and the threat of a bullet as he scrutinized rooftops. Johnny scanned Sunset. No limo.

"Who screwed the pooch here?" Heat said, frantic but not panicked.

"Nobody." Johnny was calm. "Sometimes you get blowback."

"Seriously?" Taylor was amped. "I came, I came… I was damn near on the end of that rope."

"Pinch yourself, cher. Give Baby Doll her due."

"Bitch must be a genius," Heat said. She decelerated to pissed.

"Then I'm a what?" Taylor said. "A dumb-fuck? For being involved with you two?"

"Wonder why she didn't kill us," Johnny said.

"Disappointed?"

"Curious."

"War ain't finished yet." Heat idled at anxious. "It's just a hitch in the get-along."

Taylor was incredulous. "You insane? I'm the one had a gun up my ass. Twice! I'm done here."

"But we're only inches from getting the story."

"Le Roux's..." Taylor waved at the studio. "We worked a deal. Shit rolls south, we go to the cops. We're there, Johnny. Deal's a deal. We even voted on it."

Heat grabbed Johnny's biceps. "Can't you feel it? Story's got legs. I'm going to be initiated into The Way, and Le Roux's… Le Roux's..." She couldn't kick the image of his spattered brain.

"A dot," Johnny said.

"That's cold."

"It's a fact. Not a thing we can do."

"Sure there is. We connect the dots. We're home free."

"Don't have a job."

"Exactly," she said and threw in a little body English.

Johnny gripped her shoulders. Towered over her. "No can do, boo. Too risky. Time to get you to dreamland."

Heat fumed, punched his arm and twisted loose.

"Both of you can bunk with me," Taylor said.

"Pussies. I will crack it, and when I do?" She flipped them off and stomped away.

Johnny groaned and massaged his temples. "Oh man, bed spins comin'." He battled gut gymnastics. "Has to be the Mare's Milk."

"Mare's Milk?" But Taylor didn't care. He started after Heat. Entertained the notion he'd talk sense into her.

Johnny seemed to read his mind. "She'll ride that rocket for a while."

"How long?" Taylor shoved hands in his pockets.

"Tomorrow. Dinner."

Heat continued her hike into one of America's most dangerous neighborhoods. Alone. Both Johnny and Taylor wanted to rescue her.

"Best to spectate and wait."

"In the meantime?"

"We soldier on."

"And Emma?"

"Remains a mystery." Johnny burped and stifled a tummy vault.

"That's it?"

"I don't do magic."

"You drag me down a hole that's got a nine-mil slug with my name on it at the bottom, and you say you're done?"

Johnny reviewed notes as if nothing had occurred.

"What'd they do to you when you were a kid?"

Johnny hesitated but powered on. "Fix a meet with your detective buddies and we'll show them all the dots. Go with Body-On-A-Rope, first. Sounds kind of Christmasy."

"How's any of it land us closer to Emma?"

"Doesn't. But it can't hurt. Don't forget, there's Baby Doll and the classified ads. We lay out the dots that aim at The Way. All the cops need do is draw the lines."

"There a catch, Scoop? You people never cave so easy. Especially to the police."

"You people? That's funny coming from you."

"Excuse me?"

In a second, Johnny understood his mistake. "Sorry. Didn't mean anything by it."

"Sure you did. Say it again."

Johnny shook his head.

"You being all PC now? Then allow me. Half-breed. Zebra. Oreo. Every other Sunday, black. I grew up in vanilla valley Idaho, remember?"

"So don't call me Scoop."

"You prefer slime ball? How 'bout shit surfer?"

"That's what you think of me? Doesn't matter. No gig, no point. Just as well share."

"Cases were shipped to Robbery-Homicide, anyway."

"Damn. Who's the lead? Maybe we can organize a little give and take with 'em."

"Not gonna happen. It's Hand Job."

"Homicide Special?"

"Yeah. Know her?"

"By rep."

They watched Heat. "So we leave Emma in limbo?" Taylor said.

"Worse. She wasn't even wearing a box. Plot her dots. It's a huge one on 'when.' Kinda sorta half of one on 'who.' But no clue as to 'where.' And 'why?' It's anybody's guess. So's 'how.'"

"Still got it as a murder?"

"Probably. Which leads to the biggest dot of all – how come Long and Short don't?"

Each contemplated the question as Heat vanished over a rise.

"She'll be okay," Johnny said.

CHAPTER 54

"You decent?" Taylor said. Geared up for the day in a Hawaiian print, he knocked once on Heat's apartment door. Unlatched, it swung open.

"Yeah?" Johnny said.

Surprised, Taylor ambled in. "A threesome?" Heat's hoodie, yoga leggings and bra were piled on the braided rug. "She putting on her new war paint?"

"She's late." Johnny gazed out the window, first at the bakery, then at a leaden sky that promised rain.

"Heat gave you a key?"

"Not locked." Johnny wore a fresh, ironed shirt, but their encounter with Getz had extracted a toll. His pale complexion was blotchy, and dried flecks of Le Roux speckled his slacks and coat.

"Maybe she's trying to get your job back for you."

"Maybe." Johnny raised his hat and explored the titles on Heat's shelves.

Taylor's strobe flashed as he tested it.

The cat purred.

It was an uncomfortable quiet until Johnny broke it. "Helluva night last night."

"Yeah."

"This close." Johnny held a thumb and forefinger a quarter of an inch apart.

Taylor let the thought fall. They weren't elbow-to-ass in the foxhole. The kinship of shared peril and sudden death faded as the sun climbed. "Heat give you any kind of a head's up?"

"No. You?"

"That she has info and to pop by, ASAP."

"Ditto." Johnny spotted Grenade curled on a pillow.

"You suppose she's…"

"Perturbed?"

"Had a stronger word in mind."

"Have to ask her."

The tension was palpable. Johnny stroked the kitty. Taylor unscrewed the lens. Inspected it. His phone rang. Saved from the silence. "Quigley." Listened. "Copy that." Ended the call. Yawned. Tried to shake awake a little energy. "Wanna learn how homicide operates, Scoop? See all the innards?" Taylor attached the lens to his camera and waited for an answer. "C'mon. Now or never."

Johnny was torn. Stay for Heat and her news? Or live the dream?

"You know you want to."

Yeah, he did, but a textbook tugged at his attention. Common in Heat's place, but it was all by itself near Grenade on the sleep-side of the bed. Taylor's serpent-symbol photo was stuck between pages.

"If you're coming, come."

"Can't ditch her."

"Not. She'll find us if she gets lonely." Taylor generated noise on the stairs as he bounded past the vodka bottle.

Johnny took the book and petted Grenade. "Borrowing it." He hurried to the parking lot and vaulted into Taylor's van. "Thanks."

"Pleasure. Belt."

Johnny talked over radio chatter as he buckled up. "Where's the stiff?"

"Theater Row." Taylor steered the van into moderate, mid-morning, Monday traffic. At Murder Burger, he merged onto Silver Lake, sped up the ramp to the north 101 Freeway and sliced across two lanes. He raced by Vermont and Melrose / Normandie.

Johnny opened the book he'd taken from Heat's. He compared Taylor's coffin-lid pic to one in the book. A perfect match. "Bingo. Gotta see this."

"Busy." Taylor rocketed down the Santa Monica Boulevard exit, made a hard left and drove west.

Speed and gravity banged Johnny into the door, but he didn't care. The ride was worth it.

Taylor pressed a button on the console. The siren blared. "Cool, huh?"

Johnny nodded.

Taylor flicked a toggle. "Lights, too." Cars pulled to the curb. Congestion eased. He accelerated. Had a clear path in the center of six lanes.

Johnny was ecstatic. Running hot. Second item on his bucket list accomplished. Could it be any better? He caught a glimpse of Hollywood Forever and felt a pang of guilt for leaving Heat in the lurch.

A mile-and-a-half and three minutes beyond the 101, four miles and fifteen minutes from Heat's, Taylor bounced the van on the curb and stopped on the southeast corner of Wilcox and Santa Monica Boulevard.

Johnny set the book on the floor. Swung his feet to the sidewalk. Checked surroundings. They were at The Complex, a cluster of five ninety-nine seat theaters and several rehearsal and audition studios in the heart of Theater Row. Marquees blurbed titles and performance times. Posters displayed headshots of actors. Johnny didn't recognize them. No one would.

Taylor prepped. Polished the lens, inserted a new memory card. He hopped from the van, grabbed images of the theaters, snapped pix of the intersection, and moved south. Johnny was behind him.

One building down Wilcox, two shiny LAPD patrol SUVs were grill-to-grill. They defended an alley entrance twelve feet wide. Two cops unfurled yellow, plastic crime-scene tape and secured it to side-view mirrors. Spectators stretched the barrier and strained to see the action. A young officer maintained a sign-in log. Taylor dashed off "*T N Q 3*" and indicated Johnny. "Him, too."

The reporter grinned, scribbled something resembling a signature, stooped under the tape and entered as an invited guest. Johnny had scaled Everest. He was the proverbial sponge. Soaked it up. Jotted observations and impressions so he'd remember every detail.

They weren't in an alley. It was similar to a cul-de-sac and measured twelve by twenty. Jammed with required personnel, there was space for a single LED stand.

Johnny slipped past a Scientific Investigation Division tech, a full dumpster, and a couple canvas scenery flats slanted against a two-story brick wall. He bumped one, had an "oh crap" moment, but steadied it.

Taylor, arms tucked, squeezed in. " 'Scuse me." Said it every other step and joined Walsh and Morales. Tapped her on the shoulder.

"Hey, T." Walsh smiled, then frowned. "Yo. Sam Spade. I've seen you." Johnny wore his fedora and London Fog. "Whitely Heights. The station. Returning to the scene, punk? Visiting the deed?" She yanked his collar and slapped her cuffs on him.

"Hey. I'm legal. Tell her."

"He is. Catch and release. He's mine."

Walsh appraised Johnny top-to-bottom. Approved. "So who's your new playmate?" She unlocked the restraints.

"Johnny Lincoln, ma'am. *True Crime LA.*" He offered his business card.

Walsh soured. “Ma’am?” She marched off.

Taylor photographed second-floor crank windows. “Not high enough for a dive.”

“Gold star for you,” Doctor CC Rademaker said. “She’s an OD”

“Not one of our do-it-yourselfers?”

“Nope.”

“So no Hand Job from Homicide Special?” Morales said.

“Only if you ask for one,” Rademaker said.

“Hah, hah, hah…” Morales emphasized with a familiar gesture.

“Back at ya, Bruno.”

A phone rang. Twelve people patted belts and pockets.

“It’s the victim’s,” the Medical Examiner said. “Probably a client.”

“Or pimp,” someone said.

There was a fourth ring but not a fifth. As Johnny listened to his phone, he found a clear line of sight to the body. Slumped.

“Always a bitch at first,” Taylor said. “You feel a puke coming on, leave. Embarrass yourself out by the lookie-loos. And you cannot take pictures, so disappear your cell. Comprende?” No response.

Johnny’s eyes were wet.

“What’s with you?” Taylor sensed dread. Shoved past Walsh and Morales. Saw the answer. “No.”

The ME judged the photographer’s reaction and signaled the detectives.

“Do her, too, T?” Bruno said.

They scrutinized a mess of fire-engine red hair, an open mouth and splayed legs. The left, bent at a forty-five-degree angle, formed a triangle. The right was folded, calf flush to thigh, toes by her ass. The knee jutted, an inch deep in a puddle of rainwater. She was barefoot. Green tights were shredded, and a skirt was bunched around her hips. The front of a red, laced-lined corset was ripped, and a cropped leather jacket was wedged beneath her neck.

“Who is she, T.?” Asked Walsh, sympathetic, concerned.

“Heather O’Leary,” Taylor and Johnny said.

Heat’s right arm extended above her head. A rubber tube was knotted on the bicep. Veins bulged. The needle of a disposable syringe was buried in her flesh.

“Not possible,” Johnny said.

“Yeah. Never,” Taylor agreed.

“News flash, Kemo,” Morales said. “Looks like a junkie, quacks like a junkie.”

Taylor slammed Morales’s jaw. The cop staggered.

Johnny leaped between them.

“I’ll have your balls for this. Dickhead.”

"Clam the hell up, partner," Walsh said.

"It's cool. Copacetic." Johnny said as he elbowed Taylor out of range.

"Her clothes, Johnny," Taylor said. "Check out what she's wearing. She was going to The Way."

"No."

"Yeah, she was. For you. She was doing it for you, Johnny, so you wouldn't lose your shit-scrape job." Heat's wild locks mixed with the muck of the recent storms.

"Told her not to."

"B F-ing D. You wanted the story. She knew that. It's the one thing in your life that meant anything to you." Taylor knocked Johnny on his ass. Eye-fucked him. Dropped the Nikon in his lap and stalked away.

Johnny cradled the camera.

On Wilcox, the Hoods, in their tracksuits, rested against the red Cadillac.

CHAPTER 55

"Get her packaged and wrapped. Slap on a bow and let's ship her." CC Rademaker drummed her biceps and stood over Heat. "Get swoop and scoop in here." A coroner's investigator scurried to the street.

"We ain't even near quittin'," Morales said.

"This one's a cinch. Paint-by-numbers," the ME said.

Johnny remained on his butt in the muck, slacks saturated. A criminalist bumped him and plucked evidence. The crime scene revived and resumed its pace. A heavy woman dragged a gurney. Johnny obstructed her access. She toed him and said, "Shake it, sunshine."

He stood.

Heavy and her co-worker, a skinny man who cultivated a sorry excuse of a wispy mustache and goat-tee, bypassed Johnny. *LA COUNTY CORONER FORENSIC SERVICES* was printed on their navy-blue coveralls. The racket of solid, rubber wheels on uneven, cracked cement ceased when they reached Heat.

Skinny squeezed a lever on the metal stretcher. Lowered it to six inches above the pavement. There was no mattress, just cold stainless steel, a black, vinyl square and a clipboard. The pick-up team snapped on latex gloves. Skinny wrote boxy letters on a red, 3x5 inch tag and looped its elastic band on Heat's right, big toe. He unfurled the vinyl into a body bag and unzipped it. "On three," he said and grabbed Heat's ankles. "One, two..." Heavy raised the shoulders and lifted. "Three."

Johnny fought bile as Heat's head fell back and her chin sagged. Heavy's grip loosened and she dumped the body on the gurney.

"Careful. Don't bruise the fruit," Rademaker said.

Heavy elevated the gurney waist-high. Heat's arms dangled. They were streaked with grime. Skinny slid them in the vinyl bag, then pressed on Heat's knees and straightened her legs. He tucked in the red hair and pulled the zipper from feet to face.

"Hot cargo comin' through," Heavy said. She pushed the gurney out of the alley. Hit a pothole. The bag jiggled.

Johnny's lips quivered. He swabbed snot as he trailed Heat.

Morales tried to snag the camera strap. "Give me that."

Walsh restrained him. Showed her phone. "We got this."

On Wilcox, away from the crush, Skinny huffed and puffed as he and Heavy loaded Heat in the rear of an official van parked behind the police SUVs. They secured her and shut the doors. Reflective letters spelled *Los Angeles County Department of Coroner.*

Johnny stared at the meat wagon. Heat was in there. Heat. Devastated, he didn't understand his feelings. He'd known her since August – four months - but she was a first. Not <u>the</u> first - they'd never even kissed. But the first living person to stir his emotional pot.

Taylor's van hadn't moved. Johnny's spirits ticked up a fraction as he scooted to the passenger side and opened the door. "Hey," he said, but the vehicle was empty except for Heat's textbook. Disappointed, he scanned the spectators. No Taylor. Not in the immediate vicinity. Johnny did, however, locate him on Wilcox, hunched, hands in pockets, walking towards Hollywood Station. Johnny also thought he recognized a vintage Caddy, its driver bird-dogging Taylor. The car shadowed the photographer until he reached the cop shop's public entrance. As he disappeared inside, the big old car executed a U-turn and braked in front of the bail bonds place.

Taylor surprised the lobby officer as he entered the stairwell. His heavy foot-falls echoed until he arrived at the second floor and entered the squad room.

Two detectives laughed at a joke and nodded.

The Brunette made a production of buffing his nails with an emery board. His wardrobe selection was an interpretation of a perky suburban mom set for a round of golf—pink polo shirt and an apple-green skirt. He noticed Taylor. Shot him a look. Bad vibes.

Taylor plopped in his chair. Searched his top drawer for the photos of Emma. Found them. Remembered the laughter and the caresses.

Lieutenant Hoffman sat his hefty ass on T's desk. Taylor fidgeted, shuffled the pictures and contemplated the ceiling. "I've been shooting pictures of the dead for a while.

War mostly." The LT let him crawl out that branch all by his lonesome. "But nobody I knew. Not really." He deflated. "Sure, some of the soldiers were battle buddies, but you can't get too friendly."

Hoffman nodded and ambled to his office without a word.

CHAPTER 56

"We have a stiff," Jolly Duncan announced on the public-address system. "Theater Row. Wanna-be Hollywood." He pointed at each staffer and wiggled his brows. "Eeny, meeny, miney..."

Mass, Captain Showbiz and Panther, leaned forward. All coveted a murder and the by-line. The usual, ho-hum, police-blotter write-ups bored them to sleep, not to mention ad time. Madam Speaker refused to participate in Duncan's nonsense, and Blitz didn't unless victim or perpetrator donned a jersey with a number and smashed a ball or a puck for bucks.

"Okay," Duncan said. He appeared to weigh individual pros and cons as he pursed his lips and tapped them with a pencil. He grinned, ready to announce his choice. The front door opened. The process paused. The Chief's eyes narrowed. Anger bubbled. "I gave you the heave-ho."

Johnny walked in, head down, clutching his fedora. His blood-sprinkled coat hung open.

"What happened to you, baby?" Panther said.

Duncan charged into the newsroom. "You're arse is grass." The sight of Johnny's muddy clothes slowed him and shut his mouth.

"Chief." Johnny wadded his hat and cleared his throat. "The D. B.? On Theater Row?" He strained to hide his grief. "I, uh... I was there." Summoned all his strength and fortitude. "It's Heat."

No reactions for a second, two, three...

"The fuck?" Mass said.

Panther gasped. Gushed tears. Speaker leaped to her feet. Showbiz sobbed. Duncan froze. The fog of shock rolled in.

Mass grabbed a classic .38-Special from his bottom drawer. Spun the cylinder. "Who did it?"

"That's why I'm here. To figure it," Johnny said.

"Me, I'm going huntin'." Mass waved his weapon.

"Pump the brakes," Madam Speaker said. "Before anybody goes off the rails, let's do our thing. Jolly?" Duncan didn't respond. "Chief!"

"Uh, yeah," Duncan said. "Uh, new lede means new cover art, so suck it up and jump on it. Mass. On point. Panther, cops. Captain..."

"I'll do it," Johnny said.

"You're toast."

"I saw it. Saw Heat."

"No is no, Harvard."

"Sure it was her?" Mass said.

"No wiggle room. Not a dime's worth." Hope vaporized. "It's... It's..." If Johnny spoke her name, it might be less painful. "Heat's…" Nope. Worse. "She's connected to the model piece and The Way. It's..." he hesitated. "It's my Big Story."

"For real?" Madam Speaker said.

"For real. And it's breaking."

In normal circumstances, the team would sing his praises with congrats and attaboys. Instead, they bounced their eyes from Johnny to Jolly.

Johnny hardened his gaze on the Chief. "Been working this forever. I will report it, with or without you."

Duncan snorted and snarled. Wanted to kick the crap out of him but settled for, "Yeah, yeah, yeah," and exposed a rare hint of compassion. "One-time offer. Standard free-lance rate."

"Deal." But Johnny took no pleasure in the gig.

"And considering the circumstances, I'm willing to break the rules. Once. You can park your arse at your old spot and take advantage of all our resources." He ducked into his sanctuary and closed the blinds.

"So generous," Mass said.

"Heard you…"

Johnny dropped into Heat's seat, resigned to grim reality.

"It's truly the Baby Doll thing?" Madam Speaker said.

"Yeah," Johnny said.

"So now what?" Panther said.

"We report and get it all down."

"You okay for that?"

He nodded at *TCLA's* crazy collection of writers. "Since I was nine."

Speaker rose, then Captain Showbiz. Even Blitz. Mass got to his feet and spun his revolver's cylinder again. Panther stood and saluted.

"It's yours," Speaker said.

This "how" wasn't the stuff of Johnny's dreams, but the "what" was. He cleared his throat. "Mass? Point. Panther? Police. Captain, The Way. I dug up pretty good material. I'll zap it to you ASAP. Blitz rides the desk. Everything funnels to Madam Speaker. She'll assign sidebars."

"And you?" Panther said. She knew. They all did but needed reassurance he had enough in the tank.

"I follow her," he said. "Heat."

CHAPTER 57

"He gave me a gun," CC Rademaker sang. She was loud and on-key. Dressed in violet scrubs, she pranced in her cold, fluorescent-bright autopsy suite. In each corner, she struck a match and lit the belly of a ceramic Buddha incense burner.

Forensic Services delivered a body in a bag belted to a mortuary stretcher. Heavy unbuckled the safety straps, ran the zipper and slipped her hands beneath pale shoulders. Her rail-thin partner grasped the ankles. "Uno, dos, tres," she said. They dragged the corpse onto the table and placed the feet on the down-slope. The metal slab was canted for drainage. "Bye-bye, now," she said to the ME and wandered away with a wave.

Skinny bobbed his bones to the tune. "Later, doc."

Heavy gave him a look. "You like that music?"

"Oh yeah. White soul."

Alone, Deputy Medical Examiner Rademaker reveled in the solitude of her domain. She tossed convention and decorum, grabbed the overhead mic, bopped and sang. "Poured me some wine..." Hummed the rest and pushed the mic boom towards the ceiling. Lit an incense stick, stuck it between the third and fourth toes of Heat's left foot, hiked the volume and swayed to the beat.

Heat lay tits up, face smeared with grime, locks filthy and matted. Rademaker removed Heat's muddy jacket but didn't tag it as evidence. She pitched it in a trash can and reached to her twelve-by-sixteen instrument tray. Fingers brushed a variety of scalpels, scissors, forceps, rib spreaders, hypodermic needles, coiled tubes of various lengths and widths and even a Stryker - a high-powered buzz saw used to open skulls. She gripped it. Squeezed the trigger. Seventeen thousand RPMs screeched. Rademaker returned it and selected surgical scissors. She snipped the corset from cleavage to hips and watched Heat's breasts settle into a natural position. She clipped the skirt, tugged it clear of the body and flung it in the can.

Rademaker rested the blades on Heat's bare tummy. Smiled as she slid one under the waistband of the green tights, cut to the crotch, then down the right leg. Did the same with the left and peeled them off. She pulled the retractable shower, sprayed and washed the torso. Took particular care with the pelvic area. Rademaker cleaned Heat's appendages and combed her hair straight back. "So beautiful."

"Say again? Kind of loud in here," Johnny said.

Rademaker was ruffled by the interruption. She composed herself. "Beautiful. Her."

Johnny glimpsed Heat. He slumped, drew a breath, but struggled to regain his composure as he attempted to ignore her body. He focused on the Medical Examiner.

She recognized him. "Recycle whatever I said last time."

"Actually, I'm here to make the arrangements. Procure possession of her human remains."

"You're family?"

"Well, yeah."

"Day late and a shekel short, but great try. My gang here contacted next of kin. The system's all primed and ready."

"So that's it?"

"There's a lot of work for the living in the world of the dead." Bored, she sighed. "Here's the typical SOP. Take notes. I'm not repeating it. For starters, I do the slice and dice, then sew her up and she goes in the fridge. Meantime, we contact family, give them a to-do list and a bunch of mortuaries. Then, some drone comes in and measures her for a box. They dump her in a bag, cram her in a hearse or similar mode, and she's gone."

"To where?"

"North Pole. I do not care, long as she's processed on out."

"Can I observe?"

"What?"

"When you crack open the redhead."

"Sure." Rademaker selected a scalpel and held it as if it were an instrument of affection. She touched the flat, razor-sharp blade against Heat's jugular notch – the hollow at the base of her throat. She flipped the tool, nicked Heat's cleavage and drew a speck of blood. Johnny cringed as the droplet spread a bit and pooled.

He grabbed the ME's wrist. "Okay, okay." Stared hard, released her, and walked out.

CHAPTER 58

"There's my hunk-a-hunk a burnin' wood," Panther said as she rushed into the squad room. It was lunch. None of the five people present, which included the Brunette, paid attention to her, but Hoffman did.

Panther had chucked her usual brown slacks in favor of a pleated, burgundy mini and black tights. A gray silk blouse completed the ensemble. It revealed a fair amount of skin but no meaningful cleavage. She hurried past Taylor and made a bee-line for the Lieutenant. "Hola, Tree. Wanna chow down?" She smooched him.

Hoffman's pulse spiked as he peeked at his detectives.

"Coast is clear." She slipped into his office.

"And what brings you to our fine establishment, Miss Perez?"

Taylor watched as Panther paced and counted with her fingers. It was common knowledge among the troops that Cedar Tree lacked a significant other in favor of fuck buddies. The skinny Latina fit his type. Common interests, gallows humor, cop lingo. He tilted into her and talked. Or appeared to – his chin moved.

On the office side of the glass wall, Hoffman said, "And anyway, you have way more on our cases than I do."

"Let's explore. Shall we review?" Panther said. "Victims. There's your model, slash, porn star. Your up-and-coming Black actor dude. Your 'banger, and, sources whisper, maybe even two additional bodies courtesy of this guy. My little birdie also claims you've got a semi-Asian redhead news babe on ice. I'm especially curious about her, she being a work-sister and all."

Taylor aimed his phone and snapped a couple pix of Panther and the Lieutenant as she conquered his personal space. LT's mouth flapped as she stroked his neck and played with his tie.

In the office, Panther said, "Four-plus months undercover? That's a while."

"'Specially how he does it." He eyeballed the Brunette. "He's scary good. At the infiltration."

"And info wise?"

"Sketchy."

"He holding out?"

"Nope. Targets are pros. Sullivan's hitting all the notes, but the targets are twitchy. Bosses downtown are checking their watches and Homicide Special's sniffing our butts. The thing's picking up a stink that reminds me of an old-time fix, but so far, it's all fart, no shit."

"There's a headline. 'All Fart. No Shit.' But, sadly, *True Crime LA* is a family publication, so feed me, Tree."

"Your work-sister breaks the pattern."

"So say your sleuths."

"Yep." He leaned on the edge of his desk.

Panther sashayed closer. Had she managed even a B-cup, she'd have grazed his chest. That piqued her curiosity about enhancement. But Cedar Tree enjoyed it. Yes, he did.

Panther toyed with his necktie. "My compadres speculate our reporter-sister is actually a fairly sizeable chunk of your bruhaha. Trappings and seasonings are a bit diff, but she's part of the serial."

"Doctor Death respectfully disagrees, and you know her. Long and Short are also singing the same song. Location, position of the deceased. Textbook OD. We ever recover T's camera, you'll see."

Panther frowned disbelief, then kissed Hoffman – not a peck, but a full-on lip-lock. She patted LT's ass, skipped out of his office and glided to the photographer. Hand on a hip, her movements were smoother as she sat next to him and crossed her legs. "Stunning stems, wouldn't you say?"

"Hubba, hubba," Taylor said.

"I'm honoring Heat."

"She'd be proud."

The elevator dinged. Walsh and Morales stepped out and strode to Taylor. They snubbed Panther.

"Need to talk, T," Walsh said. She and Morales flanked him. No "hiya" or "how are ya," to Panther. Just a nod at the hall. "'Scuse us." Walsh led Taylor away. Nobody noticed. The Brunette wrote on a legal pad. Another D read her computer screen. Three were huddled in quiet conversation. Hoffman hung a photo and added to his collection.

Walsh, Taylor and Morales entered Interrogation. She slid a metal chair from under the scratched and gouged government-issue table. "Sit."

He ignored her order and remained standing. "This again?"

Walsh created a racket as she sat, arms and elbows on the tabletop. It was sticky.

Morales scowled. "You forced us to shoot the stiff with cells."

Taylor bristled. "Her name's… Screw it." Not worth the aggravation.

"Wonder how a defense lawyer'll spin that?"

"I'm in here 'cuz you had to improvise?"

"Come on, T, when'd you morph into a schmuck?" Walsh said.

"About a minute after you did."

"Fill me in on your catch-of-the-day.

"Catch-and-release."

"Whatever. Who is he and where can I find him?"

"Johnny Lincoln and not a clue."

"Geezus, T, going after you sucks." Walsh jumped to her feet.

"But it's only business, right?" Taylor didn't disguise his cynicism.

"Hell no, it isn't. You're family."

CHAPTER 59

"Head 'em up. Move 'em out," CC Rademaker said. She circled a finger in the air and dodged early-a.m. rain. The Deputy ME commanded the loading dock of the three-story, early twentieth-century pile of bricks that was home and headquarters for the Los Angeles County Department of the Medical Examiner and Coroner. She clutched paperwork and sipped steamy coffee from a mug decorated with a cartoon silhouette of a sprawled corpse.

"Damn all." She didn't have a free hand to sign a form or take a packet thrust at her by a tall girl. Woman. Whatever. Couldn't have been more than twenty. Rademaker clamped a clipboard between her knees and snatched a pen offered by the youngster. The ME scrawled her autograph and exchanged it for a full, number ten-sized envelope. "Light a fire, kiddo. It's Santa night and they're circling the ranch." It was Christmas Eve dawn. Thirty hearses and vans were nose-to-ass. Engines idled as they lined up for a slot to load and transport LA's pre-holiday fatality surge.

"Aye, aye," the courier said. She dropped the paper into the pocket of a starched cotton lab jacket. "This it?" But didn't wait for a reply. She pulled, then pushed and maneuvered a gurney that carried a lumpy body bag to the rear of a hearse. Steel legs folded and the contents quivered as she rammed the litter into the back, lowered and latched the door. "See you on the flip side."

"You don't have enough miles on you to know what a flip side is." Rademaker lifted the envelope flap, breathed the aroma of an inch-thick bundle of hundred-dollar bills and said to the assembled drivers, "Keep rolling. Santa's on his way."

At the morgue's main gate, Miss Edna loitered and watched the parade of vehicles. She sported a yellow slicker and a jaunty red beret shielded by a transparent, plastic umbrella. She perked up. Thumbed digits into her phone. It rang once. "Got one coming at you from here," she said. "Nazi station wagon. Kind of gets you to ponder who won the war."

"Black Mercedes?" Johnny said.

"Ain't you paying any mind?"

"Sure it's her?" Johnny cooled his jets on Mission Road in East LA's Boyle Heights. He saw the massive county hospital behind the cupula of the coroner's building.

"Should be bearin' down on ya. See it?"

"Affirmative."

"Anything hinky?"

"Nada." The windows were tinted. Johnny couldn't ID anyone as the wagon drove by.

"Any funeral home on it?"

"Nope."

"Exactly."

Johnny watched the hearse approach an on-ramp to the I-5 / Golden State Freeway. A Metro Orange arrived. He boarded, tapped his fare card but didn't sit. He grabbed a pole and kept his eyes on the hearse as it passed the freeway entrance, drove the perimeter of a train yard, and turned onto Cesar Chavez Avenue. He lost sight of it. "Goddammit."

The driver shot him a scold.

"Sorry. Trying to tail that car up there."

"On here? Give yourself a kudo."

"But I need to catch the Sunset bus. I'll get off at your next stop."

She braked, slowed to an unscheduled halt below an overpass and opened the doors. "Best to you."

"Appreciate it." Johnny hopped to the curb, hurried around potholes to the intersection of Mission and Chavez and ducked under the bus-shelter roof. He no longer saw the Mercedes. Pressed numbers on his phone.

CHAPTER 60

"Showbiz. Job for you," Madam Speaker said. The newsroom crew was harried but subdued, not their usual loud and crazy, then Mass bellowed.

"No? Did I hear *no?* Baby Doll's KAs, instantly, or I promise I'll pop you like a ripe zit. I swear a solemn oath I'll be there before we hang up." He tucked his phone between right cheek and shoulder and typed. "Look at you, Boob-a-loo. Cooking with gas."

The hippie vendor lugged her heavy wheelie box to Heat's desk. She kissed a single red rose and laid it beside a bouquet.

Jolly Duncan hid in his office, glued to *Capital Crime*, his Washington, DC counterpart.

Blitz ignored them all. Clicked email, fidgeted, answered his line. "Sports Crimes." Listened. Offered a few, "Uh-huhs," and, "Thanks. Appreciate it." Relieved, he hung up, snatched his gym gear and beat a path to the exit.

"Get your slappy ass back here," Captain Showbiz said.

"New story."

"Only have the one."

"Shit-can him," Mass said as he aimed his pistol.

"Snip his scrote." Panther pantomimed scissors.

"Love to." Madam Speaker glowered at Blitz and transmitted a message. He received it with a cringe and increased his speed to the door. Speaker shifted her eye fuck to Jolly Duncan in his office. Made sure he saw her rip a page from a pad and wave it at Showbiz. "Go here. Poke the bear. I'll guarantee he pays you gas money." She hollered,

"Right, Chief?"

At Mission and Chavez, Johnny paced in the west-bound shelter. Rain pounded. He checked for messages. None. Typed and sent a text. Finally, a bus appeared. Onboard, Johnny did a visual out the windshield. His target was history.

Captain Showbiz, parked and idling in the *TCLA* lot, aimed his pristine, green Toyota Corolla at Sunset Boulevard. The wipers swept. Traffic flowed on wet pavement. A bottled-water truck pulled into the mini-mall. The tires of a giant, red Rapid gushed plumes of spray as it lumbered past. The Captain wondered if Johnny was a passenger. A Mercedes hearse was close behind. It bore no logo or signage to indicate a specific mortuary, which fit Miss Edna's description. Nothing inside was visible.

He looped a bluetooth into an ear. "Testing, testing."

"Receiving you loud and clear." Panther said.

"Objective acquired." Showbiz secured his seat belt and zoomed onto the Boulevard.

Nineteen minutes later, Johnny disembarked at Murder Burger. His coattails fluttered in the wind, and he held his hat as he hustled towards HQ. At the Mongol Horde, he changed his mind. Tried the door. Locked. Knocked.

Genghis, in street clothes, unlocked and bowed. "Ho, ho, ho, Mr. Johnny. What shakin'? Not food yet. It's ten in a.m. A hour, maybe."

"Can I hang?"

"Oh sure. Every-ting A-okay?"

Johnny nodded and sat in the unofficial *True Crime* booth.

"Miss Heat? She coming?"

"No." Smartphone on the table, he squared his notebook, hauled a crumpled copy of the coffin serpent, a pen and the police-band scanner out of pockets. He inserted the earbud above his left lobe.

Genghis delivered a mug filled to the brim. He knew Johnny drank it straight, so no sugar, cream or spoon. "Tell me you want any-ting," he said, and returned to the kitchen.

"Thanks." A sip and a sigh. Elixir of life. He took a bigger swallow and neared ready. Stacked a collection of business cards, plucked one, glanced at it and set it aside. Perused five more front and back. Drank again and assessed the seventh - a glammed-up portrait of a woman. It was the Leave-It-To-Beaver MILF from his earlier trip to The Baths. Beneath her chin was "Mama's" and a "323" number. A Los Angeles County area code. One of fourteen. He studied her. Remembered details of the night with Taylor and Heat. Beyond the Le Roux mess, the fire, chase and gunfight, no ideas or theories hit him. Sure, all those crisscrossed and a few even connected, but not all. He'd exhausted his leads. Johnny drummed a pen, contemplated "Mama's" info, and called. He listened. Pushed an icon, followed instructions and touched "!" and "%" on a virtual keypad. Spelled his name and e-mail on the keyboard and pressed "send." A gulp of coffee later, the notification vibrated.

His excitement at a response ebbed when he read an address that did not compute. Well, most of it did. He knew where it was and its function. He'd been there. The letter "B" after the numbers stumped him. It indicated a secondary unit. He input a web search for info and images. An expected, familiar location showed, but not a unit "B."

Johnny gathered his things and dropped three singles. "Thanks, Genghis."

"Almost lunch."

CHAPTER 61

"You are done. Finito," Lieutenant Hoffman said as he stormed into Interrogation. He glared at Long and Short and heaved his bulk forward. "What'd you do, T?"

Walsh slumped. "He knew..."

"Didn't ask you."

"I knew this morning's DB," Taylor said.

"Oh?" Surprised, Hoffman's eyes drilled Walsh. "His knowing the deceased in any way, shape or form impact your work?"

"Unh unh."

"Not an answer, detective."

"No, sir, it did not."

"Does T's previous contact with the victim add to your investigation? Subtract from it? Make it easier? Harder?"

"Yes, no, no and no."

"Watch it."

"You asked." But Walsh knew she had one foot over the line, and the other was on it. A cartoon banana peel came to mind.

"Mr. Quigley the Third. With me."

Taylor scooted his chair and tossed a nasty scowl at Walsh.

"Had to, T, she said.

"No, you did not," Hoffman said. "I hate cop-on-cop." He was offended, not angry.

"Wasn't cop-on-cop," Morales said. "He never raised his right hand."

"Oh yeah?" Taylor lunged. "Where the fuck were you when I was pushing troops and dodging bullets in the sandbox? Tucked under your blankies? All warm and comfy?"

The Lieutenant snared Taylor's collar. "Settle, T." Snarled at his detectives. "He's family. You two screwed the balance." T's excursion with Johnny and subsequent trip to Interrogation threw a wrench into the well-oiled tempo of Hollywood Division Detectives. In the military, it was designated "unit cohesion." Hoffman shepherded Taylor past Morales and out.

In the squad room, Panther appropriated Taylor's space. She chattered on her cell, "Can I quote you?" Wrote fast, fist-pumped, and ended the call as LT and the photographer arrived. "Ahh, Sherlock and Watson." Neither acknowledged her. "Dynamic duo?" Taylor motioned for his seat. "Frosty," Panther said. "Mamacita never begat no dummy." She surrendered the spot and sat her ass on the desk. Showed off her legs. Flexed her feet and ankles. "Who's gonna volunteer to dig data for me?"

"Shhhhhh..." The LT peeked at his people. Safe, he sighed and gestured to Taylor.

"Me? You sure?"

"Sure he's sure. You're not in the brotherhood of blue, and I'm not distracted by that pesky constitution." She handed Taylor her Reporter's Notebook.

He clicked on his computer screen and input a license plate number. As the relevant facts showed, Taylor, Panther and Cedar Tree leaned in.

"Damn," they said in unison.

"Yeah, ditto damn," Panther said. "Plate comes back to a prop house?" She scribbled the DMV data, air-kissed and headed to the elevator.

Hoffman watched. "She's even got shake and jiggle. Not a lot, but enough."

Panther winked at him.

"Who knew?" The LT smiled and confronted reality. "Thought you upped and quit."

"Define 'quit.'" Taylor said.

"In or out. No dry-humping the LAPD."

"I'll take a personal day."

"But you don't spend it here."

"Give me a minute to retrieve some stuff, then I'll go to the beach." He typed.

"Planning to sit under a lifeguard tower and count waves?"

"Snowflakes." Taylor jotted the results of his search.

"Hows about tracking down my camera?"

"Yours?"

"Yes, mine. My ass is almost in a sling. You don't find that camera, bosses'll chew my butt from here to hell and beyond. That happens, I put your tantrum in a report. That happens..."

"Yeah, yeah, yeah."

CHAPTER 62

"Forty-eight. Extra-long," Johnny said. He was in a men's formal-wear shop.

"Yes, you are." The MILF he'd met at The Baths inspected Johnny. Soggy fedora, scorched, blood-spattered clothes. She uttered a non-committal, "Um, um, um," stroked the gauze bandage that wrapped his neck and creased bold, vermilion lips into a sly grin.

Johnny blushed. The petticoated, fifties TV-mom was ancient history, replaced by a film-noir femme fatale. Black and white impressions of Lauren Bacall and Veronica Lake flooded his mind. But in his live, HD world, shiny tresses puffed and tumbled into blonde clouds that grazed the padded shoulders of a charcoal-gray suit. The skirt hem skimmed the tops of her knees. The fitted jacket revealed tanned skin and magnificent lady curves. No blouse, one button.

He coughed. "I'm thinking it's possible you can aim me in the right direction again."

"Already am." The MILF glided between a half-dozen mannequins exhibiting traditional black bow tie and cummerbund ensembles and the trendier floral tuxes in a variety of colors. Johnny riveted his eyes to her hypnotic rhythm of grace and seduction. Stocking seams climbed from the heels of crimson, open-toe pumps, ran the length of her calves, and vanished beneath her skirt. He imagined the garter belt. Or thigh-highs? That was speculation for another time.

She gauged a row of tuxedos. Selected one. Held it next to Johnny. "Perfect."

"Why do I need a penguin suit?"

"If you've ever had one, you wouldn't ask."

"I've had one." Johnny was a tad defensive.

"Prom doesn't count." Busted. "It's okay." The MILF patted his cheek, beckoned with a finger and stepped deeper into the store. Her outfit clung to the gentle sweep of her hips, and she exuded easy confidence as she arranged the tux on top of a glass case.

Captivated, Johnny cleared his throat. "Heard of Baby Doll Getz?"

"Of course."

"She involved at The Baths?"

"I suppose she is."

"It's part of her biz? Her empire?"

The MILF paused at a display of patent leather shoes, both Oxfords and loafers. "Size?"

"Thirteen medium."

"Impressive. But I don't want you walking on bad luck. Let's bump you a size."

"Not superstitious."

"Extra never hurt."

She retrieved a red tape measure, sauntered across thick-pile carpet and stopped less than a foot from him. It wasn't an intrusion. To Johnny, it felt like an arrival. With trumpets.

She caressed his hand. "Long." Admired it.

He inhaled her perfume. Exquisite. Struggled to remember his manners as the MILF encircled his waist with the tape. He felt the swell of her breasts as she breathed. Johnny enjoyed the moment but was impatient. "Uhh… save ya a little effort."

"No effort. Believe me."

"Thirty-eight, thirty-four."

She scrutinized the numbers. "You are correct, sir." And released the tape. As it fell, she knelt, admired the view, and met Johnny's look. She anchored one end of the tape at a pant cuff. Watched his expression as she elevated the other along the inseam, past his ACL, to within a fingernail of nudging his package. Checked the result. "Bang-on. Thirty-four."

Johnny loved the fuss but resisted a variety of involuntary reactions. "I'm doing a story."

The MILF pouted.

"Co-worker died. Writing the obit."

"So sorry." She rose and swayed her ass to the tuxedo lying on the cabinet.

Johnny watched her. "I'll bite your bait. I'm not blind. I get that you're a bird dog. It was pretty obvious when we, uh, met. But for who? Baby Doll? Yourself? The Baths?"

"So many questions. I'm a yenta."

"Huh…?"

"Google it."

"Spell it."

She slid a folded formal shirt under the satin lapel of the jacket, the pleats and collar points visible. Found a bow tie – black, accented with tiny, multi-colored swooshes - and laid it on top. "Perfect."

"Nice."

"Just nice?" The MILF removed a burgundy vest from a wood hangar. "Tall guys do so much better in these." From behind, she helped him into it, leveled the shoulders, reached around to his front, and buttoned her way up. Left the bottom one undone. Johnny glimpsed his reflection in a full-length mirror. He approved. She fine-tuned straps to a comfortable fit and smoothed the fabric.

"Why all the dress-up gear?"

She flipped her hair. "Tonight's your night if you don't mind unwrapping your gifts on Christmas Eve. And your hot buddy, too. I pegged him as a forty-two-regular."

"Him? Why?"

"Mama's partial." She eased the vest off Johnny, placed it with the tuxedo and presented him an engraved invitation. "Nine o'clock. And hire a ride. You'll prefer to be unencumbered."

"How expensive?"

"For what?"

"To get in."

"It's Christmas."

Not convinced Mama was all-in on the truth, he asked, "And for the outfit?"

"Don't be silly. You're my guests."

"Or Getz's?" The MILF didn't respond. "And after I get my present?"

"You have to ask? Oh, darlin'…" She frowned sympathy.

"You ain't making sense." Johnny took the invite. Rubbed the letters.

The MILF slipped the vest, slacks, jackets and a cummerbund onto hangers and secured them in a garment bag. She set shirts in a sky-blue box. Gathered links and studs, neckwear, socks and shoes. "It'll last forever."

"What will?"

"This Christmas. The memory of it."

"When do you want all this brought back?"

"Midnight, Cinderella."

Johnny started to protest. She touched his lips. "At your convenience." Handed him everything. "Ta-ta for now. Don't want to dally."

"We'll see."

"And waste a perfect Christmas? Such a tragedy." She blew him a kiss and spelled, "y-e-n-t-a. Yenta."

Johnny draped the bag on a forearm and gripped the handles of a hemp sack. A block and two minutes later, he sat on a bus bench, annoyed he hadn't noticed The Baths and Mama's in the same building. Johnny quizzed himself. How'd he not figure it? No excuses, but the memories of his previous foray to the heart of Silver Lake were rain, fire and bullets. He eyed Unit B and pondered what the MILF meant. He Googled *yenta*. "Gossip?" Read further. That made a little more sense. It didn't mean what she thought it meant. She'd used the common American mistranslation. Match-maker. Ah. Dots connected. Tumblers fell. Recruiter. Even a procurer. Okay. A rough outline took shape. His cell rang.

CHAPTER 63

"Sucks," Mass said.

"That's Hollywood," Miss Edna said.

"But a prop house? Odd." Madam Speaker was on her feet, arms folded. She presided over the controlled chaos of the newsroom. Phones jangled, people talked and hammered keyboards. "Anybody tell Johnny? You?" She said to Panther.

"Says he has it and he's on it." She stood in front of Speaker.

"Showbiz on the horn," yelled Mass as he waved his phone and lit a smoke.

Madam Speaker turned and stabbed a blinking light on her touchtone. "You're on squawk."

A faint, unintelligible voice trickled out of a 40-year-old speakerphone. An obsolete Western Electric. The clunky case was a five-by-four, beige, hard-plastic rectangle with dull, aluminum mesh.

"Again." Speaker cupped her ears. Garbled words seeped. She struck her gavel twice. "Order. Order." The staff clammed. "Repeat."

"They… Heat…"

"Louder."

The Captain's report eeked from the system. "…transported Heat, if it is Heat, to the First National at H and H."

"Bells, anyone?"

"No." Panther and Mass said.

Miss Edna mused for a second. "Nope."

Even the sandwich vendor considered it. "Nada."

"El Jefe?" Panther said.

Duncan, cozy in his ergo chair, read *Manhattan Murder*.

"Tits on a boar," Miss Edna said.

"Limp dick."

"That doesn't contribute," Madam Speaker said.

Showbiz sounded distant and tinny as he attempted to hail his colleagues. "Hello? Hola? Come to the Captain."

"You sure Heat's there?" Speaker was bent over her desk, her mouth an inch from the box.

"No. Not sure. It's the location of the hearse. They disappeared into a garage, so can't confirm."

"Could you?"

"With the Eighty-second Airborne."

"Canvass the neighbors. Need backup?"

"Or do I <u>want</u> backup?"

Patience frayed, Speaker banged her forehead on the desktop. "Choose."

"I'm good."

"Keep us posted." She pressed "end."

Wheels marched in, followed by...

"Baby Doll Getz," Mass said. He stared in awe. "Damn."

Tall and stately in her black dress and pearls, Getz's five-inch heels tapped a staccato rhythm all the way to Mass. She locked her cold, blue eyes on his browns. Pin-drop silence as he trembled.

"Oh, cher... you do a story on me, if you do, it's Beatrice Dolores."

"Yes, ma'am. Absolutely. Never knew your real name."

"And now you do. You are?"

"Sorry. Mass. Mass Machado. So sorry."

"Ah yes. Serial killers." Getz offered her right hand.

"And multiple murders," he said. Flattered, Mass wiped damp palms on his pants and shook. "I covered some of your handiwork."

"Did you?" She squeezed.

He realized his mistake and bowed.

She released the shake and scanned left. "You are?"

"Panther. As in Pink."

"Ahh yes. Tech crimes. Computer scams. Very popular. You?"

"They call me Madam Speaker."

"All that political corruption." Getz was puzzled. "Don't y'all have more scribes?"

"Our entertainment correspondent is on assignment."

"Of course. Captain Showbiz. Bet he's busy."

"And there's our sports dude," Mass said. "But he bugged out. Schmuck."

"And the rookie," Speaker said. "He's somewhere doing something for somebody."

"Ahhh." Getz admired bouquets of lilies and roses on Heat's desk. "Someone get married?"

"Croaked," Mass said.

"Sorry for your loss." Rote. No emotion or interest as she turned a drawn-out three-sixty. She surveyed peeling paint, ancient furniture, and equipment.

Panther looked away.

Speaker contemplated the ceiling.

Getz knew her reputation. Reveled in the fear and tension it caused. She stopped, smiled, spread her arms and said, "Eddie. Been ages, cher. Merry, Merry."

Miss Edna blushed.

"Whoa." Mass was shocked.

Panther leaned forward to ensure she heard every syllable.

"Hey, Bea," Edna said with a finger wave.

Hey, Bea? Chutzpa or insanity? Staffers held their collective breath. Wondered if Edna had taken her last.

Getz wrapped Miss Edna in a bear hug. Baby Doll was half-a-head taller. Edna gave her a couple polite pats on the back.

Speaker and the crew were stunned.

Baby Doll clasped Miss Edna's scrawny biceps. "So fantastic to see you," she said.

Edna mustered a reluctant smile.

Duncan, alerted by the silence, closed the out-of-town rag. His curiosity vanished and his pulse sprinted when Miss Edna pointed at him and curtsied.

Baby Doll paraded into the Chief's office as if she owned it. He rose on shaky legs. She allowed him to absorb the moment. "Mr. Jolly Duncan, isn't it?"

"Yes, madam."

"Editor in Chief?"

"Yes."

"Nice to meet. Long time coming."

"Yes, madam. Pleasure."

Panther, Mass and Speaker whispered, "Can you hear? What're they talking about?"

Mass rolled his chair a foot. Bumped into Wheels, positioned in a fighting stance.

Getz walked behind Duncan. Ran a finger over his Pulitzer. "I'm a huge fan of *True Crime.*" She was delighted with the pun, but her killer eyes didn't brighten. "How could I not be? Eddie and I know each other since forever. Never miss an issue. Love putting faces to by-lines. Should've done it ages ago."

Duncan hid his hands. Perish the thought anyone noticed he was a white-knuckler. As if they wouldn't know. "Glad to be of assistance." His throat was pinched by fear. "Eddie?"

"Edna. Horowitz. Jack's wife. Jack…" Getz enjoyed a fond memory. "Me 'n Jack discovered… things."

Duncan peeked at Miss Edna. She shrugged an "oh well."

Baby Doll was pleased. She'd stirred the pot and spiced it with secrets. "Appreciate your hospitality."

The Chief hoped he wouldn't pee.

CHAPTER 64

"Douglas Street," announced the automated voice. The bus stopped. Johnny secured the tuxedos and shopping bag. He exited and paid no attention to the red light as he navigated four lanes of moderate, mid-afternoon traffic to the north side of Sunset. As he walked west, Johnny ran a list. Getz, The Way, the suicides, Heat. Especially Heat. A brief inventory long on questions.

Two blocks later, at Sutherland, he passed a squat, gray, booze and burger dive. Red, white and blue bunting hung over the entrance. A neon sign flashed *Shortstop*, the beacon of a sometimes famous joint. It had been a cop bar, was occasionally a post-game hangout for big-leaguers, and always a watering hole for baseball fans pouring out of nearby Dodger Stadium eighty-one games a season. More, if they made the playoffs. But three months of El Nino remained until Opening Day.

Johnny arrived at a smog-stained edifice. A seventy-year-old fire escape flanked by windows zig-zagged four floors down the front. If the rusty, rickety iron didn't crumble in a blaze or a quake, you'd need to swan dive the final ten feet to save the family jewels – if you were lucky.

He pulled a steel gate separating an *"Abogado"* from an *"Estetica."* His Spanish was rusty to non-existent. He'd researched the translations - a lawyer and a female-grooming salon.

The gate banged, Johnny entered and climbed a flight. Dark. That was normal. Hallway bulbs were gone before he moved in. On the plus side, the summer stink was absent. December chill masked the piss-garlic-and-boiled-cabbage aroma that assailed him when he rented the place in August. He reached a door. Johnny was never sure of the color, but there were scuffed and gouged remnants of glossy brown and beige. He balanced his load and found keys. Jammed one in a shiny new lock.

"Let's talk," Taylor said, shrouded in shadow.

Johnny neither reacted nor acknowledged as he unlocked, flipped a switch with an elbow, and lit a small studio apartment. The room was painted in the ever-popular egg-shell.

"This the deluxe pad? With a pisser and shower?"

Johnny crossed red, thread-bare carpet to a closet, hung the suit bag and set the hemp sack on the floor.

Taylor eyed a tidy kitchenette. Two-burner stove and a vintage, harvest-gold refrigerator. One clean dinner plate, a single glass and a knife, fork and spoon were on the counter. "So why the mystery?"

"No mystery."

The only decoration was a *Maltese Falcon* movie poster taped above a double bed. The one-sheet featured Bogey, the bird and Mary Astor. The bed was covered by an old quilt and a fluffed pillow. He also had a thrift-shop recliner and lamp.

"This the reason you don't tell people where you live? It's a dump, but hey."

"How'd you find me?"

"Seriously?" Taylor stepped to a battered, four-drawer, wood dresser. Nine locks mounted in 6 x 10 rectangles of wood were on the top. They ranged from residential to industrial. "You practice?" He examined one. Rotated it. Tested the mechanism. "For a house?"

"Office."

Taylor replaced it and turned towards a bulletin board that spanned the entire length of the place. Actually, three boards with two-hundred-fifty, pale pink, blue, yellow and green index cards pinned to them. Johnny tried to obstruct Taylor's view.

"Cut the secrets. Level with me, Scoop."

Johnny cringed. Balled his fists. "I hate that." He weighed the odds of a physical confrontation. Taller, younger, more robust, he'd win, or so he thought. But Taylor was military-trained and a combat veteran. All the guy wanted was to lend a hand. Johnny conceded and allowed him a look.

Thirty-four vertical columns. Each represented a year, 1987 to PRESENT. Taylor read the top card in the first column. "New Orleans. Misdemeanor pandering. Eleven months. Suspended." He shifted to a green card in the next column - 1987. "Seen Port-au-Prince." Then a yellow. "Nineteen ninety. Still Haiti. Est."

"Establishes," Johnny said.

"Noted. Establishes casino and brothel catering to cruise lines. Ninety-five, returns to NOLA. Disappears for eight months." Taylor scrutinized the board. "This is a history of the contemporary sex trade."

"Yes."

"Prostitution, porn, human trafficking." He leaned in. "Holy crap. For real?"

"Which one?"

Taylor thumped a knuckle on a card. "The government of U…"

Johnny cut him off. "Yeah. And it ain't the only one."

"And these?"

"What do they say?"

"Big-time Corporate America."

"A-k-a Wall Street."

"They're all in it together? I'll scratch yours's if you'll scratch mine?"

"Pretty much. Check the next column."

Taylor did. "Don't recognize them."

"Hedge funds. Invested in the distribution companies. Sheltered, off-shore, Cayman Islands-type firms with Swiss bank confidentiality. That's where her stash of cash is."

"Computer streaming?"

"No. That's chump change to them. Loss-leaders."

Taylor continued to absorb the info on the board. "Sick and twisted. You'd have to be involved to make sense of it as a business. Product arrived. Product value. Product transferred. Product shipped. Explain."

"Distribution and price."

"I got that much. Tell me the real product."

Johnny had never discussed any of it.

"You dragged me into it. Sold it to me as my ticket back. I'd like to know. I deserve to know."

"You said it a minute ago."

Taylor shrugged. "Remind me."

Johnny mused. Talk or not? Two heads, yada-yada, BS, BS. "Human traffic. Kids. Mostly girls. Some early teens sprinkled in. A few boys."

Taylor grimaced. "Isn't that the Russian mob?"

"They work for Getz. Told you that."

"What's your part in it?"

"It's the Big Story," Johnny said.

"Baby Doll?"

"Yeah."

Taylor inspected the cards. "Two-thousand one."

"After nine-eleven. When nobody was paying attention."

Taylor continued. "Relocates to LA. Bankrolls Indian Casino. Oh-two – Buys First Nat building. Purchases porn studios. Porn retail stores. Makes them female-friendly. Controls production and distribution." Johnny's notations and comments detailed a contemporary form of lurid, perverted, indentured servitude with no hope for the victims. "I get it. It's great journalism. But why? You nursing a death wish?"

"'No. Because it is great. Better than great. It's Aces. She's Aces. Cornered an entire industry. Wrapped it, slapped her name on it and keeps laughing all the way to the bank. Or wherever she piles her fortune."

"So her being an evil, murdering bitch hasn't got anything to do with it?"

"For character development, sure. It's great punch-up. But this..." Johnny gestured. "Pure evil. Perversions for profit. Production, clubs, porn palaces. But they're all teasers. Appetizers. The real deal? She feeds the kiddie shit, then the kids, to the sickos who possess all the money and power. They buy and protect. That's the story."

"So her blowing Le Roux's brains all over us is character development? You're so full of it." Taylor opened the '70s-era refrigerator and peered in. Empty. "Nothing to drink, Scoop?"

"Don't."

"How come? All you do is dig in it." Taylor slammed the fridge. "Level for once."

Johnny indicated the cards. "It's all there."

"Those? Fine and dandy. You've done your legwork, but stuff's missing."

"Such as?"

A silent stand-off. Five seconds. Ten.

Taylor blinked. "The 'why.' Don't you have feelings for all of this?" He shook a fist at the columns. "Or about Heat?"

That dented Johnny's armor. "Monday through Sunday." Didn't say that he wondered what the hell had possessed her to hook up with Taylor.

"Fooled me."

"You decided I ought to wear black for the dead?"

"Yeah."

"Life goes on. Get used to it." Johnny removed a tuxedo from his closet.

"Did I mention you are one cold son of a bitch? It's a game to you, isn't it?"

"No."

"Sure it is. Got a board." Taylor poked the cork. "Pieces. So who wins? Most cards?" Flicked one. "Whoever's alive on New Years? Eliminates Heat." Hollered, "You do get we're down to the short strokes, don't you, Scoop?"

Johnny ambled to Taylor and held the tux jacket shoulder-high. "She had you pegged."

Taylor glared, then heard a silly ring tone. Hiccups.

The tension amped as Johnny answered. "Go. Yeah. Uh-huh, uh-huh. I'll text it." As he listened, he tossed the tuxedo at Taylor. It hit the side of the bed and fell in a heap. Taylor scooped it up but was sidetracked when he spotted a textbook in a circle of lamplight. A photo was wedged in it. He flung the clothes on the bed and scanned the tome.

Johnny was engaged on his phone. "You sure?" He said and kicked off his shoes.

Taylor turned to the page marked by the picture. It was one of his - the serpent symbol on the coffin lid - side-by-side with an illustration. They matched. He read the description and the book's title.

The Mysteries of Voodou

"Copy that." Johnny remembered to add, "Thanks," and ended the call. "Time to pin on your diapers, tough guy."

Taylor shut the book. "Damballah?"

CHAPTER 65

"How's about them Dodgers?" Miss Edna said. She wadded a lace hanky and rubbed her cheeks.

"No. Unh unh. None of your sweet, little old biddy-bitch act anymore," Panther said. She made a fist and cocked an arm.

Miss Edna dropped into Johnny's chair. Panther, Madam Speaker and Mass loomed above her.

Duncan relaxed against his office door and folded his arms. He forced back a grin, causing his lips to twitch.

"So... What do you want to hear?" Edna said.

The front entrance opened to street noise. "Hi, all," Captain Showbiz said. He hurried to his desk. Noticed his associates were miffed and had Miss Edna surrounded. "She finally flash her boobs?" No one laughed. "Guess not." He hung his blazer on a coat rack. "She's too old to sell and too skinny to rent. Right, Miss E?"

"She's pals with Baby Doll Getz," Mass said.

The statement froze Showbiz. It took him a couple beats to process. "Pals?"

"Yeah," Panther said. "Apparently, for decades."

"Gi-normus. How'd you hear that?"

"She was here."

"Who was here?"

"Baby Doll."

"No..." Showbiz was shocked beyond shocked.

"Missed a boffo performance," Madam Speaker said.

"Yes indeedie-do," Mass said.

"Hugs. Even smooches," Panther recounted. She eyed Miss Edna. "Long-lost asshole buddies. Right 'Eddie?'"

"Like sorority sisters."

"Yeah. We were. Buddies, not the other," Edna said. She tried to roll out of the line of fire. Mass blocked her with his gut.

"Spill," Speaker said. "Johnny's flying blind."

Edna peeked at Panther for a rescue. Instead, Panther said, "Anything happens to him? It's all on you, old lady. Don't wanna bury Johnny, too."

"Enough! Jeez…" Miss Edna wrung her hanky and began her tale. "Okay. My late, great hubs, Jack, Jack Horowitz, who none a you had the pleasure, rest his soul and feed it pastrami. Jack and Bea were doing the deed before he met me. His *Times-Picayune* days. He's the one dubbed her 'Baby Doll.' In his stories. It stuck."

"Bea?" Captain Showbiz said. "You addressed the crime queen of LA as Bea?"

"To her face, yeah," Panther said.

"And you aren't pushing up daisies? Buy a lottery ticket. Tonight."

Miss Edna had no desire to engage or explain but gained motive as the angry staff closed in for the kill. "Okay, okay. Bea came here, to LA, after me and Jack did, and reached out. We'd bought *TCLA,* so we knew her competition. Wrote about them almost every week and she couldn't exactly go to the cops for a briefing, so we kinda became her tip sheet. And we played some. Bea threw huge shindigs."

"So the rumors are accurate?" Mass said.

"What rumors?"

"You own the rag."

"How often you hear me say I own the joint?"

"Lots, but..."

"No buts. You're a reporter," Edna activated an atrophied editor's muscle.

Mass flared red as he revved from angry to ballistic.

"You aware of all this?" Madam Speaker said to Duncan. He nodded. "And you never told Johnny?"

"You never told us," Panther said. "Not a hint or an FYI."

"It was need-to-know," Duncan said.

"Seems a tad CIA-ish," Showbiz said.

"And you…" Panther was ready to throttle Edna. "I hold you personally responsible."

"Heard you already," Edna said.

"For Heat, and for Johnny."

"Y'all kept on about how it was best he learn on his own."

"Learn, not die."

Miss Edna's chin quivered as she eyed the cement floor. "I wrote the biography on Bea. Literally. Saw…" Shuddered. "Saw shit that'd make ol' Q-ball sprout hair. It sold, too. The paperback. But left a pile of bodies, if you get my drift, on the cutting room floor. No choice. You understand."

"Should've filled us in. Especially Johnny," Speaker said.

"Especially Heat," Mass said. Memories slammed. He yanked a piece of paper from a binder and blew his nose. Panther wiped a tear.

"But 'Eddie' here, can't make it better, can you? She did what she did, or in this case, what she didn't do. So maybe…" Speaker cleared her throat. "So maybe there's a tidbit you remember that can help."

"Not recalling."

"Useless," Mass complained.

"Come on," Panther said.

Madam Speaker seized Edna's arms and challenged her nose-to-nose. "Think."

"A blank's a blank," Edna said.

Speaker squeezed. Had an idea. "Where were the, uh, shindigs, 'Bea' threw?"

Miss Edna snuffed. Wiped her nose with a hankie. "Garbutt Mansion. Top of Hathaway Hill."

"That's her place?" Mass said.

CHAPTER 66

"Voo-doo?" Taylor said.

"Voo-dough," Johnny said. "Like bread dough."

They settled into the cushy back seats of a Town Car. Taylor cradled the book on his lap. Johnny babied a worn, brown vinyl briefcase on his.

Tuxed to the max, they wore the ensembles selected by the MILF. Stiff, white, pleated formal shirts, bow ties, onyx studs, and cuff links. Satin-lapel, shawl-collar jackets and slacks for both, with patent-leather loafers. A lot of black, except Johnny's burgundy vest.

"Why the briefcase?" Taylor said.

"Bargaining chips."

"Hand-crafted on a color laser printer?"

Johnny's reaction was a sharp look and several unasked questions.

"Heat briefed me."

"She tell you a lot?"

"I'm guessing all of it."

"Not possible."

"Welcome aboard," the driver said. "I'm Reggie." He had a squeaky voice. "And this is your chariot, your carriage, your magic carpet ride. But before we fly, need to process my gratuity." Skinny and sixtyish, he cultivated a wispy, salt-and-pepper beard and a gray rat tail. Nineteen-eighties aviator glasses hid his eyes.

Johnny protested. "Paid when I ordered."

"Paid your fare. We're talking about my tip. You'd do the same, you were me." He indicated Johnny's broken-down building.

Johnny whipped out his flash roll. Peeled off a couple twenties.

"No can do with the cash. See the sign on the back of my seat? Driver carries no cash? Your card's already in the system. It's hassle free."

Johnny wanted to haggle but changed his mind.

Reggie touched numbers on his smartphone and passed it back.

"Press the pound key to approve."

"Fifty?"

"Gotta eat."

"Invite me over." Johnny was disgusted but paid and returned the device.

"Okay then. All set." Reggie's high pitch was perfect for his scrawny frame. He put the Lincoln in gear and drove.

Taylor unbuttoned his collar. "Better."

They hit a rough patch of road. The book bounced. Taylor snagged it. "This, getting into these monkey suits, it's all about 'voo-dough?'"

"Yes."

"So… Damballah?" Taylor waved his photo.

"Serpent god. Creator of all life. Numero uno veve."

"Vay vay?"

"Voo dou symbol. Damballah is the man. The most important veve, symbol, in Haitian voodou."

"You're giving me too much to remember."

"Those aquariums at the First National Building? Puffer Fish. Stir in ol' Damballah and The Way and it all clicks. They're from the Caribbean. Haiti."

"You believe in that?"

"It's worth a try."

"Where's the dolls and the pins?"

"In the movies."

"What's with the tuxedos and limos and parties?"

"Not a clue."

"Oh boy…" Taylor gazed at trails of brake and headlights. Traffic was a bear on Sunset as they slogged past *TCLA*. At Murder Burger, Reggie steered onto Silver Lake.

"And your plan is?"

"Party hard?"

CHAPTER 67

"Christmas is canceled." Madam Speaker hammered her gavel. Mass smoked and yapped. Showbiz sorted and prioritized a stack of notes. Panther's hands were a blur as she typed. Miss Edna dawdled in *True Crime* Siberia - the outer fringes beyond Rookie Haven.

"Listen," Speaker said. No one did. Frustrated, she banged on the nearest surface. "Order. Order." Talk and work ceased. Quiet descended. "As I was saying. Panther. Hollywood Station."

"On it." She gathered her raincoat but waited to hear all the marching orders.

"Captain. Locate Johnny. Track him. Keep his ass flame-free whether he agrees or not. I do not care where he is or what he says he's doing or how much he bitches."

"Will do." He picked up his landline.

"Mass. Go up to that house Edna mentioned. See if Baby Doll still lives there and do we need to pay attention. If not, plant your butt back here."

"Yeppir."

Miss Edna raised a hand. "I, uh, can show him the shortcut and the lay of the land once we're on scene." She batted her eyes.

"Not my call," Madam Speaker said.

Mass snatched a fresh notebook and jabbed a pen in a pocket. He waddled to the front. "Better keep pace, granny."

Edna, all smiles, scurried to the door. "I know a great way to get up the hill to Apex."

"Tell me when we're in the car."

Troops deployed, Speaker felt compelled to deliver a final command. "Remember – your reporting funnels here."

"Copy that," Panther said. She followed Mass and Miss Edna.

Madam Speaker enjoyed the rare silence. Twirled a rose from the makeshift memorial of flowers on Heat's desk. "You knew all this," she said to Duncan. "About Getz and Edna." She let the accusation hang.

"Yes, I did, Betsy." He wanted to escape to his office and shut the blinds.

Speaker assembled a mental puzzle. "How long ago did Baby Doll get to you?"

"Never. Today's the first I ever talked to her."

"So who?"

"Ownership."

"Edna?"

"Yep. Swore me to secrecy."

"Wow. Never saw that. Not at all. She make you do a pinky swear?"

"Yeah."

"Serious." The dots connected, and the image was a bombshell. "Edna? Why?"

The question floated. Duncan heaved a sigh. "You think the ads cover the nut? Baby Doll holds the mortgage. Literally and figuratively. It's crazy."

"Not as crazy as you allowing Heat and Johnny to jump into a shit storm."

"Can't lay it on me. He went there on his own."

"You gave him permission. Then you gave him Heat."

"Harvard drew the lines a while ago, before he came to me. You knew. His 'Big Story.' You didn't come up with word one to divert him."

"Never knew the details."

"Unh unh. You don't get to wiggle off the hook. You didn't take him seriously. None of you did. But I kept trying to bloody well wave him away."

"Obviously, not hard enough."

"Who you kidding? They disobeyed orders. I pulled them and issued another assignment. Out of town, no less. That didn't do the trick, so I sacked their arses."

"Will Edna spike Johnny's story?"

"With Heat gone? Even Edna has to figure we're past that. She loves *True Crime.* Home and hearth. Decorates the tree, hangs the stockings. Even buys the stuffers."

A puzzle piece locked in. "And what's your stocking-stuffer for being such a good scout? Keys to a vacation place? Boat?"

"Life," Duncan said.

CHAPTER 68

"Up, up and a way-a-a," Reggie sang. Shrill and scratchy as he drove the steep ascent of Apex Avenue. "Hathaway Hill, brah. Part nine-zero-zero-three-nine, part two-six, all LA. In the clouds. Views to the edge of the earth."

Johnny and Taylor cringed, a captive audience for the travelogue. "Don't fret about earning your tip," Johnny said.

Reggie displayed too-white teeth and glanced in the mirror as he passed buildings that grew in size with the altitude. "Where you gents are whoop-tee-doing tonight was built on thirty acres in 1928. That's when it was finished and the family moved in. Actually, it was three solid years to erect 'cuz it's solid concrete." He chortled at his joke. "There's twenty-four toilets. Plenty of places to go."

Johnny rolled his eyes. "Who's the lucky owner?"

"No inkling, but it's too far east to be a film or TV star. You know them." The show biz glitterati preferred the cool ocean breezes of the Westside of LA. The braver ones ventured as far east as Los Feliz.

Reggie braked behind a stretch limo. Halogen lights lit the vehicles. Johnny saw a twelve-foot, wrought-iron fence and a thickset rent-a-cop. He wore gray slacks, a uniform blouse tucked tight over a ballistic vest, black, clip-on tie, silver badge and spit-shined utility belt. He saluted, a gate slid open, and the stretch proceeded. Security guy was joined by a woman in an identical uniform. Armed and alert, holsters strapped to thighs, their swagger broadcast off-duty police. She checked a digital pad and waved Reggie forward. A few yards later she ordered "Halt," and approached, walking on the balls of her feet, ready to react in any direction. She stopped at a spot that forced Reggie to twist his torso to see her, then made a circular motion with an index finger. He buzzed down the window.

Her partner, near the right, rear fender, rested a hand on his weapon.

She quick-scanned the interior. "Welcome to Hathaway Estates. Let me see your fares."

Reggie lowered the passenger window and revealed Johnny and Taylor.

"Destination?" She said.

"To the top," Johnny said.

"Names?"

"Lincoln, Johnny, plus one."

"And plus's?"

"Quigley, Taylor Nesbit the third. Q-U-I..."

"Yeah, yeah, got it here." She tapped the screen. "IDs?"

They reached for their wallets. Johnny presented his almost-new California license,

Taylor, his LAPD identification.

The guard compared pictures to live faces. "Of course. Now I recognize you. The crime scene photog. Remember the DB in Frogtown? The the old fart? I was on clipboard. Your tux threw me. Does you justice." She aimed her device and shot. "Anywho, I'm Nussman, he's Bumgarner. Northeast Division." She signaled. Bumgarner clicked a remote-control device. Nussman saluted and said, "Don't do anything I wouldn't do."

The Town Car entered the gated community. Reggie drove in silence for seven minutes and ascended the hill past expensive dwellings.

"Nice, but doesn't quite live up to the hype," Taylor said.

"Wait for it," Reggie said as he navigated the narrow street and rounded a bend. "In three, two..." They arrived at the crest.

"Wow." Johnny said.

A multi-level mansion crowned the summit. Floodlights formed patterns of inverted pyramids on cement walls.

Johnny and Taylor were familiar with the structure, but from a distance. If you lived or worked in that area of LA you'd seen it. To Silver Lake and beyond, the house was a nighttime beacon and a daylight mystery. A hilltop landmark no one knew a thing about, and everybody took for granted.

Reggie's car idled, fourth in line on a circular drive. He shoved the shifter into "P" and scurried to Johnny's door. Taylor let himself out and leaned against the trunk. Johnny emerged and gawked.

Seven attic garrets capped a massive roof that sloped at an incline more appropriate for alpine snow than SoCal sun. A second-floor balcony appeared stunted against the immense scale of the manse. An architectural afterthought? "We could camp out in there and nobody'd ever find us,"Taylor said.

He and Johnny were met at the bottom of an outdoor staircase by an Asian woman, no older than her early twenties. She wore a simple combo of a black, long-sleeve tee and white leggings. "And who do I have the pleasure of greeting?"

They told her. She touched a tablet. "Onward, gentlemen. Happy Holidays."

"You, too," Johnny said. Their climb of sixteen steps covered by a red carpet evolved from quiet to hushed sounds of people and muted strains of classical music. Halfway, Johnny paused and turned around. "Wow."

Below him, the Los Angeles basin twinkled postcard-clear to the Palos Verdes Peninsula, thirty miles south. To his left, the downtown skyscrapers soared. The infamous freeways radiated from them like strips of ribbons on a package. Decorations in the triangular shape of Christmas trees topped half a dozen high-rises between the Civic Center and Hollywood. Eleven miles to Johnny's right, built decades ago on a recently discovered earthquake fault, were the twin towers of Century City. Further on, the Ferris wheel on the Santa Monica pier met the dark void of the Pacific Ocean.

Taylor counted. "Four."

"Four what?" Johnny said.

"Airplanes. On final into LAX."

"How can you tell?"

"Blinking wing-tips and landing-lights. See 'em? Headlight beams in the sky?" He pointed.

"We're higher than the planes?"

"Sure. Some of 'em."

"Amazing. And they always land four across?"

"All day, every day."

They inhaled deep breaths of crisp December LA and continued up the stairs. Taylor's pulse rate rose. Johnny rubbed his palms on his pants. At the top, they were met by another elegant female. She was Black, dressed white over black. The guys identified themselves a third time. She keyed a two-way radio, repeated their info, bowed and invited them to proceed. "Tidings of the Season," she said.

Johnny and Taylor traversed a ten-yard path of Batchelder tile pavers that bisected a pristine, manicured lawn. Light from undraped windows cast rectangular glows on the grass. "It's really green,"Taylor said. "You suppose they spray it?"

"It's December." Johnny focused on red-lacquered double doors twelve feet tall. Each had a peephole, a brass knocker, and a shiny handle. "Cover story, cover story, cover story," he said, and poked the bell. Big Ben chimes and the entrance opened.

"Hi, boys," the MILF said.

CHAPTER 69

"All I do is stand and be mean-ish," Walsh said. She assumed the military stance of "at ease" and scowled.

"Piece-a-cake gig," Morales said, ass on the edge of his seat. "Raking in the big bucks for doing what's natural." He grinned. Knew she'd appreciate his sense of humor.

Walsh laid a death stare on him but couldn't hold it and smiled as she smacked a full magazine in her pistol and holstered the Glock. She slipped on running shoes that coordinated with her gray slacks. "Least I got assets." She fluffed her boobs.

"So you say."

Her loose, blue, cotton shirt hid most of those assets.

"Believe it. There's evidence and testimony. Look, but don't touch," Cedar Tree Hoffman said.

"See?" Walsh fluffed them again, not shy or modest in front of her LT and partner. But she had a more crucial issue to broach. "We good, boss? I mean the Taylor mess, and all?"

"Family spat. Not even Thanksgiving. Tuesday before, at worse."

Panther traipsed in. Her new wardrobe emboldened her. Snug, pink, square-neck top, crimson mini, paisley tights. Shoulders back, posture perfect, she projected confidence. Her heels clicked a steady rhythm. Hoffman, Walsh, and Morales watched her cross the squad room. Panther's gait was busy - an exaggerated hip swing, a lot of elbows and knees, and a smidge of shake and jiggle.

"Boss. You dog…" Morales said.

"You're outta here." Hoffman yanked a thumb like an umpire.

"Yes, sir!" The detective closed a case file and hustled to the elevator.

Walsh grabbed her blazer. "Slug a homer, L-T." She blew a kiss and hit the road.

Hoffman centered his necktie knot, straightened his wool-cashmere suit jacket and ambled to his office. "Ms. Perez?" He rolled the "r", placed the accent on the first syllable and invited her into his domain.

Panther accepted. As she entered, her butt herked and jerked as opposed to swung and swayed. Even the idea of sensual was brand new for her. To achieve graceful required additional beta testing. She sat on Hoffman's desk and scooted her ass. "Sure beats roughing it in the press hangout."

"Who'd you piss off?"

"No one. Why would you ask?"

"Isn't night cops a rookie gig? Especially on a holiday?"

"Can be, yeah. But the rookie's dick might be caught in a wringer, so here I am."

Panther flashed her best come-hither face. Under construction. The flirt was wide eyes and a tilted head, but she made her point.

Hoffman settled his large hands on her thin waist and pulled her to him. "How can I protect and serve?"

She cupped his ass. "Tell me who the tranny's chasing."

CHAPTER 70

"Yummy," the MILF said. Backlit by the brightness of the mansion's foyer, fuck-me pumps put her tits-to-chest with Taylor. She parted claret-colored lips and projected gangster's moll rather than femme fatale. She wore a black dress, nipped, tucked and belted, revealing deep cleavage, curves and great gams in seamed stockings. The MILF paraded it all but let her lady bits play with Taylor's imagination. She brushed imaginary schmutz off his lapels and kissed him. Lingered long enough to send an invitation. "Hot 'n foxy for an old broad, don't you think?" Winked. "And you, darlin'…" She reached for Johnny's briefcase. "I said unencumbered."

He didn't surrender it. "For our hostess. Consider me Santa's helper." He marched into the packed foyer.

Twosomes and threesomes giggled and canoodled. Several pairs wound their way up a grand, marble staircase. Ahead, in a congested, central corridor, partiers copped feels and stole kisses as they moved or mingled.

The MILF squeezed Taylor's bicep and led him to a vast living room. Fifty people, scattered in klatches of three, four, or five, engaged in subdued conversations and offered the occasional chuckle, but the space sounded hollow and echoey. It was impossible to distinguish single exchanges.

"Huge. Has to be what? A hundred feet?" Taylor said.

"Size matters," the MILF said.

Johnny recognized politicians and stars – film and television. He managed not to gawk. Taylor, however…

A dozen sofas, both fabric and leather, dotted the expanse. Twenty club chairs and an equal number of coffee and side tables were strategically situated to allow "flow." They weren't arranged in a rigid grid, and the room wasn't cozy, but with the planning and effort, it was livable. Johnny counted immense, antique Persian and Turkish rugs on the polished, Travertine limestone. He stopped at fourteen.

Museum-quality canvases in ornate, gold-leaf frames filled the walls. On a bet, he couldn't guess the artists but was impressed.

A dynamic work dominated from the far end. Twelve feet wide by eight high, it hung above a fireplace mantle of the same width. Vibrant colors depicted a bold woman atop a rearing horse. She wielded a sword and carried a shield emblazoned with a crown and fleur-de-lis.

Men, middle-aged to ancient, sported tuxedos and formal finery. Sleek, slim women of comparable age flirted. Outfits exposed legs, shoulders and cleavage on the forty-somethings. Hemlines dropped as age advanced. Modest evening gowns graced the elders. All dripped diamonds, emeralds or sapphires.

Johnny wanted to take cell phone pictures and notes but knew better.

Taylor summed it up. "Rubbing asses with the one percent."

"One-tenth of one percent," the MILF said. The door chimes rang. She sighed. "Duty beckons. Don't wander off." She pecked Taylor's cheek and paraded her gorgeous bod.

"She's not the reason we're here," Johnny said.

"Fooled me."

They entered the main hall. Johnny heard soft chamber music and strolled deeper into the house. Taylor lagged behind.

They passed chatterers and huggers. Men and women. A few disrobed, performing bumps and grinds. Some waved panties. Others tossed them at guys.

"Definitely puts a new spin on partying," Taylor said.

"Bet someone spiked the punch."

"Don't think they need any help."

Clapping seeped into the hall. Johnny and Taylor tracked it to an oak-paneled salon. A pool player chalked the tip of a cue. She rested her tummy on the rail next to a corner pocket and lowered her torso. Her khaki culottes rode up, uncovering toned thighs. She wrapped the stick's butt with her right hand and bridged the business end with her left.

Taylor nudged Johnny. "What?"

"That. Free-range." The player wore no top or bra. Her nipples grazed the green baize. She sighted and shot. The clack of balls generated polite oohs and aahs, but the forty spectators' interest wasn't the game. The shooter presented her well-endowed glory and curtsied to enthusiastic applause. Taylor loitered and enjoyed the view.

Johnny walked on. Heard music. "Beethoven. Ode to Joy. Ninth Symphony."

"Show off." Taylor hurried to catch up.

"Verbalizing helps imprint sights and sounds on the old noggin so I won't forget. For when I write the piece."

"If you say so."

They side-stepped a distraught man and followed Ludwig van through an archway to an oak-paneled, wainscoted lounge. It was a third the size of the living room but large by any standard.

The music was live. The guys were surprised to see a string quartet behind a barricade of music stands. The foursome fronted leather-bound tomes shelved in a built-in bookcase thirty feet long. Two seated musicians were men in white-tie and tails on violin and viola. Two ladies in white silk blouses and ankle-length black skirts completed the ensemble. A cellist sat, knees bracketing her instrument, and bowed. The bassist stood as tall as her tuning pegs. Her body was hidden by the eight-shape of the bull fiddle. The musicians didn't miss a beat and turned pages in unison.

Three chintz sofas overflowed with group gropes.

Taylor nodded at activity in a shaded alcove.

"Got it," Johnny said.

A fervent matron pinned a male against the shelving, raised a leg, balanced, grabbed his ass and tool and thrust.

Taylor's eyes landed on a corner. "Is that one O'Hara or Riley?"

"Who?"

"Remember that detective show, 'O'Hara and Riley'?" He motioned towards a once-famous TV star. She leaned into the nakedness of a maybe-legal, waifish girl whose response was a sloppy kiss and a grope beneath the star's dress.

Johnny looked. "O'Hara." He scanned the room. A dozen couples in various stages of undress. Old dude/sweet young thing, mature female/young stud, young/old girl-girl or boy-boy, fondled, unbuttoned, and unzipped. "Kinda, sorta reminds me of The Baths, only, only..."

"Rich," Taylor said.

A blonde humper screamed an "O." No one reacted. Except Taylor. He gawked.

"Be cool," Johnny said.

"I've got a pulse. You know about all this?" Partiers, mature and opulent, youthful and beautiful, pleasured all comers.

"No. Damn." Anxious, Johnny dipped to trim his height. Elbowed Taylor and nodded toward entrance.

The Hoods who had attempted to kill them twice were under the arch, eyeing the crowd.

Taylor slouched. Johnny hunched and angled in the direction of French doors. He moved at a casual pace. Wanted to blend. Taylor expected the Hoods to smack him. Or worse.

They edged past the quartet, reached the exit and slipped outside. They mingled with revelers on the banks of a body of water that resembled a movie version of a south-seas lagoon. A hundred Chinese lanterns flickered and reflected off the surface. Ferns and orchids dotted the grounds, and a waterfall cascaded over boulders. There were no swimmers or skinny-dippers.

Portable, propane heaters erected ten feet apart surrounded the pool. They burned orange. Radiant warmth attracted more players who caressed their escorts.

Johnny and Taylor eyeballed a bunch of folks engaged in what seemed to be a prime-time swingers prom, but everything was lopsided. The young ones weren't into it. They exhibited no expressions. Had dead eyes and mechanical actions as they smashed lips, tugged shirts and slacks or gowns and garters. It was sexual paint-by-numbers - one, two, two, three - lips, boob, boob, crotch – stay inside the lines, then copulate.

"Any ideas?" Taylor said.

"Aside from the obvious? Remember the powder you filched?"

"At the fish lab?" Taylor's pronunciation hit a speed bump. "Tetro-dough-toxin?"

"Yeah" Johnny was on alert. "It's that, or an extract of a certain kind of tree bark. But then it could be the Burundanga flower. Even toad secretions. Also possible it's synthetic. Scopolamine comes to mind."

"Explain."

"Drugs that zap the brain and zones them out, but they're controllable. I'd give you odds the escorts partook."

"Voluntarily?"

"Or somebody gave it to them. Most likely gave it, which is why they're so, so..."

"Vacant."

"Yeah."

Taylor was skeptical. "Would you do that? Give it all up for some vague promise?"

"It's not on my bucket list, but those classified ads? In our paper? They cater to the desperate. You lose hope there's no predicting what you'll do." Johnny sounded as if he'd experienced that truth. He ambled towards the splash of the waterfall where the assignations were frenzied, even rough, but neither intimate nor passionate.

A male snorted.

"Yes, yes, yessss." A female moaned.

"A piece of me is yelling to dive in,"Taylor said.

"Me, too,"Johnny said.

"Signs of life."

They trekked to the far end of the pool. Johnny scribbled mental notes. Taylor snapped brain images of duos and trios. "You figure out how they get here?"

"The classified ad. Web site. Called the number. And according to the available evidence," he indicated the closest escorts, "if you're hot, The Way pledges a golden parachute. I suspect a girl tells a guy or a guy tells a girl, or girl-girl, guy-guy, depending, that if you jump, it's a second chance to fulfill all your dreams. Double your money, they're assured a happy landing, so they rip the cord."

"Problem is, this is the LZ."Taylor said.

A Hispanic teen with a ponytail flattened her bare breasts and thonged pelvis against Johnny. Did a grind, rotated, twerked, then faced him and hugged. A Gothic-script tattoo on her throat spelled *EP 13*. "Hey, baby. Crave danger?" She said in a montone.

"Aren't you...?" She led with her tongue and laid a juicy kiss on the photographer before he finished the question.

"Chica's here for your pleasure."

He was perplexed. "I know you."

She performed a perfunctory stroke of his junk. "Daddy."

Taylor gripped her shoulders and repositioned her to the side.

"Oh, daddy."

"We're fine, doll,"Johnny said.

The Latina scooted to him. Rubbed her body up, down, up, down. By the book. Not sensuous at all.

"Scram."

"You get hard for boys?"

"No."

"Blondes?"

"Yeah. That's it. Now run along. We're visiting."Johnny eased her off.

She bowed. "Thank you for your consideration." Shuffled away.

"Recognize her?"

"Sure. The 'banger,"Taylor said. "She had a copy of your rag at her scene, and Walsh figured her for one of our suicides."

They watched as Elvia latched on to a TV action star.

"What's this all about?"

"Zombies,"Johnny said with relish.

CHAPTER 71

"We're rolling six tonight," Wheels said. She stood next to the boss's enormous desk, riding crop tucked between left bicep and ribcage. She wore her Stetson, jodhpurs, boots, silver English spurs, and a white, sleeveless top.

Getz, in her black dress, pearls, and fluffy, pink slippers, gazed out a window. The sea of city lights mesmerized her. She never tired of the sight.

The driver fanned six, nine-by-twelve envelopes. "Four babes, two dudes." Set them on a felt blotter. Held a seventh.

Getz nibbled her pearls. "Real ones are gritty. Cultured are smooth."

Wheels had no idea what that meant or which kind the boss owned, and she'd never ask.

Getz stepped from the view. She paused, admired her Remington and walked to the Chauffeur. She held the poise and posture of a model. A bit sway-backed due to age, but tall and true. She chose an envelope and shook the contents onto her desk. Lifted a thin, blue booklet. Embossed in gold on the front was:

PASSPORT
UNITED STATES OF AMERICA

Below it was the nation's official "eagle seal." She flicked it open with a French-tipped nail. Studied the photo of a beauty and the data of name, height, weight, and age. "Ever wonder?"

"About?" Wheels said.

"She's a baby."

"So was I."

"Yeah, me too." Getz grazed engraved letters on an eight-and-a-half by eleven-inch mock parchment. "Never fails to amaze me."

"What?"

"These. Genuine California birth certificates. And the US passports, too. Not so easy in this day and age."

"Money, money, money."

Getz tapped a yellow pamphlet the same size as the travel documents. On it was printed…

World Health Organization
Proof of Vaccination

She flipped pages. Grimaced. "Typhoid-paratyphoid? Ouch. Dengue fever?" Winced. "Hate needles…"

"Mighta gone a little extreme with tonight's crop."

"Not to worry. We do ship product to weird destinations." Getz slid the WHO information in with the other records. "And the private reserve?"

"In the cellar, waiting for pick up. Special order. Eleven-year-old twins. Client's thrilled. And finally…" She passed her boss the last packet.

"You peek?"

"Don't I always?"

"And…?"

"It's got answers."

Getz removed a sheet of thick, rust-colored paper, not blue-green, and smaller. Seven-by-ten. Read it, blotted her eyes with a tissue and blew her nose. "Who gets gratitude?"

"I emailed you a list."

Getz dabbed her cheeks with knuckles and presented herself. "Well?"

Wheels handed her a pair of sling-back pumps. "A-plus numero uno."

CHAPTER 72

"Zombies? What're you smoking?" Taylor said.

"Check 'em out," Johnny said. "What do you see?"

"Aside from the obvious?" He tossed Johnny's words at him. Grinned. The humping shifted to a higher gear. Moans and yelps echoed. "The humpees are young and hot."

"And?"

"I don't know."

"Scope their eyes."

Taylor did. "Oh..." Most were in the throes but with no hunger or lust.

"Welcome to their new existence. Remember the literature we picked up? The Way promised a ticket to a 'fresh dawn.'? They sure got it."

The Hoods opened the French doors. Johnny saw them and stooped. He prodded Taylor. They mingled. Watched a dozen men drop trou. Females shed blouses and bras. Johnny and Taylor kept their clothes on, but flirted, laughed, slapped butts, oohed and ahhed. They moved along the banks and blended as best they could. Johnny scanned people on the lagoon's rim. He didn't sense an immediate threat but didn't relax and didn't dare stand straight.

"Show's shifting," Taylor said. Caught in a tide of bodies, he and Johnny drifted to a mammoth red and white-striped tent. It covered a fraction of a broad, manicured lawn that stretched beyond the canvas big top towards the silhouette of Mt. Wilson and the San Gabriel Mountains.

Disco blared. "Retro," Johnny said.

The 70s tune appealed to the wealthy Boomers in tuxes and formals who made every effort to dance to rhythmic thump, thump, thumps. Men jabbed fists and jutted chins. Their partners swiveled hips and shook their booties into the tent. Johnny and Taylor rode the wave.

Thirty lighted Christmas trees decorated the interior. A runway four feet above a temporary wood floor bisected seating for three hundred – a hundred-fifty plastic folding chairs on either side. Revelers pulsed to the beat. Johnny and Taylor slalomed to the third row, using the throng as a convenient shield. A stage capped the runway and formed a T. A circle-spot hit a maroon curtain, and the music segued to an instrumental rendition of "Jingle Bell Rock."

The Brunette burst forth in a sparkling emerald gown. Slit to his left hip, leg exposed, he swept across the platform to the beat of the up-tempo carol.

"Fucker's everywhere," Taylor said.

At center-stage, the Brunette performed an exaggerated hip grind, popped a pelvic thrust, and pranced.

"How's he do that and not dangle his junk?"

The hot spot tracked the Brunette as he hailed the crowd with his throaty, impersonator delivery. "Hello, my lovelies. Shall we begin the festivities?"

The intensity dimmed a notch, but no one noticed. Party-goers throbbed, pulsed, and shouted to be heard.

Mic to his lips, the Brunette said, "The moment has arrived. So. Are you ready?" No reaction. Not happy, he continued. "Again, with gusto..." Added umph. "Are. You. Ready?" Again, no response. The Brunette drew a finger over his throat. The music ceased. He dropped the falsetto. "Did you not hear me? It's time." An authoritarian demand with an expectation of compliance. Not to be questioned. The onlookers quieted and settled. Anxious ladies tugged hems. Gentlemen smoothed trousers.

The Brunette signaled. Music resumed. He danced to a fast, Euro-beat version of "Hark! The Herald Angels Sing." Used his MC voice. "And now that I have your undivided attention." He admired his ha-ha and with a sweeping gesture kicked off the festivities. "Turn to your programs. Lot number ten. From It-tah-ly."

A swarthy, barefoot male in a pearl-gray Armani jacket strutted on the runway.

"College-educated in computers, programmed for all-night fun."

Well-heeled spectators ogled, expressed approval with oohs and ahs, tilted champagne flutes and sipped bubbly.

Johnny was enthralled with the spectacle.

The Brunette continued his sales pitch. "No home is complete until you plug him in. Click 'unbridled lust.' He is tested and vetted. Bundled to please. So – let's start at five, shall we?"

Excited applause as the auction item unbuttoned his coat and shed it an arm at a time. He twirled it and flung it into the crowd. Cheers for his pecs, but he didn't leave it at that. He milked a slow grind and deep thrust into a growing ovation, but his face was a blank.

"Five hundred?" The Brunette said. Fifty tipsy women, aged forties to sixties, hooted and hollered. The Brunette was delighted. "Do I hear six?" A bunch of hands remained in the air.

"What are they bidding on?" Taylor said.

"Vincent Parnelli," Johnny said.

"Suicide by oven?"

The Brunette exuded excitement. Only he knew if it was genuine. "Seven. Do I hear seven?" He said. There was one taker. A wealthy Asian old enough to be Vinnie's grandmother. She wore a standard-issue black dress and enough gold bangles and baubles to finance a hostile merger. The Brunette combed the audience for more buyers. "Eight? Eight hundred?" Nothing. "Last chance. Mr. Italy's at seven hundred thousand, and, going once..." He regarded his bidders. Goaded them. "Tapped out? Progeny blow the bank?" A final look-see. "Seven hundred twice." The Brunette knew the offer was maxed. "Sold American. Seven-hundred thousand on the barrel-head. An astute investment." He aimed claps at the winner.

Vincent Parnelli jumped into the crowd. His buyer squeezed the goods.

Taylor whispered, "What'd we just see?"

"Cover story. Twenty-first-century slave market. High-end human traffic."

CHAPTER 73

"Seriously. Could you turn your nose up at this?" The MILF said. She raked her hair and struck a pose for a tall Latina greeter. Back arched, pelvis thrust, flaunting ass and boobs, her attire functioned as designed.

"Not ever," the greeter said.

The MILF was vexed. Nobody blew her off. Not many, anyway. She searched for Taylor. Inventoried the men in the foyer, examined each male on the staircase, eyeballed the living room. No luck. She rushed into the hall. Bumped a babe who clamped her teeth on a guy's zipper. Ignored others engrossed in various stages of sexual activity. She peeked at the billiards game.

The topless shooter stroked her cue, but Taylor wasn't among the bystanders. The MILF used her radio. "Paul, Marcel?" The Hoods emerged from the library, signaled thumbs-down, and ducked into the salon. The MILF pondered. Ahh. A thought. Strode to the front. Keyed the talk button on her two-way. "Appears Mutt and Jeff are off the leash."

Thirty hands rose to ears. Staff, uniformed guards and plainclothes operatives throughout the mansion listened. "The boys bolted," the MILF said, and joined the flow of merrymakers. All personnel with earpieces and wrist mics scrutinized guests as they flocked towards large doors at the rear of the house flanked by security agents. The MILF hurried to one. "Seen a hunky mixed-race dude and his tall friend?"

Detective Walsh arched her brows. That was all the surprise she allowed herself. "Uh, no."

CHAPTER 74

"Nine-hundred-thousand. Sold American! He'll keep you toasty on those icy Moscow nights," the Brunette said. He led the applause as Andre, in white thong, leaped down and landed beside his new, pale, bony-assed owner. Weathered cleavage swelled as she buckled a spiked collar on his neck.

"Fuck," Taylor said. "Last I saw him, brother was dead on a bed."

Music amped and the beat quickened to a hyped "Handel's Messiah." The Brunette strutted and clapped. "Feel it? Come on..." Clap, clap, clap... He channeled a fight announcer. "Are you ready?" Cupped an ear.

Heard a lukewarm, "Yes."

"Uh, uh, uh... we practiced this." Wagged a finger. "Are you ready?" Dragged it out at the top of his voice.

"Yes."

"What?"

"Yes," the multitude screamed.

The Brunette pranced. "And now..."

A bugle sounded the "Call To Post" – the fanfare trumpeted at horse races 'round the world – and was followed by a head-banging "Joy to the World."

A flawless young woman high-stepped on stage. A sheer teddy draped alabaster skin as she glided along the runway.

"A thoroughbred," the Brunette declared. "Give it up for number one in your program."

The magnificent blonde spun a sensuous pirouette. The teddy billowed and the crowd thundered.

"I'm sure you'll agree. You will want this angel to cap your tree. She is beyond mere expectations. She hails from the Bluegrass State and was born to ride. Feast."

Beauty paraded with long strides. Attendees coveted her youth. They believed only one successful bid stood between them and the first item on their life lists. ED pills kicked in.

Taylor sat three rows back, stunned, fists clenched. "It's Emma!"

"But wait. There's more." The Brunette tittered. "Our goddess does it all. She's an acquisition you won't regret." He rubbed her butt. She didn't react.

Furious, Taylor launched. Johnny grabbed his sleeve.

Beauty twirled and revealed a vacuous expression – mouth parted, eyes blank. Johnny remembered the pale, nude blonde curled on the hardwood in Whitley Heights. Recalled Taylor's pictures of better days. It was, without a doubt, Emma on the auction block.

"She is such a treat, isn't she?" The Brunette said. "So special. The auction must, I insist, must commence at a million with increments of half-a-mil. A one-time protocol, I assure you. You understand. If you are the winner, you will tender immediate payment using cash, bearer bonds or black card prior to claiming possession. And remember. Your, uh, donation is tax-deductible."

Lights rose on the audience. The Brunette saw most of them slumped and discouraged, priced out of the market.

"I feel your pain. Truly." He patted his chest to convey empathy. "But - shall we begin? Yes?" He explored the onlookers. "Do I hear one million?"

An Arab in traditional, checked keffiyah and white thobe, touched his mustache.

"And, away we go..." The Brunette mimicked a track announcer. "One to one-and-a-half. One-and-a-half? Do I hear one-million-five-hundred-thousand?" He rotated Emma.

A bald gentleman scratched an ear.

"Thank you, sir. Two?"

A plump mature removed her bifocals.

"Superb. And up a half?"

Taylor's temper flared. He shot his right hand skyward.

"Oh, crap," Johnny said.

The Brunette recognized Taylor but overlooked him. "Two-five? Two-point-five?"

A casting director's version of a US president tugged an ear lobe.

"Excellent, sir," the Brunette said. "Who'll give me three?"

"Three." It was Taylor.

The Brunette, cold as a silver dollar in a snowdrift, stared at Taylor and Johnny. "Three-five?"

The Arab flicked his mustache again.

The Brunette focused killer eyes on Taylor and spat syllables. "We are at three-and-a-half million. If we may proceed."

"Bucks?" Taylor said. "Okay. Four." He pumped his fist. The drunks loved it. Cheered him on.

Johnny cringed and wondered what came next.

The Brunette could have killed. Would have, at another location. "Very well. Four-and-a-half?"

"I'll climb that ladder." Taylor gloated.

"You're bidding against yourself, sir."

"Love the challenge."

"Afandim?" The Brunette said. The Arab gave an indifferent nod. Relief. "And, we're headed to five. Who'll give me five?"

"Yeah, I'm there," Taylor said.

The Brunette's shoulders drooped. "Five it is." He squinted a plea at other bidders. "Five-and-a-half?" No response. Eyed the Arab. "Five-five? Five-and-a-half?"

Taylor, on pins and needles, fidgeted.

Johnny tried to determine the repercussions when the moment of truth arrived. He needed to develop a plan. Racked his brain. Nothing. They'd have to wing it.

"Five-and-a-half?" The Brunette ground his jaw. Paused a few seconds, but it felt like forever. "Five going once." He hoped for a lifesaver. "And twice?" One last scan of the bidders. "Sold American. Five million takes her."

A roar of approval.

"Pay the man," Taylor said as he pushed Johnny towards the stage.

CHAPTER 75

"Fuck, fuck, fuck." The MILF plopped down on the bottom step of the grand stairway, elbows on knees, chin in her hands. Her orders had been clear - stick to Johnny and Taylor like grim death. It was death that worried her.

Security agents darted room-to-room. Guards sprinted outside to the yards and gardens. The female greeters attempted to wrangle visitors, but antics and activities intensified as people shed clothes. A cheer wafted from the billiards game. Down the hall, the string-quartet bowed baroque, unable to compete with the sights and sounds of humping bodies.

Alberta Hand marched across the foyer. She didn't possess a spec of sympathy or compassion as she lobbed a two-way radio at the MILF. She caught it, hesitated, pressed talk and whispered, "Go." Raised the device to her ear. Trembled. Her breathing accelerated and her pulse soared. She lowered the walkie-talkie and gathered herself. Smoothed imaginary wrinkles.

"Suck it up," Hand Job said as she snatched the radio. "Least you'll make it home."

"Promise?" The MILF hiked into the night.

CHAPTER 76

"Emma. It's me. We won," Taylor said as he sprang out of his chair.

She was alone at the end of the runway, trapped in the bright beam of a spotlight. Unprotected by the lingerie, she shivered, but her heart-shaped face displayed no emotion.

Johnny ran interference as he and Taylor made their way from the third row. Well-wishers grasped for a piece of the winner – a handshake or pat on the back - and toasted his good fortune. Lucky dog.

The guys reached Emma. Taylor cradled her butt with a hand and caught her as she fell off the stage. "Babe?" Emma showed no trace of recognition. Her teeth chattered. He covered her with his tux jacket.

The Brunette sneered at them from the stage. "And how do you intend to pay for her, sir?"

Johnny wedged himself between Taylor, Emma and the Brunette. Clicked the latch on his briefcase. The Brunette squatted. Johnny popped the lid and allowed the Undercover a peek. He recoiled. Johnny said, "Gotchya."

The Brunette composed himself. Into his microphone he announced, "My dear, dear friends. Attention. The auction has concluded. Repeat – we are finished. Be safe and wish Santa a very merry."

The audience booed. They craved a fresh item but obeyed instructions and dispersed, bobbing and dancing to the rockin' carols.

The crowd pitched and flowed towards the exit. Jostled, Johnny tossed an elbow here, a shove there. Took a quick look. Checked that Taylor and Emma weren't engulfed by the horde. "Big smiles, kids. Remember, you scored the prize of the century." Emma's head lolled. Taylor tightened his grip around her waist.

The Brunette jumped into the crowd and pursued. Unsteady on spike heels, he smacked a tux-clad man and plowed over women.

Johnny led Taylor and Emma into the chilly night. Outside, they accelerated. Dodged clusters of drunks and escorts. Skirted a knot of writhing bodies that resembled a rugby scrum. Used them as camouflage.

Johnny searched for an escape. "Sneak back into the tent?"

"Nope," Taylor said. "We'll be cornered."

They faced bare lawns and gardens that traversed the hill. "Overland seems clear."

"Now, yeah. But we go there they find us fast and we're in a turkey shoot. As the turkeys. We stay here, it's worse. Let's get inside the house. It's congested. We disrupt. Creates confusion and a diversion. Gives us a chance."

"Next time, you better get us a chopper." That bent the tension.

"Promise." Taylor gauged distance to the French doors. "Ten yards to go."

"First down."

"We only get one."

Johnny jogged towards the music salon. Taylor embraced Emma's waist. Her knees collapsed. She sagged against his right hip. He lifted and carried her. At the doors, Johnny glanced behind. Saw Taylor struggling with Emma. He doubled back. Together, they hoisted her.

Near the waterfall, the Brunette summoned a staffer and borrowed a radio.

Johnny and Taylor carry-dragged Emma into the mansion, past the musicians and the group gropes to the central corridor. They tried to blend and lose themselves in the crazy pack of drunks and escorts. Johnny navigated. Threw several punches to clear a path. He didn't notice the dozen security agents yapping into wrist mics. No one moved to intercept. They could have restrained Johnny, secured his briefcase, separated Emma and Taylor and terminated the threat without risk to anyone.

Johnny entered the jammed foyer. He joined a hundred alarmed, bewildered folks. Taylor propped Emma with his shoulder. Forward progress was glacial, but the entrance was in sight. Twenty feet. Fifteen.

Plainclothes and uniformed personnel deployed and barred the exits. Taylor recognized one of them. It took a moment for the disbelief to recede. He widened his eyes and raised his brows in a silent appeal to Walsh. She unbuttoned her blazer and revealed her holstered weapon. Taylor spun Emma in the opposite direction. Johnny turned, too. Three guards cut off their getaway. Six closed from the rear.

Auction patrons flooded the area. They rushed Walsh. Bumped and jostled, she lost her footing but not her Beretta. Other guests shook the knobs. Locked and blocked, they were crammed cheek-to-jowl with nowhere to run.

Knuckles hammered Johnny's kidney. Excruciating pain erupted. He staggered but didn't fall. A pistol poked his neck.

"Really went and did it now," the Brunette said.

Someone shouted, "Gun!" A seismic wave of freak-out swept the room. An unintentional human ring encircled Johnny, Taylor, Emma and the Brunette, accompanied by a faint melody performed by the quartet.

Johnny heard the music. "Mozart. Eine Kleine Nachtmusik." He hurt like hell but yawned. "Sure you wanna head down this road, Bucko?"

The undercover cop answered by chambering a round.

Amped and edgy partiers surged, fueled by terror arcing at warp speed.

Taylor shielded Emma. He relaxed as Detective Hand approached. She seized the moment and jabbed her gun barrel into Emma's cleavage. Taylor couldn't do a thing.

The Brunette hid his anxiety and smiled. "Calmly, everyone. Things're fine. A couple interlopers is all." A collective sigh rippled. He grabbed Johnny's briefcase.

Johnny wrenched it back. "Careful now. Ask yourself what might trigger it."

Screams. The throng pitched and heaved. A woman was knocked to the Travertine. Another was tripped. Stampede.

Johnny, Taylor, Emma and the Brunette were swept up in the frenzy to escape. The Brunette fought to hang on to the case. Tough to do in heels. Bodies smashed him. He flailed and slipped. Johnny surfed the swell. Hoped he'd ride the confusion to safety.

An air horn blasted. Three seconds of ear-splitting loud followed by instant quiet. All movement halted. "Johnny, Johnny, Johnny." Baby Doll's voice sliced the silence.

The naked and almost naked squirmed and strained to conceal their private bits. The tuxed and gowned watched their hostess amble down the stairs. Tall, thin, aging elegance. Her dress fit like a glove. She was flanked by the Hoods and trailed by Wheels who wielded the horn. "Thought we had a deal, kid." Getz was disappointed.

"Cum see, cum saw," Johnny said.

"Whatchya got there?"

Johnny balanced the briefcase on his right palm, gut-high. "Little giftie for the holidays." He turned a slow semi-circle. Cranked the fright-level.

"For me? A present?" She clapped with mock glee. Sucked an angry breath. Her lips moved. Johnny wondered if she was into a ten-count.

"Take a gander." He brandished his case. "Might be your last."

"Such drama, Johnny. Okay, I'm in. Want me to guess?" Phony grin. "Answer is - C-4 plastique. Or maybe Semtex?" Getz did a game-show hop. "Is it? Is it?" High-fived her driver. "Did I get it? Do I win?" Her expression shifted to stone killer. "You ruined Christmas. Coal in your stocking."

"Oh well. There's still New Year." His mind raced. He needed a play.

Baby Doll demonstrated all the patience in the world as Wheels scrutinized the skittish partiers and auction attendees crammed into the foyer.

"Figure it out yet?" Getz winked. Not the retort Johnny imagined.

She nodded at the Hoods, but before they acted, Johnny toyed with the briefcase handle – up down, up down.

People whimpered and cried.

Getz was annoyed. "You are distressing my friends."

Again, her response astonished him. "Tell you what, Baby Doll."

"Ain't my name." Anger flared.

"Sure thing, Miss Beatrice. Let's talk, me and you. Work it smooth between and betwixt. But everybody else gets a pass. Them, too." He lifted the case towards Taylor and Emma.

Baby Doll scanned the foyer, then peered into the living room. Was it possible to resurrect the evening? She calculated the night's shutdown versus future losses. Sighed. No choice but to bite the bullet. Baby Doll addressed her angry customer base. "And look at you, my friends, all pumped for Santa. But sadly, Mr. Claus will have to find you in your own beds." She signaled Walsh. The detective threw open the front doors.

Taylor, relieved beyond words, mouthed thanks to Johnny and scowled at Walsh as he nudged Emma into the cold.

The mansion emptied. Auction attendees elbowed and scurried, but Johnny didn't twitch a muscle. The Brunette targeted his skull with a Beretta. Hand Job settled into a shooting stance ready to pump a 9mm double-tap into Johnny's chest. Walsh maintained her post and aimed her Glock at him, too.

"Three of you?" Johnny supposed his life expectancy had deflated to a minute or so. Gestured at the Brunette. "One dirty cop. I can buy that. Him I get. But the crown princess of RHD?" He frowned at Hand. "And you?" Sniped a nasty glance at Walsh. "Especially you." She racked the slide on her pistol.

Getz, Wheels and the Hoods watched from the staircase. Baby Doll beamed. "Okay, okay, okay. Enough of that." She smiled at Johnny and spread her arms. "Welcome to my home. You like the place, son?"

CHAPTER 77

"Ow," yelped Emma. Her right foot met something sharp. She bounced on her left and cried. Taylor felt a tad relieved. It was her first reaction to anything.

A terrified partier sprawled into them. Taylor teetered and twisted but cradled Emma. The mob of men and women wearing remnants of evening regalia inundated lawns and gardens. They shooed their escorts towards the circular driveway.

Limousines and luxury cars kissed bumpers all the way to the property's main gate, a hundred yards. Clients dumped their zombies and scrambled into limos. Didn't make a difference whose. They'd sort it out later. Engines revved, horns blared. It was gridlock on the hill.

Taylor carried Emma to the top of the outdoor red carpet stairs. A page-one banner popped into his head - *Escape From Hathaway Hill.* Nope. Reminded him of matinees he'd seen as a youngster. Taylor's professional instincts kicked in. He framed imaginary pictures. Nobody in a position of power, private or public, would believe the mass panic without evidence. But done is done. He'd surrendered his camera. He weaved and evaded, shielding Emma, but the spectacle was too much. Each blink was a could-have-been photo, every step a change of perspective and context. He steadied her, drew his phone from his jeans and captured video of the stampede.

Taylor focused on a hefty baldie stripped to tighty whities, a sleeveless undershirt and patent-leather loafers. The dude hauled a nude female and bellowed, "Onward, dammit." The escort displayed no fear, no sense of urgency.

A guard blindsided Taylor. Banged a pistol between his eyes. "House. Now."

"Hey. . ." Taylor cocked his arm for a punch. No match for a pistol. "Day late and a buck short," he said. "You should run. Police'll be here any minute."

The security guy flashed a PD badge.

CHAPTER 78

"Johnny, you've crossed paths with Paul and Marcel but ain't officially met," Getz said. She prompted them, one on either side of her. "*Soyez poli.*"

"*Bonsoir*," they said. Their tone was average, not four-ball. Not the image Johnny conjured of the buff enforcers who walked through fire at Le Roux's. Or later, emerged unscathed from the crash of their airborne Caddy.

"Voodou witch doctors," he said. "Awesome."

"Respect, Johnny. Respect. Voodou priests."

"Which is why you went after the pharmaceutical company. To steal psycho-hypnotics." Johnny's virgin cover story took shape.

"You be catching on. Yep, they help a lot. But to possess a soul, you go way past that. Way past. You must control its desires. You gettin' all this?" She gestured at Dennis positioned on the second-floor landing.

He shoved Heat. Clenched her flannel nightie and squashed her tummy against a banister twenty feet above Johnny. She didn't resist.

The sight of her ripped Johnny apart. "Heat," he said. She didn't respond to her nickname. "Heather!" No recognition. He was ripped apart. Elated she was alive. Devastated by her state of being.

Dennis tightened his grip on Heat and whispered in her ear. She responded in a monotone. "Sir?"

He grabbed a fist full of red hair, jerked her head and trained her eyes on Johnny.

"Not me. Him. Remember him?"

"No."

"He remembers you."

"How may I be of service?"

"He didn't hear you."

Heat said with a loud voice, "How may I serve you, sir?"

Dennis murmured orders. She swung a leg over the rail, straddled the banister, shifted her weight and wobbled.

Getz snapped to attention, with exaggerated ceremony, extended her arms towards Heat and the heavens and commanded, "Fly."

Excited, the Hoods and Wheels looked up. "Always the best part, this," she said.

"No," Johnny yelled. Unnerved, he ran towards the stairs. Didn't make it. Hand Job tripped him. He fell and skidded. Watched Heat as she dangled her feet above the long drop and wiggled her ass forward on the rail.

The Brunette and Walsh shared a silent, "What the fuck?"

Sergeant Hand, fascinated, lowered her weapon.

Heat shimmied closer to the edge. She teetered on the railing.

"Stop." Johnny was on his knees.

Heat's weight shifted. She lost her balance. Tilted forward. Dennis jerked the flannel. Interrupted the fall.

Devastated, Johnny dug deep. Searched mind and gut, but death was death. If it came to that, he'd cope. He'd witnessed some. But what they'd done to Heat was worse.

He tried in vain to dissect Getz's mind. Each waited for the other to crack the silence. A tick. Then five. Baby Doll signaled Dennis.

He yanked Heat off the rail. She crumpled.

The Hoods and Wheels slumped. "*Zut,*" they said. Damn it.

Walsh and the Brunette breathed easier.

Perplexed, Hand Job said, "Why?"

On his knees, Johnny exhaled.

"Impressed?" Baby Doll smiled.

Johnny didn't say.

"Oh, come on. Admit it. It's pretty groovy, yeah?" She wanted a reaction. He did not give it. "Possession of the soul, Johnny. You remember that, you'll zoom to the top of the class. So man up."

Johnny rose. Flexed his muscles. Inventoried aches and pains. "Me and she, we hike out of here."

"Big thinker. Yeah, I approve."

"And I give you this." He presented the briefcase.

"You're smart, cher. Why you suppose I allowed you so much living? All da time to run around and dig in my stuff?" She smirked and let it sink in. "Use your noggin, boy."

He considered the attempts on his life by Paul and Marcel. The fire, M-4 rifles on a loading dock, car chase. "Okay. I get it. No one's that lucky."

Getz shrugged but grinned. Sashayed down the grand staircase to the floor.

"Thanks. Appreciate you keeping me alive and all, but I told you the deal already."

"Well, I ain't told you mine."

Johnny tensed. Lifted and lowered the handle.

"Cher… You really pack boom-clay in there? Where'd you get it at?" Getz knew he had no answers. "You couldn't pile the bucks to buy it even if you do know how to find it." She studied him. Deliberated. Came to a conclusion. "Join me, son. You'll be my number one." Baby Doll touched his face. "My heir."

Johnny didn't flinch but felt as if he'd been kicked in the *coullion* and bestowed the keys to the kingdom. Questions swamped him. About his history. His future. But only two mattered. Would he become the greatest crime reporter in the world? Or the greatest criminal?

"You're a chip off. We'd be the A-Team." She stroked his cheek. "Finally got to the heart of your story, cher."

CHAPTER 79

"Wanna keep your badge? Join the crowd," Taylor said. He and Emma were corralled by gun-point at the crest of the red carpet steps.

Agitated, the guard whacked Taylor's scalp with his pistol. "Quiet." He glanced at the landscaped grounds in a futile effort to locate an ally. "Shake it. You've been summoned."

There wasn't a clear route to the house. The crush of Baby Doll's guests was intense. Half-dressed females endeavored to cover themselves, with little luck. Many of the men struggled to put on jackets in mid flee. Some dragged partners and knocked anyone slower out of their way. A few were on their own.

A stunned matron in a silk slip meandered alone, dazed. "Sonny? Sonny? Sonny?" She called.

Taylor blocked a frightened runner from plowing into Emma. Didn't make much difference. The security agent prodded and whipped her ass. She collapsed.

"Hey, schmucko." Taylor pivoted and punted the off-duty policeman's crotch.

The cop's mouth opened. His eyes bugged. Worst. Pain. Ever. He doubled over and fell nose-first.

Taylor snatched the firearm from the grass and leveled it at the guy. No need. He writhed, cupped his vitals, curled into a fetal position and moaned. Taylor jammed the nine-millimeter in his waistband, stabilized Emma and deflected the onslaught as she sagged.

CHAPTER 80

"The redhead, or I swear…" Johnny wrestled with the urge to hug Getz. He stomped on a thousand angry "whys" that flooded his brain.

Baby Doll grinned. "Just like me." She wondered if Johnny possessed all the goods. He owned strong and resilient, even brave. Possessed enormous balls. His current situation proved it. Not many grew them that large. But it was impossible to discern a hundred percent.

Johnny fixated on a single word. Son. It was the premise of his search. Had been forever. He'd unearthed evidence. Granted, it was circumstantial and not buried deep. She'd disappeared for eight months the year he was born. Reappeared for Thanksgiving the weekend he'd arrived into the world. She'd donated beaucoup bucks to St. Agnes School, where he'd attended before entering the foster-care system at age nine. Those dots and more were written on index cards tacked to a small bulletin board hidden in his closet. They were his life events. Milestones. Most nights, he studied them for connections to Getz. He knew it was an exercise in futility that always resulted in one unresolved issue.

"Why'd you leave me?" He said.

"No. No. We get to that maybe a little later. Right now, I call," Baby Doll said.

"Boss!" Wheels said.

"Pourquoi?" Paul and Marcel chimed in.

"What ya got, Johnny?" Baby Doll said.

The three detectives in the foyer had no clue about the personal histories at play.

"The girl. Redhead. Give her to me we're cool and I'm gone."

"I called." Getz reached for the briefcase. "Means you gotta put up or shut up."

"Okay." He yanked off the handle. Held it high. "Everybody get a look."

Getz froze. The Hoods and Wheels ducked. Walsh prepared to run. Hand Job and the Brunette were right behind.

"Ten seconds and we vaporize." Johnny made sure everyone saw the handle. "Nine..."

"Once again, you impress me, son."

"Eight..."

"Don't you wanna know who you are?"

"Seven…

Getz paused a full, torturous second.

"Six..."

"Give her to him," she said.

Dennis released Heat, slapped her ass and pushed.

"Five…"

She bounced into Wheels.

"Four…"

Lurched towards Johnny.

"Three…"

He re-attached the handle and caught her.

Sighs of relief. Even the toughest of the tough and meanest of the mean had no desire to die that way - vaporized, with nothing to bury but air.

Johnny steadied Heat. "And Baby Doll?" His New Orleans accent surfaced. "We might share some past, cher, but we ain't a stitch similar, me and you. Not at all. Un unh."

Her Seventh Ward breeding emerged. "So why da hell you tink I'm your momma?"

"'Cuz it makes sense."

"Why?"

"It's complicated?"

"No. Really?" She grinned. "Been keeping my eye on you for ages. Why you reckon you landed your job, a kid, no experience? Bet you tinkin' it's 'cuz I be your momma. Pullin' strings. Ponder it a lot, do ya boy? Two? Three thousand times?" She stood so close he smelled her perfume. Delicate. "Answer my question."

"There's so many."

Baby Doll hated challenges. She narrowed her eyes. "Why you tink I'm your momma? Dat one."

Johnny shrugged.

"Here's what you been waitin' on. Ready for your answer? I didn't leave you. Been with you your whole time." Getz snapped her fingers. Wheels gave her an envelope. "Here. Proof." Baby Doll slid out the engraved, rust-colored document. Displayed it. "This. It's you. Birth certificate. Yeah. Big how-do-you-do, no? Real name and all." She waited for Johnny to take it. When he didn't, she poked it. "Where it say daddy?" She smacked an empty line on the paper. "Big-ass blank."

Johnny deadpanned her - not a flicker or a blink.

Infuriated, she yelled, "And where it has who is your momma?" She thumped it. "Junkie Whore. Junkie Fucking Whore." Screamed, "She worked for me."

That stung him, but no way he'd reveal the hurt. Especially to her. Johnny was within an arm's length from the prize he'd hunted his entire life. Why not grab it? He was desperate to learn the truth.

"Take it." She threw it at him. Seethed. The certificate fluttered to the floor. "Take it!" Wiped a tear.

Johnny ignored the birth record and led Heat past the Brunette and Walsh. He stopped. Not his wisest decision, but necessary. He locked eyes with Getz. "I know my real name."

CHAPTER 81

"Johnny. This way," Taylor said. Through the swarm of panic on the mansion's grounds, he glimpsed Johnny and Heat. As bodies flew by, he saw Wheels framed and backlit by the house's open entrance. She raised her 9-mm.

Taylor wrapped an arm around Emma. Shielded her. Hailed and hollered, "Johnny. Down. Get down." Lost sight of them. Hang on a minute. Heat? Nah, not a chance. He'd seen her lying in the mud and muck of that alley. But who else had a fire-engine-red mop?

Johnny and Heat trudged from the house. Barefoot and brain-fried, she tumbled. He stooped to lift her. She kneed his jaw. Hammered his teeth. Stunned rather than hurt, he shook it off.

Taylor dodged and weaved but recognized the unmistakable silhouette of a woman in the mansion's open entry. She assumed a shooting stance. Feet twelve inches apart. Elbows bent and tight. Not Wheels – no hat on a mountain of hair - but whoever it was aimed an automatic.

Johnny and Heat slogged across the wet lawn. She slipped. He fought to keep her upright.

Taylor spotted them. "Johnny!" Heard two shots. Frantic, he couldn't see beyond the crush and surge of panic.

Johnny reacted to the gunfire. He pushed Heat down and shielded her. Glanced at Getz's manse. Saw D-III Alberta "Birdy" Hand, outlined by the doorway, crumble to the threshold. The Brunette and Walsh, weapons drawn, rushed her. The Brunette kicked Hand's pistol, and Walsh flipped her tits down. Johnny was surprised when the Brunette cuffed Detective Hand's wrists. Where'd he keep those? Johnny thought. Not important. Focus.

Walsh picked Johnny out of the crowd and smiled at him. The Brunette flashed thumbs-up. That blew Johnny's mind. He was one of the good guys? Walsh, too? On-duty and undercover? And Hand Job? Homicide Special's star was a baddie? Fantastic story.

An explosion rocked the second and third floors. Shock waves slammed Johnny and Heat onto the damp grass. He struggled to his knees. Sucked deep breaths. Nodded some sense into his head. "Heat?" He said. No response. "C'mon, cher, we gotta git." She didn't move. He placed fingers on her jugular. Felt an irregular beat which was better than the alternative, but not much. He draped his tux jacket over her shoulders.

Another blast shattered windows. Johnny screened Heat with his body.

Shrieks and cries filled the night. Party-goers and escorts fled in panic as a million shards of glass rained. A third explosion collapsed the chimneys. Bricks flew. Flames billowed. Dense smoke mushroomed.

A shrill whistle was followed by a bang. A gold Chrysanthemum burst in the sky. A sparkling red, white and blue ball soared. Explosions rocked the hill. Pyrotechnics as majestic as the Fourth of July lit Christmas Eve.

Johnny embraced Heat's middle. It took a couple tries to hoist and balance her against his hip. She slumped, rag-doll limp.

"No, no, no." He slapped her. Not hard hard, but hard enough to startle her. Heat's eyes flew open - wild, angry. Then closed. She faded fast. Drooped. "Have to boogie. Come on." Johnny scouted the grounds. Hundreds of escorts, guests, guards and greeters scurried in multiple directions. There was no sign of Baby Doll Getz or her crew - Wheels, Paul, Marcel, Dennis.

Walsh keyed a radio and talked. The Brunette covered Hand Job with his Beretta as she elevated her chin half an inch. Not dead yet, but her odds were lousy. Unless 9-1-1 sent a helo, she'd bleed out before paramedics and a rescue ambulance battled past the tangle of limos. Johnny couldn't drum up any sympathy. What'd the cops call it? NHI? No Humans Involved? Yeah. Hand Job certified as NHI.

He secured Heat and lugged her away from mesmerized revelers who slowed the stampede to ooh and aah at the fireworks.

Twenty yards later, Johnny and Heat made it to Taylor and Emma at the top of the steps. Thrilled, Taylor pounded Johnny, but the joy was tempered. Heat was Raggedy-Ann floppy. In much worse shape than Emma, who'd been prepped and prettied for auction. Johnny strained to keep her from crumpling.

"You must've brought one humungous stack of chips in that case," Taylor said.

Johnny unlocked his briefcase. A digital clock, LED numbers, a pre-paid cell phone and a red wire taped to a full laundry detergent box. No C-4. No Semtex. No nothing. "People assume if they'd do it, you'd do it," he said.

"Cool, Scoop."

A 30 million candlepower NiteSun from a helicopter lit the estate. The pilot's amplified voice echoed. "This is the Los Angeles Police Department. Halt. Remain in place."

The richest of the rich scattered like roaches, but escorts complied and plugged their ears as a Fire Department chopper landed on the front lawn.

"Johnny!" Mass breathed hard as he and Miss Edna ascended the last outdoor stair.

CHAPTER 82

"Crime Queen of LA. Crime Queen of LA," Ink said. It was early in the a.m. – seven-ish – two days after Christmas. The first streaks of morning sun touched the roofs of buildings across the street. The crusty news vendor's half-block of papers, magazines and books cast shadows as he paced the southeast corner of Hollywood and Cahuenga. "*True Crime LA*. Read all about it. Crime Queen dethroned. Five bucks." He flexed. SoCal's December dawn chill played havoc with the old coot's joints.

A second bundle of *TCLAs* flew off a delivery truck and bounced with a thud on the sidewalk. Ink slashed the binding with a box cutter and repeated, "Crime Queen of LA dethroned." A customer grabbed a copy and tendered a five-dollar bill. Ink snatched the money and stuck it in a nylon pouch under the orange vest.

Another customer snagged one. Ink smiled. "What's shakin'?" He said.

"Just my bacon, Ink, just my bacon," Wheels said. She offered to pay.

He shooed the cash. "Tell the boss hello." Winked.

"Will do." Getz's driver folded the bill and tucked it in an inside pocket of a tailored fox-hunt jacket. "Later, handsome." She shimmied her ass and skipped to a late model Ford Taurus. Slid in, smoothed the tabloid, scanned the bold banner and sub-headlines.

SEX SLAVES OF LA
BILLIONAIRE BOFF BASH BUSTED
COPS CLOBBER COP
ROUND-UP AT THE RHD

The cover photo presented crazed, near-nude escorts as they escaped Getz's burning manse. Wheels thought it captured the pandemonium and panic in a single frame.

A smaller shot featured the Brunette and Walsh as they hauled Hand Job. Arms and legs flaccid, her head hung. Blood soaked her clothes. She'd raised her eyes and looked at Taylor the instant he took the picture. Wounded, overwhelmed with dread, her expression was a plea for help.

A third photo revealed a bewildered man in a rumpled suit escorted by LT Cedar Tree Hoffman. The caption identified him as the Captain of Robbery-Homicide. Hand's boss.

Wheels opened *TCLA*. Page two displayed additional images of the hilltop hubbub.

A red and white LAFD chopper on the lawn.

SWAT wrangling the partiers.

Fireworks.

Identical, eleven-year-old twin girls swathed in blankets, escorted by a female officer.

On the inside front was the headline.

BUH-BYE BABY DOLL

Followed by…

SEX SLAVES SAVED – AUCTION AXED

Next came the credits.

Special Report by
Heat O'Leary and Harvard Lincoln
Photography – Soldier Boy Quigley, III
Contributors – Mass Machado, Captain Showbiz Simkins, Panther Perez, Madam Speaker Butler, Eddie "The Owner" Horowitz.

There were two rows of portrait pix below the fold – Baby Doll Getz, Emma and the recent "suicides."

Wheels snorted a giggle. Passed the paper over her shoulder, buckled her safety belt and drove. A backseat light turned on.

CHAPTER 83

"Hot off the press. Hot off the press," Miss Edna said. She cradled a bundle of *True Crimes*, flapped a brand-spanking-new edition and tossed it. Then another. The frenetic jumble of newsroom activity ground to a stop. The only noise was the slap of thick *TCLAs* as they landed. Miss Edna started to toss one on Heat's desk but instead laid it among the flowers and bouquets of the improvised shrine.

Panther, Speaker, Mass, Showbiz, even Blitz, snapped open their papers and scrutinized the story.

"Wow," Blitz said. High praise.

"Who's gonna be me 'n Eddie in the movie?" Mass said. "I mean, us saving your bacon and all."

Miss Edna cackled. "Leo and Kate."

"Together again. Perfect."

Johnny and Taylor were as proud as new papas.

"Here's a winner," Captain Showbiz said. "The parents of recuperating zombie-sex slave victim Emma McConnell arrived at an undisclosed LA-area hospital from their home in Lexington, Kentucky. In an exclusive interview, they confirmed their model-daughter is on the mend."

Duncan interrupted. "Yeah, yeah, yeah. Already know that." He grabbed a copy from Miss Edna and admired the photograph of wild, half-naked people. Read the heads for the hundredth time. "Boffola! Best damn issue ever. Best crew ever. Let's hear it for Harvard and his big story." Johnny blushed and bowed. Duncan, the writers, Miss Edna, even the sandwich maven, rattled their copies. "And Heat," Duncan said. Sadness descended on the staff. The Chief was perhaps a tiny bit concerned. Maybe had a micro feeling. "Yeah, it's too bad. We'll send her one, no charge. You'll get it to her?" He gestured at Johnny and Taylor, elbow-to-elbow in the center of the room. They ignored him, their gaze glued to the entrance.

Heat stood in the doorway surrounded by a rectangle of sunlight. She was an angelic vision in powder-blue bowling shirt, black mini skirt, yellow tights, Purcell tennies and spikey red hair. Her face and eyes were blank. Void. Zombied.

"No," Panther said, on the verge of tears.

"Oh no," Captain Showbiz said.

Johnny's heart ached and Taylor's jaw dropped.

Mass was sad and yearned for better days as he waddled to Heat. "Miss you." He snuffed. Looked her up and down. Her blank stare provoked a sob from him.

"Boo!" Heat said.

Astounded, Mass froze, mouth agape.

She laughed.

Johnny scrambled. Wanted to swoop her off her feet. So did Taylor. They bumped, tripped and stumbled.

Panther led Heat and paused long enough for Mass to lay on a bear-hug. "They are real," he said as he blushed.

Heat, tongue-tied and full of joy, pecked Showbiz and embraced Madam Speaker. She felt like a shy adolescent as she approached Johnny and Taylor. Sniffled and wiped.

Johnny fought his emotions. Or tried to. "I'm so sorry. Never should have..."

Heat shooshed him. "Bring it in." They buried their chins in each other's hugs.

"Rent a room," Duncan said. "And get to work. Every last bleedin' one of you."

Panther and Showbiz hurried to their desks. The sandwich lady squatted on her cooler. Miss Edna scooted to the Christmas tree. Mass plopped in his chair, and the pulse of *True Crime LA* recovered a steady beat of phones and keyboards.

Johnny, Heat and Taylor wiped tears of joy. Heat used her pinkies. Johnny, his knuckles. Taylor, his palms.

"You three, too. Get cracking," Duncan said.

"Uh, Chief?" Johnny said as they uncoupled. "Our cover? The best ever? Best journalists on the planet? Your words."

"Not exactly accurate."

"Close enough. But it's a freelance piece, remember? You give us our checks, we'll be out of your hair."

Duncan cogitated, contemplated the ceiling, pursed and patted his lips, and pretended to tap out. "Okay. Safe word is ouch. You got your jobs."

Heat fiddled with a button and tugged her hem.

Panther fist-pumped a yes.

The Captain clapped his fingertips.

Speaker nodded.

Mass waved a double thumbs-up.

But Johnny, Heat and Taylor didn't respond to the Chief yay or nay.

"Oh, all right. Geezus H. Quit twisting the blade. A hundred-a-week raise."

"Yes," Heat said with a skip and a hop.

"Generous of you to dust the vault, Chief," Johnny said, "but I'm afraid we can't accept. What can I say?"

"Try 'yes,'" Duncan said.

"No can do. Your turn. Make a counter."

"Counter what?"

"Offer. Me 'n Heat were offered a better deal elsewhere. Naturally, Taylor's included in the package."

"Really?" Heat said.

"Oh?" Taylor said.

Duncan, skeptical, squinted. "How much better?"

"I could buy a car, better."

"Impressive."

"Hey, tough guy?" Johnny said to Taylor. "Wanna pin on your diapers again?"

No response.

"Typical," Heat said. She verged towards angry.

"I love the two of you," Taylor said. "But I'm done with the dead."

Johnny dug in a trench coat pocket and extracted Taylor's Nikon. "Sure?" He tendered it with respect and admiration.

Silence, as everyone held their breath.

Taylor eyed his camera. He remembered that terrible day with Heat, believing she was a fresh corpse in the alley. The sense of loss, the feelings of guilt, and wondered if he even wanted the Nikon. It filtered him from both good and evil. Life through a single-lens reflex was less painful but less authentic. He eyed Heat.

"Don't look at me," she said.

Johnny draped the strap around his friend's neck.

Taylor didn't resist. The Nikon hung against his chest for a moment, then he made it a threesome, aimed the camera. "Selfie."

"Well, hell," Duncan said. "Figured it'd happen sooner or later."

'You did?" Heat blew her nose.

"Sure. Outgrow your britches. Leave us in the lurch. Bite the digits what feed you." Duncan loped to his office. "Check's in the mail."

"Chief. My man. That's how you wanna leave it?" Johnny said.

Duncan slammed his door and sat in his ergo chair. Rocked.

"Guess it is," Taylor said.

"Nah, he doesn't mean it," Mass said.

"Course not," Miss Edna said. "Now go."

Johnny, Heat and Taylor let the new reality soak in.

"I just got back," Heat said.

"You earned a new gig," Speaker said.

Heat hugged Mass, the Captain and Miss Edna. Whispered in Panther's ear, "Adore the new you."

Johnny shook hands.

Taylor nodded his farewells.

They shared a final round of "see-ya-soons," ambled to the exit and departed the *TCLA HQ* for blue sky and bright sun. Standing on the sidewalk, they watched moderate, mid-morning, Sunset Boulevard traffic.

Heat was the first to say something. "We going to the *Times*, Johnny? Or one of those tabloid TV shows? Yeah, TV. That'd be fan-fucking-tastic."

"I say we hit the Horde," he said.

"At ten-thirty?"

"The Horde?" Taylor said.

"Where's the new gig, Johnny?" Heat said.

He hesitated. "Sure you don't want something to eat?"

"Johnny..." Heat dragged out his name. Added o's and n's as her suspicion grew.

"Uhhh – I thought we'd up the ante. Work him for more."

"You didn't…"

Taylor laughed. "Lost that one, Scoop."

"Don't call me Scoop."

"A slow death," Heat said, happy to throttle him. "Very, very slow."

"No. Not to worry. The Chief'll churn a few brain cells then beg us to come back."

"And if he doesn't?"

Johnny searched for an answer. The answer. Any answer.

Taylor chuckled.

Heat fumed.

Johnny found it. "It's LA, doll."

She relented, stepped between them and arm-in-arm, they walked to Murder Burger and the bus stop.

ACKNOWLEDGEMENTS

It's not a good idea to work in a vacuum, so I don't. Christina Hoag was key and critical to whipping the manuscript into shape. I'd like to thank my good friend Kevin Anthony for his time and notes. Thanks to the gang at USVAA. I read parts of an early draft to them and they opened my eyes to excellent points that had escaped me. Longtime friend David Freed was a huge motivator, and this is the first he'll know of that. And I'd like to thank my former screenwriting partner, Glenn Benest.

ABOUT THE PUBLISHER

Onward Press (www.onwardpress.org) is the publishing imprint of the United States Veterans' Artists Alliance, Inc. a 501-c-3 educational non-profit (www.usvaa.org). Our mission is to publish well-written, compelling books by military veterans, spouses, military brats and other family members, as well as people who served in other government agencies and their family members.

Onward Press books available at Amazon:

Zippo Boys: Serving Gay in Viet Nam by Dave Lara
Welcome to Blackwater: Mercenaries, Money and Mayhem in Iraq by Morgan Lerette
Baghdad Underground Railroad: Saving American Allies in Iraq by Steve Miska
Skin of Tattoos by Christina Hoag
Girl on the Brink by Christina Hoag
Chica al borde by Christina Hoag

The United States Veterans' Artists Alliance (USVAA) is an award winning, multi-disciplinary non-profit arts organization founded in 2004. USVAA provides opportunities for veterans by highlighting their work in the arts, humanities and the entertainment industry. As a voice representing the veterans' community and in our endeavors as artists, the organization strives to address issues of concern to veterans and their families, including the transition from military to civilian life, education, employment, the effects of wartime and military-service injuries, including posttraumatic stress disorder (PTSD), traumatic brain injury (TBI), military sexual trauma (MST) and homelessness.

www.ingramcontent.com/pod-product-compliance
Lightning Source LLC
Chambersburg PA
CBHW030538310726
48979CB00010B/1951/J

* 9 7 8 1 9 5 4 9 8 8 1 2 5 *